Secret of the Ruby

OTHER BOOKS BY A. E. SMITH

Journey of the Pearl

Quest of the Sapphire

A Gift for Gracelyn

Secret of the Ruby

A. E. Smith

RESOURCE *Publications* · Eugene, Oregon

SECRET OF THE RUBY

Resource Publications
An Imprint of Wipf and Stock Publishers
199 W. 8th Ave., Suite 3
Eugene, OR 97401

www.wipfandstock.com

PAPERBACK ISBN: 978-1-7252-7988-9
HARDCOVER ISBN: 978-1-7252-7987-2
EBOOK ISBN: 978-1-7252-7989-6

02/15/21

For Ken, Kenna Marie
And my parents

Preface

————⊗⊗⊗————

Centurion Adan Clovius Longinus, the man in charge of crucifying Yeshua of Nazareth, has once again stepped out of history and onto the pages of this historical drama. *Secret of the Ruby* is the third and final book of the Gemstone Trilogy. Adan and his adopted brother, Nikolaus, set out to resolve their suspicions surrounding the death of Nikolaus's family and the mystery of the Prophecy Box. Adan has also been given the task of delivering John's Book of Revelation to followers of the early church despite the emperor's efforts to acquire the scroll for himself. Along with the emperor's mercenaries, bounty hunters are also in pursuit when warrants for the arrest of Aurelius and Pomona are made public.

Drawing on historical facts, the Prophecy Box is based on the Antikythera Mechanism housed in the National Archaeological Museum in Athens, Greece. This analog computer was invented about twenty-two hundred years ago and reveals that early scientists knew precise workings of the sun, moon, earth, and five other planets. The same scientific facts were lost during the Dark Ages and not fully accepted by most of the population until the 1700's.

For the purpose of this story, certain historical events have been moved on the chronological timeline. For example: the apostle John really was imprisoned on Patmos Island and the generally accepted author of the Book of Revelation, but not when Centurion Longinus would have been in his early forties. Any emperors mentioned in this book will be in the order that they were in power but not according to the actual years they ruled.

Words in italics are either direct quotes from the Bible, words of emphasis, or words in a language other than English.

Chapter 1

Death Strikes the Unworthy

A red stain spread across the tiles of the mosaic floor. Nicandros Kokinos stared in shock as he stood paralyzed with the realization of what he had done. The chief astrologer of Athens was dying. Nicandros had shoved the elderly man so violently he lost his balance and struck his head on the corner of the table where a wooden box stood. Nicandros stumbled back as fear twisted his features. There was no going back. The deed was done. He had to let the injured man die or face arrest and execution.

Nicandros ran a hand across his mouth with mounting panic. No one would believe the old man's death was an accident. He would be convicted and crucified. Just the thought made his vision swim. His gaze, once again, fell on the blood pooling on the intricately tiled floor. He watched as the mosaic image of a griffin was slowly disappearing under the red stain. The monster was portrayed with the classic back legs and body of a lion, and the front claws, wings, and head of an eagle. It stood on a mountaintop with wings spread and a front leg raised to warn away intruders. The dying man lay across the creature with his hand appearing to grasp an outstretched wing in a last plea for escape. Seeking the path of least resistance, the blood spread across the mosaic tiles of the monster's head. Nicandros stared in horror as the red stain followed the grout lines of the tiles. The yellow eyes appeared to be bloodshot and angry. The dreadful effect made the horrified man believe the griffin was watching him.

The blossoming red pool made Nicandros look at the star ruby in his signet ring. The letters N and K etched into the cabochon-fashioned gemstone seemed to mock him. The signature ring was a symbol of a man's honor and used to confirm his identity on documents. He looked from his ruby ring to the slashing talons of the griffin.

"If you could rise up and avenge your master, it would be justice," he muttered.

Nicandros Kokinos forced himself to look into the chief astrologer's eyes. Finally, their gaze became fixed and unblinking. The man was dead. Nicandros looked at the cypress wood box sitting on the table. Its innocent appearance belied the violence that had just transpired. How could anything so beautifully crafted cause such tragedy?

Only the night before, Nicandros had gone for a long walk to dull the pain of yet another rejected building design. Bankruptcy was staring him in the face and it bore an evil expression. Selling himself into slavery to pay his mounting debts would not be enough and he knew what every Roman court of law would demand. He could be forced to sell his wife and children as slaves. He stopped in a tavern and settled in a dark corner to drink himself into oblivion. Two young men came in and sat nearby. They were quiet, at first, but the more they drank the louder they became. Nicandros found himself listening. What he heard gave him hope.

Their mentor was a man of the *Magi*, the great School of Magic in the Far East. This *magus* possessed a mysterious box that the two men spoke of with awe. They called it the Prophecy Box. Yet, they exchanged condemnation for the cavalier treatment of the great treasure. It seemed that the *magus,* its guardian, left the box unattended in his upstairs library as if it was nothing more than decoration. At first, Nicandros thought they were exaggerating the box's abilities until he heard more detail. As he listened, he realized it could save his fortune, his career, and his marriage, if only he could steal it. He wondered if he actually had the nerve to take such a chance. Yet, he was encouraged when he heard how easy it would be to locate it once he was in the home of the owner. Desperation fed his denial of the risks. He reasoned that if the *magus* treated the box so casually, he deserved to have it stolen. He convinced himself that his need for the box was far greater than the old man's. As he pondered the alleged power of the box, he realized that it could enable him to do much more than pay his debts. This mysterious box could make him rich and revered like none other. He told himself that the *magus* did not fully comprehend its potential, thus, his disrespect for the object. Surely, he could unlock its secrets once he had the box in his possession.

Nicandros followed the two young men when they left and made note of their address. He returned the next day and watched the house. The same two men left after a while and no one else came. He was about to approach the villa when two more men left the house. It unnerved him since he did not know there were others in the villa. Finally, after convincing himself it was safe, Nicandros hurried across the street. He opened the front door carefully and slipped inside. He quietly mounted the stairs and easily found the library. There on a table was the wooden box. Nicandros thanked his good fortune and hurried to the table. The door to the hallway opened as an elderly man stepped into the room. Nicandros knew he was the chief astrologer by his distinctive apparel. The startled man tried to cry out. Panic ensued and things happened in quick succession.

It was far too late for second guessing. Nicandros approached the wooden box and ran his hands over an iridescent, golden stone and a pearlescent pale-blue stone at the top corners of the lid. Their colors shimmered as he looked at them from different angles. There was a peculiar stone at the bottom of the lid that looked like sand dunes under a dark-green, starry sky. He opened the lid and read some of the instructions etched in Greek on the framework of the first wheel. Nicandros surmised what the cabochon-fashioned stones represented. The golden stone was the sun. The blue stone was the moon. The landscape-looking stone represented the earth. It all made sense.

Never before had anyone been able to correctly predict the appearance of signs and wonders in the skies. Some soothsayers claimed they could interpret celestial events, but none of them predicted when those events would occur. This device had to be the Prophecy Box, the object the two men in the bar were discussing. His nerve gave way and he backed away from the table. Something about the box warned him away.

A voice sounded from the figure sprawled across the tiled griffin. Nicandros nearly fainted. He thought the man was dead.

"Unworthy. Die now." A raspy breath escaped the chief astrologer's lips. It was his last.

Was the dying man speaking of himself? Or would Nicandros suffer the same fate—an unnatural death? The chief astrologer's muffled words raised a new panic in him. When he eavesdropped on the two men, he had also heard them speak of a curse. The device was invented by Greek mathematicians and astrologers who had been dead for centuries. They left no records, except for a warning carved on the inside of the lid. Nicandros opened the hinged lid and read:

Beware the Guardians of the Stones
Death will strike the Unworthy.

It didn't occur to Nicandros that death would eventually "strike" everyone. In his mind, to defy the guardians was to invite an imminent disaster. The students apparently believed the same thing. They talked of how the chief astrologer reported that whoever tampered with the device, died within days, even though he had scoffed at the notion. He claimed that any deaths were coincidences or baseless rumors. The chief astrologer was planning to take the device apart for a few visiting *Magi* who wished to see its inner workings. The two men joked that their mentor might "arouse the Guardians." That same man was now dead. Nicandros could not dismiss the possibility of supernatural intervention. He closed the lid and stepped away from the table.

Nicandros started to leave. Then he stopped and stood still. The enticing object seemed to whisper into his ear, subverting his better judgement. He returned to the table and took hold of the box. Why should he leave all this magic for someone else? He knew the visiting astrologers would gather this same evening. The box would be out of his reach forever. He would be forced to accept an insignificant assistant's job or watch his family be enslaved.

The young architect's building designs were being roundly rejected and his only prospect was to accept a position he'd been offered as an assistant to the most successful architect in Athens. It paid less and was less prestigious. The architect was also younger and less experienced than Nicandros whose pride outweighed his fear of bankruptcy, even though his wife had recently delivered their seventh child, putting an additional burden on the family finances. He couldn't bear selling his family into slavery, as the law could require, but he would never work for a sniveling "youngster" who brandished his authority over his subordinates. The Prophecy Box was the solution to all his problems.

Nicandros whispered a quick prayer to Soteria, goddess of protection, and Zeus, ruler of Olympus. He muttered prayers to other various gods, just to be on the safe side, and snatched up the box. It was a little longer than his forearm, as wide as his spread fingers, and as thick as his palm. He wondered how the most powerful object in the world could be so small. Yet, due to its weight, he had to carry it in both arms.

Nicandros stepped out into the hallway. He heard distant voices and knew that the servants must be in the kitchen at the back of the ground floor. He hurried from the villa and made his way along the streets of Athens until he reached his home. He hid the box as best he could. After the body of the astrologer was found the whole city talked of nothing else, and Nicandros lived in fear. As the days passed and no suspects were arrested, Nicandros heard that the death was ruled an accident. No one knew what he had done. No one in the house had even known he had been there. Out in the street, a beggar took notice of a man he had not seen before leaving the house, the day the old man died, carrying a wooden box but no one thought to question him.

When the Prophecy Box could not be located, the *Magi* assumed that it had been stolen and the chief astrologer had been murdered. They declared his death an accident to keep the matter to themselves and the theft of the box a secret. Still, the city fairly buzzed with proposed conspiracies and counter conspiracies. One such theory was that the visiting *Magi*, themselves, had murdered their colleague out of jealousy. In time, the Athenians turned to other gossip and speculation, leaving behind the interest in the old man's suspicious death.

The other *Magi* did not lose interest. They gathered and debated and finally came to a solution. The chief astrologer's assistant, a man named Balthazar was assigned the task of finding the murderer and the box. Balthazar vowed to succeed, no matter the cost.

Nicandros was initially relieved to learn the ruling of accidental death for the old man. Then doubt wormed its way into his thoughts and dreams. His fear grew as the weeks passed. He began to "see" shadowy figures watching him from doorways and alleys. As he struggled to understand the workings of the box, fear gnawed at him every waking moment.

Then the final straw shattered the camel's proverbial back. Nicandros wanted to see if the visiting *Magi* were still at the old man's residence. If they believed their mentor's death was truly an accident, they would be gone. As he approached the villa, he saw the beggar who was usually found across the street. He was talking to Balthazar. The beggar was gesturing and the young man was intensely listening. Then the beggar framed his hands as if he were describing a box. Nicandros drew closer. He heard the beggar say, "about your height, carrying a wooden box. Saw him the day before, watching the house. I never saw him before that, but he looked at me as he hurried by."

The young man replied, "Will you describe him so I can draw a sketch?"

The beggar grinned, revealing more gaps than teeth. "For ten silver coins. Yes."

Nicandros turned and fled to his house. He immediately made preparations to leave the city as quickly as possible. He took his family from Athens, claiming to his wife that he had a job offer in Thessalonica. He took the first job offered to him, even though he was overqualified for the menial position as clerk in a law office. In his free time, he would study the box with diligence and test the results. He hoped his predictions would entice a wealthy man who needed an architect.

His plan eventually worked. After a number of successful predictions, word reached Emperor Tiberius in Rome. Much to Nicandros's delight, an offer to serve as the emperor's chief architect arrived with instructions if he accepted the offer. The emperor's agents would arrive at the house, pack up his family's belongings, and convey them to the nearest port. There, the family would board a ship selected by the agents. The passage was already paid. The young architect was ecstatic. Not only was he assured a life of luxury and respect, he had a legitimate reason to leave Greece where he no longer felt safe.

Nicandros's success at predicting certain events was also reported in Athens, arousing the suspicion of Balthazar. He sent a message to a colleague in Thessalonica asking for a description of the author of the predictions. The response closely resembled the sketch he had made from the beggar's description. The *magus* found his way to Nicandros's home before the emperor's agents arrived and angrily confronted him. Threats were voiced. Nicandros's young daughter, Dionysia overheard the argument and saw the man leave.. Nicandros's fear for himself and his family rekindled. Then, his eldest son, Nikolaus, caught him manipulating the dials of the Prophecy Box that same day. The boy observed his father long enough to know that the box was special. Nicandros's terrible secret was struggling to come to light. The Kokinos clan of the ruby was in deadly danger.

Nicandros was not only afraid; he was riddled with guilt. He had killed a man. He had stolen a priceless, supernatural object, and others were eyeing him with suspicion. Then a great realization came to him. What if he hadn't fully comprehended the power of the Prophecy Box? What if it could predict much more than celestial events, eclipses, and occultations of the planets and the moon? What if it could actually predict human events, wars, plagues, famines, or floods? What if it could predict the ultimate—the end of days? Nicandros shuddered at the terrible implications. What if he learned how to use the Prophecy Box to its full potential? He knew he would be incapable of keeping such predictions to himself. The day the emperor's agents came, Nicandros secured the box in his clothes chest and vowed not to use it again until he was safely in Rome. Tragically, he, his wife, and five of his children, would be dead before the ship ever reached the shores of *Italia*.

***

Many years later, in a cottage in Caesarea, Centurion Adan Longinus jerked awake in the black of night. A crash had awakened him. It was near midnight and a downpour was drenching the land. The wind pushed through the pelting waves of rain, as if trying to escape the torrent. A blinding flash of light filled the room and another crackle of thunder sounded almost immediately. He gently touched Dulcibella's arm, but she made no response. Somehow, the storm had not disturbed his wife, but he wondered about his sons, Aquila, and Marco. Adan left the bed and padded down the hall to their bedrooms. The obliging streaks of lightning revealed that his sons were asleep. Adan, Marco, and Aquila had only been reunited with the family a few months after searching for Marco who had ran away on an ill-prepared quest. The anxiety of those months was still fresh on Adan's mind. Marco's quest to free his previously enslaved Aunt Dionysia had taken more twists and turns than the swirling storm outside, but had resulted in saving the lives of Dionysia, her husband Decimus, his two slaves, and the former slave, Calais Antipas.

Adan returned to the bed and slipped under the blankets as quietly as he could.

"Were they asleep?" a voice sounded from the other side of the bed.

"Did I wake you, Dulcie?"

"No. But your absence did." She turned to face her husband. "If this storm causes road washouts, we may have to postpone our trip to Jerusalem. Aurelius will be so disappointed."

"Yes. Probably," Adan whispered as he nestled Dulcibella in his arms. "He has a limited amount of time since he is scheduled to pick up another cargo in a week. The *Child of the Ocean* will need to be on her way to Cyprus if he is to keep his shipping schedule current. But this might be his only chance to meet Pomona. We've got to try."

"And we will," assured Dulcibella, "as long as it is safe to travel."

"Safe or not, I am determined to repay my debt to Pomona for helping me find Marco. She is Felix Valentius's daughter, after all, and she could have just as easily done him harm."

"You never retaliated against Valentius," murmured Dulcibella. "Why would she harm any of us? Wouldn't her anger be more rationally focused on Theophilus Salvitto? He's the one who arrested Valentius and had him thrown in the pit."

Adan arched an eyebrow. "I think the key word was 'rationally.' The man hated me with all his heart because of my grandfather's harsh words and the false assumption that Father paid to have Aurelius murdered. Valentius could have poisoned her against me."

A gust of damp wind burst through the window lattice and Dulcibella snuggled closer to her husband as she spoke. "Even if he did, she apparently rose above it. I look forward to meeting Pomona and telling her how grateful I am. From what Marco tells me, he didn't make things easy for her. At least he apologized for his ugly comments about Valentius. He shouldn't have said them but it's understandable. Marco and Aquila have heard the stories from their Uncle Nikolaus and Serapio. Maybe now, they'll remember that there are several sides to every story."

Adan snorted. "I doubt they will have to learn that lesson only once."

Dulcibella playfully punched his arm. "Have some faith in your sons, Adan. Has your stubborn nature so rubbed off on them?"

Adan grinned. "I'm afraid so. No doubt, they will always need to learn things the hard way, just like me."

"Heaven help us," sighed Dulcibella. "They've only come of age this year. What adventures are we destined to survive now that they're facing adulthood?"

"Well, let's hope it will not be as traumatic as Marco getting shipwrecked and Aquila being falsely accused and arrested, only to flee for our lives from the eruptions of *Mons Vesuvio*. I could stand a little boredom for a while."

Dulcibella laid a finger across his lips. "Shhh. Don't say that. You'll jinx us."

"Are you superstitious, Dulcie?" teased Adan. "I thought you were the practical one."

Dulcibella snickered. "Are you so easily fooled, my love? Or am I better at playacting than I thought?" She hesitated for a moment. Her tone grew serious. "Are you still going to search for the Prophecy Box?"

"I admit it gives me pause, but I feel compelled. The truth about the deaths of Niko's family will cause him pain, but to *not* know the truth could be deadly if someone is searching for him, thinking he has the box."

"Surely, after all these years, no one would still be looking for it."

"Time does not extinguish greed or the desire for power. Look at how long Valentius carried his grudge against my grandfather and father."

"True." Dulcibella sighed in agreement. "Do you think the box has something to do with the *Magi* of the Zoroastrians?"

"I think it's likely. The *Magi* are the most learned in astrology and magic. If there is any device that can truly predict the future, they would be the ones to invent it."

"Magic," she snorted, "I don't believe it exists. It's clever trickery that only looks like magic."

"I'm sure you're right. What may appear to be magic to the common man may be scientific knowledge to the *Magi*. Think of what Aquila and Marco did when they fooled Simon Magus who claimed to be a great sorcerer. They appeared to be supernatural werewolves and threw blue and green flames from their hands. As identical twins, they fooled Simon into thinking they could appear and disappear in the blink of an eye. Yet, it was not magic, but creative science and identical biology. As you said, what may look like magic is really just clever tricks."

"Ignorant people who cannot explain an event leap to the conclusion that it has a supernatural cause," admitted Dulcibella. "Perhaps the box is a product of trickery as well."

"Perhaps. But if Niko's family was murdered to steal the box, then it must have some very powerful effect, one way or another."

"If the box was invented by the *Magi* who we know live in the Far East, how did Nicandros come in contact with them? Niko told me that they never left Greece until Emperor Tiberius persuaded Nicandros to come to Rome."

Adan had often thought about that dilemma. "I don't know, Dulcie. Maybe some of the *Magi* had brought the box to Greece for some reason."

Dulcibella started to ask another question when lightning lit up the bedroom. It was a few moments before the thunder sounded with a tumbling rumble.

"The storm is moving away," said Adan. "We should get some sleep."

"Perhaps our dreams will reveal all these mysteries to us in one night."

Adan leaned over and kissed her. "I hope not. That would ruin all the fun."

Chapter 2

The Destiny of Emperor Domitian

———— ✦✦✦ ————

Within the eastern Aegean Sea sat an island isolated, barren, and void of human good will. Emperor Titus Flavius Domitian considered it his personal prison for convicts, sorcerers, and mystics. Domitian was a man buffeted about by his fear of the future and his thirst for power. He craved power more than any other thing. Riches enabled power. Vast territories and resources enabled power. Loyal armies enabled power. Yet, there was only one way to retain control of power and that was knowledge of the future. If one knew the future, preparations could be enacted with full confidence. Disasters and disease could be avoided by being in the safest places at the worst times. Wars would be won by knowing where and when the enemy would attack. Profits could be made if times of bounty were predicted to offset times of famine. Domitian even had dreams of controlling the weather. What better way to destroy an enemy's army than to beat them to death with hail or whisk them away in a windstorm?

Emperor Domitian craved the knowledge of things to come. He wanted his soothsayers to whisper wonderful things in his ear and soothe him with assurances of his grasp upon the might of the Roman Empire. He welcomed any man of wisdom as long as he wisely spoke only what the emperor wanted to hear. Still, in the dark of the night when sleep alluded him, when his thoughts were infected with the shadows of broken promises and betrayals, he paced the halls. He raged against the unfairness of being the most powerful man on the planet but powerless against what would come. Foreknowledge was the one treasure that Domitian could never possess. His soothsayers were wrong more than half the time. No visions took shape within his dreams. No feelings of portent ever stirred his inner being. If only there was some way to know—*everything*.

Jealousy curled its tentacles around the emperor's heart. Why wasn't the gift of prophecy given to him? Why couldn't he look upon the stars and know within his soul what was to be? He despised and mistrusted the very men he gathered into his private circle. The more prophecies he heard, the more he doubted their sincerity. His fear of being manipulated by the same men he desperately sought added to his despair. In fact, Domitian feared, above all else, the men connected to the most mystical man he had ever heard of—Yeshua of Nazareth. They called themselves Christians or followers of the Way. Soothsayers whispered rumors of Yeshua's prophecies and Domitian hungered for more. Yet, he murdered every Christian he could get his hands on, infuriated by their refusal to worship him despite the threat of cruel and public executions.

When John, the son of Zebedee came before him, he sentenced him to death by emersion in boiling oil and the impossible happened. John came out of the oil unscathed. Yahweh, who John worshiped and obeyed without reservation, revealed to the people of Rome that Domitian was powerless against God's will. Not even a blister appeared on John's skin. Afraid to attempt another execution of John, he exiled the man to the Island of Patmos, to work him to death in the mines.

Then one of Domitian's soothsayers had a dream of an eagle dipping its talons in the blood of a sacrifice and writing wondrous things on stone tablets. The soothsayer suggested that the eagle was none other than John. He swore that the words in blood would predict that Domitian would rule Rome forever if he, himself, would read the words aloud to the people.

Domitian devised a plan. John was safely imprisoned on the island. Escape was impossible so his location was secure. The emperor was afraid to send for John and demand for him to reveal his visions since he may not have had them yet and interference might cause the visions to never occur. However, if Domitian sent a few men to watch what John did, he would be in control over his prisoner. He would instruct the "guards" to make sure John had papyrus, pen and ink and time to record whatever he wished. Then the emperor realized there was a problem. What if his spies took away John's writings before he had finished? They would have no way of knowing if more visions were to come.

The emperor discussed the matter with a few of his councilmen and one suggested that if the captive turned his writings over to someone to deliver elsewhere, then it would be assured that he had written all he was going to write. With no expectation of escape, no promise of pardon, Domitian believed that John's only power was to dream. He didn't understand that any true follower of Yeshua had the greatest power of all—Yahweh's eternal love.

The emperor poured over his lists of servants, aides, and clerks. He thought of the spies he employed and eliminated each one. He ordered his entourage of soldiers and slaves to take him to the temple on Capitoline Hill to pray and pay homage to Jupiter. Surely the king of the gods would show him a sign of who he could trust with such an important job. The man must be crafty and resourceful but controllable. He must be intelligent and ruthless. Most important of all, he must understand that failure would not be tolerated.

Domitian returned to the palace and waited with growing agitation. Finally, a slave trader who specialized in highly skilled men asked for an audience with the emperor.

The slave trader was well past any prime he may have known in his life. He was balding and tried to hide it by securing a few strands of hair across his shiny head with pig grease.

The man bowed and waited to be told to rise. In the meantime, Domitian studied his posture and demeanor and judged the man to be unimpressive. He nodded at his chancellor and the man clapped his hands twice. The visitor regained his normal posture.

"Your Excellency, I am a businessman of some renown and have purchased a *gladiator* that fits your specifications of intelligence, skill, and allegiance to you. I first saw him battling Rome's previously favorite *gladiator*. Obviously, he won the battle."

When the emperor did not order his immediate removal, the slave trader looked over his shoulder and gestured at three men standing just inside the archway. "Your Excellency, this is Celsus, a true-hearted Roman who has passed all of my stringent tests with the highest degree of success. I present him to you at the price you offered."

Domitian looked at the tall, muscular man with sun-streaked, brown hair, dark eyes, and an expression of mild curiosity. There was no fear in his demeanor. Domitian saw that his eyes lingered on the guards and their weapons as if evaluating how best to overwhelm them. His right earlobe was missing, bitten off by a Scythian woman who liked the taste of blood, but no one knew this other than the two of them. Emperor Domitian ordered that the man be brought before him and forced to knell. Celsus had a better idea. He moved too quickly for the two guards to defend themselves. Before they could struggle to their feet, Celsus took a step toward the emperor, knelt on one knee, and bowed his head.

The slave trader raised a rod to punish Celsus for his audacity. He struck the slave across the back. The man did not flinch but, instead, slowly turned malevolent eyes on the slave trader.

"Do that again and I'll kill you," Celsus stated in a low, deadly tone.

"You won't need to," interjected the emperor, impressed with Celsus's boldness. "My guards will do it for you."

The slave trader cringed and backed away a few steps. "My apologies, Your Excellency. I only punished him out of respect for you."

Domitian ignored him and addressed the slave. "You show promise. If I sent you to perform a very delicate errand for me, what compensation would you expect if you are successful?"

"None, Your Excellency. I wish for nothing but the pleasure to serve."

Domitian chortled with delight. "This is the man that the great Jupiter has sent to do my biding." He glanced at his chancellor. "Pay the trader the agreed price—minus half—for striking my property. Have my new emissary treated to whatever his heart desires for tonight. Celsus, select two men to accompany you. Make sure they understand that if either one of them disobeys you, you have my permission to kill them."

Domitian held up a finger. "But if you run, my spies will find you and you will die on the cross. If you are unsuccessful but return willingly, your death will be painless. If you bring me the prophecies of which I seek, you will be paid what you richly deserve, and nothing less."

Celsus heard the promise of riches and determined to succeed at any cost.

Domitian continued the instructions. "Go first to Jerusalem. Inquire after any followers of the Nazarene named Yeshua who was crucified. Search their homes for any writings of prophecy. If you find nothing in Jerusalem, then go to Patmos Island. I will give you a letter of employment at the prison. Find John, son of Zebedee and make sure he has papyrus and ink. Wait until John gives the prophecies to a messenger. Steal the prophecies and bring them to me. Do whatever you wish to the messenger. Do you understand?"

"Yes, Your Excellency."

"Do I need to repeat any of it?"

"No, Your Excellency."

Emperor Domitian signaled two guards to escort Celsus to a luxury room in the palace. At least, until tomorrow, the former *gladiator* did not have to wonder if it was his last day to live. He was led out of the state room. The slave trader was escorted to the treasury office to receive half of what he had originally been promised. He did not complain.

Domitian walked out onto the balcony and gazed out over the city of Rome. Ever since he had been told about Emperor Tiberius's obsession for a prophecy device owned by the *Magi* and how the old man never got his hands on it, Domitian had scorned him. How could the most powerful man, at the time, fail so miserably? Emperor Caligula, the incompetent lunatic with a self-image as fragile as a butterfly, didn't even understand the value of the device. Then Emperor Claudius determined that the device had been destroyed and didn't even attempt to look for it. What a fool the man must have been, thought Domitian. Then evidence came to him proving that Claudius had been correct. The prophecy device of the *Magi* was forever lost and no mention of it had been reported in many years. He had grieved at the loss for, he too, had craved to own it just as Tiberius had done. He had sent many men to try and find it. All had failed and died for their failure.

Yet, a new hope swelled in the emperor's heart. This slave, Celsus, had the eye of a predator and the heart of a warrior. When the man chose to bow before him, rather than be forced, he revealed the spirit of a champion. Perhaps, if the man was successful in bringing back John's prophecies, he would keep his promise of a reward. If the slave failed, he would make sure Celsus wished he had never lived.

Chapter 3

The Trap Is Triggered

Adan and Dulcibella were on the road to Jerusalem after breakfast along with Aquila and Marco. They stopped in Caesarea at the Ocean View Inn to meet up with Captain Aurelius Hadrian, the son of Centurion Felix Valentius, and Nikolaus, Adan's adopted brother. Nikolaus kissed his wife, Marina, and assured his family he would return within a week. At the crossroads to the Caesarea garrison, Adan's group met the squad of soldiers he had requested to accompany them. Adan introduced *Principales* Neziah and the other three soldiers to the group. They continued south to Joppa and spent the night with their long-time friend, Simon the tanner. Nikolaus gave Simon and his wife a gift of flour from his mill. They happily accepted the flour even though their hospitality never came with a price. Marco also presented a female goat which had been abandoned by its mother. He had nursed the kid goat back to health and confirmed the quality of its milk by also including a portion of cheese. Simon declared that gifts were never necessary, but he was honored by their generosity.

Dulcibella smiled at the elderly man's graciousness. "Simon, we show up on your doorstep unannounced every time we travel to Jerusalem. We are the ones who are honored by you. We are hopeful that when we return, you will allow one more guest. Her name is Pomona and we hope to bring her with us."

The evening passed with good food and everyone's favorite pastime, storytelling. Captain Hadrian had more than enough tales of his sea adventures. Simon and his wife also wanted to hear about their near escape from the eruptions of *Vesuvio*. Marco showed them his leather-corded, purple sapphire and explained how the etched crystal had convinced him to find Dionysia. It was late when they finally settled down for a restful night.

The group was up early the next morning and eager to be on their way. Adan and his family were looking forward to seeing Serapio and Fabiana, their long-time friends. Aurelius Hadrian was apprehensive about meeting his half-sister but eager to meet

Adan's friends that he had heard so much about. Adan had told him stories of how he and Serapio first met and how Adan had lived with Serapio's family for some time after a heated argument with his father, the retired *minor consul*, Aquila Clovius Longinus. Dulcibella told Aurelius how Serapio had been half blinded in the arena, but Simon Peter, an apostle of Yeshua, healed the ruined eye. Aurelius was skeptical that anyone could restore sight to a blind eye but kept his doubts to himself, not wanting to offend Dulcibella and the others.

The travelers reached the western gate of Jerusalem without incidence. Adan and Dulcibella debated on whether they should go to Pomona's house before seeing Serapio and Fabiana. Aurelius cleared his throat and they looked at him expectantly.

"I'm not trying to be selfish," Aurelius said, "but should we retrieve a certain scroll that reveals how I faked my death, first?"

Adan's brows shot up. "Ah, yes, we need to pay a visit to the business office at the Antonia. Dulcie, Niko, you'll need to go to Serapio's shop. Neziah, you and your men wait for me at Serapio's as well. Marco, Aquila, you'll come with me. Aurelius, I think it's best if you stay with the others. We'll meet you there. Take Marco's horse. He'll ride with Aquila. Marco, bring your *cucullus*. You will have need of a hooded cloak. Only two of us will enter the front gates of the Antonia but you will enter another way."

"Will you bring Pomona to Serapio's place afterwards?" asked Aurelius.

Adan paused in thought. "I think we will come back here to fetch all of you first, then go to Pomona's. And it might be best if you don't mention anything about her to Serapio. He and Fabiana are in a precarious position here in Jerusalem. Serapio will want to go with us in case there's trouble. I don't want to involve him. It's too risky."

Dulcibella and Aurelius agreed. Nikolaus was glad Adan wanted him to go with the others to Serapio's. He had no desire to be inside the walls of the Antonia Fortress, once again.

The atmosphere inside the city walls of Jerusalem was stifling as the group rode through the streets. Hostility permeated the air like a foul smell. Many more patrols were on duty than Adan had ever seen. There were even more than when King Herod was looking for Simon Peter after he vanished from the Antonia. The soldiers looked surly and harassed. Angry glares were shot at Adan and his squad. The men kept Dulcibella in the middle to protect her from any attempt at harassment or assault. Adan explained his plan to Marco and Aquila as they slowly made their way among pedestrians, wagons and carriages.

Aquila looked back at Marco and grinned. "This should be fun. It's not like we haven't pretended to be the same person before. Right, brother?"

They were riding along Commerce Road when Adan stopped two intersections from Sheep Gate Street. "We'll leave you here. Marco, climb on behind Aquila. Nikolaus, could you take Wingshadow?"

Marco dropped from the saddle and climbed up behind his brother on Nighthawk.

Adan addressed *Principales* Neziah and the other soldiers, "I am trusting you to keep everyone safe. I know you will do your best."

The men assured Adan that they would. Nikolaus took Wingshadow's reins and he, and the others, continued to Serapio's. Adan and the twins headed for the Antonia Fortress.

"Marco, you probably suspect," explained Adan, "every fort has, at least, one secret tunnel. If it hasn't been blocked, I'll need you to go through it and I'll be waiting for you at the trap door inside the fortress. There will be a vertical shaft you'll need to climb. There should be a ladder up to the door. I'll be there to let you in. Come on. It's this way."

He led his sons to a congested tumble of decaying buildings next to an outer wall of the Antonia. It was a storage area for items discarded for the poor to scavenge. Early every morning, soldiers routinely dumped trash over the wall. Adan slipped from Blackfire's saddle and motioned for Marco to follow him. Aquila stayed with the horses.

Adan scanned the area for people picking through the trash heaps. It was a common practice for people to search for bricks or blocks of limestone from demolished buildings, unwanted furniture, or cooking pots. A small group was slowly making their way over a fresh pile of leftover food. One of them looked over his shoulder at Adan. His ears and most of his nose and lips had been torn away. He raised a hand to pull a scarf farther over his face. His fingertips were missing. Adan forced himself to not grimace at the signs of leprosy. Instead, he reached into his pouch and approached the man. He showed the man a silver coin and set it down near him. The man was shocked, having expected the centurion to shout at them to leave. Yet, he did not move until Adan had backed away.

He picked up the coin. "Thank you, Centurion. You have exchanged this silver coin for a golden crown in heaven. God be with you." He turned away and urged his group to move on.

Adan turned back to this son. "Marco, stomp your feet as you walk." He covered his nose to stymie the stench of decomposing trash.

"Why?" Marco took a closer look. "*Ohe*, never mind."

Rats and roaches scattered as they progressed. Marco cringed at the foul smell. It was easy to see why the hidden passage was safe from accidental discovery.

Adan made his way behind the crumbling buildings, piles of discarded pottery, and broken furniture until he found a single limestone slab lying on the ground next to the fortress wall. Marco helped him clear the trash partially hiding it and pushed it aside. They stared into a small opening to a steeply slanting tunnel.

"You'll have to crawl through there, then feel your way along the tunnel and keep your head low. You'll find the trap door at the top of a shaft, at the end of the tunnel. The ladder is sturdy enough—at least, it was when Tribune Salvitto showed me the passage. The trap door is secured from inside a storage shed."

Marco slipped into the tunnel opening. Adan replaced the limestone slab. The centurion threaded his way through the debris back to Aquila and jumped into the saddle.

They rode around the Antonia's outer wall until they approached the gates. Adan introduced himself and the usual ripple of recognition passed among the soldiers. He announced that he was there on official business and they waved them through. The two rode across the central quadrangle toward a separate building near the soldiers' barracks. Adan stopped in front of the building and tilted his head toward the sign over the door which read—*Negotium Officium*, the business office. They continued around to the back of the building, out of sight. Aquila stayed with the horses while Adan walked toward the barracks. Seeing that no one was paying attention, he slipped behind the building and approached the storage shed which was huddled between it and the outer limestone wall. He unbarred the door of the shed and went inside.

Adan paused to let his eyes adjust to the low light. The pungent smell of dust and stagnant air was unpleasant. He pulled the front of his tunic over his nose and mouth. He stepped around battered wooden cases and cracked shelves until he found an old cabinet and pushed it over the hard-packed dirt floor until a wooden trap door was revealed. He grasped a brass ring, pulled it open, and called to Marco.

There was no answer.

"Marco! Are you there?" Adan tried to see into the darkness. Anxiety tightened his chest as he called again.

"Father, I'm down here," called a disembodied voice from the void. "Apparently, someone made use of the ladder elsewhere. I was trying to see if it was left somewhere in the tunnel."

Adan lay flat on the shed floor and extended his hand. "Here, grab my hand."

They grasped each other's wrists and Marco used the tunnel wall to brace his feet as he climbed from the pit. He clambered over the edge of the opening.

"Marco, throw one side of your cloak over your left shoulder, and pull up the hood. Make sure it hides your face. You'll look like one of the resident musicians hired for entertainment. Trail behind us until we're inside the office. Leave the cloak on Blackfire's saddle. The horses are behind the business office. You know what to do."

Marco arranged the cloak and slipped out of the storage room. Adan replaced the bar to secure the outer storage door and rejoined Aquila.

"Let's go," said Adan to Aquila. "Now it gets tricky. You might have to improvise."

Father and son strolled out from behind the office building and pulled the door open. They did not close it. The startled clerk leaped to his feet at the sight of Adan's centurion attire.

"Sir!" exclaimed the soldier. "How may I serve you?" As Adan approached the counter, the man's eyes widened in recognition. He blinked rapidly with agitation as he took a step back.

"I am Centurion Adan Clovius Longinus. This is my son. It occurs to me that I should retrieve my old *testamentuem* since I have a more recent one on file at the Fortress in Caesarea. I keep forgetting about the old one whenever I'm in Jerusalem so I made a point to not forget this time."

The office clerk swallowed anxiously. He knew this centurion was the *Lupus Legatus* that had been executed by Herod's order and here he stood. Aquila moved closer to his father to block the view of the door and stared at the man. The clerk's attention was drawn to another pair of wolf eyes. The man's lips moved slightly as he silently prayed to Mars, the god of war, for protection. Aquila coughed loudly and Adan glanced at him with appropriate concern. Marco heard the signal and crept from behind the open door. He scurried into the office hunched over and crouched behind the counter.

"Will you get me a request form, soldier? I'll fill it out as you search for the document," said Adan.

The man reached beneath the counter and set the papyrus sheets before Adan.

"Aquila, go help him."

The man turned to walk into the second of the eight rooms housing shelves of cubicles. The first two were for centurions, only. Aquila followed him into the room. Marco padded silently into the first room housing the cubicles for A-K. He had to find the scroll sent by Aurelius Julius among all the centurions' last testaments and other documents. It had been there for about twenty years and may have been misplaced to make room for more recently filed scrolls.

As soon as the soldier and Aquila disappeared into the second room for L-Z, Adan called out, "Excuse me, *Legionary*, I'll need a pen and ink."

The clerk left Aquila and took the items from his own desk. The man again started for the second room.

"You'll need to look for *Adas* Clovius Longinus, not Adan. I changed my *praenomen*."

"Yes, Centurion. As you wish." He started to return to the second room yet again.

"I was here not too long ago," said Adan, drawing the man back, "and became acquainted with Commander Lysias. I went with him to deliver the prisoner, Paul of Tarsus, to Caesarea. There was an incident and his slave died. Do you know if he bought another stable boy? The commander rented out his other slave to tend to the centurions' horses."

The soldier relaxed under Adan's amiable manner. "I do remember the slave you speak of. He was a fair-haired Greek. Well, maybe not. Lysias probably made him dye it to mark him as property. He took poison right there in a horse stall, so they say."

"That must have angered the commander. Losing a good slave."

"Yes, Sir, he called for an investigation about the poison. Wanted to know how he got it. They finally decided he had made it himself from an oleander bush growing in back of the stables. Commander Lysias had the bush pulled up and burned. A couple of slaves nearly died just from the smoke. Leave it to ignorant slaves to have no idea how poisonous oleander is. Even wild animals know better than to eat it."

The soldier made a dismissive gesture. "But stable slaves are cheap enough. Lysias had him replaced within the week but the new slave has scars from the pox." He ran his hand over his face. "No one wants to look at him." He smirked. "Or use him for anything else."

Adan's expression hardened. The sneer on the clerk's face vanished and he lowered his eyes, embarrassed at his failed joke.

Adan waited a moment before he spoke, "Our horses might need their hooves cleaned and filed later today? Does the commander rent him out like he did the Greek slave?"

"Yes, Sir, he does. Do you want me to make a reservation with the commander?"

"Perhaps later. If we have enough time, I'll stop by when we finish our errands." Adan returned to the task of filling out the lengthy request form.

This conversation not only kept the soldier busy while Marco searched for Aurelius's letter, it also confirmed that Commander Lysias was convinced that Calais was "dead." Marco's plan to fake Calais's death had succeeded. Adan would send the good news as soon as he returned to Caesarea.

While Adan talked with the soldier, Aquila moved the scrolls around in the cubicles to make enough noise for the clerk to hear. When the soldier returned to the room, he started to rummage through the L's.

"Sir, I already looked," said Aquila. "It's not there. I was about to check the M and N cubicles just in case it was misplaced."

"Go ahead. I'll look in the O and P cubicles."

By the time the clerk finished with the O's and P's, he was grumbling under his breath. The clerk finally went back to the L's and removed all of the scrolls. He checked each one before he replaced it in the cubicle.

In the first room, Marco found Aurelius's letter surprisingly without difficulty, in fact, it was on the top of the pile of scrolls in the proper cubicle. Something about the scroll didn't seem right. It was too light for two letters. He checked the wax seal. It looked fresh. The scroll ends weren't even dusty. He pulled back a corner of the papyrus and read a part of a few lines. It was the letter Aurelius had written to Tribune Theo Salvitto, but the letter for Demitre appeared to be missing. Marco carefully put the scroll back into the same place it had been. While Aquila and the clerk searched for Adan's scroll in the second room, he padded into the main room and around the counter. He gave his father an unhappy look and shook his head as he quickly slipped out the door. There was no time to explain.

The soldier and Aquila reentered the main room. "Centurion Longinus, I am very sorry. We both searched carefully but your *testamentuem* is not there. Could it have been sent to the garrison in Caesarea? Perhaps the clerk there filed it and forgot to tell you."

"That is a real possibility, *Legionary*," agreed Adan. "I'll check on that as soon as I get back." He added a note at the bottom. "Here is the request form. I have indicated that the document could not be found. Come Aquila, we have more errands this afternoon." He handed the form to the clerk who glanced over it to be sure nothing was left blank.

While Adan and Aquila were busy with the clerk, Marco headed for the shed behind the barracks. In his hurry, he forgot to retrieve the cloak thrown over Blackfire's saddle until he saw a group of soldiers talking among themselves. He started to retrace his steps toward the business office.

"You there!" shouted one of the men. "What are you doing here? Why don't you have a visitor's sash?"

Marco slowly turned to face the soldiers. They started toward him, when one of them stopped and hurriedly whispered to his companions.

"Forgive me," said the man who had shouted at him. "You must be the son of Centurion Longinus." He tilted his head toward one of the other men. "He said he saw you come in with the centurion. Go about your business."

Marco hurried on his way. He ducked behind the barracks and watched to see if the men would see Adan and Aquila leave the office. The men didn't move on and continued with their conversation. Marco knew that his father and brother would leave any minute. He had to do something before the men saw Aquila on the opposite side of the quad. Marco approached the men. He anxiously pointed toward Holding, the building where prisoners were held.

"Sirs, I am sorry to interrupt but I think I saw a woman crouched down behind that building. She seemed very upset."

The soldier who had shouted at him pointed in the same direction. "Behind Holding? Over there?" Marco nodded eagerly.

They hurried away in the opposite direction from the business office. Marco ran to the shed to wait for his father and brother. They soon rounded the corner of the barracks and joined him.

"Marco! Was Aurelius's scroll gone? You looked carefully, didn't you?" asked Adan as he removed the bar securing the shed door.

"Father, the scroll was right on top, in plain sight but the letter for Demitre was missing. There was only the letter addressed to Tribune Salvitto. So, I put it back. The wax seal looked fresh and it looked like the scroll had been handled. It wasn't even dusty. Would they have left such an outdated document on top of the pile? It would have to be moved out of the way anytime they wanted to find another scroll."

"Lysias," Adan hissed, "he must have the letter addressed to Demitre. Aurelius explained everything about his new identity in that letter. Lysias knows Aurelius is alive and willfully deserted the army. Leaving the scroll was a trap. He must have given standing orders to arrest anyone who tried to walk out with it." He sighed wearily and shook his head. "That was quick thinking, Marco. You did the right thing. Come on. Let's get you out of here."

Marco tried to hide his gratification at hearing his father's praise. He glanced at Aquila who smirked good-naturedly, not missing Marco's reaction. Both brothers treasured their father's rarely spoken praise.

Adan pulled the door open and they entered the shed. He and Aquila helped Marco drop into the tunnel. Adan secured the cabinet over the trap door and he and Aquila left the shed. He re-barred the door and they mounted their horses. They leisurely trotted across the quad and out the fortress gates. They circled around the Antonia and found the limestone slab among the trash heaps. Father and son moved the slab aside to find Marco waiting for them. He climbed out and they replaced the stone slab. They mounted up and headed for Serapio's shop.

***

Back at the Antonia, a centurion came into the business office and asked for his *testamentuem* to make a few changes. When the clerk found the document, he noticed that the scroll from Aurelius Pomponius Julius was disturbed. A corner of the papyrus was bent as if someone had pulled it away. The commander had instructed all the soldiers who worked as clerks to give the scroll to whoever asked for it so it would be in his possession when the guards stopped him at the gate. Seeing that the papyrus was damaged, he ran to the commander's office when his replacement came on duty at shift change.

"Enter!" called out Lysias when a knock sounded at his door.

The *legionary* entered and came to attention. "Commander Lysias, you instructed me to report if the scroll written by Centurion Julius was retrieved. It was not but it's been damaged. Centurion Longinus, the one they call the Wolf Commander, came asking for his *testamentuem*, but it wasn't there. It was after he and his son left that I noticed that the scroll had been disturbed."

"Was he ever out of your sight?"

"Yes, Sir, when I went to get his *testamentuem*."

"Could he have gone into the first room then?"

"No, Sir. The request form was completed. It would take the whole time I was in the second room for him to finish filling it out."

"You said, his son was with him—just one. Where was the other one?"

"Which other one, Sir?"

"He has identical twin sons."

"Centurion Longinus and one son came in the office, Sir. He called him Aquila."

"Go next door and get my *principales*."

The clerk returned with the commander's aide. Lysias sent him to the gate sentries to inquire about the centurion. When he returned, he confirmed that Longinus entered with only one son. Lysias dismissed his aide and addressed the clerk. "Was he angry when you failed to find his *testamentuem*?"

The soldier looked confused for a moment. He realized that anger and a threat of punishment would have been the standard reaction. "No, Sir. Now that you ask, I realize he was quite agreeable and accepted the situation. There was no reprimand, Sir."

Lysias frowned. "So, he comes all the way to Jerusalem to get his *testamentuem* and doesn't care that it's not here. How kind of him." The commander mulled over the facts for a moment. "Why would Longinus want his old *Testamentuem* after all this time?

It has been, at least, twenty years. Besides, there would have to be a new one on file in Caesarea."

"He said that he kept forgetting to get it whenever he was in Jerusalem," offered the soldier.

Lysias grunted. "Why did he feel the need to explain his actions to an insignificant underling?"

The soldier blinked anxiously, not sure if he was supposed to answer.

Commander Lysias contemplated the situation while the clerk waited at attention. He felt insulted that Centurion Longinus had denied him the courtesy of a visit. He remembered how proud he had been to have the great *Lupus Legatus* by his side when they escorted Paul of Tarsus to Governor Felix but Longinus had rebuffed his admiration. He had been treated this way by many native-born Romans with family entitlements. He was a Greek with a *Peregrini Latini* citizenship, which cost him a great deal of money. It allowed him to vote, own property, sue in court, have a legal trial, and be protected from torture, including crucifixion. Yet, he was a semi-citizen with only half the rights of a native-born Roman. It rankled his self-image to know that he was considered only one step above a freed slave. He also knew that he was only given command of the Antonia because no one else wanted it. Jerusalem had become a hotbed of rebellion and if insurgents should succeed in driving the Romans out, he would be the sacrificial scapegoat.

"He was up to something," grumbled the commander. "Every time he shows up, something unusual happens. Could his son have ever slipped into the first room?"

"No, Sir, I would have seen him. Besides, I could hear him checking the scrolls. He never left that room."

"Did Longinus ever have time to find the scroll and inspect it?"

"No, Sir. Not only was the form completely filled out, I could hear the pen scratching on the papyrus, now and then. It had a dull nib."

Lysias slammed his fist down on his desk. "Then how in Hades was the scroll damaged? Did you inspect it when you first came on duty as I instructed you?"

The soldier gulped. He had forgotten. "No, Sir, I did forget but only this once."

Lysias jumped to his feet. His face was red with anger. "Only this once? Liar! I should throw you into a sack of snakes!"

It was a common punishment for more serious offenses but it would take time for someone to catch enough of the reptiles to make it meaningful. "Go muck out the stalls of every centurion's horse with your bare hands!"

"Yes, Commander!" The *legionary* rushed from the room. He was grateful that he escaped being tied in a dead-body bag with dozens of the slithering creatures. A venomous viper, or even a sand boa, was often included in the punishment. Sand boas were not poisonous but they used their teeth to get a good hold before squeezing the prey to death. He only hoped that Lysias's slave had already cleaned most of the stalls.

Commander Lysias left his office and walked to the *negotium officium*. He told the clerk on duty to get Centurion Julius's scroll. He snatched it from the clerk's hand and left. He pondered the situation as he returned to his office. Why had Longinus come to the Antonia for a non-urgent errand, yet deliberately avoided him—especially since he *outranked* Longinus? An informal greeting was not only polite; Lysias considered it protocol. It was so typical of the high society elite to snub any foreigner, especially one from a Roman occupied country. The Romans denigrated the people they conquered and admired any people who opposed them. The best way to gain Rome's respect was to fight to the death. Either way, Rome would gain the region's resources and the survivors for slaves. Lysias's own father had sold him to the Roman army when he turned eight years old. He never saw his family again. He understood his father's reasoning and did not blame him. However, his early experiences with his Roman trainers left him with a deep resentment against those he saw as pampered and privileged.

Lysias entered his office and sat down behind his desk. He fingered the damaged papyrus and thought to himself, "I see the problem. If someone knew there should be two letters, it's obvious that there's only one." He grunted in frustration. He should have included a copy of Aurelius's letter to Demitre.

The clerk said he could hear Aquila in the second room moving the scrolls as he searched and Longinus filled out the form with a dull pen, scratching all the while. How did Longinus manage to find the scroll, determine the inner letter was missing, put it back and still keep filling out the form in the main room?

"That was careless of you, Centurion," thought Lysias. "Damaging the parchment like some careless slave." His eyes widened and eyebrows arched at the implication of his own words. "A careless slave."

His expression darkened as he thought back on Longinus's last visit earlier in the year. His slave, Calais, had killed himself right when Longinus and his sons showed up. He remembered how one of Longinus's sons was the first to raise the alarm. Longinus had been the one who confirmed Calais was dead. He also suggested Calais had taken poison and found the vial easily even though it had dropped into the straw in the stall. Then he had insisted on arranging and paying for Calais's cremation. Why care so much about a slave, especially one he didn't own and had not even seen in twenty years?

Lysias paced the floor, and then he stopped. He hadn't been in the business office since Aurelius's scroll was brought to him and he replaced it as a trap. He had no way of knowing if his clerks *ever* checked the condition of the scroll, so it could have been damaged before today. He had heard how the centurion was partial to a group of stable slaves and how loyal they were to him. Calais had been one of them. What if the previous time Longinus was here, he asked Calais to sneak into the business office and find Aurelius's scroll? Longinus discovered that the incriminating letter was missing and had Calais put it back, damaging it in the process. Using this task as leverage, Calais demanded that Longinus help him run away. Instead, Longinus poisoned the slave to end the attempted blackmail. His conviction that Longinus murdered Calais gained momentum like a boulder set loose on a mountaintop.

He thought the scenario through to the present. Longinus showed no surprise or anger that his *testamentuem* was missing. He knew it wasn't there but used the task as an excuse to enter the office. If so, why? Why would he come back? He smiled and picked up the scroll.

"That's it," declared Lysias out loud. "You wanted to see if it was still there. You would have had time to do *that*." If the scroll was gone, that would mean the hunt for Aurelius had been called off. If it was still there, the hunt was still on. Why would Longinus care either way? And why now?

He remembered that King Herod used Aurelius's "death" against Felix Valentius in Longinus's defense during the execution of Simon Peter's guards. Aurelius had faked his death two years before Longinus ever met Valentius but could they have become friends since then? Herod proved that Aurelius must have hated his father, Valentius. Longinus must have also hated Valentius. The answer came to him as if someone had whispered it in his ear. The two men had become friends somehow. Adan needed to know if Aurelius was still in danger. Why now? Aurelius must be in Jerusalem, *right now*.

Lysias clenched his fists in frustration. He couldn't prove anything but all the facts indicated that Longinus had not only made a fool of him by circumventing the trap, he killed Calais, his most valued property. The *Lupus Legatus* may have fooled his fellow Romans, but Lysias knew the truth. Adan Clovius Longinus was a fraud.

Lysias found a sheet of papyrus, his pen, and inkpot. He wrote a brief letter explaining the circumstances surrounding the second letter to the deceased murderer, Alexander Nisos, who used the alias, Demitre, and was the uncle of Aurelius Julius. He needed proof of a connection between Aurelius Julius and Adan Longinus before making such radical accusations, especially directly to Herod, bypassing the chain of command. Lysias had been waiting a long time for someone to ask for that scroll. Perhaps it was time to stop waiting and to act. Surely, Aurelius and Longinus were here together in Jerusalem for an important reason, one worth the risk of Aurelius's capture.

The commander strode from his office and found his aide in the office next door. He instructed the *principales* to find the centurion and make note of who was traveling with him. "Start with the one-eyed furniture maker," he ordered. "Longinus is known to favor him. Do you remember what Felix Valentius looked like? You were here then, yes?" The soldier answered affirmatively. "If you spot a man who looks like Valentius, with Longinus, follow them. When you're satisfied that they are interacting like friends, come back and report to me."

If his aide returned with the news he hoped to hear, he would send Aurelius Julius's original letter, intended for Demitre, to King Herod Agrippa, in Caesarea. He knew Herod carried a grudge against Longinus. When the letter was received by the king, Commander Lysias was sure that he would be rewarded for his diligence and Longinus would suffer the same fate as Calais.

Chapter 4

The Hunt for the Innocent

———— ∞ ————

A dan decided that they had no time to waste after they reunited at Serapio's shop. He hated cutting their visit short, but a sense of urgency was gnawing at him. Unusual for Serapio, he had not tried to convince them to stay longer. In fact, he and Fabiana had seemed anxious and distracted. Adan wasn't surprised, considering the volatile atmosphere in Jerusalem. Distracted with his own situation, he didn't see the soldier sitting on his horse at the public water fountain in the middle of the intersection. He kept glancing toward Serapio's shop. When Adan's group trotted past him, the soldier stared at Aurelius. He followed Adan's group from a safe distance.

Principales Neziah and Adan took the lead as the others followed. The group kept to the center of the hard-packed, dusty streets and avoided making eye contact with the inhabitants. The three escort soldiers stayed behind the group and often glanced over their shoulders for signs of trouble. The most observant of the three noticed a Roman soldier who appeared to be following them. He was about to move up next to Neziah to inform him when Adan raised his hand for the group to slow to a walk. His brow creased with concern as he turned onto Pomona's street. There was something very wrong with her house. The door lay in the street, ripped from the hinges. Her fruit sign, advertising her shop, was trampled, and she was nowhere in sight. The group reined in their horses and dismounted.

Principales Neziah and his men stayed on their horses as Adan strode into the house. "What has happened here?" he said aloud to the walls. Fear made his mouth go dry as sadness clouded his features. The scant furniture was trampled and curses were scratched on the walls. He remembered that Valentius had bought this house for Pomona and her mother, Eliana. She would never have left it willingly to be vandalized in her absence. Where was Pomona? He prayed that she was alive and safe. Aurelius joined him and stood ashen faced as he read the curses on the wall. He was devastated to think that he had learned he had a sister only to have her taken from him before they could meet. Dulcibella lightly touched his arm and whispered something to him but could offer little comfort.

A voice sounded from the doorway. "She got away. I warned her." It was the young boy who had once taken Pomona's message to Adan, informing him that Marco was in her home. His face was taunt with grief. "Pomona was always kind to me. She gave me samples of her best fruits and overpaid me when I worked for her."

Adan approached the boy. "You did well to warn her. Do you know why this happened?"

The boy stared at the floor. He shuffled his feet and bit his lower lip. "They said she was consorting with Roman soldiers."

"So, what if she did?" snapped Aquila from the doorway. "She had a right to have visitors!"

The boy's expression hardened with sudden anger. "That's just it. She didn't. Except," he pointed at Adan. "for you! And you!" He pointed at Aquila. He blinked in surprise when Marco entered the house but recovered quickly. "One of the other fruit merchants accused her and stirred up the crowd."

Marco clenched his fists in frustration. "This is my fault! If I had not come back here after I thought Calais was dead, she would be here now!"

Adan gestured with impatience. "Our presence was a convenient excuse to accuse her. We're wasting time discussing this." He turned to the boy. "Do you have any idea where she went?"

He shook his head. "You'll never find her. If you could, so could they, and then they'll kill her." The child wilted with grief. "It's not fair! She did nothing wrong."

"Do you know that for a fact?" demanded Marco.

The boy tried to dodge around him, but Marco grasped the child's arm. "Please, we need your help. What happened here?"

The boy blinked nervously at the sight of Marco's wolf eyes. Then he looked from Adan to Aquila and back to Marco. "Do you promise not to eat me?"

Aquila looked at the boy with stern sincerity. "We promise if you help us." Adan shot a look of disapproval at Aquila. Dulcibella bit her lip and looked away.

Aurelius stepped closer. "It is true. They can control their hunger *if* they are not angered."

The boy swallowed hard and looked at Adan and his sons. They nodded solemnly, not being above using any means to find Pomona.

The boy turned his attention to Adan. "The merchant told his customers that Pomona was in league with Romans and selling them information about us. I ran to tell her. When they came banging on her door and shouting, Pomona was scared, but she tried to reason with them. They wouldn't listen. They dragged her into the street but she fought back. I'm not sure how it happened, but the man who accused her got tangled up with the others and knocked down. He fell on a knife. I couldn't see if it was his knife or one of the others'. They blamed Pomona, but I tried to tell them that she was nowhere near him when the man fell. They wouldn't listen to me. Then soldiers came and, in the confusion, I grabbed her hand and pulled her away. I think the soldiers figured she was a mother trying to protect her child from a street fight." He looked away in defeat. "I don't know where she went." He spun away and ran from the house.

"That was clever," said Adan. "His quick thinking probably saved her from being arrested."

"But she's gone. What do we do now?" asked Marco.

Dulcibella looked at Adan. "You asked us not to say anything about Pomona to Serapio and Fabian but they may already know about her. If I had to run for my life because a centurion came to my home, I would run to that centurion's closest friends."

"Pomona has no idea who my friends are," countered Adan.

"Yes, she does," said Marco. "When I was hiding from you, I mentioned that I couldn't go to Serapio's house because that would be the first place you'd look."

"Even if she didn't run to Serapio," said Dulcibella, "his customers would tell him the town's gossip. Serapio and Fabiana may have heard something helpful."

Without another word, they left the house and climbed back on their horses.

Neziah signaled to Adan, "Sir, one of the men spotted a lone soldier following us. He's hanging back on the other side of that courtyard wall. You can just make out his shadow, there." He pointed to a corner of the street. "What are your orders?"

"Take your men and approach him," answered Adan. "Ask him to carry a message to Commander Lysias for me. Tell him that I regret not being able to visit with him earlier and beg his pardon. Tell him *Primus Pilus* Tacitus will be pleased with my report on the Antonia. I'm leaving this to you because it will appear too defensive if I confront him myself. Lysias has no business tracking me or anyone with us. If he asks anything about Aurelius, claim no knowledge of the man. Keep your wits about you. Then wait for us at the western gate."

Neziah could not resist a smile of appreciation for Adan's trust in him. "Yes, Sir. It will be done." He and the other three soldiers turned their horses toward the street corner.

Adan's group trotted back to Serapio's shop, but they were in for another distressing surprise. Serapio's door was uncharacteristically shut. He always kept it open to signal that he was open for business. No one came to the door at their knocking.

"They're not here, Adan," said Dulcibella. "Look through the window lattice. Some of the furniture is gone." The distress in her voice belied her attempt to remain calm. "What could have happened? They said nothing about leaving when we were here."

"First my sister is missing," exclaimed Aurelius, "and now they're gone. Can this get any worse?"

"I'm afraid it can, Aurelius," said Adan. "I haven't had a chance to tell you but your letter to your Uncle Demitre was missing from the scroll. Lysias must have it and knows you're alive." He thought about telling Aurelius about the soldier that had been following them but decided he didn't need to know. There was nothing he could do about it. "I am so sorry. I have failed you on every count."

"This is not your fault," declared Aurelius. "If anything, this must be fate's way of paying me back for deceiving my father and dishonoring my oath as a centurion. I think our departure from this accursed city is overdue. We should leave."

Adan agreed and spun Blackfire around, but Dulcibella called out to him. "Adan, wait! We have to talk about this. They must have had most of their things already packed when we showed up earlier. I thought the two of them seemed out of sorts. We must have delayed them. But we have no idea where they went."

"Father," offered Aquila, "Serapio would go to the one place in Judea where he would be welcomed, no questions asked. He would go to Caesarea."

"Aquila is right," agreed Marco. "He will be headed for the western gate."

"I did tell him," said Nikolaus, "that I would help him establish a shop near the Ocean View Inn if he should ever leave Jerusalem. I even reserved a plot of land for him."

"Would he request an escort at the Antonia?" asked Aurelius. "Should we inquire there?"

"No," said Adan. "The Antonia is the last place he would go for help now that Theophilus Salvitto is gone. My sons and Niko are right. Serapio would head for Caesarea. Come on!"

They formed a tight group with Dulcibella in the center and trotted through the congested streets of the city. A few residents shouted curses at Adan as they passed but the catcalls went unheeded. If they had guessed incorrectly precious time would be lost. They met up with Neziah and his men who were waiting one street up from the gateway.

"What happened with the spy, Neziah?" asked Adan.

"He was embarrassed that we spotted him but he recovered. He described Captain Hadrian and asked his name. I said it was Cornelius. Then I asked why he was inquiring about your family and by whose orders. He said Commander Lysias had sent him concerning a relative of Felix Valentius. I asked him if he was referring to the traitor executed by Caligula."

"That was quick thinking. Lysias knows my father-in-law is Marcus Cornelius," said Adan.

Neziah continued, "He asked outright if the man with you was the son of Valentius. We laughed in his face. I said, 'I just told you his name is Cornelius. Do you really think Centurion Longinus would associate with the son of the man who tried to kill him every chance he got?'"

"How did he react to that?" asked Adan.

"He turned kind of red and didn't ask any more questions, Sir. I gave him your message for Commander Lysias. Then he turned his horse and left."

"You did well, Neziah. Come on. We have to find Serapio and his family. Apparently, they are fleeing the city." They continued the remaining short distance to the western gate.

They craned their necks trying to see among the pedestrians, wagons, animals, and beggars. Adan spotted two wagons moving in single file and the leader had a mane of unruly gray-streaked, black hair. Adan breathed a sigh of relief when he recognized his friends and their wagons. They were waiting in line to have their possessions checked for taxable merchandise, but something didn't look right. The line was much longer than normal and twice as many soldiers were on duty. The men looked surly and they were being more thorough than protocol required. Adan signaled for his group to stop. He scrutinized Serapio and Fabiana with narrowed eyes and a scowl.

"What's the matter?" asked Dulcibella.

"She's not talking."

"Who?" Dulcibella studied their friends.

"Fabiana. She never just sits there," said Adan with deepening anxiety "Unless she's really worried about something. And why are they searching the wagons so carefully?"

Aquila nudged his horse closer to his father. "When I was imprisoned in Rome, our guards looked like that when they were searching for contraband. Could they be looking for Pomona?"

Adan addressed the others, "All of you stay back until I have Serapio out of the city. Neziah, you and the men follow my lead. We will act as if we have orders to escort Serapio and his family to *Primus Pilus* Tacitus."

The soldiers acknowledged the centurion's order and moved their horses behind Adan and *Principales* Neziah. Adan rode past the other wagons in line and approached Serapio's wagon.

"Ah, fortune smiles upon us!" Adan shouted. "I went to your house and was afraid I wouldn't find you before you left the city. I have orders to escort you to the garrison in Caesarea, by command of *Primus Pilus* Tacitus. He did not want you to make this journey without protection and he apologizes for not sending me sooner. Apparently, there was a miscommunication about your departure time."

Serapio's relieved surprise flashed across his face for a second before he lifted his chin. "Well, Centurion, you are a most welcome sight indeed. Tacitus expects us in Caesarea no later than the day after tomorrow so we were forced to leave without you. But here you are!"

Adan saw the *legionaries* eyeing him suspiciously despite his attire and weapons that signaled his status as a centurion. Their lack of immediate acknowledgment of his authority told him how serious the situation was and it rankled his ego.

He spotted a soldier wearing the belt of a *principales* and beckoned to the man. "Are you in charge here?"

"Yes, Centurion. I have strict orders to search every wagon for a Samaritan woman who knifed a Roman citizen. I hear she slashed him from neck to knee." The soldier approached as he spoke until he stood to the side of Blackfire. He peered up into Adan's face. He stepped back when he recognized him. "Forgive me, Sir, but are you the *Lupus Legatus*?"

Adan made a disgruntled face. He hated the nickname. "All you need to be concerned about is that I am Centurion Longinus with orders to escort this man and his family. I understand you have orders from Commander Lysias, but I will save you the trouble of searching these two wagons. There is no one to arrest here or merchandise to tax."

The *principales* was recently promoted and eager to establish his new position. "I mean no disrespect, but Commander Lysias outranks you and I have direct orders from him. I will search quickly."

Adan's irritation was blatantly evident at the soldier's dismissal of his status. "How dare you question my authority! *Primus Pilus* Tacitus outranks you, me, *and* Commander Lysias combined. But I appreciate your need to obey. So, I'll give you two choices. Go ahead and search." He waved a hand at Serapio and Nebetka's wagons.

The soldier's features relaxed and he started toward Serapio's wagon.

"However," Adan dropped his hand to the hilt of his sword, "if you don't find your fugitive then I will report to Lysias *and* Tacitus how you interfered in *my* duties. There is nothing here besides household belongings. Nothing to be taxed. Do you really think this man, summoned by the highest-ranking commander in Judea, would be stupid enough to aid a runaway criminal, *under my escort*?"

The soldier hesitated with indecision.

"Regulus Novius Serapio," called out Adan. "Are you harboring a knife-slashing, crazy woman along with your wife, son, and *grandchildren*?"

Serapio uttered a deep, growl of a laugh. "Of course, I am. I brought her along to make the trip entertaining. I so hate to be bored."

The soldier's face reddened with embarrassment as the other *legionaries* tried not to smirk. They were pleased to see the man's overinflated ego knocked down a few notches.

Adan glared at the soldier. "What is your decision? I'm losing daylight and—what is your name? *Principales* Neziah, make note of this man's name for my report."

The soldier stepped farther away. "My name is Domitius, Sir. I apologize for inconveniencing you. I was only doing my job." He bowed his head and backed out of the way. He shouted for his men to make a path through the traffic. "Clear the way! Nothing here to be taxed!" He gestured impatiently at the men to reassert his authority. "Stop standing around gawking like old women or I'll have you scrubbing the *latrines* for a week!"

The soldiers jumped into action and shouted at the other travelers to make room for Adan and the two wagons. Adan and Neziah took the lead as Serapio and Nebetka followed him through the city gates. The other escort soldiers followed behind. Blackfire's muscular frame and high-stepping gait persuaded pedestrians to quickly move aside.

Dulcibella and the others eventually joined Adan outside the city gate. The road branched several times and other travelers became sparse. Even the breeze no longer carried the sound or smell of the city as they reached the far side of a wind-chiseled hill. Adan spied a cluster of oaks and led the group off the road for a rest. Everyone dismounted as Serapio and Nebetka helped their families get down from the wagons.

Adan turned to Serapio and Fabiana. "What has happened to make you abandon your home without telling us? I know you would never leave unless hellfire was biting at your heels."

"That is exactly what is happening in Jerusalem. I knew if I said anything to Dulcibella or Nikolaus, they would insist on staying with us. I am so sorry that I cannot give you a profitable return on the money you invested on my shop, but once I get reestablished, I can pay. . ."

"Stop right there," said Adan with a raised hand. "That shop was a gift from me, not a loan. You are free to do with it as you please. Do not forget I lived with you for years and you and Fabiana treated me like a son." Adan stepped closer and put a hand on his friend's shoulder. "Now tell me, what is going on that makes you and Nebetka suddenly vacate your houses."

Serapio sighed and glanced at Nebetka and Fabiana as they joined them, "Jerusalem is primed for revolt. The people are suffering under unbearable taxes and injustices showered on them at every turn. Men, women, and children are murdered in the streets without consequences. Soldiers openly steal from the citizens and laugh at their protests. This cannot go on, Adan."

"I hear you but the republic was dissolved a long time ago and we are ruled by an emperor who cares nothing for the rules of law. I doubt Emperor Domitian has even read them. He prefers making up lies and meaningless executive orders to serve his own purposes. He has given free rein to the commanders loyal to him to do as they please as long as they fill his coffers with tax payments."

"Perhaps Rome has taken debauchery to a new level," suggested Dulcibella as she put a supportive arm around Fabiana's shoulders. "People will only tolerate so much before they retaliate."

Fabiana looked away, dreading her next words. "There is one other matter." She looked at Serapio anxiously.

Serapio cleared his throat and gave his wagon a sidelong look. "Yes, there is that."

Adan looked from one to the other. "What are you talking about?"

Nebetka walked away to join his wife who was standing by the wagon with their children.

"Now, don't be angry, Adan," said Serapio. "It was the right thing to do." He walked to his wagon and began lifting pieces of furniture and other household goods out of it.

Adan realized what was happening. "You've *got* to be kidding me!"

Fabiana looked at him with frustration. "What would you have done?"

Aurelius, who had been listening in silence, frowned in confusion. "What is going on?"

Nikolaus, who had been listening without comment helped Serapio remove enough of the wagon's contents to expose a false bottom. They lifted the wood panel off and Serapio reached inside. "It's safe now. You can come out."

Aurelius and Adan walked to the wagon and peered over the side. A small, middle-aged woman sat up and looked around apprehensively. She saw Adan and murmured, "So, we meet again, Centurion."

"Pomona!" Adan stared in shock. "Serapio, if those soldiers had found her, all of you would have been. . ."

"Let's not talk about what could have happened since it didn't," said Serapio with an impish grin. "Let's just be thankful that you came along just when you did."

Aurelius stepped closer. He never looked away from Pomona's face as he offered a hand to help her down from the wagon. He studied her features so intently, she blinked with concern.

"Do I know you, Sir?" she asked as she surveyed his features. Her expression altered as she realized who he must be but she doubted her senses. "I know your face—but not you."

"You have his eyes. Intelligent and deep," said Aurelius. "But you have none of his sharpness. Your mother must have been quite beautiful."

A slow smile lit Pomona's face as her doubt evaporated. "And you have his strong jaw and high cheekbones and brow. You must be Aurelius. We meet at last. Am I foolish to think you have come to Jerusalem to find me?"

"Not foolish," said Aurelius as he slowly shook his head.

Serapio and Fabiana stared at them. "Do you know each other?" Serapio asked.

Pomona smiled at Serapio. "No, not yet, but we will. We have the same father." She turned back to Aurelius. "He is my half-brother. Our father was Felix Pomponius Valentius. He dearly loved his wife, Julia, but found solace with my mother, Eliana, when he was gravely injured and very much alone."

"Pomona," said Aurelius as he reached for her. "You are the only family I have left."

Without hesitation, she took his hand. "Can this be possible? Can you ever think of me as family? My mother was your father's mistress, after all."

"Yes, my father dishonored my mother, but that is not your fault. He also dishonored your mother, which was not her fault either. My father and your mother held each other's lives in their hands, did they not? But why should we let the sins of the father stop us from being brother and sister? Over the years, I have felt the sting of choosing a world without family. I had no idea how lost that would feel when I stole the name, Hadrian, from a dead man."

Pomona shook her head. "Can I trust you?" She looked around at Adan and the soldiers. "Can I trust you as well? I am accused of murder, which I did not commit. Some men dragged me from my home. One of the men pulled out a knife. I clawed at his eyes as father had taught me. The man lashed out wildly with the knife but I dodged under his arm. His thrashing about with the knife caused confusion and the men released me to avoid being slashed. People were yelling and jostling each other. My attacker was knocked to the ground and I saw that he was bleeding. Others cried out to a passing patrol but they came in shouting and brandishing their swords. People scattered every which way. I ran and never looked back." She lowered her head and closed her eyes against the pain of so much loss. "Father bought that house for my mother. It was the only home I remember."

"The boy's story fits with yours," said Adan. "Did he help you escape?"

"The boy I sent to you when Marco was there? Yes, he tried to explain that you were the only Roman soldier to ever come there and you were only trying to find your son. They pushed him aside and wouldn't listen. Then everything happened at once and someone pulled me away. Was it that sweet child?"

"I believe it was," said Adan. "I hope he does not suffer for defending you."

Pomona frowned at the sad thought. "If they harm him, I would never forgive myself."

"How did you get to Serapio's shop?" asked Dulcibella. "Could someone have followed you?" She nervously glanced along the road toward Jerusalem.

"I can't remember which streets I took. I just ran and melted in with the crowds."

"I found her in our barn," said Fabiana. "We have known each other for some time. She always had the best peaches. Besides, we knew Pomona was innocent. Not only do I believe her, but there was no blood on her or her clothes. And before you wonder if she could have stolen someone else's clothes, see these fruits decorating the neckline? I embroidered them, myself, in exchange for a pot of grape and honey jam."

Serapio gently rested a hand on Pomona's arm. "I also believe her. As a *gladiator*, I know it is impossible to kill a man without being splattered with his blood. Adan, we couldn't let her be arrested. There would be no justice for her. The man was going to kill Pomona without cause. It was an accident that her accuser was killed but it was also justice in disguise."

The group discussed a few more details. Then Adan took his soldiers aside and explained the situation. He gave them permission to abandon the mission if they wished to do so. The soldiers expressed their wish to follow his lead. They had seen their share of corrupt commanders and knew that Adan Clovius Longinus was not one of them.

Adan gathered the group together. "Come on! We can make it to Emmaus before nightfall."

"Let me help you in the wagon," said Aurelius to Pomona. "Sit here at the back and my horse will keep pace. We have much to talk about. For one thing, you will need a new identity. I happen to know something about that." He lowered the tailgate of the wagon and helped her in.

The others smiled with approval as he made sure she was comfortable before he secured the tailgate. The group was soon on their way to Emmaus. Adan discussed possible strategies with Dulcibella, Niko and Serapio. Aurelius and Pomona talked about memories of their parents and the course of each other's lives.

Pomona considered Aurelius's suggestion. "A new name?" She uttered with a sigh. "I suppose it would be wise."

"Since you are my sister, your *cognomen,* of course, will be Hadrian, your *nomen* will be Pomponius and your *praenomen* will be Hadriana. How does Hadriana Pomponius Hadrian sound? Fits right in with tradition."

"I cannot think of ever being called anything but Pomona. It is, after all, the only name I have ever had." She raised her hands in mock surrender. "However, I will not resist. Hadriana Pomponius Hadrian has a nice sound to it."

"Do not forget, the name Hadrian protects us both. You do not know me, yet. I could be the worst scoundrel you ever met. But I have freely shared my darkest secret with you and you have admitted to being a fugitive to me. Until we can learn to trust each other from our hearts, we can trust each other from our mutual desire to avoid being arrested."

Pomona snickered at the twinkle in his eyes. "Good point. Getting arrested would be most annoying. But I am very partial to the name Pomona."

"Then, Pomona should be your *agnomen*. It is a nickname that fits with Pomponius; does it not? Pomona Hadriana Pomponius Hadrian, sister of Captain Aurelius Pomponius Hadrian—at your service," he announced with a flourish of his hand.

Pomona laughed. She hadn't felt such heartfelt joy in a long time.

Chapter 5

Trouble and Treasure

"**E**nter!" barked Commander Lysias when someone knocked on his office door. His *principales* stepped inside and stood at attention. "Ah, you're back quickly. Did you find Longinus?"

"Yes, Sir. He is traveling with a large group including a woman. I saw the twin sons as well."

"I don't care about them," Lysias grumped irritably. "Did you see a man that favored Valentius?"

The soldier hesitated. "Sir, there were two other men and four soldiers with the group. One of the men looked Greek and the other one looked—different."

"Different from what?"

"From Centurion Valentius, Sir. He was about the right age to be his son, but his features were not like I remember Valentius. This man has a strong jaw like Valentius, but his other features are more appealing. No one would have said Valentius was handsome. Besides, I spoke with the centurion's *principales* and he said the man's name is Cornelius. The father-in-law of Longinus is *Primus Pilus* Cornelius. I believe the man in question is the son of Cornelius. He also said that Centurion Longinus had a message for you." He relayed Adan's message.

"Did Longinus confront you, himself?"

"No, Sir. He seemed unconcerned that I was there."

Lysias curled his lip and glared at the soldier long enough to make the man gulp down his increasing anxiety. "Leave," he ordered with an impatient wave of his hand. The man fled from the room.

The commander snatched up his incomplete letter to Herod and clenched his teeth. The proof he had coveted had alluded him. He began to pace the office as was his habit when he tried to think. He stopped and looked out the lattice of his window. He watched two soldiers dragging an unfortunate slave toward the Pit House, a miserable place infested with rats, roaches and human excrement.

It was a huge risk to circumvent the chain of command. The letter should go to *Primus Pilus* Tacitus first. However, he knew this was information that Herod would value and, as king, he had the authority to suspend any military policy as long as Rome's interests were upheld. There were no guarantees in life, only opportunities. An image flashed in his mind of being thrown in the pit and he shuddered. It was a recurrent nightmare that surfaced when he was stressed or ill.

Lysias knew this might be his last chance to get even with Longinus. If he let it go, he would be no better than a coward. He sat at his desk and wrote down his accusations. He addressed the letter to King Herod and sealed the papyrus with his signet ring. He muttered a prayer to the Roman goddess of luck, Fortuna, and left his office to tell his *principales* to send fast riders to deliver the letter. King Herod should have it in two days.

***

Within a few weeks, another opportunity literally knocked on Commander Lysias's office door. A man named Celsus requested an audience with the commander. He claimed to be on business for the emperor and had a letter of introduction to prove it.

The man was shown in and Lysias scanned the letter. "What can I do for you Celsus?" He glanced at the man's missing earlobe. "What happened to your ear?"

Celsus didn't hesitate. "I was hungry and didn't have anything else to eat."

Lysias chuckled. "What do you need?"

"Emperor Domitian has sent me to Jerusalem in search of any men claiming to be prophets who were in league with the Hebrew named Yeshua who was crucified. I thought it best if I asked you since you know the city better than anyone. The emperor is particularly interested in any prophecies concerning the Roman Empire. Do you know of any such men?"

Lysias was about to admit his ignorance of such matters. The last man he had contact with who claimed to be a follower of Yeshua was Paul of Tarsus. The thought of having to escort Paul to Caesarea made him think of Longinus. As Celsus frowned at the commander's hesitation, a terrible idea took shape for Lysias. Celsus was about to repeat the question when the commander raised a hand.

"I beg your forgiveness," drawled Lysias. "I have thought of someone who might be quite helpful. There is a man named Adan Clovius Longinus, a centurion. Rumor has it that he has rejected allegiance to the Roman Empire and has become a follower of this dead Hebrew. He is great friends with Paul of Tarsus who is under arrest for stirring up the people against the empire."

Celsus raised his eyebrows in interest. "A centurion, no less. That is highly foolish of him but what could he have to do with prophecies?"

"I understand he is also great friends with the man called Simon Peter who Herod arrested for heresy against the empire and another is named John, son of Zebedee."

Celsus waved a dismissive hand. "Yes, yes, we have John. He is imprisoned on Patmos Island. Still, you have not answered my question. How is Longinus connected to prophecies?"

Lysias leaned forward with a sly smile. "Longinus has secrets the emperor would sorely want to hear." The commander waited for Celsus to react while he tried to think of something incriminating. "I have heard that the man called Yeshua, that so many thought to be the Jews' Messiah, told Longinus great secrets as he was dying. Longinus is fluent in Hebrew. I've heard him talking to Hebrew soldiers when we escorted Paul. There were reports throughout Jerusalem that this Yeshua came back from the dead— just like Longinus. Do you think that is a coincidence? Ah, I see I have your attention. Longinus may not be a prophet himself but he is friends with all three of the prophets I mentioned. I have no doubt that Longinus knows many secrets about Rome, the emperor—and who threatens both in the future." Lysias raised his eyebrows and gave a knowing smile as if that would assure Celsus he was telling the truth.

Celsus's felt a wave of satisfaction. "Where can I find this centurion?"

"He was here in Jerusalem a few weeks ago. I was told that he was asking about John's whereabouts," he lied. " I imagine that by the time he learns that John is on Patmos, you could beat him there and simply wait. If he shows up, then you have your answer. If he does not, you can find him in Caesarea. He is stationed there. Tell me, will you arrest Longinus? Will you interrogate him under torture?"

When Lysias saw Celsus's shocked expression, he quickly added. "I'm only joking, of course. You would never torture a Roman citizen, much less a centurion."

Celsus leaned back in his chair. Implying that a centurion should be tortured was not a joking matter. The commander's bluster made him suspicious. "If he has information I will get it out of him, one way or another." He watched an expression of pleasure crawl across the man's face. "What have you got against Longinus?"

"Me? Nothing much, really. He killed my slave. I can't prove it but I know he did it."

"Killed your slave? For what reason? Centurions are supposed to be honorable men."

"Honorable?" Lysias grunted in disgust. "Longinus is only 'honorable' when it suits his purpose. He has everyone fooled. Trust me. Why else would he think he could kill my slave and suffer no consequences? I just wish I could prove it."

"Why can't you? Were there no witnesses?"

"None that would testify against him since the only witness was his own son," growled Lysias. "So, take care, Celsus. He is a dangerous man. And favored by Dolos."

"Dolos? Who is that?"

"Many pardons," said Lysias with a bow of his head. "You would not be familiar with the Greek gods. Dolos is the god of trickery, the master of treachery. I overheard

Longinus beseeching the clever Dolos. He was speaking Greek, of course, and didn't realize a native speaker was nearby."

"I thought you said he was a follower of this dead Hebrew, Yeshua? Why would he also pray to one of your many useless, Greek gods? The man is a native-born Roman."

Lysias felt his face grow hot. He hoped Celsus thought he was angry at the insults rather than embarrassed at his mistake. He tried to deflect. "I suppose you think your Jupiter is more powerful than Zeus? Hardly! Besides, I only told you what I heard. If you want an explanation, ask Longinus, if you can catch him. He just might outsmart you."

"Did he outsmart you?" Celsus leveled a calculating stare at the commander.

"Of course, not! Why do you insult me after I give you this information?"

Celsus rose to his feet. "Yes, thank you for that information. You have been most—shall I say—revealing."

"You will tell the emperor of my aid?" asked Lysias, still smarting at the man's evident dismissal of his accusations.

"Of course, I never forget an informer." He smiled readily, yet his eyes remained cold. "If you will excuse me. I will not take any more of your time."

Celsus left and joined the two men traveling with him who had waited outside. "That was informative but not in the way I had hoped," he told the others. "We'll spend a few more days searching for any self-proclaimed prophets in Jerusalem. If we find nothing, then we're off to Patmos Island. Our duties as 'guards' at the prison await us. Let's hope our efforts are better rewarded there or things will not go well for us."

"Will we be starving in the street with the beggars and lepers?" whined the youngest of the three men.

"You will beg for that before Domitian gets through with us," grumbled Celsus. "We won't live long enough to starve."

Commander Lysias watched the three men mount their horses and ride out through the Antonia gates. "You have laughed behind my back long enough, Longinus. Now, I have the last laugh on you."

***

Adan and his group traveled safely to Joppa to stay with Simon, the tanner, as they always did. Simon and his wife beamed with pleasure at the jars of sage, oregano, cloves, cayenne pepper, and zaatar that Fabiana and Serapio gave to them to express their gratitude for welcoming the whole family. Pomona was surprised at how readily they also welcomed her, considering she was a Samaritan. Dulcibella explained that Simon and his wife were Christians and did not follow the old covenant laws of Israel, hence their welcoming attitude toward Jew, Samaritan, and Gentile, alike.

The men trooped down to the shore by way of a twisting path cut into the cliff face. They rowed out in Simon's boat and tossed fishing nets to gather in a substantial quantity of fish for dinner. The women prepared yeast bread, spiced olive oil, grilled fish and boiled peppers, onions, and cucumber. Nebetka's older children milked Simon's goats and they all enjoyed the rich flavor of fresh goat's milk. Baked pastry filled with fig preserves was the dinner's finale. They sat out under the stars telling stories until the children began to nod off. Life had taken a new turn for Pomona and Serapio's clan. Only a day ago, they were dealing with the constant threat of violence in the maelstrom of Jerusalem. That was the nature of change. Just like the natural processes of the earth, change could be slow and unnoticed, but it could also be sudden and catastrophic. The one common denominator was that the outcome was never guaranteed. Unexpected events were the constant shadows that stalked every moment in time.

Adan's troupe bade farewell to Simon and his wife the next morning and made good time to Caesarea. The following weeks would be busy for Nikolaus and Marina as they helped Serapio temporarily set up shop at the Ocean View Inn while construction was begun for their new shop and home. Serapio only had enough money to get the building started but he hoped that he would be able to borrow the rest. He refused any help from his friends but Adan and Nikolaus hoped he would relent and accept their offers of aid.

In the meantime, everyone returned to their previous activities. Adan reported for duty at the Caesarea garrison and the family settled back into their comfortable routine.

Aurelius introduced Pomona to the crew of the *Child of the Ocean*. Pomona was again surprised at their acceptance of her. She had lived under the stigma of being barely tolerated for so long, she had become accustomed to belligerence at best and open hostility at worst. Aurelius was satisfied with the crews' usual repairs on the ship and planned to cast off with his new cargo as soon as it was loaded. They would be taking a shipment of olive oil, Israel's chief export, to Neopolis. For the time being, Pomona decided to accept her brother's offer of traveling with him.

Aurelius took her on a tour of the vessel. Pomona was impressed with, not only, the good condition of the ship, but also the demeanor of the crew. They greeted their captain as if they were pleased to see him back. Since she had experience with running a business, Aurelius offered her the job of managing the accounts. She looked the logs over and was already seeing ways to make the record keeping more efficient. She had always been good with numbers. Her father had insisted that she be taught the same lessons as a son would receive.

Brother and sister ended the tour in Aurelius's quarters. He ordered his cabin boy to bring them wine and refreshment as they sat down to talk. Pomona saw the wooden chest in a corner with the name Hadrian carved on the lid. She walked over to inspect it.

"This looks like you haven't opened it in years. Or do you leave it dusty for a reason?"

"Actually, it isn't mine. I never touch it."

Pomona gave him an understanding glance. "It belonged to the man who drowned."

"I suppose I really should open it someday," Aurelius muttered.

"Perhaps that day has come."

Aurelius gazed at the wooden chest as if, finally, it was giving him permission. "It's locked. I don't have the key," he said without conviction.

"Any lock can be broken." Pomona walked back to her brother and laid her hand on his shoulder. "Aurelius, would this man want to be forgotten? You said he had no family, was traveling alone, so he must not have had close friends. He tossed himself into a world of strangers." She patted his arm. "I believe you owe him a chance to reveal who he was. Let us remember him since no one else will."

"Perhaps you're right," sighed Aurelius. "I have grieved at the loss of my family, but at least, I had one, and now you. To have no kin in this world is like a ship without sails or an anchor. Maybe we can be 'family' to this man, at least in our hearts."

He got up and inspected the lock. It was a simple internal lever lock and only needed something to catch on the grooves and twist it open. He opened a hidden compartment in his desk and took out the key for the desk drawers. It took some maneuvering but he managed to turn the lock. Pomona came to stand by her brother as he opened the chest.

Inside was a top layer of tunics, robes, and other items of clothing. Very little water had seeped into the chest after the *Scarlet Jade* sunk so there appeared to be little damage. Aurelius lifted the clothes out and Pomona set them on the desk. There was another wooden chest in one corner. They were not surprised to find gold, silver, and bronze coins inside, but there were also three small leather bags closed with draw strings. Pomona opened one and gasped at the pearl that rolled onto her hand. It had a beautiful color like fresh cream. Each of the other two bags also held a pearl. They were not large or perfectly spherical but their baroque form was highly prized.

"A good way to transport wealth," commented Aurelius. "I suppose it would be easy enough to sell a pearl as the financial need arose."

Pomona thought for a moment. "I don't think he had a permanent home. Was he setting out from Rome for the first time?"

"I think so. The way he talked, it sounded like he had just sold his business."

"I don't think we should keep these," said Pomona.

"You mean sell them?"

Pomona thought for a moment. "Do we lack anything? Don't you own this ship outright and make a good profit?" She looked at Aurelius to see his reaction. "To honor the life of this man we should give these away."

"But to whom? We should select the recipients carefully."

"Three answers will come to us when the time is right," Pomona assured him. "And thank you for agreeing to do this. I see the same kindness in you that I saw in our father."

"*Kindness?* Are we talking about the same father?"

"*Ohe*, don't be a rascal."

"So, I've gone from a kindhearted brother to a rascal?" He grinned at her mischievously.

Pomona teasingly slapped his arm. "Stop that!"

Aurelius laughed. "Let's see what else Hadrian has for us."

They found more items that a man would need on an extended journey. There was a copper mirror, an obsidian-bladed razor for shaving, wooden prongs supporting a few strands from a horse's tail for flossing one's teeth, an ornately carved comb, and several pairs of sandals for different occasions. There were bottles of scented oil to soothe abraded skin after shaving and a glass bottle of leeches in vinegar used to dye hair black. Aurelius wondered if Hadrian was older than he looked since he must have dyed his gray hair. They were both surprised that after all these years the leeches were nearly intact.

Pomona pointed to some embossed leather partially hidden under a fine silk robe. "What is that? It looks like a book. Father had one, despite how expensive they are. He read from it to me when I was a child. That was the only book I have ever seen, until now."

Aurelius carefully pulled the book from the chest. "It's a journal. See the dates heading the passages."

They sat down on the bench next to the main portal in the cabin. In silence, they scanned the passages while Aurelius slowly turned the pages.

"I guess I was wrong," he admitted. "It looks like he had already traveled quite a bit. Here, see what else you can find in these entries. I've got to check on my crew." He handed the journal to his sister and left. She soon became absorbed in reading.

Hours later, Aurelius returned. "Are you getting hungry? I'll have my slave bring us dinner."

"That would be nice, but you've got to see this." She handed the journal to him. "Look at this entry. Hadrian spent time at the Temple of Serapis, a branch of the Library of Alexandria in Egypt. All the knowledge of the world is stored in countless scrolls. They have books as well. This is exciting. Listen. Hadrian writes, 'I dined with one of the chief librarians last night and today, he showed me writings of ancient Israel. There was an account of a census that was taken soon after the implementation of the new calendar system by decree of Julius Caesar. The account was written by a *magus* of the School of the *Magi*. It told of a great child king who was born in Bethlehem. The *Magi* found evidence in ancient text that a celestial event would announce the birth of this great king who would rule all mankind. They watched for the sign. When it appeared, they started out on their journey. They met with many misadventures before they presented themselves to King Herod in Jerusalem but eventually found the child nearly two years after his birth. They brought him many gifts but there were three special gifts befitting for a king. *When they had opened their treasures, they presented gifts to him: gold, frankincense, and myrrh. Then, being divinely warned in a dream that they should not return to Herod, they departed for their own country another way.* The story went on to say that King Herod, being afraid for his position, sent soldiers to Bethlehem to kill all the male babies of two years or younger.'"

Pomona shook her head in grief. "Did that really happen? How horrible! How could anyone snatch an infant from his mother's arms and kill the helpless babe? I'm sure men and women were also killed when they tried to protect their children."

Aurelius looked away, clenching his teeth, but said nothing. Silence hung between them until he grumbled, "I guess the child was killed since we've never heard of any such ruler."

Pomona was about to speak but there was a knock at the door. The cabin boy entered carrying a tray bearing dinner and goblets of wine. He set the tray on his master's desk and asked for instructions. Aurelius waved him off.

"Wait," said Pomona, "have you eaten?"

The boy shot a look at his master and blinked in fright. When Aurelius did not reprimand him, he answered with a shake of his head.

"Then take my dinner," replied Pomona. "I will not eat if anyone on this ship goes hungry."

Aurelius rolled his eyes. "I don't let anyone starve. Eat your dinner, Pomona. Boy, make sure you get your fill tonight. Tell Cook he can check with Pomona if he has any doubts. Apparently, she is the new kitchen manager." He threw her a look of surrender.

Pomona beamed at her brother and then addressed the boy. "What is your name?"

The boy again looked inquiringly at his master. Aurelius replied, "Answer her when she asks you a question."

"Samuel. My name is Samuel, my lady."

"Samuel. That's a strong name, one of honor. Do you try to live up to your name, Samuel?"

"I will do my best for you, my lady."

Pomona smiled and tilted her head toward the door. "You have done well. Now, go, and eat."

When Samuel was gone, Pomona tapped her finger on the journal. "I'm thinking about this last detail about how the men in the caravan were divinely warned in a dream to avoid Herod. Would a divine power warn the *Magi* but let the child be killed? That doesn't make sense."

"Good point. Why protect the *Magi* but not the child? Would this divine power be the Hebrew God? We should show Adan this journal since he and his household worship him."

"Yes, let's eat and then go to his villa. Dulcibella told me the way and said to come visit any time." She held up her hand. "But first, I'd like to suggest a few things."

"What sort of things?" he asked suspiciously.

"Improvement things. Such as keeping the crew healthy. They will work so much better for you if they are well fed and their ailments are treated. If you take good care of them, they will take good care of you. Have you not ever seen the infected blisters on an oarsman's hands? How well will he row if he is in pain? How useful will he be if he dies of that infection?"

Aurelius sighed. "I have taken a heart of kindness onto the *Child of the Ocean*. Perhaps I should change my ship's name to *Mother for the Lost*. The port masters will laugh me out of business."

Pomona puckered her lips in mock disapproval. "Don't be annoyed, dear brother. Goodness begets goodness. Maybe not immediately and sometimes compassion falls upon the ungrateful. But how will you know the results if you don't try it? Let's make a bet. Give me three months under my suggestions and we'll see where your profits go. If they are higher than the previous three months, I get one wish. If they are lower, then you get one wish. A reasonable one, of course. What say you?"

Aurelius could not hold back a smile of satisfaction. "Three months, Pomona. No more, starting today. A bet for a wish. I already know what I will ask for."

"So do I." Pomona put out her hand and they shook on their bet.

They ate their dinner amid conversation on other matters. Afterwards, they hired a carriage at the pier to take them to the estate of Marcus Cornelius. Pomona eyed the view of the ocean from the cliff top as they stepped down from the carriage. The setting sun sent glimmering rays across the bobbing waves. She sighed to see such beauty and thought that she could never tire of looking upon it. Aurelius offered his arm and she looped her arm through his. He pulled the bell cord at the front door. Footsteps sounded from inside the house and the door opened. Marco smiled when he saw who it was.

"Welcome to our home!" he exclaimed. "Come in, come in. We've just finished dinner and were about to go out on the terrace." The young man stepped back and motioned for them to enter. Then he stepped out of the door and called to the coach driver. "Are you in need of refreshment while you wait? Go around to the kitchen door and Cook will find something for you. Andreas will bring hay and water for your horse." Marco saw motion out of the corner of his eye. "*Ohe*, here he comes now. Thank you, Andreas!" he called out to their long-time estate manager.

The carriage driver was so surprised that he looked around to see if Marco was addressing someone else. Marco pointed in the direction of the kitchen door. "Cook will be expecting you."

He closed the door and led Pomona and Aurelius to the terrace to join the others. He hurried over to the back door and spoke with Cook, before joining the others.

Introductions were exchanged. Marcus and Iovita welcomed their visitors and invited them to sit. Adan asked if they needed refreshment but they declined the offer.

"I finally took your advice, Adan," volunteered Aurelius. "Pomona and I opened Hadrian's storage chest and we found this," he handed the journal to Adan. "There are entries about a child king whose birth was honored by the *Magi*. They traveled from the Far East to find him and took him royal gifts. Do you know anything about this?"

"Not much. May I see?" asked Adan. "Allow me to dismiss your carriage and stay the night with us." When the siblings accepted with pleasure, Adan addressed Marco. "Could you tell the carriage driver he can go. Get a few copper coins out of my desk drawer and pay him for waiting."

Marco took off at a trot and Aurelius handed Adan the journal.

"Here it is. Looks like his visit to the Temple of Serapis was during his first year of travel. Hadrian gave me the impression he was just setting out but there are years of entries in this journal."

Adan found the passage and read it aloud. Dulcibella and Iovita gasped in horror at the description of murdering the male babies. Marcus swallowed hard and glared at the sea, refusing to meet anyone's eye. He was grateful that he had not been a part of the slaughter but grieved that he had been a willing member of the same army. Defending one's homeland was one thing. Butchering harmless babies was barbaric.

"I have heard of this travesty," muttered Marcus Cornelius in a subdued voice.

"Was the child murdered?" asked Aurelius.

"Not then," said Adan. "But he was later. His name is Yeshua."

Aurelius frowned. "You say, 'his name *is* Yeshua? Don't you mean *was*? How do you know he was murdered?"

Everyone directed anxious looks at Adan. Marco hung his head. Aquila chewed his bottom lip. They had once used their father's most grievous confession against him.

Adan didn't hesitate to answer, "I know because I murdered him. I crucified him, as I was ordered. I plunged a spear into his heart to make sure he was dead. Then, a few days later, he greeted me in the garden where his body had been laid but had disappeared from inside the sealed tomb. I know this because I was guarding his tomb until a divine being rolled the stone away, showing that it was empty. His name *is* Yeshua because he has always lived and will always live. He is the Son of Yahweh."

Aurelius's jaw dropped in shock at the unbelievable statements. He looked around at the others to see if they shared his dismay but they were smiling with relief.

"Are you saying that he came back to life?" demanded Aurelius. "Even after you pierced his heart? He was just a man, Adan."

"Let me start from the beginning." He told Aurelius the story of Yeshua.

Marcus added how an angel of God told him to send for Peter and how he and his household were baptized into the faith. Aurelius and Pomona listened without interruption. Bits of news that Aurelius had heard about a great Hebrew healer came to mind.

Pomona had heard many accounts while she lived in Jerusalem, but her father had convinced her that Yeshua was nothing more than a skilled healer. She addressed Adan, "Do you remember what I told you about the slave, Calypso, my father gave to my mother? I told you her father worked for the *Magi*. She told me once that her father had traveled with the *Magi* to Israel to visit a great king. Could it have been Yeshua?"

Pomona explained how her father told her the Roman authorities didn't know what to do with this unusual rabbi since he never spoke against Rome. Instead, he condemned the Sanhedrin for corruption and hypocrisy. In fact, Yeshua told the people to love their enemies, even the Romans.

Marco told Pomona about his adventures, which were inspired by his belief that God had a mission for him. Aquila added his own adventures and how he learned from them.

Then Adan turned to Aurelius. "Have you told your sister how you saved our lives?"

Pomona looked at her brother with astonishment.

"*Ohe*, that answers my question," said Adan at seeing her expression.

Aurelius told Pomona about the catastrophic eruptions of Mt. *Vesuvio*. Pomona was fascinated. They talked late into the night until everyone grew tired and decided to call it a night. Pomona started to follow the others into the house but Adan called her back. Dulcibella started to leave but Adan gestured for her to stay.

"Pomona, I need to find Calypso," said Adan. "How will I know she's the right one?"

"That's easy." She lifted a hand to the side of her neck. "She has a birthmark right here. It looks like a butterfly."

"On the right side where you have your hand?" asked Dulcibella.

"Yes." Pomona lowered her arm. "She used to tell me a sweet story about a butterfly that she rescued from a spider's web. It gave her the mark to protect her from stinging insects. I always loved that story as a child."

"Where should we look first?" asked Adan.

"Pergamon," said Pomona. "If she's not there, others may know where she's gone."

He thanked her and she walked toward the villa.

Adan held the journal up in his hand. "Dulcie, I have to show this to Niko."

"As a matter of curiosity, or do you have a more pressing reason?"

"The latter. I'm wondering why the *Magi* came from such a great distance to pay homage to a carpenter's son. How did they know he was the Messiah? And what was this sign that announced his birth? I'm wondering if the Prophecy Box had anything to do with their knowledge of the omen. The *Magi* keep coming up, like signposts on a treasure map."

"A treasure map that you're hoping will lead to the Prophecy Box?" Dulcibella looked doubtful. "Are you sure you should encourage Niko to delve into this secret? What he discovers might tear him apart."

Adan was conflicted. "I know. Somehow I feel that not knowing the truth could be very dangerous, eventually. It is suspicious that Niko's father had the box. People may still be looking for it and might determine that his son has it. Niko's success and wealth could lead them to that conclusion."

"Why? What do those things have to do with the box?"

"Why does anyone murder someone to steal something? It usually has to do with power or wealth or both. I think the Prophecy Box supplies both motives. And the *Magi* are powerful and rich. There's enough of them to carry on a search for decades. Time is no protection in this case, I'm afraid."

"You think Nicandros killed someone to steal the box? Could the *Magi* have killed Niko's family?"

"I suppose it's possible, or maybe someone connected to them. Or it could be someone else entirely. Someone powerful. Like a king or a governor."

"Or an emperor," suggested Dulcibella.

"Or an emperor. Tomorrow, I'll go see Niko. I'll check on Serapio, too. Want to come along?"

"Absolutely. It'll give me a chance to visit with Marina and Fabiana."

Adan slipped his arm around her waist. They walked across the terrace and up the hill to their cottage.

Chapter 6

Shadows of the *Magi*

⸺⊱⊰⸺

The next morning, Marco and Aquila volunteered to drive Aurelius and Pomona back to the ship in the family carriage. Before Adan had to report for duty at the garrison, he and Dulcibella rode over to the Ocean View Inn. Serapio was already at work, supervising the construction of his new home and shop. Dulcibella greeted him with a hug and excused herself to find Fabiana and Marina in the inn. Adan satisfied himself that Serapio had the construction crew well in hand. He found his brother sitting on the back deck with a scroll in his hands. The breeze off the sea was cool and steady. Billowing clouds hung in clusters, mimicking faces and animals if the observer was imaginatively inclined. Nikolaus and Adan were entertained by a school of manta rays suddenly leaping from the water, arching through the air, and landing nearly flat on the water with loud slapping sounds. The creatures eventually disappeared under the waves.

"*Ohe*, that was unexpected!" Nikolaus set the scroll aside. "I guess that's why sailors call them thunder fish. What brings you out this refreshing morning?"

Adan sat down to join him. "Something I think you'll be interested to hear. Aurelius and Pomona opened the sea chest that belonged to the real Hadrian. They found a journal of Hadrian's travels. He visited the Temple of Serapis and was shown some of the documents stored there. He found a passage in one of the scrolls about the *Magi* traveling in a caravan to find a child king whose rule would never end. The text referred to a star that signaled his birth. The timing is right for that child to be Yeshua."

Nikolaus raised his eyebrows questioningly. "That is fascinating. How did they know where to look for him?"

"I have no idea. All I know is that the *Magi* went to Jerusalem first and asked King Herod where the child was so they could worship him. Herod asked his soothsayers and they said Bethlehem, so that's the direction he sent them. Then the star appeared again right over the house where the child was living."

"Do you think the Prophecy Box may have helped them identify the star?" asked Nikolaus.

"Maybe. If we can find a *magus* who traveled to Bethlehem, he should know if the Prophecy Box helped in any way."

"And why my father had it," said Nikolaus. "We have to find Calypso."

"Yes. Calypso's father worked for the *Magi* and went with them to pay homage to the child," added Adan. "We really do need to find her."

Nikolaus considered his options. "I cannot possibly leave now so soon after our travels with Marco and Aquila."

Adan agreed. "Tacitus has always been supportive of my requests but I don't want to overreach. Perhaps it would be best if we wait through the winter and consider leaving in the spring."

The two brothers were mutually conflicted. "Why does that feel like a bad idea?" asked Nikolaus.

Adan shrugged. "Maybe something will happen that suggests otherwise. Besides, the Olympic Games are approaching and I have to help with security for the visiting athletes and their dignitaries. Herod Agrippa will be presiding over the events and we have to protect him as well."

Nikolaus chewed his lip in thought. "Marina will understand whenever we decide to go. In fact, she might be eager for me to get some answers about my family. Also, Serapio is here now and it has turned out well with my daughter and her husband helping to manage this place. Let's hope for the best and prepare ourselves. Who will go with us?"

"We have plenty of time to give that some thought."

"We need Pomona to join us," said Nikolaus, "but it sounds like she won't leave her brother."

"The obstacles do seem insurmountable. However, if our journey is God's will, it will happen. We just need to be patient. For now, let's talk this over with them and see where Aurelius will be going over the next few months."

Nikolaus agreed and they went to the stables to saddle his horse. They found Mariana and Dulcibella talking with Fabiana and told them they would be gone for a short errand. They rode down to the pier where the *Child of the Ocean* was docked. Aurelius was on deck and waved for them to come aboard.

"What brings such fine gentlemen to my ship?" called out Aurelius.

Adan and Nikolaus strode up the gangplank and greeted their friend. "We were wondering if we could speak to you and Pomona if it's convenient," said Adan.

Aurelius led them to his cabin. Pomona was sitting at the table, inspecting the latest cargo inventories. She looked up and smiled. "What can I do for you two?" She waved a hand for them to join her at the table.

Adan gave a brief summary of their interest in finding Calypso.

Pomona's expression hardened. "You want me to help you find Calypso? After all these years? I don't really know how I can possibly help."

"Perhaps if you told us anything she said about her previous life, places, names of people, memories of events," said Nikolaus patiently. He understood her reluctance.

Pomona considered whether she wanted to remember anything about the woman she had loved like a second mother but had abandoned her when Eliana died. Calypso may have been a slave, but Pomona had viewed her as an equal. She remembered how her mother would scold her for talking back to Calypso. Eliana would say, "Treat her with love and she will love you." Pomona believed her mother, but in the end, her love for Calypso had not mattered. She left anyway. However, Pomona felt indebted to Adan and Nikolaus for helping her to flee Jerusalem.

"She said that her husband was killed while they lived in Jerusalem and she became destitute. Her daughters were grown and married, but their husbands did not want to take her in. She had sons but would only shake her head if I asked about them. They caused her great pain, or, at least, something did. She didn't speak much about them, but sometimes she cried when she thought no one was looking. I always thought it was the loss of her husband. She said he was a kind man and a good father."

Pomona remembered how Calypso used to sing her to sleep. She would never forget those soothing lullabies. She looked up from her reverie. "There is one thing she let slip. Father came to visit. He loved to tell me stories about his adventures and once he mentioned Pergamon. He said something about the Caicus River and she corrected his pronunciation, under her breath. He didn't hear her but I did. I asked her later if she had been to Pergamon. She said she grew up there."

"Then we'll start there," said Nikolaus. "Perhaps she had family and friends there that will remember her. Anything else?"

"She made the most delicious pastries. In fact, Father told me that was one reason he offered to buy her as a slave." Pomona looked away and frowned in concentration. "I have a vague memory of Father telling me that he would have bought her son as well but he was short on money. He said that someone who outranked him took pity on the boy and did not want him sold to the mines. He never mentioned anything about Calypso's son again. But I don't think she held anything against my Father. She always made sure there were honeyed-fruit treats for him when he came to visit. I don't know if that helps."

"Pomona, they can travel with us and you can go to Pergamon to help them find this woman," said Aurelius. "I usually procure a full schedule of cargoes to deliver in that area of the Aegean. We can go after I come back here with a shipment from Cyprus. Adan, you, and Nikolaus are welcome to travel on my ship. I can accept a cargo slated for Smyrna which isn't far from Pergamon."

Nikolaus and Adan looked at each other with hope "Thank you for the offer. That would be extremely helpful," said Nikolaus.

"It depends on whether I can get away from my duties," said Adan. "We'll have to wait and hope for the best."

***

A few days later, Pomona and Aurelius had a task they needed to complete before they set sail for Cyprus. They took a carriage to pick up Adan and Dulcibella first, and then on to the Ocean View Inn and found Nikolaus talking with Serapio as they looked over the beginning construction of Serapio's new home and furniture shop. They would have to double up the occupancy of the home since it would be some time before Nebetka and his family could afford their own place. While Pomona talked with Serapio, Fabiana came out of the inn to join them. The two women hugged in greeting.

Aurelius pulled Nikolaus out of earshot of the others. "Niko, tell me, how are Serapio and Nebetka paying for all this? Adan said they may have difficulties."

Nikolaus gave him an anxious look. "Serapio has enough saved up to get started but he'll have to borrow the rest. Adan and I offered to help but he refused both of us as I'm sure Adan told you. Honestly, he might be in debt for many years, especially with needing two homes."

Aurelius tilted his head at the others. "Come on. I think we're going to need your help."

Aurelius walked back over to his sister. He took a small leather purse from his coin pouch and handed it to her. "Serapio, Fabiana, we need to talk with you," Aurelius said.

Pomona explained, "Aurelius and I opened the clothes chest of the real Hadrian that drowned. He left something that we want the two of you to have. Now, before you refuse, let me tell you how this is going to work. You risked your lives, all of you, to get me to safety. You gave up your homes and the shop. You did this with no expectation of reward. However, if you refuse this gift—remember, it was a gift to us as well—I will turn myself in at the garrison."

Serapio and Fabiana stared at her in astonishment. "What are you talking about?" demanded Serapio.

"This." Pomona took his hand and set the little purse in his palm. "I mean it, Serapio. If you so much as even *try* to give that back, I will run to the garrison and throw myself in the pit."

Serapio didn't move. Fabiana picked up the purse from his hand and carefully opened it. She gasped when the pearl rolled out. "This is worth a fortune, Pomona. We can't possibly. . ."

"Ah! I mean it," declared Pomona. "Straight to the pit." She whirled around.

"Stop!" Serapio waved his hands in the air. "Fine! You win! You're a hard woman to refuse." He looked at Fabiana and they both started laughing. "But a very easy woman to love. From the bottom of our hearts, Pomona, we thank you and you, too, Aurelius, since we suspect you had something to do with this 'blackmail' you have so *generously* threatened us with."

They laughed together and marveled at the beauty of the cream-colored gem. Seeing the pearl made Adan and Dulcibella smile at each other in fond memory of the blue pearl they gave to Paul. The money from that pearl, along with many donations, kept hundreds of thousands from starving during a severe famine.

Aurelius turned to Adan. "There is something we need you to do for us." He and Pomona grinned at each other. "You'll know when the time is right so we're leaving that up to you."

Adan gave a sigh of long-suffering. "More 'blackmail' I suspect. And I'm to be a co-conspirator. Yes?"

Brother and sister enthusiastically agreed. Aurelius took another small purse from his coin pouch and handed it to Adan. "Choose well, Centurion."

Chapter 7

Herod's Malicious Mission

⸺⸻⸺

Hosting the Olympic Games in Caesarea instead of Olympia was causing a great deal of work for *Primus Pilus* Tacitus and his centurions. The *legionaries* were accustomed to long hours and exhausting work, but the five days of competition were hectic and unpredictable problems arose. The Saxons with their dyed hair and beards of orange, green and blue demanded certain foods. The Greeks, since they invented the Olympic Games, wanted the prime lanes for the foot races. The Egyptians wanted images of their gods to precede them as they entered the arena, instead of a single banner. The Romans, of course, demanded the best of everything. Tacitus and his men were grateful The Games were held only once every four years.

The weeks before The Games involved the usual logistics of organizing any large event, but Adan remained optimistic throughout the ordeal. Each afternoon when he rode Blackfire home, he anticipated the return of the *Child of the Ocean*. On the third day of competition, a young man trotted up to him and extended a scroll. The messenger explained that the letter would have been delivered days ago, but there was some confusion on where to find him. The messenger had been instructed to give the letter directly to the centurion and no one else. Adan thanked him and unrolled the letter. It was from Calais Antipas.

> *Greetings to you,*
>
> *I have settled in Patmos Island. None of my family remain here, but I did manage to earn an apprenticeship with a bakery called* Pristina eum Caesar, *the only bakery that supplies the prison complex. A friend of yours is here. He said that you once told him a story about a three-legged donkey. Now he would like to tell you a story. If at all possible, please come to Patmos Island at your first opportunity. You will find me at the prison's bakery.*
>
> *Your faithful servant,*
> *Antipas*

Adan was glad that Calais Antipas had not said anything incriminating in the letter in case it had fallen into the wrong hands. The mention of his childhood pet was code for John, son of Zebedee. It was disturbing to learn that John was imprisoned on Patmos but Adan didn't get a chance to consider travel logistics. An aide rushed up to him, saying that Tacitus requested his presence immediately. Adan hurried to the central office at the garrison. He knocked on the commander's door.

The familiar deep voice called out, "Enter."

"You summoned me, Sir," said Adan as he stood at attention and waited for instructions.

"Come sit down, Centurion," responded Tacitus. "I'll get right to the point. Herod has summoned you for a meeting and it doesn't look good for you. Apparently, the son of Felix Valentius did not drowned. He is very much alive. Valentius sought revenge against you and your father due to this deception. Correct me if I'm wrong but Aurelius Julius was supposed to have met his death when the *Scarlet Jade* sank. He faked his death to avoid obeying his father's orders. Of course, it was an illegal order since family members are not allowed to serve together." Tacitus expelled a puff of air as if it had a bad taste.

"Herod has learned of this deception due to a letter from Aurelius to Demitre, that 'slave' who was actually the brother-in-law to Valentius and the murderer, Alexander Nisos. Commander Lysias sent it to Herod along with accusations against you. Said he discovered it hidden away in the Antonia archives. What concerns me is that Herod seems to believe what Lysias told him about you. Herod wants you in his audience room at the palace immediately. I thought you should be warned."

A knot of fear rose in Adan's throat. Did Lysias also implicate Aquila, or did he know that Marco had handled the scroll? Also, Aurelius was due back to Caesarea any day. He was trying to think if there was any way he could warn him off when he realized Tacitus had gone silent and was glaring at him.

"Did you hear me, Centurion?"

"Many pardons, Sir. The mention of Valentius distracted me."

Tacitus curled a lip. "I suppose that is understandable. You better get over there before Herod issues a warrant for your arrest." He didn't sound like he was joking.

Adan's head was in a fog. The last person he ever wanted to summon him was King Herod but there was no way around it. He trudged over to the stables and saddled Blackfire himself. The ride to Herod's Palace on the harbor was over much too quickly. Blackfire even pulled impatiently at the bridle as if bored with the slow pace. Adan found himself ushered in and standing before the king before he could think straight. Then he heard that familiar voice in his head. *Do not be afraid. I AM with you.* Adan took a deep breath and exhaled slowly.

King Herod was watching him with a malicious stare. The exaggerated smile twisting his childishly small mouth gave an impression of Cupid. His lids drooped over his eyes like miniature hoods. His hair was jet black, just like the last time Adan stood before him two decades ago. Herod's vanity clearly did not tolerate gray hair. He was clean shaven in the tradition of prominent Roman men. His dominant ears fanned out from his skull like mollusk shells.

"So! Here you stand before me once more, Centurion. Did I not warn you to never give me cause to summon you again?"

"Yes, Your Excellency. You did. Yet, I obeyed your summons."

Herod leaned back on his throne and chuckled. He picked up a roll of papyrus and slapped it against the palm of his hand. "Do you know what is written in this letter?"

"No, Your Excellency."

Herod grunted with pleasure. "It is proof that the son of Felix Pomponius Valentius did not die all those years ago. Aurelius Pomponius Julius is alive. Seems the idiot, Valentius, sought revenge against you based on this lie. What do you have to say about that?"

Adan pretended to take a moment to absorb the information. He looked away as he opened his mouth in "shock" at the news, wanting to say something, but unable to find the proper words.

"Ah, do I detect an element of surprise in your expression, Centurion? If so, well played. You should volunteer in the amphitheater. The truth is, there are those who suspect you have known about this for some time. Commander Lysias, for one, has implicated you in a plot with Aurelius Julius as your co-conspirator. Lysias hinted that you sought to steal Julius's scroll of incriminating evidence by forcing his slave, Calais, to bring you the scroll. When you discovered that the letter intended for Demitre was missing, you made the slave return the scroll and he damaged it in the process."

King Herod's eyes fairly glittered with pleasure. "Then something you didn't expect occurred. The slave, knowing that you were vulnerable, demanded that you help him escape. You complied. He did escape—by way of death after you poisoned him." Herod watched triumphantly as Adan gaped at him. A guttural laugh permeated the room. "So, you murdered the slave to cover up your misdeeds? Is that correct, Centurion?"

It took Adan a moment to speak. "Your Excellency, Lysias is accusing me of murdering his slave so I can protect the very man who, by his cowardly act of deception, turned my commanding officer against me to the point of seeking my death? Do I understand this situation correctly?"

"You do. Did you kill the slave?"

"No, Your Excellency, I did not. I was present at the Antonia when his body was discovered by my son. It was obvious to me, at the time, that the slave had committed suicide by poison."

Herod's lips curved into a sly smile. "Good answer, Centurion. I looked into the accusation against you. I was. . ." Herod thrust out his lower lip in a pout, "disappointed to learn from one of my spies that Lysias, himself, conducted an investigation and determined that the slave used oil from the oleander plant to take his own life. The spy reported that there was no evidence of forced poisoning. There's no human ignorant enough to allow one bitter droplet of the oleander on his tongue unless he means to die.

It seems you have made yourself yet *another* enemy who outranks you, Centurion. You seem to have a gift for that. I would advise you against ever meeting the emperor."

Herod paused in anticipation of watching Adan unravel. "My spy reported that you appeared at the Antonia a few weeks ago. Lysias believes you wanted to see if the scroll was still there. If it was not, then Aurelius Julius would be in the clear. Finding the scroll still in place told you Julius was still in danger of being arrested. He reported that a man who could be Julius, himself, was with you in Jerusalem. So, now you're consorting with a known traitor? What do you say about these scathing accusations, Centurion?"

"Your Excellency, I cannot make sense of Lysias's assumptions. I went to the Antonia to check if I had left an old *testamentuem* on file. I was accompanied by my wife, her brother, my brother, and my sons to also visit our long-time friends in Jerusalem. I was on leave with my commander's permission. I had an escort with me as well. Perhaps he believes one of those men was this son of Valentius. I do not understand Commander Lysias vendetta against me. My only other interaction with him was to help escort the prisoner, Paul of Tarsus, to be interrogated by Governor Felix. Perhaps the commander feels that I received too much credit for successfully bringing Paul to the governor even though it was not my doing. It was the excellent training and discipline of the soldiers and God's protection against the insurgents in Jerusalem."

Herod arched an eyebrow. "I see. Yes, fortunately, for you, Centurion Longinus, I do see what is really going on here. Lysias is a fool! He has the head of a loaf of bread. His skull is full of air and fermented yeast. What else should we expect, umm? He is a half-breed citizen with a shop-bought citizenship. He's a pathetic Greek desperate to make a name for himself so he goes after the legendary *Lupus Legatus*. I know what you're thinking. Somehow, you found out that Lysias set a trap with evidence proving Julius was alive. You wanted to discover if the warrant for Aurelius Julius was still in effect *without* letting Lysias in on your plans. *You* want to arrest Julius yourself. You want to haul the traitor, bound in chains, before me and throw him at my feet to earn my good graces. Tell me I speak the truth!"

"No, Your Excellency. I do not wish to bring him before you in chains. I wish to see Aurelius Julius floating upon a shark infested sea."

King Herod roared with laughter. "And you shall get the chance to do just that, Longinus as soon as your duties during the Olympic Games are over. I knew you would prove to be useful someday. That is why I spared your life for a second time in Jerusalem."

Adan struggled to keep a straight face. The five thousand soldiers demanding his release might have also been a part of Herod's decision to spare his life.

Herod snapped his fingers at Blastus, his long-time chamberlain. "Give him the warrant for Julius's arrest. Now find that slimy toad of a traitor for me, Centurion. If you should have need to end his life, bring me proof of his death. I believe a head, without the body, of course, should suffice." Herod's piercing gaze leveled on Adan. "I give you six months to present him for execution or *you* will take his place. Do you understand? You have your orders. Now leave me!"

Blastus handed Adan the document. The blood red and bright yellow seal on the warrant for Aurelius Pomponius Julius signified that deadly force was approved. Adan left the room under Herod's gloating smile.

Blastus addressed the king. "With all due respect, Your Excellency, how can the centurion possibly find Aurelius Julius after all this time? He might even be dead."

Herod clicked his tongue behind little puckered lips. "Blastus, you are incredibly naïve. I think that's why I keep you around. I sincerely hope that Julius is dead. I would be sorely disappointed if Longinus, somehow, actually presented the man to me. In fact, my dear Blastus, if he does, I will deny that the prisoner is Aurelius Julius. I will declare that my spies already 'found' him and killed him. I will add an accusation of deliberate deception against Longinus. This will be my third attempt to execute this man. Even God, *himself*, will not stop me from succeeding this time. I *will* see his blood flow like the mighty Jordan!"

Herod ran his thick fingers over his cleft chin "Tell my spies to keep watch over the Longinus family. If they see any hint of departure, I want to know immediately. Longinus has run for his life before. What's to stop the entire family from doing the same?" He grinned at Blastus with satisfaction. "I have been itching for an opportunity, *any opportunity*, to avenge my humiliation when I was forced to release him the second time I ordered his death." Herod raised a clenched fist. "I've got him this time! Either he dies or his precious wife and children will."

Herod pushed his lower lip in and out in contemplation. "Send a message to Commander Lysias. Tell him his efforts will be rewarded in six months. I intend to give him the pleasure of executing the man." Herod laughed at the look on his aide's face. "Oh come, Blastus. I know Lysias is a delusional fool. He is a mere puff of chaff but even discarded chaff will feed a goat. Everything has its uses, even jealous buffoons. It will please me to see Longinus's reaction when he realizes Lysias will be his executioner. The centurion has been a thorn in my side for long enough!"

"Your Excellency, what of *Primus Pilus* Marcus Cornelius and *Minor Consul* Aquila Longinus?" asked Blastus. "They could cause problems for you."

"See, there you go again, Blastus. You have such innocence. That would be *retired* Marcus Cornelius and *retired* Aquila Longinus. Their titles and importance are also— *retired*. Let them try to interfere. Besides, who can stand against me in all of Judea? I am King Herod Marcus Julius Agrippa II!"

Adan stood outside the audience room, warrant in hand. He knew Herod's plan was to see him die and had no interest in the capture of Aurelius. He stared at the warrant in despair but tried to shake off the dread. He reminded himself that much could happen in six months. Still, he knew there was no way out. This time, he had a family Herod could use against him.

He left Herod's palace and returned to the garrison. He found himself outside the office of *Primus Pilus* Tacitus. As if he were disconnected from his own body, Adan felt like he was watching someone else's hand rise to knock on the door.

"Enter!" called out the baritone voice. Adan stepped inside. "Ah, Centurion, back so quickly. I see you still have your head." He gestured at a chair. "That's always a plus."

Adan swallowed at the unfortunate choice of words. "Yes, for now. Herod has a mission for me. I am to leave as soon as The Games are over."

Tacitus was surprised. He didn't think Herod trusted Adan with any special assignments. "What is the mission?"

Adan handed him the warrant. "Lysias has made trouble for me. I have no idea why." He filled Tacitus in on the details of his meeting with Herod including the threat to his life.

Tacitus scowled as he listened. He sat in silence for a moment when Adan finished. "Not only has the commander lost his mind, he has failed to follow the chain of command. Any complaints he had against you should have come to *me*, not Herod. Lysias may truly believe you killed his slave but the rest of his story is pure fabrication. Anyway, you'll need to go by the business office and withdraw enough funds for your search. But, Centurion, you must report back here in six months or Herod will issue a warrant on you."

"Do you think he'll go after my family?"

Tacitus made a face. "He wouldn't dare. Your father and father-in-law will give him pause." At Adan's doubtful expression, he added, "If it will ease your mind, I'll have a squad check in with Marcus two or three times a week."

"I appreciate that, Sir."

Tacitus cleared his throat. "Six months, eh? If you haven't found Aurelius Julius by then, you never will. He could even be dead. As for Herod's threat against you, we'll cross that bridge when we get to it. It's not like we haven't swayed his opinion before. While you're out on his useless mission, I need you to evaluate any garrison you visit. Send back reports for each one. The emperor is gearing up for a major rebellion in Israel and wants to know the condition of the troops. We might even work your efforts into a reason to override Herod's demand for your execution."

"Do you really think that will work, Sir?"

Tacitus sighed. "No. But we'll think of something."

Adan tried to take comfort in Tacitus's unconcerned demeanor but his commander had not seen the glint of hatred in Herod's eyes. He was about to speak when the door flew open.

"Sir, forgive my interruption!" cried a *principales*, "there has been a fight in the barracks. Two men have knifed each other."

Tacitus groaned and headed for the door. "Centurion, we'll discuss final instructions for your mission after The Games." He left with the agitated soldier.

Adan stood and picked up the warrant for Aurelius from Tacitus's desk. A pile of warrants were also on the desk that had not been there at their first meeting. Out of curiosity, Adan scanned through them. He saw that most were for runaway slaves and a few thieves. Then one caught his eye and his heart sank. It was for Pomona. The charge was for murdering a Roman citizen in Jerusalem.

"*Ohe!* What next?" he muttered to the empty room.

***

The Olympic Games were over and the athletes were gone. Adan's last day at the garrison had arrived. He withdrew the required funds at the business office for his mission but he had one more task before he could leave, which Pomona had entrusted to him. He went to the soldier's barracks and found *Principales* Neziah.

"Find the men who went to Jerusalem with us and bring them to my office," ordered Adan. Neziah hurried to obey. Adan didn't have long to wait for the four men to report back. They stood at attention and waited.

"Men, you have shown yourselves to be more than loyal by the way you fulfilled your duties in Jerusalem. Don't think I have forgotten the bonus you forfeited by following my orders and not revealing the identity of a certain traveler. You have asked for nothing in return. However, there is one who wishes to compensate you for protecting her. You must understand that this reward does *not* come from me. That would be seen as a bribe and you four are above such dishonor."

Adan opened a drawer of his desk and took out four leather bags secured with drawstrings. "The one who wishes to express her gratitude recently came into the possession of a small gem which a friend of mine was able to sell for a fair price." He handed each soldier one of the bags. Their hands dropped under the unexpected weight. They needed both hands to support them. "The *aureuii* is a gift from one unjustly accused. Your defense of her was both honorable and courageous."

The four men gaped at Adan, speechless and wide-eyed.

"Centurion, Sir," exclaimed Neziah, "there must be more gold in this bag than each of us would receive for our retirement—combined. I," he glanced at the other men, "*we,* don't know what to say. This is most generous."

"I will tell her what you said, *Principales* Neziah," replied Adan. "On occasion, the greater good demands that we listen to our conscience. She is, in fact, innocent of the charge against her. There is nothing more deplorable than to execute one who is innocent. There was one time that I was ordered to crucify a truly innocent man and I obeyed."

"Did he curse you, Sir, as he suffered?" asked Neziah.

"No. He forgave me."

The four soldiers, simultaneously, dropped their jaws and stared.

"That is a story for another day, gentlemen. As for this," he pointed at the bags of gold, "it did not come from me. However, I wish to reward your obedience during a difficult time. Therefore, I have also recommended the four of you for promotions, effective immediately. You have consistently performed your duties above my expectations as long as I've known each of you. You will need to go to the business office and sign your acceptance of your new pay grade. Be safe, gentlemen. I would suggest that you deposit that gold in the *Aerarium* in town. The public treasury will be much safer than hiding it under your bed in the barracks. Dismissed."

The men adamantly thanked Adan and left his office. He could hear them happily talking, mostly at the same time, as they trooped over to the business office. He grinned to himself as he watched them go.

Adan took care of a few last details, left the garrison, and made straight for the Ocean View Inn to tell Nikolaus that all was prepared for their journey. Now the path was clear. Adan had begun to feel that the assignment to find Aurelius was a blessing in disguise. There was no copy of Aurelius's warrant in the stack that held Pomona's warrant. That could mean only one thing; he had the only copy of the warrant because Herod did not really care if Aurelius was found. For now, he had to put Herod's threat aside and pray for some type of solution.

However, professional bounty hunters would be searching for Pomona. Another danger was for Adan, himself. If bounty hunters located her in his presence, they would wonder why he hadn't arrested her. That fact would be reported to Tacitus and King Herod. They would have to be careful and stay prepared for any possibilities.

Adan considered telling Marcus about Herod's threat. Then he thought better of it since Marcus would only worry and might even try to intervene while Adan was gone. He would tell everything to Marcus when he returned home, knowing that his father-in-law and former commanding officer would do everything he could to help. For now, Adan would keep Herod's threat to himself.

When Adan returned home that day, he pulled Marcus aside and they went out on the terrace. "I need to talk to you about some developments that I do not want anyone else to know. Tacitus knows, of course." Adan gave Marcus the details on Lysias's accusations and Herod's response but left out the threat to execute him if Aurelius was not captured or killed. "Tacitus also assigned me to send evaluations of our forts to him. Seems the emperor needs readiness information. Do you think I should tell Aurelius that I have been ordered to find him?"

Marcus pursed his lips in thought. "No. It will force him to either trust you or grow suspicious of you. It will put a strain on your developing relationship, possibly a dangerous one if he should ever doubt your motives."

"But I did not turn Pomona in after Serapio revealed her presence. Doesn't that count for something?"

"Yes, but that was after she had escaped and in the presence of your best friends. How easily could you have snatched up Pomona in front of Serapio, Fabiana, and Nebetka? No, Adan, I would not advise giving Aurelius a reason to doubt your intentions. Suspicion is like barnacles on a ship's hull, one by one they slowly gnaw at the wood until suddenly, the ship sinks. As far as he knows, you're searching for the Prophecy Box and evaluating Roman garrisons. However, he does need to be warned that Lysias sent his secret letter to Herod. Aurelius will know to be careful, for himself, and not just his sister. What about Pomona? What is her status?"

"I saw a warrant for her arrest on Tacitus's desk."

"That is to be expected and you should tell Pomona the search for her has been officially authorized. That is all brother and sister need to know."

"Agreed," said Adan. "Could you tell them the situation when they get back from this next delivery if you see them before I do? There won't be time for the news of Pomona's warrant to get around for months and they don't need to worry about this now."

"I will. You should tell the family tonight. They will want to pray and ask God to watch over the four of you. Will you tell Niko about Herod's assignment?"

Adan considered his options. "I think not. He is going to be stressed enough as it is. We're trying to find out if his family was murdered because his father stole the box. I think he doesn't need another burden besides that."

"I understand your reasoning, but consider one thing, Adan. Niko is your brother. You think you're protecting him? He might think that you don't trust him. There is something I learned as the commander of thousands of men and that is, people can confront a difficult situation if asked to do so. Expect little; receive little. Expect much; much can be given. It's called faith, Adan. Have faith in your brother. It might even help him to deal with his family's darkest secrets if he knows *you* have kept no secrets from him."

Adan looked out over the sea. A group of gulls were gathered on the beach, fighting amongst themselves over a stranded fish. Their raucous noise was distracting as he tried to consider what to do. He remembered when Niko proved himself worthy of his faith in him when, as a slave, he returned from running away in the middle of the night.

"You're right." Adan frowned and looked away. "I would be terribly hurt if he kept any conflict from me. Yes, he should know everything I've told you." Adan wanted to tell Marcus about Herod's threat but his instincts kept him silent. Frustrated, he threw himself on the terrace bench.

"What is it? As if I can't guess," said Marcus with a knowing glance. "Your conscience is killing you. You'll have to lie to Tacitus about Aurelius and Pomona, the man who encouraged five thousand men to save your life. I know you, Adan. Lying is a bitter poison to you."

"Yes. Deceiving him does not sit easy. The man stood up for me against King Herod and could have been executed for appearing without a summons. He was the first to announce his intention to appear before Herod. The worst part is that I will have to lie to him about Aurelius and Pomona every time either one of them is mentioned."

"I understand your dilemma," said Marcus. "Tacitus is a dear friend to me and a trusted ally. You are, indeed, betraying his trust. But which is the greater wrong? Deceiving your commanding officer and benefactor? Or, allowing two innocent friends to die on the cross? As far as I'm concerned, Aurelius is innocent of treason since Valentius gave him an unlawful order. Family members cannot serve at the same garrison. Aurelius was in an impossible situation. If he reported for duty, he would be a co-conspirator in the deception. If Aurelius reported his father's illegal orders, Valentius would have been expelled from the army and forced to forfeit his pension."

Marcus gestured with incredulity. "It is obvious that Valentius did not care that he was endangering himself and his son. At this point, you cannot sustain your loyalty to Tacitus and protect two people who do not deserve to die."

"I can only ask God to forgive me for deceiving Tacitus."

Marcus nodded in agreement. "There is one other thing I would suggest. Leave your centurion attire and those weapons behind. They could attract unwanted attention. I have a sword and dagger that are suitably sharp but not works of art like yours."

Adan considered the advice. "I think my centurion status will 'open doors' considerably better than a common citizen could do. As for my weapons, I couldn't bear to leave them behind. I have grown very attached to their elegant efficiency."

Marcus pursed his lips in disapproval. "Be careful, Adan. Do not let the beauty of an object subvert your better judgment. They are only works of metal, not the personification of your personality or spirit. They will set you apart within a crowd you might want to hide in."

"Don't worry, Marcus. I'll be fine."

"Will you tell Dulcibella about Herod's assignment?"

"Yes. I don't even need to think about that. Her wisdom has strengthened me countless times."

Marcus smiled. "She takes after her mother."

***

The family gathered that evening to discuss the coming journey. "How often will you need to send reports to Tacitus?" asked Marcus. "Did he tell you which garrisons to visit?"

"He did not specify either matter but I'll try to send a report from every major port."

"You have a complicated journey ahead of you," said Dulcibella. "You need to help Niko find the truth about his family, find John on Patmos Island, evaluate garrisons for Emperor Domitian, and try to protect Aurelius and Pomona from bounty hunters. Is there anything else we should know?" She watched for Adan's reaction. He met her eye and a silent communication passed between them. She knew Adan had more to tell her—much more.

Knowing adventure was involved, the twins begged to go as well, but Adan insisted that they stay in Caesarea to pursue their budding careers. Aquila was studying architecture with several engineers and Marco was studying under the chief *veterinarius* at the garrison.

Later that night, when Adan and Dulcibella nestled into their bed, Adan turned on his side to face his wife. She had been watching him and waiting for the right moment.

"Are you ready to tell me what you won't tell the others?" She managed a smile even though her heart ached with fear.

Adan took her hand and brought it to his lips. They lay facing each other, hands held between them. "Herod ordered me to find Aurelius and said I would be executed in his place if I failed to do so. He gave me six months."

Dulcibella took a deep breath. "I see. Herod has kept his vendetta against you all these years. We shouldn't be surprised. Bitterness builds over time. Herod will keep us under surveillance in case we try to flee. I would if I were him. He means to extract revenge one way or another. I see only one way out of this threat."

"What is that?"

"We ask God to take care of it."

Adan was relieved at her acceptance of both the threat and their inability to combat it. "You are right, of course. I will do what I can, but besides Tacitus, you are the only one who knows about this. I know you will guard this secret as well as you guard our love. If God wants us to live, we will."

She let go of his hand and reached for his face. "God is with us no matter what any human can do. I love you, Adan. God knows that. Either in this world or eternity, God will always love his children."

Adan gently pulled her into his arms. "I know. That's why he gave us each other."

✳✳✳

The Child of the Ocean was due back in Caesarea in the next day or two. Adan and Nikolaus discussed strategy on various ways to locate Calypso who seemed to be the best first step in their search. Traveling all the way to the School of the *Magi* was not an option. Adan did not believe that he and Nikolaus were led to Pomona simply as a coincidence. They only hoped that Pomona's help would be enough to locate the woman whose father worked for the *Magi*. Even that connection was a long shot. They could only hope for a fruitful result.

Concerning King Herod's intention to see Adan executed, despite Tacitus's cavalier attitude, Adan knew nothing would change Herod's mind. Not this time.

Chapter 8

A Warning for The Golden One

———⌘———

Two mornings later, the *Child of the Ocean* appeared on the horizon. Adan was at Serapio's construction site, the twins were with their instructors, and Nikolaus was checking inventory with his managers at the flour mill and the wine shop. Marcus Cornelius spotted the ship from the terrace and asked Andreas, his estate manager, to saddle a horse for him. Marcus rode down to the harbor to watch the ship come in. Aurelius was at the helm and recognized Marcus. He waved a greeting and Marcus waved back. Soon the two men were talking together on the deck and Pomona joined them.

"Good to see you, Marcus," called Pomona as she crossed the deck. "What are you two discussing with such serious faces?"

Aurelius tried to smile away his anxiety. "It is nothing we didn't expect. Marcus was telling me about the warrant issued for your arrest. Also, Lysias has acted on the letter I sent Demitre all those years ago. Herod has it now."

Pomona threw her hands to her mouth. "No! He will send men after you. We must leave at once. Forget loading a cargo." She anxiously scanned the pier for soldiers.

"Pomona, all is not lost," reassured Marcus. "Lysias overplayed his hand by making ridiculous accusations against Adan. He claimed that Aurelius and Adan have joined forces. Herod had his spies check into Lysias's story and found no evidence to support it. However, Herod is vindictive and he might twist the situation to his advantage. So, you and Aurelius must always be careful."

Pomona breathed a sigh of relief. "Pray to your God that bounty hunters don't find us."

"Pomona, you believe in God. Believe also in Yeshua. Your prayers will be heard." As Marcus and Adan had agreed, he did not tell Aurelius that Adan had been ordered to present him to Herod.

"What a pair we make," drawled Pomona as she glanced up at her brother. "It is a good thing our surname is common and even better that we live on a ship. Two fugitives sailing over the ocean, as free as the seagulls over our heads."

Aurelius smiled at her imagery. "Since I don't know what cargo I will pick up in any port, we should be one step ahead of anyone on our trail, unless I have to wait too long to get another cargo, then someone might catch up. That can be avoided if I forfeit a profit, occasionally, and leave without a cargo. Perhaps Pomona's prayers to your God will help."

"Prayers always help," said Marcus. "God will watch over both of you, Adan and Nikolaus. Of that, I am sure. I have known Adan since he was seventeen. He has more than just the eyes of a wolf, but also the cunning and courage. If anyone can find a way to keep you safe, it is him. I would suggest altering your route occasionally. You don't want anyone to pick up on a pattern."

Marcus invited them to join the family for dinner that evening and took his leave. They accepted eagerly and watched as the former *Primus Pilus* centurion walked down the pier to his horse.

Aurelius looked up and down the length of his ship. "We will find safety on the high seas and then as the months turn into years, they will forget about us. Time and distance can be a great protector. I only hope that we will always have the *Child of the Ocean* as our home."

Pomona's face lit up with a broad smile.

"What?" Aurelius asked. "Why are you grinning at me like that?"

"You don't even realize what you said. You said, 'we' and 'our' when you were talking about being on the high seas and the ship being a home. It makes my heart sing to be 'us' and not 'you' or 'me.' There is nothing more precious than our relationships."

Aurelius returned her heart-felt smile. It did feel good to have the warmth and security of a companion he could trust. His smile faded and he frowned at a long-past memory.

"What is it?" Pomona lightly touched his arm.

He hesitated to answer but her open expression comforted him. "I was planning to kill both Adan and Nikolaus when I first saw them outside the court before Nikolaus gave testimony against our father. I've never told this to anyone else, Pomona. I spotted them, standing with Adan's father, Aquila. I had a dagger hidden inside my sleeve and I slowly approached them. Then Adan saw me and looked me in the eye. I thought he would be condescending, arrogant, entitled, like so many wealthy Romans. He was not. In that moment, I doubted my intentions. He looked at me with open curiosity and was about to say something, I think. When he was distracted by the summons from the court clerk, I slipped away. I had almost made the worst mistake of my life but I didn't know that until I saw Father just before he was executed"

Pomona gasped. "What happened?"

"I bribed the jailer so I could confront him. Things didn't go as I planned. He asked me to thank Adan for not killing him when he had the chance. He said Adan forgave him, instead. He said that if Adan had taken his revenge, he would never have known I was alive. Then Father said he had always loved me even when he didn't love himself. That changed my whole life."

Pomona reached for his hand. "Aurelius, it breaks my heart that you didn't get to know him the way I did. I suppose that when he was with me and my mother, he became someone else. It was as if he stepped through a portal into another world. I know he dearly loved you and your mother but we only saw him occasionally. He was not there when we were ill or having other difficulties. I knew him under very different circumstances. But when he thought you had died, a part of him died, and never recovered. The opium he was addicted to certainly didn't help. When Adan showed up at the Antonia," she shook her head sadly, "he turned into someone ugly and cruel. Not toward us, but toward others! It was a grievous thing to see."

"Isn't it ironic that Father tried to destroy the same man who brought us together? The *very* same man who has sworn to protect us now."

"Life has a way of twisting reality into unexpected outcomes." Pomona patted her brother's arm. "You think they'll serve clam stew tonight?"

"I sure hope so. It's delicious." Aurelius grinned. "I wouldn't turn down cake, either."

***

Dulcibella and Marina arranged an elaborate dinner the evening before Adan and Nikolaus boarded the *Child of the Ocean*. Prayers were pronounced by each member of the family. Their departure would be a sad occasion but everyone hoped that great things would be accomplished and they would return soon.

At the harbor the next day, the family exchanged farewells and lingering hugs. Adan stepped up to his father-in-law last and reached to clasp his hand. Marcus grasped hold but didn't let go. Instead, he pulled Adan in slightly.

Marcus whispered in his ear. "Herod doesn't care a mite about Aurelius, does he?"

Adan pulled back in surprise. "What do you mean?"

"Adan, I know Herod Agrippa. He is vindictive but very patient. You have publicly shown him up twice and he will never forgive that. He intends to execute you if you fail to present Aurelius. Yes?"

Adan bowed his head. "He does."

Marcus leaned in. "Let him try." A slow smile curved his lips.

"What do you intend to do?" asked Adan anxiously.

"Pray."

The two men, both soldiers, both familiar with impossible odds, looked into each other's eyes and saw strength. Not the strength of a human arm or will, but the strength of faith in the greatest power of all.

When Nikolaus and Marina stepped away from the others, Dulcibella and Adan did the same thing. They held each other closely as Dulcibella peered up into her husband's golden eyes.

"I suspect Herod will send spies after you," she whispered. "Or activate those he has stationed throughout the empire. I'm sure he sent letters out as soon as you left his presence."

"I'm sure you're right. That's what I would have done if the roles were reversed."

"Then will you consider a disguise. Leave your military attire and weapons here. Your eye color will not give you away from a distance but everything else will announce, 'Centurion Longinus is here!' Are you sure that is wise?"

"Have you been talking with your father?"

"Do not dodge the issue, Adan. You need to blend in, not stand out like a tree among shrubs." She studied the expression on his face and knew her advice would be ignored. "Fine. If you insist on being stubborn about this, I can only pray that God will protect you. Don't be surprised if you get reprimanded for your mule-headedness."

"Don't be angry, Dulcie. I'll be careful. I just think. . ." He wasn't sure what he was thinking. Instead, he gathered her in his arms and kissed her good-bye with all his love.

It seemed like a flash of a few moments before the family was waving good-bye from the pier as the *Child of the Ocean* set sail and headed toward the western horizon.

As the brothers stood in the bow of the ship, feeling the brisk breeze on their faces, they contemplated their uncertain future. Nothing in this world meant more to them than their families, yet, once again they bade farewell to their loved ones and struck out on faith. The waves lapping at the ship as it sliced through the water made Adan think of his own life. He had chosen a philosophy of life that carved a new path every day, one that often ran counter to his own culture as the prow of a ship cuts through the waves. Putting the needs of others before his own brought satisfaction but came with a price. Leaving Dulcibella and his family behind was one of those prices. However, ignoring the possible dangers involved with the secrets of the Kokinos clan could be much worse. Adan wanted no regrets. He had to help Nikolaus learn the truth and to prepare for consequences from the past.

"Niko, do you want to see Athens again?" asked Adan pensively. He remembered how the streets of Rome made him nostalgic and nervous at the same time.

"I do think of Athens. I might go by our home, out of respect. I'm not sure how that shows respect—looking at a villa occupied by another family—but I feel a certain yearning to see places of my childhood. My childhood *before* I was a stable slave, of course."

The mention of Nikolaus once being a slave reminded Adan of Calais's letter. He invited Nikolaus to his quarters to read the letter for himself.

After Nikolaus read it, he commented, "I know you fear for John. I do, too."

Adan frowned. "Calais would not make such a request for a trivial reason."

"Our first stop is Paphos, on the island of Cyprus, right?" asked Nikolaus. "Then from there to Patmos Island. How much time will you spend on evaluating the garrison there. Or is it only a prison?"

"There's only a prison and a handful of soldiers. I won't send a report from there. Tacitus does not care about my search for Aurelius any more than. . ." Adan realized his error too late.

"Any more than who?" Nikolaus looked at his brother intently.

Adan pursed his lips and looked away. "Marcus was right. I can't keep the truth from you."

"*Ohe*, you mean how Herod doesn't give a rat's tail about someone who disappeared decades ago? How he intends to order your execution when you fail to bring in Aurelius?'

Adan threw his hands in the air. "How is it that everyone knows about this?"

"Really, Adan, it wasn't too hard to figure out when Marcus huddled with you on the pier. You looked at him as if he'd caught you stealing goodies out of the cookie urn. Has anyone ever told you what an expressive face you have? You're a terrible liar, you know. I mean, Herod has Aurelius's letter, right? What is the most evil thing he could do with that? Go after you. Give me some credit, brother."

"If you figured it out so easily, why didn't you say something?"

"I wanted to see if you'd tell me first. I was going to be annoyed with you if you did not." Nikolaus punctuated his statement with a jab at Adan's chest. "*Seriously* annoyed!"

Adan let loose with the most heart-felt laughter he had done in weeks. "You truly are my brother, Niko. What would I do without you?"

"Be bored to tears, no doubt. Who else would go on adventures with you? You're with me for my search. I'm with you for your survival. That's what brothers do."

Adan nodded and gave Nikolaus a bemused grin. "We're not made for sitting on benches and sipping honey ale, are we?"

"Not in this world."

They relaxed in a comfortable silence as they watched the ship's bow slice through the slate-blue water of the Mediterranean. In the distance, they could see a pod of whales surface and dive as if they were taking turns.

Nikolaus finally broke the silence. "What if Aurelius doesn't secure a cargo for Patmos? Will he still want to stop there?"

"He said that he usually picks up a cargo at Chios in Mysia, northeast of Patmos. It would be standard procedure for him to resupply the ship along the way."

Assured that their path looked clear, the brothers began to relax and enjoy the voyage. They passed the time by keeping journals to share with their families when they got home and holding long conversations with Aurelius and Pomona. The two half-siblings seemed to get along as if they had grown up together. Surprisingly, they enjoyed sharing stories of their mothers but Pomona was careful to not speak too much about their father, since she had much better memories of him than Aurelius. The relationship between father and son had been dominated by guilt and resentment. The relationship between father and daughter had been affectionate and carefree.

Every evening, the four of them would share dinner together. Pomona was usually content to listen more than talk but not this evening.

"Do you know why Father chose Aurelius for your *praenomen*?" she asked.

"Why do I think this story will be embarrassing?" he asked with a sheepish smirk. "Can I trust it to be the truth or will you make it up as you go?"

"I assure you; it is quite true if Father is to be trusted. I'll let you be the judge."

The others leaned back in their chairs, anticipating a story that would be amusing at her brother's expense, considering her mischievous expression.

"It seems that even as a baby, just beginning to crawl," Pomona declared, "you loved to get into your mother's cosmetics. Father said you were fascinated with the bottles of different shapes and sizes. You loved to chew on the cork stoppers. Your sweet, patient mother never scolded you, Father said. She would laugh if you got face rouge or eye color in your mouth. You would squish up your lips at the bitter taste and try to spit it out especially if you got red chalk or alkanet rouge on your tongue from trying to lick it off your fingers."

Adan and Nikolaus grinned at the look of suspicious disbelief on Aurelius's face. "You should know that I can spot a lie even if it is spoken with a pleasing voice."

"No, no, dear brother. It is quite true. One day you managed to get your toddler's hands on a bottle of saffron dye which you 'acquired' from a neighbor's house. You know that's used to turn dark hair to blonde."

"Like the blonde hair of a prostitute?" asked Nikolaus with an exaggerated look of shock.

"*Ohe*, everyone knows a few high society men and women dye their hair blonde, at least in Rome," objected Aurelius with mock severity. "Let's not jump to conclusions. It was a good neighborhood."

Pomona snickered. "Perhaps, but apparently there was one little thief lurking about. This particular bottle seemed to have magically appeared in the house because no one claimed it. But you had gotten a hold of it and managed to chew off the stopper. When your mother tried to rescue the bottle from certain destruction, you upended the whole thing right over your head. Your black hair was streaked with bright blonde. From then on Father called you Aurelius, the 'golden one.' The name outlasted your golden waves of hair—obviously."

Her brother looked around at the others with a straight face. When the others stared back at him with apprehensive expressions, he burst into laughter. "Ha! Did you think I have no sense of humor? Besides," Aurelius ran his fingers through his thick, black hair, "I think blonde highlights would look quite attractive on me."

The others laughed and exchanged puns on the questionable virtue of blonde-headed Romans.

Pomona declared, "Father always said you were impressed with your own good looks. He said you could stay amused 'forever' with a mirror. He would say, 'He gets his features from his mother, thank the gods, but he did get his manly jawline from me.' He would stroke his chin and I would laugh."

Aurelius leaned back in his chair and grinned. "I remember that. I loved playing with Mother's mirror. I thought the polished copper was fascinating and I liked flashing reflected sunlight at the neighbors windows. When I saw someone looking out, I'd stop so they couldn't figure out where the flashes were coming from."

Pomona shook a finger at him. "So, you were a scoundrel and a prankster! No wonder, I like you so much."

Aurelius took an appreciative bow. The others hooted with laughter.

Chapter 9

Predictions of Peril

T he cargo was successfully delivered at Paphos and Adan sent a brief report on the garrison to Tacitus. The next cargo was picked up at Chios Island, the fifth largest Greek island. Patmos Island was the next stop. They made port in Skala, the only port on the island. Adan and Nikolaus lost no time in hiring a carriage to take them to the prison located next to the mine entrances. The stark, rocky cliffs contrasted with the low, inland, scrub trees nestled between barren hills. The road that led to the prison was rough and the carriage struggled as the iron-shod wheels impacted protruding rocks and pebbles.

"Perhaps we would be better off walking," muttered Nikolaus. "One more bump like that and my spine will crack."

"You're probably right. Besides, I think that's the prison headquarters." Adan asked the driver about the mud brick buildings and he confirmed that they had reached their destination. "Then you can stop here."

The men climbed out of the carriage. Adan paid the driver half the agreed price and asked him to wait there. They walked the final distance to the mud brick structures. The breeze was soft with moisture from the ocean and warm for that time of year. They talked little as they trudged along the road, trying to avoid jutting stones of basalt and feldspar. The island was rich in igneous minerals such as quartz and pyrite, hence the mines scattered between the low hills. Quartz was used for talismans and healing potions. Pyrite was used to light fires and the iron sulfate was leached out of the mineral for curing anemia. It was brutal work to chip and pry the minerals from the mine tunnels using only smokey torches for light.

As the two men drew closer to the entrance of the complex, they were surprised to find only one guard on duty. The man's tunic was dirty and his face hadn't felt a razor in days. He eyed the uniform belt and *caligae* of a centurion before looking Adan in the eye. An expression of sullen resentment sharpened his expression as he glared at the two men.

"I am Centurion Adan Clovius Longinus and this is my brother, Nikolaus. We request permission to enter."

"Why are you here?" demanded the guard. He caught sight of Adan's sword and tilted his head. "That's a fancy wolf's head you have there on your sword. That must have cost you a fortune. It would be a real shame if you lost it." He slowly raised his head and leered at Adan.

Adan moved so fast the guard didn't have a chance to react. A dagger was at his throat and the man was pressed against the solid wood of the massive gate. "You dare to show me such disrespect again and you will regret it," Adan hissed.

The soldier sputtered and threw his hands up in surrender. "Please, Sir, I apologize. Out here, we forget our manners. I meant no disrespect."

Adan pushed off from the man. "Open the gate! Now!"

The guard obeyed and continued to apologize. They walked into the complex grounds and didn't look back as the gate swung back into position.

"*Ohe*, remind me to never get on your bad side," Nikolaus muttered under his breath.

Adan grumbled something unintelligible and kept walking. His good humor didn't return until they entered the main office. He made introductions to the soldier in charge of visitor registration and the man asked them to sign in. While Nikolaus took care of the registration, Adan asked for directions to the bakery. It stood in between the laundry shop and one of several wine shops. They had no trouble finding the laundry shop since the smell advertised its presence. Human urine was used to clean soiled clothes since the acid content eliminated most stains.

They entered the open doorway of the *Pistrino eum Caesar*. The chief baker was a deeply tanned woman who looked to be in her fifties. Her arms were muscular and her hands were unusually large. She had pleasant features, despite the wrinkles from too much sun, and gray-streaked black hair. She looked the two men up and down.

"You two don't belong here," she declared. "What do you want?"

Adan looked at her doubtfully. "Do you know every single person on this island?"

"No," she drawled, "just every single centurion and you're not one of them." She looked back and forth from Adan to Nikolaus. "You both have strange eyes."

"Do we? No one's ever said that before," quipped Nikolaus.

She cackled at his sarcasm. "So, what can I do for you?"

"We're looking for a friend of ours," said Nikolaus. "I believe he works for you. Calais Antipas. Is he around?"

She turned her head toward a doorway that opened to the work area and shouted. "Boy! Are you back there? You have visitors."

The sound of something heavy dropping on a table was soon followed by Calais appearing in the doorway. His curly hair was fully back to its natural, dark color, which set off his grayish-green eyes. A broad grin brightened his face when he saw Adan and Nikolaus.

"You came! And so quickly," cried Calais as he wiped his hands on his tunic and shook their offered hands. He turned to the woman. "I need to take my friends to see John."

The woman curled a lip. "I don't pay you to be someone's tour guide." She looked over at Adan. "Even if he is a centurion."

"What if I pay for his time?" offered Adan. He pulled a *denarius* from his coin pouch.

A smile replaced her frown at the sight of the silver coin. "You can have him all afternoon for that much," she said. "Send him back in half an hour and I'll prepare refreshments."

Calais thanked her and hurried out of the shop. "John has a task for you of the greatest importance," whispered Calais. They had to lean in to hear him. "I have offered to do this so many times I've lost count but he insists it has to be you, Centurion."

"Why are you whispering?" asked Nikolaus, glancing around. "We're the only ones here."

"And why are you calling me Centurion? You know I prefer Adan."

"Sorry, just a habit on both counts. Come on. This time of day he will be in the prisoners' quarters. Even here they let the prisoners rest when the sun is hot. I suspect it is because the guards don't want to stand around in the heat."

Calais led them past several rows of cubicles that had three walls of mud brick and the outer wall of bars and a wooden door. The roof offered some protection from the elements, but the barred outer wall offered none. Several guards started to challenge Calais even though they knew him and who he came to see. They only wanted to impress the visiting centurion in case he would report on their diligence. Adan didn't give them a chance. He waved them off as they approached.

Calais stopped at the last cell in the row. John was lying on his narrow cot against the far wall but the cell was so narrow, Calais was able to touch John's arm through the bars. Adan could see a small table at the end of the cell. If John sat on the end of his bed, he could sit at the table. The prisoner jerked away and threw a startled look at the three men. A smile lit his face when he saw Calais, Adan, and Nikolaus.

"Ah, you came! And so quickly!"

"That's what Calais said," Adan replied. His expression sobered as he took in John's condition. "But it greatly pains me to see you in this place." Adan turned to the closest guard and ordered him to open John's cell. The guard hurried to find the key and unlocked the door. John waited for the guard to move away and then pulled a scroll from between the bed and the brick wall.

"I must give this to you now while I have the chance," said John as he thrust the scroll into Adan's hands. "Guard it with your life and take it to Priscilla and Aquila in Corinth. Paul lived with them for a time and the three of them worked their trade of tent making while they preached the Good News to any who would listen. You will find the couple at their tent shop."

Adan looked at the scroll. "What is this?"

"Come, we need a private place to talk," said Calais. He led them to a building that served as an interrogation facility. They sat at the only table while Calais left to get the promised refreshments from the bakery.

John looked from Adan to Nikolaus solemnly. "God has sent his Spirit to me to instruct his seven churches of Asia and to reveal the future judgement of mankind. There are letters to Ephesus, Smyrna, Pergamon, Thyatira, Sardis, Philadelphia, and Laodicea. I also recorded the visions revealed to me. Not one particle of parchment can go missing, neither can a single letter be altered in any word. Do not lose it. This might be the only chance I have to record my visions. Aquila and Priscilla will make sure each church receives a copy."

"Have you seen visions of war?" asked Adan. He was thinking how horrible it would be for him to be torn away from Dulcibella and his family.

John lowered his head to his hand for a moment before he looked up at the men. "I have seen terrible things. War? Yes. And disease, starvation, fire ravaging the land, attacks of wild animals, the ocean heaving and tossing in agitation. Desecration of the temple in Jerusalem. It will be the time of the Tribulation. Yet, somehow, the Good News will be preached throughout the world even while these terrible things take place."

"The Gospel will be preached everywhere?" exclaimed Adan. "How will that be possible? It takes a great deal of effort for someone to preach to more than a few people at a time. Even letters can take months to get from one city to another."

"What of the seas and the waves roaring?" asked Nikolaus. "What will cause that?"

John replied, "I can only tell you what I saw in my vision."

"There are storms that pass over the sea," said Adan, "but they only last a few days. Perhaps there will be storms that won't stop."

"We know for a fact that huge ocean waves hit the land after flaming mountains erupt and earthquakes shake the land," said Nikolaus. "Perhaps 'waves roaring' has to do with those events."

John passed his hand across his creased brow. "I have recorded all my visions on that scroll. One must hold on to faith in Yahweh and Yeshua to be spared this terrible trial."

"This Tribulation—why will it happen?" asked Nikolaus.

"God does everything for a purpose," explained John. "There would be no purpose for the Tribulation if everyone involved is doomed to condemnation. I also saw two witnesses who will preach God's message. They will be killed and their bodies left for the whole world to see. I cannot explain how the entire world can see this at the same time but after three and a half days, they will come back to life. Many will give glory to God. This means that salvation is possible during this time. Also, there would be no purpose to subject faithful followers to the Tribulation since they already believe. Yeshua told us, '*Therefore, watch always and pray that you may be counted worthy to escape all these things that will happen and to stand before the Son of Man.*'"

"How will one be counted worthy?" asked Nikolaus.

"Love God and Yeshua above all. Follow Yeshua's example. If you do that, you will be spared the terrible events I saw in my visions. Yeshua told the faithful, '*Because you have kept My word of patience, I also will keep you from the hour of temptation which shall come upon the entire world, to test those who dwell on the earth.*' Yeshua's promise is true and his faithfulness never ends. Yeshua said that two will be working in the field, one will be taken, the other left."

"Taken? How?" asked Adan.

"Yeshua gave no detail on that." John made a gesture of acceptance. "In reality, it doesn't matter how. We can believe that it will be done."

"You said there are letters for seven churches. What do they say?" asked Nikolaus.

"The letters praise or admonish believers according to their faith and deeds. Salvation is offered to everyone but God knows our hearts and sees our deeds. Following Yeshua's example is a daily task as long as we live. Temptation and distractions occur, causing some to fall away. The letters will help guide the believers in these churches to continue in their faith."

"What about other churches, like ours in Caesarea?" asked Adan.

"Understand this," John clarified, "these letters are intended for all churches of believers. Those that exist now and will in the future. The church is the 'family' of believers and not a city or a temple. The church is the people who love Yeshua and God, wherever they may live."

"Will the future emperors persecute God's believers as much as the Roman emperor does now?" asked Nikolaus.

John hung his head in sorrow. "There will be only one ruler of the world during this time. Many will be deceived and will follow him. He will be the Antichrist who gets his power from Beelzebub, who is the first Antichrist. Those who are not deceived will know the Antichrist by his name. *Let him who has understanding calculate the number of the beast, for it is the number of a man: His number is 666.* This will be his sign."

The brothers looked at him questioningly. "Let me explain," said John. "Greek and Hebrew letters, as you know, are used to express numerical values. The name of the Antichrist spelled in Greek or Hebrew letters will add up to 666."

"Do not forget the numerical system in Latin," said Adan. "The letter I is one, V is five, X is ten, L is fifty, C is one hundred, and D is five hundred. That adds up to 666. That may not mean anything but it's odd that three major languages use letters for numerical values that add up to the same number."

John shrugged his thin shoulders. "Even I do not see the sense in some of my visions. I only know that is what was revealed to me.'

"Have there been other prophets who saw visions?" asked Adan.

"Yes. The prophet, Daniel, a thousand years ago, had a vision of four beasts. The beasts represented empires. Babylonia, Persia, and Greece. The fourth beast was different from the rest and will be the final empire which will rule the world for a short time until Yeshua destroys it for all eternity."

"How will the Antichrist take power?" asked Adan.

"The Antichrist will pluck out three horns, which are three kings and will take their places and their countries. I also had a vision of this beast but the one I saw had ten heads which represent ten nations that will form an alliance under the dominion of the Antichrist. *I saw one of his heads as if it was mortally wounded, but his deadly wound was healed, and the whole world marveled and followed the beast.* The head with a deadly wound that is healed is a nation or empire that collapsed but will revive itself."

"What country will the Antichrist come from?" asked Nikolaus.

"The prophet Micah wrote, '*When the Assyrian comes into our land, and when he treads in our palaces, then we will raise against him seven shepherds and eight princely men. . .He,* the Christ, *shall deliver us from the Assyrian.*' Being an Assyrian could mean a philosophy and not a nationality. It could also mean that he came from another country but when he takes the place of three kings, he will assume their citizenship."

John gave Adan a penetrating gaze. "There were those who believed the Messiah would deliver us from Rome. When Yeshua did nothing to confirm that belief, they rejected him as the Messiah. They did not understand that Yeshua delivered us from *sin*, not a government. When he returns he will have a double-edged sword in his mouth, which means, he will only have to speak and the Antichrist and his followers will be thrown into the fiery pit for eternity."

Adan and Nikolaus sat in silence, trying to absorb the implication of this prediction.

Nikolaus cleared his throat. "Which ten nations will form the final empire?"

"Daniel described and then interpreted a dream of King Nebuchadnezzar," explained John, "in which a statue of a man revealed a history of conquest. Babylonia fell to Persia. Persia fell to Greece. Greece fell to Rome, which will be split into two empires, and then it will fall, hence the two legs of iron representing the Roman Empire. The feet of the statue were made of iron and clay, ten toes, representing ten nations. The ones made of iron are strong. The ones made of clay are weak. Then a mountain, not cut by human hands, will fall upon the feet of iron and clay. They will be crushed by the mountain, which will remain forever. That mountain is God's kingdom."

"This Antichrist you speak of," said Adan. "Is he the only antichrist?"

John shook his head. "There have been other antichrists and there will be many more, but there will be only one Antichrist known as 666. There will be many signs and specific world events leading up to the Tribulation. No one should be surprised."

"What kind of signs and events?" asked Adan. "Niko and I were in Jerusalem recently and I've never seen so much hostility and tension. Will Rome eventually bring war against the city?"

"Yeshua told us, *'Jerusalem will be trampled on by the Gentiles until the times of the Gentiles are fulfilled.'* As I said, the people of Israel will be scattered throughout the world. Then, in a single day, God will cause Israel to become a united, sovereign nation, once again. After a time, Jerusalem will be restored to the Jewish people as well. Then another event must take place."

"In Jerusalem?" asked Adan.

"Yes. The temple will be rebuilt," answered John.

"Rebuilt? It's standing now as we speak," pointed out Adan.

John answered ardently. "Yeshua told us when we were boasting about the magnificence of the temple that *the days will come in which not one stone shall be left upon another. When you see Jerusalem surrounded by armies, then know that its desolation is near.* The second temple will be destroyed. A third temple will be built in the future."

Adan and Nikolaus looked at each other with concern. They suspected that Jerusalem could be destroyed in their lifetime. If ever there was a time for Rome to ransack the city, it was now.

John offered encouragement. "As Yeshua said, God will collect those whose names are written in the *Book of Life* and they will be spared the Tribulation. Yeshua told us that only God knows the exact day and hour when we will be taken up, but we can know when the time is approaching. That is why you must take this scroll to Aquila and Priscilla. They and others will make copies for each of the seven churches. Do not make or deliver copies to any of the cities, yourselves. You must find the tent makers."

Adan felt his throat tighten with the magnitude of the task. "John, I have to ask. Why me?"

"That is a simple answer with a complicated reason. You are the *Lepus Legatus*. Imperial guardsmen to *gladiators* will hesitate to attack you. Just before I was banished to this place, word came to me that the emperor was seeking prophecies. I believe he hopes to acquire this scroll. I have been supplied with papyrus and ink, which was not done for my benefit, but for the emperor. No matter who the emperor sent to get this scroll, you will give them pause. Your fame is much wider than you realize. But more importantly, God will be with you."

Adan looked at the scroll. Was he holding the future of mankind in his hands? He thought of Herod's threat to his life and wondered if he would live long enough to finish the task. He wanted to refuse for fear of failure when a reassuring voice sounded in his thoughts. "*Do not be afraid.*" A breath of relief passed his lips. He knew he would succeed.

"Rest assured, John," said Adan, "the scroll will be delivered. I am not alone."

Nikolaus squared his shoulders with determination. "No, you are not."

The door swung open. Calais appeared with a tray holding several mugs, fresh bread, and olive oil. He set the tray down on the table and joined them. "Did John tell you about the visions?"

Adan confirmed that he had. "I can understand war and hunger killing off much of humanity," said Adan, "but how will the beasts of the earth cause that much death? Very few people ever come in contact with the great beasts, lions or bears and such."

"When John told me about this vision," said Calais, "I gave it much thought. You are assuming the beasts will be the great predators. Maybe not. I have noticed that where there are a great many rats, there is much disease and death. The more vermin, the more disease. Perhaps the deadly beasts will be small animals. Perhaps even insects like hornets, scorpions and mosquitoes might develop venom that causes disease. You can't destroy insects with arrows or spears. There are too many of them and they're too small. I have heard of clever soldiers that put beehives in the heads of human figures made of wood and cloth. When the invading soldiers shot their arrows at the figures, the bees attack. The invaders run away in panic."

"Hornets and scorpions certainly have venom, but not mosquitoes," pointed out Adan. "Besides, mosquitoes live in swamps and few people live in those places."

Nikolaus rubbed his chin in thought. "I think Calais could be right. The air over swamps causes *mal aria,* the bad air disease. But what if the mosquitoes could fill themselves with the bad air and carry its poison far away from the swamps?"

"When these events occur," said Adan, "hopefully, thousands of years from now, will the world be the same as it is now?"

John frowned, remembering what the prophet Daniel had written. "I think not. Daniel said that in the last days, there will be a great increase in knowledge and travel. Many things would have to change for that to happen."

"Why has God revealed these things to you in particular, John?" asked Adan.

"I don't know. I don't need to know. I do not question the actions of God." He darted a look at Calais. "No one should." Calais met his stern look with defiance but then he faltered and looked away. He tightened his lips into a thin line as if literally biting back his words.

Adan and Nikolaus thanked Calais for bringing the refreshments and took up the mugs of diluted wine. Calais tore the bread loaf into pieces and each of them took their share.

"Your visions must have been numerous and detailed," observed Adan. "This scroll is thick. May I read it?"

"Of course. Both of you should. Do not fear these events. God will gather the believers before the final days take place. No one will know when that will happen and there will be no warning, unlike the Tribulation, which will have ample warning. When Yeshua spoke of taking the believers away, he said, '*But of that day and hour no one knows, not even the angels of heaven, but My Father only.*' As you can see," he touched the scroll, "in contrast, the Tribulation will be proclaimed in many ways."

John set his hand on the table as if to steady himself. "Of the twelve that Yeshua chose, I am the only one left. I was also the only one of the twelve that stood with him at his crucifixion." He looked over at Adan. "Did you see when he looked me in the eye, then moved his head to look at you? Then he looked back at me and I knew immediately that you and I would be connected. That is why I didn't hesitate to meet with you when you asked Jamin to set up a meeting. Peter was suspicious, of course. I didn't blame him. We sat on the hilltop above the garden the whole time you were there. When Jamin demanded to know how long we should wait, Peter said, 'As long as it takes.' But I knew that we had nothing to fear from you. I said, 'We've waited long enough. Any man who gives water first to his dog before he drinks must have goodness in his heart.' I went down to you and the others followed."

Adan's expression brightened at the mention of the dog, Tigula. "I remember. Our first meeting was in the garden where Yeshua's tomb was located. You encouraged Peter to trust me. You didn't even become upset when Malchus showed up. Tigula didn't bark at you. And you weren't afraid of Tigula. You weren't afraid of me either."

John smiled at his friend. "My only fear is for those who ignore the words of Yeshua."

The four friends talked about other subjects and were in no hurry to bid farewell. They finally walked John back to his tiny cell but before they left, John motioned to Calais to speak to him privately.

"Calais, my friend, I do trust your intentions and abilities. That is why I hope you will go with them to Corinth. You will be needed. However, Adan must carry the scroll."

"If you won't let me take the scroll, then why should I leave you, John?" Calais looked away with a sulking expression. "You think I would fail on my own, don't you?"

"God has a plan for you and it no longer requires you to be on this island. You must go with Adan and Nikolaus. You can refuse me but it never works out for those who try to refuse God. You must go with them because you will *not* fail."

In spite of John's soft voice, the brothers overheard enough to understand the problem. Adan whispered, "Niko, just like John knows that Calais will be needed, I have known things, at unexpected times, before they happen. There is no glimmer of doubt because the knowing comes from God. Like in Herculaneum when I announced that we had to leave *right then*? Decimus didn't want to leave and Dionysia would have stayed with him. After I said we had to leave, *Vesuvio* began erupting. Remember?"

"I do," he answered and looked over at Calais. "Your insistence saved all our lives."

"It was not *my* insistence. I was only the messenger," declared Adan with finality.

Calais continued speaking to John. "I hate to leave you. I will obey out of respect for you but it grieves me. You shared Yeshua with me and for that, I will always be grateful." The two men hugged each other farewell. Adan and Nikolaus moved off as John gave final instructions to his friend.

When the three men started to walk away, John called out. "When you go to Pergamon, beware of the Nicolaitans and those who follow the doctrine of Balaam. They do not follow the teachings of Yeshua. But you must go there."

Adan and Nikolaus exchanged startled glances. "Did you say anything about Pergamon?" asked Adan. Nikolaus and Calais shook their heads.

Adan turned around one last time. "Peace be with you, brother."

John placed his hand over his heart. "And with each of you."

Chapter 10

A Dangerous Intention

———⁂———

T he three men headed back to the bakery for Calais to tell the owner he was leaving and to collect his meager belongings. The woman was angry at first when Calais gave notice. She had grown fond of the young man but admitted that prison employment was not a good career choice. She even wished Calais good luck before the three men left the shop. Adan stopped at the main office and wrote a brief evaluation of the facilities for Tacitus. The prison garrison was understaffed and the island did not have a strategic location but the mineral deposits would be sorely missed. The centurion in charge assured Adan that he would dispatch the report at the first opportunity. Adan thanked him and the trio headed for the prison gate. The same guard was still manning the entrance but this time he moved quickly to swing the portal open. He avoided making eye contact.

Adan and Nikolaus were relieved to find the driver was still waiting. He was asleep on the floor of the carriage. He had allowed the horse to wander a bit as it hunted for decent grass but being still harnessed to the carriage prevented it from going too far. Calais was quiet as he climbed into the carriage. He hated leaving the only friend he had made on Patmos Island, but he still smarted under John's refusal to let him convey the scroll.

The carriage ride to the pier in Skala took considerably longer than it had going the opposite direction. It seemed the driver was determined to spare his horse. The man even stepped down from his seat and led the horse when the road was a bit rockier. Adan was beginning to think the driver expected to be paid by the hour. The travelers were unaware that three men on foot trailed behind but the driver noted their progress with furtive glances over his shoulder.

One of the men trailing the carriage cursed under his breath. "That imbecile is going to give us away if he keeps looking back."

The other two men made no comment. They knew better than to speak when their leader was angry.

He turned to one of the men. "Have you posted my message?"

The man nodded.

"Good. Our employer will know the prisoner has finally finished the scroll and the courier has possession of it—for now."

He grinned at his companions. They smiled back, relieved that his anger had passed. Out of habit, he brushed the back of his fingers along his missing right earlobe.

"I will enjoy crossing swords with a centurion. In Rome, they called me Celsus, the centurion killer."

The youngest of the three men had often watched Celsus brush his fingers along his ear. His curiosity finally overcame his better judgement. "You do that a lot." He mimicked the gesture. "What happened?"

Celsus focused on the man's face. "I pinched it off and forced it down a man's throat for asking too many questions."

The two companions clamped their mouths shut. That was the last time either one of them asked Celsus a personal question.

Meanwhile, Adan rubbed the back of his neck, which was stiff with tension. Apprehension settled over him now that he was responsible for delivering John's Book of Revelation. He had no idea how or when he would get to Corinth. The magnitude of the task weighed heavily on him but it didn't explain the unsettling feeling he had of being watched. He scanned the landscape but didn't see anything out of the ordinary. Perhaps, he was only anxious to get back on the ship. Somehow, he always felt safer there.

The three men stalking Adan saw the travelers board the *Child of the Ocean*. The ship soon set sail. It was too late for Celsus and his men to attempt to join the crew.

Celsus swore vehemently under his breath. "I didn't expect that. I thought they would have to wait for passage. We need to find out where that ship is going."

The three men made their way to the pier as they watched the ship sail for the horizon. Celsus found the harbor master. "Where is that ship going?" He pointed angrily.

"You mean the one that the *Lupus Legatus* just boarded? They're headed for Chios."

"What?" cried the younger of the three men. "The *Lupus Legatus*! The wolf-eyed centurion that came back from the dead?" The man licked his lips nervously.

"Don't be such a coward," snarled Celsus. "He's just a man like any other."

"No, he's not! He's a werewolf!"

The other man ran his hand over his bald head. "We'll have to steal the scroll when he leaves it at an inn or someplace. You can't win against a werewolf."

"Who put you in charge?" demanded Celsus. "You'll do as I tell you. I don't care what foolishness you believe." He asked the harbor master if another vessel would be leaving for Chios and was told the name of the ship. The three men walked along the pier and Celsus hailed the captain. They hired on as oarsmen and were soon on their way to Chios.

***

Aurelius stood on deck watching the oarsmen who were filing up the gangway. They almost always lost a few crewmen at every port and hired a few to take their place. It was an easy way for a man to find work.

Aurelius was about to go below deck when he spotted a horse lumbering down the rock-strewn pathway, pulling a jolting, bouncing carriage. His arm shot into the air with a hearty wave. Adan, Nikolaus and someone else, who looked familiar, climbed down. He welcomed the men aboard and smiled when he saw Calais. "So, we meet again. Are you seeking employment or do you wish to pay your way?"

Calais answered eagerly. "I prefer employment if you can make room for me at the oars." He was still getting used to working for his own earnings.

"I'm sure you can squeeze into the rotation. Stow your belongings with the others' and find Junius, my Master of Oars. He's not the same man I had when we left *Vesuvio* behind. Junius is the short one, built like a bull. He sprouts horns when he's angry. Be cautious."

Calais thanked him for the job and went below deck. Adan greeted Aurelius; then went straight to the guest quarters. Most ship quarters were furnished with a security cabinet that was bolted to the floor to prevent it from thrashing about during heavy seas. Being bolted down also prevented theft. Adan tested the lock and found it to be efficient. He placed the scroll inside, locked the cabinet, and put the key in his coin pouch. He sighed with relief; the scroll was safe for now.

Nikolaus lingered on deck to chat with Aurelius. The ship was soon back out to sea and headed for the Greek island of Chios. Unlike their usual habit of staying on deck, Adan and Nikolaus sequestered themselves in Adan's quarters to read John's scroll. They discussed the meaning of the visions and how the world would be affected. Many empires had risen and fallen throughout the history of humanity, yet still life went on. Catastrophes occurred in different regions but did not affect the whole world. Life recovered in those areas or moved away. They discussed the possibility that many ancient civilizations could have existed that died out. Their cities could have been buried beneath new cities. Adan pointed out how coastal cities in *Italia* sometimes slipped beneath the waves as land mysteriously sank to lower levels. Yet, all the recorded events in history never adversely affected the entire world. John's visions predicted that all of the Tribulation events would affect every country, every city, every single person. They shuddered just to think about it.

"Think of Pompei, Herculaneum, and Stabiae," said Nikolaus. "They were completely buried in the course of a few days. Our generation will remember them, but what of the generations to follow? Even if someone wrote down the account of *Vesuvio* erupting into a flaming mountain, will anyone believe it?"

"I'm sure someone will," said Adan. "*Praefectus* Pliny, an admiral in our fleet, lived south of *Vesuvio*. He would have seen the eruptions. Cornelius Tacitus, our most famous Roman historian, will want to record any eye-witness accounts, I'm sure."

"Yes, probably. I think the cities will be rebuilt," said Nikolaus. "Maybe they will be even better. It's hard to admit but Rome brought in many improvements to Greece over the years. I wonder what men will do a thousand years from now? Two thousand years from now?"

"I can think of a few things I wish we'd do," said Adan.

"Me, too. It's too bad we can't carry coins or other items in our clothing without sewing it into the hem of a tunic or robe. A coin pouch is so easy to steal. You can carry a *loculus* over a shoulder or on your belt but those types of satchels are cumbersome. A coin purse or pouch doesn't hold much, either. I've thought about asking Marina to sew a piece of cloth on the inside of the front of my tunics. Then stuff wouldn't fall down to my belt. You could get to it easier as well."

"That's a good idea," agreed Adan. "Maybe have her embroider the stitching on the front to make it more durable."

"What improvements can you think of?"

"A better saddle," declared Adan. "For those who use slaves to 'back' them up, they see no need. Snap your fingers and a slave drops to his hands and knees and up you climb right off his back. Yes? But for someone like me who jumps and pulls himself up, it would be so much easier if there was some type of foothold. Maybe even on both sides of the saddle. It would be much easier to stay on your horse, especially if you're galloping along, trying to shoot an arrow or throw a spear. Our greatest weakness is how easily a man can be pulled from his horse when he has the reins in one hand and a weapon in the other."

Adan rolled his eyes in frustration. "We build beautiful villas and temples and aqueducts and huge ships. We have water powered flour mills. We have plumbing to take water from the well to the boilers to the house, all nice and warm. Yet, we don't have a better way to get on a horse. But then, maybe we won't always ride the backs of animals to get from here to there. Can you imagine a carriage that doesn't need horses?"

Nikolaus laughed at such a wild notion. "That's crazy. You have quite the imagination."

"Where do you think my sons get their wild ideas from?" said Adan. "Certainly not from Dulcie. She's too practical for fantasies and day-dreams."

Nikolaus looked thoughtful. "I'm thinking more along the line of nightmares. I think future weapons may be different. When John said he saw visions of a fourth of the world's population killed in war, I think weapons will not be swords, bows, or spears. Maybe we'll invent deadlier weapons using Greek fire or the sun's rays reflected off polished copper. Can you imagine burning up an invading fleet from the safety of the clifftops?"

"It is true that man's ability to make war is limited by the strength of his arm," said Adan. "Perhaps that is a good thing. Think about it, Niko. What if there were weapons that could cause destruction like earthquakes and flaming mountains can do? That's good if you use the weapons to defend against an invading enemy. What if your enemy has the same kind of weapons? Both you and the enemy could wipe each other out. Then who is left?" Adan put the scroll back in the cabinet. They grew quiet as they considered that possibility.

"Let's think of something less depressing," said Adan. "Let's play a game. We'll call it Impossible Ideas. Here's the rules. Daniel predicted there would be an increase in knowledge and travel, so our ideas have to fall in those two categories. We each present one idea per round."

"Why not?" agreed Nikolaus. "It's not like we have anything else to do. You go first."

"All right. My first idea is for knowledge," drawled Adan. "What if everyone, and I mean every man, woman and child, knew how to read at least one language?"

Nikolaus looked startled. "That would dramatically increase knowledge. It would change society if information could be distributed to the whole population at once." Nikolaus twisted his lips in thought. "Ummm, let me think. Ah, here's one for travel. What if a type of carriage really was invented that didn't need horses? A *machina* would make the wheels turn. One could travel much further since the machine would not get tired or need water and food."

"Well, your machine would need fuel. Like wood to keep a fire burning or something," suggested Adan. "But it's a good idea as far as impossibilities. What do you say? Round one is a tie?"

Nikolaus grunted in agreement, licked his finger, and drew two invisible lines in the air.

Adan thought for a moment. "Round two. This one's for travel. What if you wanted to eat breakfast in Caesarea, lunch in Rome, and dinner in Athens—on the same day? You would get in your *machina volatilis* and fly through the air like a bird."

Nikolaus grinned. "Suitably impossible! All right, let me think. Got it. What if you could put all of the knowledge from the Library of Alexandria, Library of Ashurbanipal, Library of Pergamon, the writings of Flavius Josephus, and Cornelius Tacitus into a *single* book that you could hold in your hand? You could call it a *liber nanno*."

Adan smiled approval. "Not bad. A dwarf book, but how would you read the words? They would be too small to see."

Nikolaus was momentarily stumped. "Umm. I got it. You would ask a question into the *liber nanno* and it would *tell* you the answer. How 'bout that?"

Adan tapped his chin in thought. "Since we know birds can fly, your idea is much more impossible. You win the second round. Round three. What if I could invent, for knowledge, a tiny machine that was designed to heal damaged organs from *inside* the body? You just swallow it and it knows where to go and how to fix wounded organs. You could call it a *machina de sanatio nanno*."

"A dwarf healing machine! Very clever." exclaimed Nikolaus. "*Ohe*, how 'bout this? You talk to me and I talk to you but we're two thousand cubits apart, maybe, even leagues apart but we can hear each other. We each use a *machina* that teleports our voices over great distances."

"How is that knowledge or travel?" asked Adan.

Nikolaus made a disgruntled face. "We could be sharing knowledge. I say, 'General Longinus, the enemy is sneaking up behind you.' You say, 'Really, how do you know? You're on a ship.' Then I say, 'I'm looking right at them. They just left their ships and they're coming for you.' Can you imagine how that would change everything? You leave spies all over the place; give them each a *machina de lanuae magicae* and no more surprise attacks."

A slow smile curved Adan's lips "Wouldn't your machine of magic language be sharing previously known knowledge? Our impossible ideas have to be about newly invented knowledge." He gave Nikolaus a thumbs down. "I win round three."

Nikolaus blew air from puffed cheeks. "Ah, so *now* he clarifies the rules. Are you going to give me another chance?"

"No," said Adan flatly. "Round four. Here's my next idea. It's for knowledge. What if we knew how to *replace* damaged organs? Not just fix them. For instance, a man is dying from the coughing disease so his lungs are bad. Another man has good lungs but he just died from a broken neck. So, the *medicus* does a *trans plantare* by replacing the bad lungs with the healthy lungs. Everything is stitched back together and the man can breathe like a horse in a chariot race."

The corners of Nikolaus's month curved down. "Would be messy. Wouldn't such complicated surgery make him bleed to death?"

Adan grunted with annoyance. "Good point. But it's still a good idea. Your turn."

"This one is for travel," Nikolaus clarified. "You want to get from Caesarea to Rome as fast as possible but there's a huge naval battle across the entire sea. So, you use a *machina* that swims underwater like a shark, the whole way to Rome, and you never have to come up for air. You could call it a *machina sub aqua*."

"I like it. An underwater machine," said Adan. "You wouldn't have to deal with bad weather or seasickness."

Nikolaus considered their ideas. "I think round four is a tie. I wish we really could fly like eagles and falcons or swim like barracudas and sturgeons. Imagine what you would see."

The two were quiet as they pictured their fantastic ideas. A mischievous grin spread across Adan's face. "My turn. Round five. This is for travel. A special *machina* is invented that can, not just fly through the air," he pointed upwards, "but go all the way—to—the—Moon! You could call it the *machina de Luna itinerantur*. Men will trot around, looking for a good place to camp out. They'll look back at earth and be so far away, they won't be able to see people and buildings, even the colosseum. The ocean will look like a lake."

Nikolaus was dumbstruck. "A Moon travel machine? That's *too* impossible! Does that fit in the rules? I thought it had to be travel on earth. Besides, why would anyone go to the moon?"

Adan tried not to laugh. "Because they wanted to see what it was like. Because no one had ever been there before. Because they wanted to build a fancy villa with moon rocks."

Nikolaus gave Adan a blank look, then burst into laughter. Adan started laughing and the two nearly fell out of their chairs from laughing so hard.

"You're the winner," Nikolaus declared "I can't beat that. Taking a stroll on the moon will never happen even in *ten* thousand years. Impossible is impossible forever. Yes?"

Adan grinned at his brother. "Could be. I'm out of ideas." He leaned back in his chair and interlaced his fingers behind his head. "Actually, I can beat my own impossible idea. It's not about travel or knowledge." He lowered his hands. "It's about life. What if slavery came to an end?"

Nikolaus grunted with dismay. "Even if there were machines to do the work of slaves, there will always be wars and prisoners of war, tragedy and orphans and widows, people facing bankruptcy. There will always be powerful people taking advantage of poor people. Even if the culture of slavery is outlawed by some incredible feat, it will still exist under another name."

"Very pessimistic of you, Niko. You think humanity is hopeless?"

Nikolaus rubbed his jaw in thought. "Maybe not completely hopeless. If we were, we wouldn't exist. We would have killed each other off long ago. Maybe someday, a father will not have the legal right to murder anyone in his family without question. Not his wife. Not his children. Not his slaves. Parents will not be able to sell their children into slavery. Parents will not have the legal right to toss healthy infants on garbage dumps to slowly die from neglect. A woman accused of adultery, even with evidence, will not be fed to hyenas for the entertainment of the masses. Criminals will not be nailed to crosses to die from days of torture." Nikolaus paused and sighed. "Will that ever happen?"

Adan raised his chin with confidence. "Yes."

"How can you be so sure?"

"Because Yeshua's message will be taught to the entire world. That message will change attitudes and laws. The value of human life will increase. The enforcement of laws will change. Murder will no longer be legal under any circumstances. Children of any age will be valued and protected by law. Widows will not be thrown into the street. The accusation of adultery will be a matter between spouses and God, not a source for cruel entertainment. Prisoners of war will be released when the war ends. It's so basic—Yeshua's message—treat others the same way you want to be treated. If we pass and enforce laws that uphold that premise, there is hope."

The tension eased from Nikolaus's face. "Maybe even impossible things can happen."

Adan remembered something his father told him. "I've got a story that illustrates what you just said. It's about Emperor Gaius, you know, Caligula."

"You mean when Caligula appointed his thoroughbred, Incitatus, to be a senator? That kind of impossible?"

Adan wagged his finger. "Even more impossible. There was a councilman who worked for Tiberius, named Thrasyllus of Mendes. Father said he told the senate that Caligula had 'no more chance of becoming emperor than of riding a horse across the Bay of Baiae.' So, you know what Caligula did?"

"I can't wait to hear this," said Nikolaus.

"Caligula made the navy line up ships like pontoons, with bridges in between, from Baiae to the port of Puteoli. It took over one hundred thirty ships. He rode Incitatus across the bridges and ships, across the Bay of Baiae, to prove Thrasyllus wrong. At the taxpayers' expense, of course."

Nikolaus's mouth dropped open. "You're making this up."

Adan slapped a hand to his chest. "No! Centurion's honor. It really happened."

"Did the Senate denounce him?"

"A few wanted him to pay for it from his own coffers but many others thought it was amusing. Father said Caligula had granted favors to those men who had suddenly acquired a sense of humor."

"What did Father think of it?" asked Nikolaus.

Adan stood up and assumed his most imposing stance in a perfect imitation of his father when he once gave speeches. "He said in his no-nonsense voice, 'Why doesn't the halfwit simply make that blasted stallion the emperor and spare the rest of us his astronomical absurdity? At least when Incitatus prances around, it suits him.' You should have seen the look on Father's face. You'd have thought he swallowed vinegar."

The brothers burst into laughter.

"Adan," Nikolaus managed to say, "can you imagine Father addressing Emperor Incitatus? I bet he could do it with a straight face. 'Honorable Emperor Horse Face, may we brush your royal tail? Polish your noble hooves? Get you another handful of imperial grass?"

"Ha!" Adan mimicked *Consul* Aquila's most pompous expression. 'Shall we also tend your majestic mane, your Royal Horseyness?' I can really see Father doing that. You know, speaking of Baiae, I thought of something else. Did I ever tell you why Father decided to be an architect?"

"I assumed it was simply the opposite of soldiering since Grandfather Livius dragged him from one battle to another."

"No, there was a specific reason and Grandfather Livius actually introduced Father to the idea. Grandfather's burial urn would explode if he knew. Livius had to attend meetings of the military high council in Baiae, *Italia*. You might not realize that Baiae is the center of Rome's power. It is in Baiae that life-altering decisions are made every day and all Roman rulers gather there to confer and to pleasure themselves any way they can. It is an unwritten rule that what happens in Baiae is buried in Baiae. Anyway, Grandfather Livius took Father there and left him to entertain himself. Father went to the tunnels that lead into the bowels of the earth. It gets hotter and hotter the deeper you go. Many believe Baiae sits atop the gates of Hades. Oracles sit at the end of the tunnels and for a fee, will tell you what your future holds."

"*Ohe*, that sounds unpleasant," grumbled Nikolaus. "Why do they set up shop in the tunnels if it is so hot?"

"They say the fumes coming up from Hades gives them the power of prediction, but the oracles pay a price. The heat is stifling and the fumes make people sick. Still, they make too much money to leave the tunnels. But what really intrigued Father were the underwater rivers of hot water. There are grand villas along the coastline and every one of them has tunnels underneath their homes that carry the heat of the underground rivers. They build the floors of their homes on short pillars so the heat will fill in the space underneath the tiled floor. The villas stay warm all winter. In the summer, they block off the tunnels."

"That's ingenious but where does the heat come from?"

"You can't guess, Niko? What turned *Vesuvio* into a *mons igneus,* a flaming mountain?"

"Of course. There must be a great cauldron of fire beneath the surface."

"Yes, a great furnace that takes up a great amount of space. The whole structure of the city fascinated Father to such an extent, he decided to study architecture to see if he could improve on the techniques used in Baiae. Father told me that something is happening to Baiae."

Nikolaus's tone sharpened. "Don't tell me it is about to explode, too."

"Nothing that dramatic. The city is built up against a narrow cliff which follows the coastline. There are private theaters and bath houses above the cliff. The villas are ocean front properties all the way to the shoreline. Unfortunately, Baiae is sinking. Fishermen were the first to notice. The boat docks become submerged at high tide. After Father became established in his career, he received a letter from the *proconsul* of Baiae to design new docks farther inland. He turned them down. He determined at the present rate of sinking, Baiae will be two cubits under water within a few hundred years. He believed there would be problems with the renovations within his lifetime. Father would be forced to make additional improvements at his own cost. I told Aquila, junior, about Baiae and he thinks the burning rock that explodes from the nearby flaming mountains, comes from under Baiae, leaving a vacuum, and making it sink."

"Nephew could be right," agreed Nikolaus. "We saw what *Vesuvio* did in less than two days. All that ash and molten rock had to come from somewhere."

A new idea suddenly came to Adan. "Remember what John said about massive fires in his visions? Could world-wide fires be caused by flaming mountains? Think about it, Niko. No one knew that *Mons Vesuvio* was a flaming mountain. What if other mountains are flaming mountains, just like *Vesuvio*, but haven't erupted yet? There were all those earthquakes before *Vesuvio* exploded. Do you think the earthquakes caused the eruptions? What if these terrible earthquakes John saw in his visions also set the mountains to erupting, which sets the world on fire? He said catastrophes will come one upon another, and another, and so forth."

Nikolaus rubbed his chin in contemplation. "Let me see if I understand. Yeshua said that there will be no warning before he takes the believers away to heaven. Then later, there will be omens in the sky warning that the Tribulation has begun. Yeshua comes to earth, again, at the end of the Tribulation to destroy the Antichrist and rescue the last remaining believers. Yes? Yeshua said that only God knows when the people who already believe will be taken, sparing them the trials of the Tribulation. So, no one can predict when this will happen. But what about the celestial signs, which will come later, warning of the coming Tribulation? If the exact dates of the omens of the Tribulation could be foretold, many more people might be saved before it begins."

Adan didn't like the implication of Niko's question. "How could they be predicted?"

"With the Prophecy Box," declared Nikolaus. "What if it has the power to predict the omens? John said he had visions of signs and wonders in the sky."

An uncomfortable chill went up Adan's spine. "Niko, no human could ever devise anything that could predict God's actions. Remember, even Yeshua said he did not know the exact time."

"No, I'm not talking about the actual wars and famines and such. I'm talking about events in the sky. John said that Yeshua warned them about signs in the sun, moon, and the stars."

Adan's expression tightened. "Niko, if we find the Prophecy Box, what do you intend to do with it? You're not thinking about using it, are you?"

Nikolaus didn't answer, at first. "I hadn't thought about it till now. It would be a shame to not take advantage of its power. If I could use the box to predict when these unusual celestial events would happen, it would give people more reason to believe in Yeshua."

"Again, there is no manmade device that can foretell when God will send these omens," insisted Adan. "God reveals his intentions through people, not through a *machina*."

Nikolaus shrugged passively. "It was only an idea."

Adan rubbed his hand across his forehead. "I know you have good intentions, Niko, but once a person gets a taste of great power, it can warp even the strongest will."

Nikolaus was irritated at his implied criticism. "If you think the Prophecy Box is too dangerous to use, why are we trying to find it? This was your idea!"

"It's not that I want to find the box as much as the person who *has* the box. If we're going to find out what happened to your family, we need to start with the present owner."

Nikolaus's expression grew sullen. "What if I don't care anymore. They're dead and gone. My father's ambition got them killed and put me and my sister on the auction block. As far as I know, they died from sickness." He got up from the table and began to pace the short distance within Adan's quarters. He stopped and slumped into the chair again.

"I know you *do* care, Niko. You've always cared about your family. Maybe I was wrong to start this investigation. Maybe it is better if we deliver John's scroll in Corinth and return home."

Nikolaus tamped down his anger. "I know you mean well. And you're right. I do want to know why they died. And you're probably right about the box as well. Maybe it really is dangerous. Besides, like you said, we only need to talk to the owner." He pressed his lips into a tight line. He determined to keep his ideas about the box to himself from then on.

Nikolaus gave Adan a sidelong glance. "You said we should give up and go home? Have you forgotten what Herod intends to do when you get back?"

Adan slowly met his brother's gaze. "Actually, I had. For the moment, I was more concerned about you than about my own situation. Thank you for reminding me."

Nikolaus lowered his head. "I'm sorry, Adan. That was cruel of me to say that. Of course, the box is not our objective. And I really do want to learn what happened to my family."

"It's all right, Niko. Let's take this one day at a time," suggested Adan, relieved that Nikolaus agreed with him. "We'll get through this together."

"We'll go to Pergamon for Calais. Then to Corinth, to deliver John's scroll. And then we'll be free to find the owner of the box."

"Hopefully, if we find Calypso, she'll be able to send us in the right direction. Let's go on deck. We both need the fresh air."

Nikolaus stood up and went to the door without another word. The confinement of the close quarters was making him anxious. Adan's rebuff of his ideas on the Prophecy Box only made him more determined to pursue the idea. Perhaps, if they found the box, he would be able to experiment with it—without Adan's knowledge.

Chapter 11

Curse of the Sorceress

T he *Child of the Ocean* sailed from Patmos to Chios and then on to Smyrna. Aurelius informed the crew that he had acquired a cargo in Smyrna to be delivered to the port in Troas, north by northeast of Pergamon. He informed Adan, Nikolaus, and Calais that they could hire a carriage to go from Smyrna to Pergamon, which was inland, north of Smyrna. It would take less than a day to get to and from Pergamon and he would be gone about four or five days. He told them he would pick them up again on his return trip to Smyrna. From there, he would sail west across the Aegean Sea for the eastern port in Corinth. The plan was agreeable to the travelers. They docked in Smyrna and exchanged farewells as Adan, Nikolaus, and Calais left the ship.

While the cargo was being loaded, the usual exit of a few crewman took place as others filed on board, hoping to be hired. Junius took down their names as the new crewmen went below deck to stow their knapsacks until he had the required quota. One man stood out due to his flowing, blonde hair and pale, ice-blue eyes. Junius let the blonde man give his name and then stopped those behind him.

"That's it for this trip, men," announced Junius. "We've got all we need."

The unselected men grumbled with disappointment and filed back down the gangplank.

"You there," Junius called out to the last man. "Where are you from?"

"*Germania.* Does that matter?" the man grumbled with a belligerent tone.

"What's your name again? I didn't write it down."

"Folke. It means 'chief' in my country."

"Well, you're not in your country anymore, Folke. Here, you're just an oarsman."

The man gave Junius a curled lip and surly eyes. "If you say so." He turned and followed the other men to the lower deck to stow his knapsack.

By this time, Pomona's presence had made a positive difference for the crew. She had successfully implemented her new rules. Aurelius had to admit that her efforts were paying off. Junius reported that he rarely heard complaints among the men anymore. The first rule was that everyone was to have three full meals a day. Pomona insisted on extra provisions, which cut into Aurelius's profits until he realized that the men could work more efficiently when they were well nourished. They reached ports more quickly, which enabled him to secure more cargoes. Another new rule was that each oarsman was to line up before breakfast and show her the palms of his hands. If anyone had blisters, sores, or infected lesions, she would treat the wounds with vinegar, aloe salve, or honey, and wrap the hand with bandaging. At first the men complained about the sting of the vinegar but she would poke fun at their masculinity with good-natured banter until they were too embarrassed or amused to complain further. Her treatments caused the injuries to heal faster and greatly reduced infections. Pomona also insisted that each oarsman was to have more frequent water breaks. She instructed Samuel, the cabin boy, to carry the water bucket and ladle among the men to make it easier for them to get a drink. It wasn't long before the men referred to her affectionately among themselves as *Mater*, Mother.

Samuel was beginning to feel confident enough to look the men in the eye when he handed each a ladle full of fresh water. A few would even thank him, which was virtually never expressed to a slave. A few days into sailing for Troas, Samuel was cleaning up the crew's quarters when the ship was hit by an unusually high wave that sent the boy tumbling against the bulkhead. Instinctively, he grabbed at anything to prevent falling. He heard linen rip and saw with horror that a crewman's knapsack hanging from a hook had been torn. The boy's first thought was to throw himself overboard before he could be flogged for committing such an error. Then he looked more closely. A roll of papyrus had fallen out of the torn knapsack. Why would an oarsman have such a thing? Papyrus was expensive. Being a slave, Samuel knew there was one occupation that required carrying rolls of papyrus.

Samuel had not been born into slavery. His father was an educated scribe and had taught him to read both Hebrew and Latin. They were a happy family until a minor skirmish erupted in Samuel's small Jerusalem neighborhood. A *legendary* was accidently killed which drew the ire of the Antonia soldiers. They indiscriminately killed everyone in the area. Samuel was away on an errand, which saved his life, but left him without a family. When no one offered to take him in, he sold himself into slavery to keep from starving to death.

Samuel unrolled the sheets with trembling fingers. One of the sheets was titled, Pomona, Samaritan, Murder of a Roman citizen. He saw the embroidered name along the strap of the torn knapsack. It was Folke. Samuel stuffed the papyrus down the front of his tunic and ran to find the Master of Oars.

Pomona and Aurelius were going over the supply list when they heard angry shouting from the top deck. Brother and sister looked at each other with concern. They jumped up and hurried out of the captain's quarters. The first thing Aurelius saw was that all the oars were standing vertical in the at-rest position. Pomona saw the men crowded into a group near the life rails.

"What is going on here?" shouted Aurelius as he plowed through the men. Pomona followed in his wake.

Junius had one of the oarsmen by the front of his tunic while two other burly men held the man's arms. The men were shouting for the oarsman to be thrown overboard.

"Captain!" cried Junius, "Folke has come aboard under a false pretense. He is a bounty hunter." He looked over his shoulder at Samuel. "Show him the warrant."

The boy handed the papyrus to Aurelius but he didn't bother to read it. He stuffed the document down the front of his tunic. He stepped up to face Folke. "Is this true? Was this warrant in your possession?"

Folke's eyes darted from the captain's face to the other men surrounding him. "And what of it? She's a murderer. She knifed a Roman citizen. I have a right to make a living, don't I?"

The other men howled with rage and pressed in. Junius tightened his grip on the man's tunic. "We don't care what your filthy warrant says. Pomona is no murderer. All we have to do is throw you overboard and the problem disappears!"

The men holding Folke doubled their efforts to lift him as several other men grasped his legs. Shouts of encouragement sounded as Folke was lifted into the air, his long, blonde hair went flying. Aurelius took hold of Samuel's shoulder and pulled him back from being accidently trampled. Folke shouted and cursed in anger as he struggled. His smug superiority had vanished as he looked over his shoulder and saw only slate-blue ocean waves. The furious men lifted him and with one great shout of victory, they tossed him into the sea. Cheers rose up as the men jostled each other to get to the life rails. They shouted obscenities at the floundering man as he tried to keep his head above water.

"*Stop!*" Pomona pushed Aurelius and Junius aside. "What have you done?"

She frantically looked around and spied a coil of rope. She lashed one end to the life rail and threw the remaining coil toward the drowning man. He grabbed the rope and pulled, hand over hand, to the side of the ship. He used the ship's hull to get a footing and the rope for leverage to get close enough to grab the life rail with one hand.

"Help him!" Pomona ordered.

The men looked at her in shocked silence.

"Please," she pleaded. "I'm asking you, please!"

Reluctantly, the oarsmen grabbed hold of Folke and hauled him over the life rail. He crumpled to the deck and looked up into the serene face of his rescuer.

Folke's arrogance snapped back in place. He figured that no one would dare touch him now. He slowly came to his feet and faced the others. "This doesn't change anything." He pointed at Pomona. "She's the one they want. Look at the description. She matches it perfectly."

"We don't care what your warrant says," declared Aurelius. "She *is* the one they're looking for."

The crew gasped and turned angry frowns on Aurelius.

"I also know that she did *not* kill anyone." He faced his men. "I have the testimony of eyewitnesses. A boy who witnessed the incident said that the man who falsely accused her and riled up the neighbors against her, fell on his own knife. She escaped and ran to the shop of a former *gladiator*. He told us that Pomona could not have knifed the man because there was not one drop of blood anywhere on her. A *gladiator* would know of such things."

The men listened and nodded approval of his defense for his sister.

Folke sullenly eyed Pomona. "I don't care if she's guilty or not. That's for the court to decide. I just want my fee."

The men growled with disgust. The call to throw Folke overboard again sounded and the men took up the chant. "Throw him over! Throw him over!"

Pomona stepped up to Folke and turned her back on him. She faced the crew and waved her hands up and down until they quieted. "Gentlemen, please listen to me. I love all of you as brothers. You have shown great faith in me by trying to protect me. It is because I love you that I cannot let you do this terrible thing. This man's blood would be on your hands if you do this. I cannot let you suffer this guilt on my behalf. Please, let him be."

One of the men jabbed a finger in Folke's direction. "He is the one at fault! He is guilty, not us. He cares nothing for what is good and right."

"Perhaps." Pomona placed her hand over her heart. "But I do. It isn't right to murder this man. It is true that I am innocent of the crime I am accused. I am also sure that I will not see justice in a Roman court. However, we all must die, some day. I wish to live, yes," she looked at Aurelius with sadness. She reached for Samuel and he came to her. She clutched him to her side. "But not at the cost of putting the sin of this man's murder on your heads. I will *not* let you be guilty of the very crime I am accused. I love each of you too much to stand by and do nothing."

Pomona faced Folke. "I will go with you. Do as you must."

Folke blinked in confusion. He looked at the shocked expressions on the men's faces. He saw the captain bow his head in despair and how the slave boy clung to Pomona. Then he thought about the rest of the voyage. He still had to be among them. The woman may not do anything in retaliation but what of the men? What of her brother? Would they let him take her away as his prisoner? It would take only one of them to murder him in his sleep.

"Sir." Samuel was tugging on Folke's wet tunic. "It isn't much but you can have all that I have." The boy reached into his coin pouch and took out every coin he had saved. He lifted his cupped hands up. Automatically, Folke put out his hand and the boy poured the coins into his palm. "That's for your fee so you can let *Mater* stay with us."

Folke frowned at the money. An uncomfortable feeling came over him which he had not felt in a long time but he quickly dismissed it as weakness. Junius stepped up and dumped the content of his coin pouch at Folke's feet. One by one the men filed past and dropped silver, copper, and bronze coins onto the growing pile. Pomona stood next to Aurelius with her hand over her mouth. She let tears of gratitude run freely down her face. Aurelius put an arm around her shoulders. Samuel gave up all pretense of restraint and threw his arms around Pomona's waist.

She kissed the top of his head and whispered to him. "I am your mother from now on. You are my son." She looked up at Aurelius. "So now you know my wish on the bet we made about your profits. I wish for you to free Samuel. A woman's son should not be her brother's slave."

"Ah, Pomona. What will I do with you?" said Aurelius with a patient shake of his head. "You spend my profits on dried meat, fruits and olive oil for the crew and now you want to adopt my cabin boy. What next?"

"You could declare our bet nullified and we will both have our wishes."

Aurelius looked at the bounty hunter as he stood pressed against the life rail. "I could wish for him to be thrown back into the sea but that would be unsporting. So, I'll stick to my original wish. Father had a favorite board game called *Ludus Latrunculorum*. Did he teach you to play?"

"Game of Mercenaries? Yes, he did. He even let me win sometimes."

"Then my wish is for you to teach me how to play. I will buy a game set in Troas."

The sound of Pomona's lilting laughter brought smiles to the men's faces. "Done!" she declared and they shook hands, sealing the deal.

Junius strode up to Folke and looked at the heap of coins. "If I have my numbers right, this is more than your usual fee. This is a mercy you do not deserve." He pointed at Pomona. "She is an innocent, good-hearted woman. I have served on many ships and never have I seen anyone care about the welfare of the crew like she does. Does that sound like a cold-blooded killer to you? What say you, Folke. Will you relent?"

The bounty hunter looked the crew over. His pride squirmed in his heart. To relent would be admitting defeat but he wasn't stupid. The amount of coins were truly more than his usual fee, and again, he thought of the days left before they reached Troas. It occurred to him that he could always pursue her later, now that he knew where to find her, and collect another fee.

"Yes, I relent. She is free to go." He tightened his belt before he knelt down to scoop up the coins and drop them down the front of his tunic. He stood and faced the hostile stares of the men. "My only question is—must I sleep with an eye open and my hand on a dagger?"

"No," answered Aurelius. "You will be confined to the guest quarters. You will not lift another hand to the oars or collect a single coin in pay from this moment on. You will also pay for your passage and your food starting today." He stepped closer to Folke. "If you try to arrest her later or you get someone else to do it, I will find you. And I will kill you—slowly."

The rest of the men glared at Folke as if daring him to even speak. The bounty hunter squared his shoulders and took a deep breath. He let it out slowly. "I believe you." He turned to Pomona. "You have nothing to fear from me, my lady."

"Go in peace, Folke," Pomona said as she clutched Samuel to her side.

Samuel pulled away from her embrace and approached Folke. "We cannot see what you are doing when you leave us but *Yahweh* does. *Yahweh* sees everything, even into your heart."

The bounty hunter looked at Samuel, then at Pomona, then at the men. He didn't believe in anything except himself. He did as he pleased and took pleasure in hunting the most challenging prey of all—human beings. He had learned a long time ago that people believed what they wanted to believe. Even when he lied straight into someone's face, they believed if it was what they wanted to hear. Folke didn't believe he was accountable to any person or anything greater than himself. To give his word or take an oath was only a means to an end. For now, he had to live long enough to get off this ship.

Folke put his hand out to Aurelius. "I swear to honor my pledge. May I have the warrant?"

Aurelius pulled the papyrus from his tunic and handed it to him.

"I disavow any knowledge of the person named on this warrant." He ripped it into shreds. "If I break my oath, let me be torn as this warrant has been." He tossed the fragments into the sea.

The crew cheered and spoke approvingly among themselves.

Folke pushed away from the life rail. The crew made room for him as he walked to the steps leading to the lower deck. The following days would be agonizingly long for the bounty hunter as he huddled in the cramped guest quarters. He played the scene with Pomona over and over in his mind and his anger mounted. To be at the mercy of a mere woman was bad enough but to actually be rescued from a raging mob by a woman was a demoralizing humiliation. His deflated pride screamed for revenge and he plotted how best to lay in wait for an opportunity to lure her from the ship. He would have to be patient and follow behind from port to port until the right time revealed itself. Fortunately, the crew had given the means to do just that when they donated their own money to his "fee."

He would watch and wait for an opportunity to snatch her off some pier, some city street, whatever it took. He considered the situation and knew he needed to protect his fee from other bounty hunters. He had a strategy that always worked. He would circulate the story among other bounty hunters that he had found the Samaritan woman who turned out to be a sorceress. He would claim she used a *cursus pupa,* a doll stuck with pins, to cast a spell on him. When he fell to the ground, she held up a *defixiones,* a lead curse tablet, and threatened to write his name on it with disgusting and frightening curses. He knew they would want details. He would tell them the vilest things he could image.

When they reached Troas, Folke was allowed to disembark from the *Child of the Ocean* unharmed. He walked to the end of the gangway and onto the pier without a backward glance. He headed for the Roman garrison. It was easy enough to pick up another warrant for the woman. She was now his number one priority. He prided himself on never accepting charity or pity from anyone. The way he saw it, he would never owe anyone anything, not even for saving his life. He was his own master and everyone else was a slave and slaves weren't human. They were chattel.

Chapter 12

The Brass Bull and the Butterfly

―――――⊶⊙⊙⊙⊙⊶―――――

Once Adan, Nikolaus, and Calais left the ship in Smyrna, they went looking for transportation to Pergamon. Adan hired a carriage after some haggling over the cost. The ride was pleasant with a constant, soft breeze from the sea. Wildflowers grew in sparse bunches among the rocky, semi-barren cliffs and mesas with an occasional scrub oak, gnarled from the winds. The roots extended out across the ground in some places like tangled tentacles reaching for ever elusive moisture.

Calais was hoping to find any of his family in Pergamon but wondered why Adan and Nikolaus were going with him since Corinth was in the opposite direction on the coast of Greece. His curiosity finally made him ask, "Why did you two decide to go to Pergamon? The sooner you get to Corinth, the sooner you can unload John's scroll."

"We're trying to find a woman that Pomona once knew," answered Nikolaus. "We haven't mentioned it before but now that you're asking, we'll fill you in. Remember how I told you when we were both slaves that my family died suddenly when we were sailing from Athens to Rome? Adan thinks they were murdered. A family heirloom was missing after the tragedy and we think if we can locate it, we'll find answers. We think the object was invented by the *Magi*. Pomona said the slave woman claimed her father once worked for the *Magi*. She might be able to send us in the right direction. Pomona said she was from Pergamon. We're hoping she returned there."

"What was her name?"

"Calypso," answered Adan. "Pergamon is the only clue we have on her location."

"Calypso. I don't remember anyone by that name but I was young when we left for Judea," said Calais. He frowned in thought. "What else do you know about her?"

"Pomona said she was an excellent cook," said Nikolaus, "especially breads and pastries and that she has a butterfly shaped birthmark on her neck."

"My whole family used to bake pastries for several cafes in Pergamon. Mother would have me grind the nutmeg and cinnamon but I usually made a mess of it and my sisters would have to take over." He screwed his lips up in concentration. "A birthmark on her neck. Umm. Doesn't bring anyone to mind."

"Pomona is very sure of that fact," said Adan. "But you couldn't have seen, much less, remembered everyone in the whole city?"

Calais shrugged. "True. But such a feature would be memorable. Unless, Pomona just remembers it that way. I suspect some of my own memories have altered over time. Like the time I remember Valentius and my mother talking rather heatedly out in the street in front of our house."

"Your mother knew Valentius?" asked Adan. "What were they talking about?"

"I couldn't hear all of it. I saw them through the window so I sat on the floor and listened. I didn't want them to see me. Mother was saying things like, 'You can't do this now,' and he was saying stuff like, 'It's either that or nothing.' Something like that. They went back and forth and then she came in the house. I don't remember what happened next."

Adan gave Nikolaus a curious look. "Calais, how did you come to be Theo Salvitto's slave?"

"My mother took me to him. He asked me questions and told me that I would have to work hard but that I'd never go hungry. Mother looked awful. She was pale, and shaking, and trying not to cry. Then Tribune Salvitto counted out a few *aureuii* into her hand and she was gone. At first, I thought I was supposed to wait for her to bring back whatever Salvitto had bought from her. That maybe I was supposed to stay to assure her return with the item. Then I found out that *I* was the item. That night was when I met Onesimus. It helped having a friend." He gave Nikolaus a quick glance. "You, too, Niko."

When they reached the town of Pergamon, they located an inn that offered clean rooms and good locks on the doors. Calais was eager to ask at every bakery if anyone knew of his brothers and sisters. While Calais talked with the bakery owners, Adan and Nikolaus also asked about Calypso. A few knew of women by that name but none fit the description. Calais's questions about his siblings were often met with an odd reaction. Some people hesitated before shaking their heads without looking Calais in the eye. Some hung their heads as if ashamed. Finally, after a fruitless search at every bakery, Calais headed for the public water fountain in the center of town. He slumped to a low bench near the fountain and lowered his head to his hands.

"I don't understand," he muttered. "I felt so sure that some of my family would have come back here after Father died."

"We've hit our own dead end," said Adan. "It seems that Calypso did not return here after Pomona freed her and we're out of leads. Any ideas, Niko?"

"None." He sighed and sat next to Calais.

Adan scooped up a handful of water and splashed it on his face. "Maybe we're asking in the wrong places. Who seems to know more about the townspeople than anyone? Temple priests. There certainly are a lot of temples here. Let's get some dinner and a good night's rest and try talking with the priests tomorrow." They agreed and headed back to their inn.

The next morning found the three travelers hopeful once again. By mid-morning, they had made the rounds of most of the temples. Again, the reactions from the people they questioned seemed to hint that they were withholding something. One priest who claimed that he had only lived in Pergamon a few months, suggested that they go to the court of registry to check records of marriages and deaths. They headed for the building of registry according to the man's directions. They were surprised to see the image of a brass bull set on a stone foundation in front of the building. Adan curled a lip in disgust at the figure. Nikolaus turned his head and spat on the ground. Calais stared at the hollow sculpture as a wave of nausea hit him. The brass bull was used to torture people to death.

Adan faced the other two men. "Why don't you two wait out here. Let me talk to the clerks alone." Nikolaus and Calais walked away from the offensive sculpture to wait for Adan.

Nikolaus tried not to look at the thing but it kept drawing his eye. "Why would they have such an evil contraption here. You can see where they burned the wood under the belly of the bull. And there's the trap door like a saddle on the monstrous thing. Burning anyone alive should be outlawed. I wonder how often the punishment is far worse than the crime."

"I've heard that they don't make the fire too big so the victim doesn't die quickly," said Calais. "John talked about how God loves us but I cannot imagine why. We do such horrible things to each other."

The two men didn't notice a stranger eyeing them from across the way. He was thin and wore a filthy tunic and robe. His sandals were made of hemp twine and tree bark. He carried a small ceramic pot to hold any alms that might come his way as he begged for food or coins. He approached the men and spoke hesitantly. "Will you spare a copper coin?"

Calais looked at the beggar with aversion and was about to send him away but the despair in the man's eyes gave him pause. "I'm looking for anyone in my family that may live here. Have you lived here long?"

Hoping he might be paid for information, the man answered quickly. "Many years. Long enough to see that put to use." He pointed at the brass bull. "The Nicolaitans threw a good man into the bull's belly not too long ago."

"Why would they that do?" asked Nikolaus.

The beggar grinned, revealing gaps where teeth should have been. "I can tell you all about it for a few copper coins. You can spare that much, can't you?"

Nikolaus and Calais exchanged glances. Nikolaus took a few coins from the pouch on his belt. "Tell us what you know."

The man snatched the offered coins from Nikolaus's hand as if he feared they would sprout wings. "He was a foolish man, talking, always talking nonsense but he was harmless. He talked of a Jew who died and came back to life. He talked of the hypocrisy of the rich." The man cackled with laughter. "Was it smart to poke the leviathan with a stick?" When he saw that his joking was not appreciated, he grew serious. "But he prayed to his God and the people were healed. They came to him with every illness and deformity. He asked for nothing in return. This angered the doctors and priests. Then he condemned the worship of Zeus and Artemis and others. You can see the care we take in our statues and wall sculptures. Pergamon loves her gods and goddesses. Yet, Agios healed all who came to him. Naturally, the common people overlooked his words of condemnation."

"You said his name was Agios," asked Calais. "Greek for 'saint.' What was his real name?"

"I know only that name."

"So, the doctors and priests had him thrown into the bull?" asked Nikolaus.

"They wanted to but they feared the people. For a while. Then Agios told them to stop buying images of the gods, talismans, and charms. He declared he would no longer heal anyone who bought these things. That angered the merchants. The wealthy citizens became united against Agios. They threatened the people with starvation if they interfered on his behalf." The man held his palm out. "Do you want to hear the rest?"

Nikolaus handed him another *dupondius*. "Go on."

The beggar dropped the coin into his clay pot. "Two, maybe three months ago, a mob dragged Agios here. They threw him into the brass bull. They piled wood soaked in oil under the creature's belly and lit it on fire. I was there. I saw it."

He put his hand out, again, but footsteps sounded behind him. The beggar spun around and gasped. "Centurion, Sir, I meant no harm. They allow me to beg for alms here."

Adan held up his hand and spoke softly. "Finish your story and I'll pay you a *denarius* if you help us find someone."

The beggar blinked up at Adan, and then at the others. "Yes, Sir. I will do my best. There was a crowd. They grew quiet and waited for the screams to begin. As you must know, the bull is like a *furnus* for baking bread. But there were no sounds. Nothing. They piled on more wood and waited. Still nothing. After many hours, ten times longer than it would take to kill a man, they put the fire out. When the bull had cooled, they opened it up. Agios was lying there, dead, but his hands were folded on his chest as if asleep. His clothes were scorched. I could even smell the charred linen." The beggar took a deep breath and eyed them dramatically.

"Go on," demanded Calais.

"You will not believe me," the beggar declared, hoping to stir their curiosity.

"Maybe not but tell us anyway," said Adan impatiently.

The man leaned in excitedly and put out his hand. Nikolaus gave him another coin.

"I followed a few of the men up the steps and looked inside. Agios was smiling! Yes, yes! His expression was peaceful. He was dead. But it was plain to see. Agios did *not* suffer. His skin was not singed. Neither was his hair. Only his clothes."

Adan looked intently into the beggar's face. The man flinched but didn't look away. "You say that they called this man, Agios—Saint. What was his surname?"

The beggar blinked apprehensively at Nikolaus and Calais. "I—I was afraid when you asked his name." He looked back at Adan. "If I lie to a Roman soldier, it could go badly for me."

"So, you lied to us," said Nikolaus. "Tell us his name, now, and all will be forgiven."

The beggar shot a glance at Adan to make sure he agreed. "The men who hated him refused to call him Agios. They called him Antipas."

Calais's head jerked up. "Did he have green eyes like mine and dark hair?"

The beggar looked more closely. His expression changed to recognition and quickly to fear. "I was only a witness!" he cried. "I had nothing to do with his death. In truth, I see it now. He looked like you, just older."

"That was my elder brother! They killed him. And for what? For praying for them to be healed?" He grasped the beggar by the shoulders. "Tell me everything you know!"

"I have, Sir! Everything. I know nothing else."

"You must know more details."

The man held up a hand as if to ward off a blow. "That's all I know."

Calais turned away in sorrow. To come this close to finding someone in his family, only to learn of his death was worse than not hearing of him, at all. Nikolaus tried to comfort his friend but Calais wouldn't listen. He looked over his shoulder and said something about the inn and wanting to be left alone. Nikolaus let him go.

"Can't you think of anything else you can tell us?" asked Adan.

The beggar glanced toward Calais as he hurried away. "If you want to know more, you should talk to the woman who feeds the lepers. She and Agios sometimes went together."

"How do we find this woman? What is her name?" Adan demanded.

"She lives on the west side. Her house is near a huge tree," the beggar answered. "The townspeople shun her because she goes among the lepers. They call her Petalouda."

Adan and Nikolaus exchanged surprised glances.

"Why do they call her Butterfly," asked Nikolaus.

"The burn scar." The beggar placed his hand on his neck. "Looks like a butterfly."

"Take us to her and I'll pay you two *denarii*," promised Adan. The beggar didn't hesitate as he set off for the western side of town.

Chapter 13

Past, Present, and Possibilities

T he beggar led the brothers to the house of Petalouda but she wasn't there. The poor man profusely apologized, thinking he had lost the chance of being paid. Adan calmed him with the suggestion that they ask the lepers if they had seen her.

"Even your centurion status will not protect you from leprosy," whined the beggar with obvious disgust.

"I only need to ask a few questions—from a safe distance," Adan assured him. "Where do they congregate?"

The beggar motioned toward a hillside studded with tombs, some sealed with stones, others open and unused. "They live in the open tombs."

The three men followed a narrow path that wove among shallow escarpments and sporadically vegetated gullies. As they approached the hillside, they could see people scattered over the area. Some were sitting in the openings of tombs while others sat around a central campfire. Two men were tending to several fish cooking on stones placed about the embers.

A gasp of excitement escaped the beggar's lips as he pointed to a woman talking with another woman standing by the fire. "That's her! Petalouda. Will you keep your word, Centurion?" He held out his grimy hand.

Adan eyed the man. "When I'm sure she is the woman I am seeking. Ask her, politely, if she will join us."

The beggar grumbled under his breath but moved to comply. He approached the woman tentatively and spoke to her. She glanced at Adan and Nikolaus and seemed to be asking the beggar questions. He slapped his hands together as if beseeching for mercy. She turned her back on the beggar. He wrung his hands and spoke to her again. He seemed to be imploring her. Her expression changed and she started toward the men.

Picking her way among the scattered rocks, she walked over to the brothers. The beggar trailed behind her.

"What do you want with me so badly that you're willing to pay this man two *denarii*?" the woman demanded as she gestured at the beggar standing beside her.

Adan saw a pinkish, keloid burn scar on her neck. The skin had puckered along a central line like the wings of a butterfly. Before he answered, he handed the beggar two silver coins. The man's delighted surprise was unmistakable. He expected to be cheated. The look of gratitude he shot Adan was received with a subtle smile. The beggar scurried away without looking back.

"My name is Centurion Adan Clovius Longinus. This is my brother, Niko—Nikolaus. We are searching for a woman named Calypso who served the family of Centurion Valentius."

The woman took a step back. "I am a freed woman and no longer serve Valentius."

Adan softened his tone. "Yes, we know. Besides, Valentius is dead. Our concern is for his daughter. Pomona still grieves for the loss of Calypso and wishes to see her."

The woman took in a sharp breath. "Describe her to me. And her mother." She realized her mistake and quickly added, "I assume she had a mother."

"You spoke of her in the past tense. Do you also assume she is dead?" added Nikolaus.

Her cheeks reddened at her unintentional slips.

"Her name was Eliana," said Adan. He told her why Pomona had to leave Jerusalem. "Niko and I have been able to unite her with her half-brother, Aurelius, the son of Valentius and his wife, Julia."

"Now I know you're lying," the woman hissed. "Aurelius is dead. He drowned in a shipwreck." She began to step away.

"Aurelius is very much alive but another man who looked like him died in that storm." Adan explained the details of Aurelius's 'death' when the *Scarlet Jade* went down. "However, I will understand if you don't want to go to Pomona since she is considered a wanted criminal."

The woman frowned and backed away further. "What if I'm not the woman she seeks? I could notify the authorities of her whereabouts to collect the reward for her capture."

"You could, "admitted Adan. "But you won't. You are the woman who Pomona loved like a second mother. You have the mark of a butterfly." When Adan told her the story about freeing a butterfly from a spider's web, her eyes welled up with tears.

Choking back her emotions, she asked, "Then answer me one more question, Centurion. If Pomona loved me so much, why did she free me? Did she wish to be rid of me?"

"She didn't, on both counts. Eliana freed you on her deathbed. Pomona only fulfilled her mother's wishes but she has grieved for you ever since."

She covered her mouth with her hand. She could no longer hold back her tears. "You are right. I am Calypso. I have grieved for her as well."

Adan and Nikolaus exchanged relieved smiles. Adan spoke gently. "I can take you to her. Aurelius's ship will be docked in Smyrna by the time we get there. Pomona has found a new home with her brother on his ship."

Disappointment crossed her face. "I cannot leave these people." She waved a hand toward the hillside. "No one else will bring them food. They'll starve."

"You must decide for yourself," said Nikolaus. "We will not try to talk you into it but if you will not go with us, may we talk with you about something else. Is there a place we can sit?"

Calypso remembered that Adan had kept his word with the beggar even though he could have easily run the poor man off. Perhaps she could trust them as the beggar had. She showed them the way to several flat-topped, sandstone boulders near a stand of shade trees.

"What do you want to know?" she asked.

Adan took the lead. "Perhaps we should start with the *Magi*. Did your father really work for them?"

For the first time, Calypso smiled. "You really do know Pomona. I never told anyone else about that, not even my own family. Yes, Father was the assistant to one of the chief astrologers when we lived in Persia."

"Did your father travel with the *Magi*," asked Nikolaus, "when they went to Jerusalem to pay homage to the Child King? This would have been during the reign of King Herod the Great."

"Yes, we all went, including me and my mother. The master loved her cooking and would allow no one else to prepare his meals."

Nikolaus could no longer contain his eagerness. "Did the chief astrologer have a wooden box with three stones set in the lid? A box with dials and wheels inside of it?"

Calypso was stunned. "You're describing the Prophecy Box. How did you know about it?"

"Do you know how it worked?" Nikolaus asked, ignoring her question.

"No. I never even saw it. Father said its great power was only for the *Magi*."

"Great power to do what, exactly?" asked Adan.

"To predict eclipses of the sun and the moon, ten, maybe twenty years in advance. To predict the movement of the planets and phases of the moon. To foretell the time to celebrate new moon festivals and host the Olympian Games. They are held every four years, but the month and days must align properly with the full moon and the positions of the planets to please the gods. Do you understand the value of this power?"

"Do you mean a value beyond predicting future history?" asked Nikolaus.

Calypso laughed softly. "The box does not predict human events. It predicts the cycles of the celestial bodies. Let me explain. Wealthy cities throughout the Roman Empire vie for the honor of hosting the Olympic Games, which are profitable for the local merchants. If a city magistrate knows the exact month and day the Games will be scheduled, he can prepare his city ahead of time, so, he pays the *Magi* to learn the dates. The men who select the location for the Games send out inspectors to see which city is best prepared. The further in advance the magistrate knows the dates, the better prepared his city can be. However, the fee goes up according to how far in advance you want the information."

"Let me get this straight," said Adan. "The *Magi* determine when the Olympic Games will be scheduled according to moon phases and planet alignment. They sell that information to city magistrates, raising the fee the further in advance the magistrate requests."

"Correct," said Calypso. "The *Magi* set the dates, so the men who select which city will host the Games also pay them. They have to know when to hold the Games."

"I can see how this can add up to quite a fortune," said Nicholas.

"Add in wealthy landowners who will also pay to know the best times to plant, to reap, and to schedule feasts. The Prophecy Box brings in a great deal of money. Yet, the men who pay the *Magi* for this information do not know how the predictions are determined."

"You mean, these men don't know about the Prophecy Box?" asked Adan.

"That's right. They think the *Magi* use supernatural abilities to make the predictions. That is one reason they are so revered. Anyone who can afford their services think they are great mystics and soothsayers. They are very knowledgeable and intelligent but they are only men."

"Crops are planted according to the seasons," interjected Nikolaus, "and harvested when ripe. Why would landowners pay the *Magi* to tell them what they should know by experience and their own senses?"

Calypso smirked. "Precisely. That is the power of the box. Men doubt their own knowledge and depend on a *machina* they don't even know exists. They think the *Magi* use sorcery to determine these things. They would feel so foolish if they knew that anyone can read the directions on the metalwork of the box and decipher what they want to know. It's just a machine. It's not a supernatural oracle."

"So, the *magus* who owns the box becomes incredibly rich?" asked Nikolaus.

Calypso shook her head adamantly. "No single person owns the box. It actually belongs to the school. The man in charge of it is called the guardian. All of the proceeds go into funding the School of the *Magi*. Once a year, the funds are sent to the Far East. Therefore, the *magus* who becomes the guardian of the box is chosen very carefully."

Nikolaus and Adan sat in silent contemplation. Everything was beginning to make sense. The box was a source of great wealth and perceived power for the *Magi*. If copies were made and wealthy men learned that a machine was the source of the predictions, they would stop paying the Magi and buy their own Prophecy Box. A fortune and personal esteem would be lost to the School of the *Magi*.

"What did the *Magi* do when the box was stolen?" asked Nikolaus.

"What? It was stolen? When?" Calypso looked from Nikolaus to Adan.

"Just before Emperor Tiberius died," said Adan.

"I don't know anything about that. My parents died and we left Pergamon for Judea. My husband wanted to return to the land of his birth."

"Do you know if the Prophecy Box had anything to do with the *Magi* predicting the birth of the Child King?" asked Adan. "They knew that a star would signal his birth. How did they know that and how did they know which specific star would be the omen? There are countless stars in the night sky."

"That I cannot tell you."

Adan's hopeful expression faded.

"But I know who can," she volunteered. "If he is still alive. One of the *Magi* who traveled in that caravan is living in Athens, last I heard. He goes by the name Daniel, even though that is not his given name. There were three main sects of the *Magi*; one studied the planets, one studied the moon and the sun, and the other studied the stars. Father told me that each sect assigned their chief astrologer to present a special gift to the Child King. There were other gifts because each *magus* brought his own gift, but each sect chose one very special gift that would symbolize the phases of the child's life. I did not witness this myself but Father said, '*When they had opened their treasures, they presented gifts to Him: gold, frankincense, and myrrh.*' Father heard that the little boy stood and said, 'Your gifts will never be forgotten.' Father said that the Magi were amazed at how eloquently he spoke, for being so young."

"Who were these *Magi* and how many came to pay the Child honor?" asked Nikolaus, trying to visualize the event.

"They were Jewish descendants of the Babylon exile. There were thirty-six, plus servants, and armed guards. I remember because it was my job to open the tent flaps for each master at sunrise. They were men of great intellect and love for Yahweh but they were humble. They owned no slaves or excessive property. Some did not even own their own homes. They each took only one assistant that they would mentor until their deaths. Their one extravagance was that each of the *Magi* had his own private tent. I would count them as I went from tent to tent to make sure I went to each one."

"Did you see the Child, yourself?" asked Nikolaus.

"No, only the *Magi* and their assistants were allowed into the house."

"You saw the star in the east," declared Adan. "What did it look like?"

Calypso sighed with wonder at the memory. "It was much brighter than the planet Venus as if it was the sun seen from a greater distance. It just appeared one night and all the *Magi* went berserk. They acted like bees when a rock hits the hive. Lots of meetings and ordering of supplies. They knew, of course, that it would take many months to travel to Jerusalem but they were eager to go."

"How long was the star visible?" asked Nikolaus.

"I don't remember exactly but it had disappeared by the time we left for Jerusalem. When we finally arrived in the city, they were surprised when we asked where the Child could be found. We were amazed at this. I heard some of the *Magi* saying that King Herod, who had not noticed the spectacular star, '*determined from them what time the star appeared. And he sent them to Bethlehem.*' I was confused when I heard this. Why didn't King Herod and his astrologers see the star for themselves? Why didn't the people of Jerusalem know it signaled the birth of the long-awaited Messiah? How could the sign of the Messiah escape their notice?"

She paused, trying to remember every detail. "There was something else about the star that was highly unusual. I remember the *Magi* discussing it when I would help serve their meals." She frowned and pressed her lips in concentration. "It was the reason the *Magi* knew it was the sign of the Messiah, even more than its brightness. I wish I could remember what it was?"

"Another important question to me is how the *Magi* even knew that a star would signal the birth of Yeshua," stated Adan.

"Yeshua, yes, that is his name," she softly replied.

"You said 'is' not 'was.' Are you a believer?" asked Nikolaus. She glanced anxiously at Adan. She had not meant to reveal her belief to a Roman soldier. Adan assured her that she was safely in the company of fellow believers.

Calypso closed her eyes for a moment with relief. "As for your question, Centurion, I do not know. Father didn't either because I asked him. He said that the *Magi* have insight that common people do not have. Ancient scrolls and books and teachings. They are the descendants of the Israelites exiled into Babylon. It stands to reason that they know the prophecies and mystical secrets of their ancestors."

"How did the *Magi* know which house to go to in Bethlehem?" asked Nikolaus.

"The star reappeared as soon as we left Jerusalem. *The star which they had seen in the East went before them, till it came and stood over where the young Child was. When they saw the star, they rejoiced with exceedingly great joy. And when they had come into the house, they saw the young Child with Mary, His mother, and fell down and worshiped Him.*' We all knew that what was happening was a single moment in the history of humanity. That star was a supernatural creation. But that is all I can tell you. Daniel actually saw Yeshua. He would know things that I do not. Daniel was only nineteen at the time. He was the youngest of the *Magi* in the caravan. Daniel was the apprentice to the chief astrologer in charge of the frankincense."

"Calypso, could you take us to Daniel?" Adan asked. "If there is someone you trust here in Pergamon, I will pay that person to bring bread to these lepers every day that you are with us. Is there anyone you trust?"

Calypso considered her options. Slowly, she shook her head. "There is no one—anymore. There was a great man who healed the people by the grace of God. He was a gentle soul and said nothing in his own defense when the Nicolaitans falsely accused him. Then the city authorities ordered his execution." She ducked her head and brought her hand to her brow. She bit her lower lip to force back her tears.

"Are you speaking of Agios?" asked Nikolaus in a hushed tone.

"Yes. He was the only person I could trust with my life—as he once trusted me with his."

"What do you mean?" asked Adan.

She only shook her head and refused to answer.

"There is a young man with us who wishes to know more about Agios," said Nikolaus. "Will you at least come with us to talk with him?"

Calypso didn't want to go. It had been a long day and she was tired. She was about to refuse but didn't have the heart to turn them down when she saw their pleading expressions.

"I will go with you to speak with your friend but then I must return to my home. My work here is never done."

They left the hillside area and made their way through the city streets until they reached the inn. They entered the gate into the courtyard and went to the door of Calais's room. Adan knocked and called out to him. Calypso waited patiently behind Adan and steeled herself to speak calmly. Her grief at Agios's murder left a deep despair in her heart that nothing could heal. The door opened and she heard a young man speak to Adan with a sullen tone. He turned away but left the door open, a begrudging permission for them to enter. Adan stepped aside and motioned for Calypso to enter first.

Calais refused to turn around. "I told you I wish to be left alone."

"I understand," said Adan gently, "but we've brought Calypso to speak to you about your brother."

Calypso threw her hands to her face and cried out, "His *brother*? It can't be!" Calypso reached out for him.

Calais spun around at the sound of her voice. *"Mother!"*

Calypso rushed into his arms. *"Calais!* How is this possible?" She gently pushed him out to arm's length to get a good look at his face. "You must hate me! You must think me the most horrible mother on this earth."

Calais pulled her back into his embrace. "No! I could never hate you. I know you did what you thought was best. You even sold yourself into slavery. I can't believe this. You were only a few streets away from me all those years."

Overwhelming regret made her stammer. "Y-you were kept in Jerusalem?"

"At the Antonia. I was a stable slave for many years."

Rage swept across Calypso's face. "He lied to me!" She stepped away and fresh tears ran down her face. "Valentius broke his promise to buy both of us, and then lied to my face! He said the man who bought you, a tribune named Salvitto, had given you to his brother who lived in Rome."

Unable to keep his silence, Adan exclaimed, "Salvitto's brother was dead long before he bought Calais." Nikolaus touched Adan's arm and shook his head. He tilted his head toward the door and Adan followed him out of the room. Nikolaus closed the door quietly.

Calais brought his hand to his brow. "Why would Valentius do that?"

Calypso bit her lower lip and frowned. She looked into her son's handsome face, at his muscular physique. Thinking with a mother's instinct, she knew. She moaned in despair. "I know why. When he first promised to buy us both, he hadn't seen you yet. Then he came with the slave contracts for me to sign. He came in the house and you were there. He just stared at you. Then he rolled up your contract and stuffed it under his belt. He said he had changed his mind."

"I was an eight-year-old child. What did he think he was looking at?"

"A man-child who would grow up and steal his daughter's heart. He knew how lonely she was. Calais, you have to understand. Pomona adored her father. In return, he lavished attention on her. He read to her and taught her to read to him. He told her stories and encouraged her to ask questions. Together, they would try to solve the mysteries of the world. When he had to leave, the poor little thing would cry herself to sleep. Pomona was Valentius's escape from the harsh reality of his life as a soldier and an addict. He was fond of Eliana but he doted on Pomona. He couldn't take the chance of her falling in love with you. It didn't matter if you fell in love with her or not. You would eventually come between Valentius and his daughter."

Calypso rubbed under her eyes with the back of a hand. "Pomona had no friends. No one would even give her a smile. Valentius knew you two would become best friends, growing up together. For a half Roman, half Samaritan, to marry a Greek slave would have been a sentence of poverty and persecution for both of you. A marriage of a hated half-breed and a slave would have offended everyone, especially the Romans and the Jews." She turned away and walked to the window. She bowed her head and leaned her forehead against the lattice. She looked back at her son. "I wonder if it's possible that Felix Valentius was concerned for *both of you?*"

Calais considered her words. A childhood memory came to him. "One time I was saddling Valentius's horse and two *legionaries* came into the stall. They were both drunk. They started in on me. I was powerless. Then the stall gate flew open and suddenly Valentius was there. He grabbed hold of both them. I remember him shouting in their faces and ordering them to scrub the latrines for the rest of the day." Calais looked into his mother's eyes in shock. "I remember now. He told them he would have them flogged if they ever abused me again. Then he snatched the reins from my hand and he was gone."

Calypso brought her fist to her mouth. "Forgive me, Lord God. I have judged him unfairly. Perhaps Valentius did care about both of us, after all."

Calais reached out and gently pulled his mother's long hair away from her neck. "How did this happen? Pomona thought it was a birthmark. But it's from a terrible burn, isn't it?"

Calypso pulled her hair back over her neck. "It doesn't matter now. It happened after you were sold to the tribune. Before I went to Eliana."

He saw the pain in his mother's eyes and let it go. But he had other questions that begged for answers. "Mother, how did you become Centurion Valentius's slave, in the first place?"

"He was asking around for an educated Greek woman who would serve his concubine and young daughter. I went to him. He asked if I could read and write Greek and Latin. When I showed him that I could, he offered to pay off all of your father's debts in exchange for my enslavement. I told him about you and he offered to buy us both. It was all agreed upon. Then he saw you. Nothing I said made a difference. He only offered to tell the tribune about you."

"And all this time," said Calais sadly, "I thought you sold only me and left the country."

She bowed her head in shame, knowing the pain he had felt. "How did you gain your freedom?"

"Adan's son, Marco, tricked my master. Lysias thought I was dead and Adan and the others saved me—twice."

She frowned in confusion. "Twice?"

"They saved me from Lysias and then they saved me from *Vesuvio* when it turned into a flaming mountain in *Italia*. I will tell you the whole story later. For now, let's talk about you. Why do you use the name Calypso?"

"The slave trader had forgotten my name so he mumbled something he made up. The centurion thought he said Calypiseo. Pomona couldn't pronounce it. She called me Calypso. Centurion Valentius and Eliana never corrected her." She raised her hands in mock acceptance. "Who was I to correct a sweet child? Then I grew accustomed to it. But when I came back here; they called me Petalouda without even asking my name. Again, I accepted it. What does it matter what people call me when God knows my real name?"

She affectionately touched his face and gently pushed his hair back. "You have your father's beautiful dark hair but you have my eyes. He would be so proud to see what a fine young man you have become."

"Father would be proud of all of us, especially Antipas."

"Yes, he would. So, tell me. What do you plan to do now?"

"After I go with Adan—Centurion Longinus, I will come back here and live with you, if you'd like that."

Her face brightened with joy. "I would love that more than anything in the world. Do you really have to leave at all?"

"I promised my friend, John, that I would help them take an important scroll to friends in Corinth." He angrily pressed his lips into a thin line.

"If you don't want to go with them, then don't."

"It's not that, Mother. John didn't trust me to take the scroll. I was right there! Yet, he asked me to send for Adan. All the way from Caesarea. As if I can't take care of myself. I've survived worse than most people and I am deeply loyal to him. He knows that. Still, he insisted that Adan must come to Patmos so *he* could take the scroll. I don't understand. Why wouldn't he let me prove myself?"

Calypso cupped her hand to his face. "You haven't changed, Calais. You still want your 'father' to approve of you even though his name is now John. Don't you understand? You don't need to prove anything. When others ask for help, do what they ask. Not more. Not less. We don't know how things will turn out so don't assume that your friend does not trust you. Would he have sent you to go with them if he didn't? But I can't bear to tell you good-bye, even for a short absence. I would feel like I am abandoning you once again."

"Then come with us, Mother. It will only take two or three weeks and you would have time with Pomona. She really wants to see you and she understands why you left."

"I can't leave these poor people. They suffer from disease *and* the cruelty of others."

Calais understood about cruelty. "Mother, please come with me. Surely, someone will help out for the short time we'll be gone. And I promise you, that when we get back, I will help you care for them."

"That would be a wonderful answer to my prayers. I have missed your brother so terribly, even to the point of wanting to die. But now, you are here so we can heal together and be a family again. Selling you into slavery was the hardest thing I've ever done and has caused me the greatest guilt. But I couldn't let you die of starvation. I had to give you up to save your life." She paused and frowned in despair. "But it sounds like I saved you from one horror in exchange for another just as bad."

"Tribune Salvitto treated his slaves better than most, but he assigned me to the stables. There were others at the Antonia who took advantage of the youngest slaves. I was one of them. Adan put me and others under his protection but that didn't last long." He explained what happened as briefly as he could. Calais didn't like to think about that terrible time, much less, speak of it but he continued. "Then things got even worse when Tribune Salvitto retired from the army. He sold me to Commander Lysias." He pressed the back of his hand across his forehead as if it would wipe the memory from his mind. "I hate that man. John told me that I should never hate anyone, that it poisons the soul, but. . ."

When he fell silent, Calypso touched his arm. "Your friend is right. Hate is deceitful. It spurs you to take revenge, yet when you do, you feel nothing but emptiness. It leaves you feeling like there is nothing left to live for. After your brother died, I wanted to burn this whole town in that beast of bronze. That only made me feel worse. I have left his murderers in God's hands and now with every loaf I give to the lepers, I feel I am having my revenge in another way. The men that killed your brother wish the lepers would go away or die but they don't dare raise their own hands to violence, as if they are not already covered in the blood of their victims. So, I care for the sick and I know God is watching. He sees what I do and blesses me for it. God will be my avenger."

"Your brother helped me to rely on God instead of my own hatred. I used to ask Antipas why God let the Romans live but he never answered me. They are so cruel. Valentius once told us that a man named Lucius Pedanius Secundus was murdered by one of his slaves. Because of the law, all four hundred of his slaves were condemned to crucifixion. Some in the senate tried to prevent it because there were so many women and children among the four hundred but they were all crucified, anyway. The senators in favor of the crucifixions said it was tradition. And it was done." Calypso wiped at the tears on her face. "There is so much evil in the Romans. I wish God would wipe them out."

"No, Mother, then the good-hearted Romans would die, too. Adan Longinus, his wife, his sons and daughter, his whole family, are good people. I would never want all Romans wiped from this earth if it meant Adan and his family would also die. I was very angry with Marco when I thought he had betrayed me. I was angry with Adan when I learned that he had chosen Niko over me when he freed him. I realize now that Salvitto would not have let me go, anyway. But when it counted the most, Adan, Marco, Aquila, and Niko refused to leave me on the dock in Herculaneum. The mountain was exploding, but I refused to go with them. Then they stepped off the ship. They wouldn't leave me behind. I saw their expressions. They were at peace and were willing to die with me rather than abandon me." Calais took a deep breath and sighed. "As for the Romans, sometimes, we have to take the bad with the good. Let's hope the good stays close by and the bad stays far away. Come on. Let's find Adan and Niko. There must be someone who will take food to the lepers."

Chapter 14

Predators in Pursuit

The four of them made inquiries to find someone to temporarily take Calypso's place. They met with no success until Adan found a baker and his wife who had a slave girl of about ten years old. She had been orphaned and left to starve on the street. The baker and his wife took her in to work for them. She was no longer starving but she cried at night at the loss of her family.

Adan took his time chatting with the couple and watched how the girl interacted with her master and mistress. When he saw that she was a diligent worker, he asked if they would be willing to let him pay for the child to take bread to the leper colony.

"We will be gone about three weeks," explained Adan. "If the lepers confirm that they had ample bread every day, I will pay you the same amount again through Calypso, I mean Petalouda, when she returns."

Calypso explained to the shop owners that she would pay for the bread in advance. She also gave several names of the lepers that served as spokesmen for the colony and that they could be trusted to wait for the slave girl to leave before they collected the bread.

The slave girl had been studying Calais with shy glances. She cautiously approached him. "Sir, please forgive my asking but was Agios your brother?" She backed away as if expecting a reprimand for speaking without permission. She lowered her eyes and waited.

Calais reached out with an open hand, palm up, the universal gesture of permission for a slave to make eye contact. He gave her a gentle smile. She looked at his open hand first before slowly raising her eyes to meet his.

"Yes, he was my brother. And Petalouda was his mother. My name is Calais Antipas and our mother's name is Calypso. You may call her that if you'd like."

"Will the lepers try to touch me?"

"I have spoken with them. You have nothing to fear. They only wish to be left alone to die in peace. You can leave the bread on the flat rock near the mouth of the largest cave. They will wait until you're gone before they come out, as my mother said. They have access to a well but any wine your master might have to spare would be a welcome relief to their suffering, at least, for a little while."

"How can I know that your words are true?"

"You cannot until you get to know me. But did Agios every break a promise? Did Agios tend to the sick and dying even at the cost of his own life?"

The slave girl solemnly nodded her head. "He once put his hand on my head and blessed me and gave me a loaf of wheat bread. Me, just a slave with no family. He had the kindest eyes." She looked away bashfully. "You could tell his smile was true. His eyes would light up."

"I hope to win your trust as did my brother." Calais thought of something that might help. "I will leave a symbol of my trust in you so that maybe you will trust me." He reached into his coin pouch and withdrew the little carved owl. "This is Sofi, my most prized possession. My father carved this little owl for me on my sixth birthday. I entrusted her to the centurion's son, Marco, and because he kept her safe, even after he thought I was dead, I knew I could trust him." He reached for her hand and pressed the wooden owl in her palm. "Now, you know that I will return and I am trusting you to keep Sofi safe until that day."

The child closed her fingers around the little owl. "I will protect Sofi as best as I can." She opened her hand and smiled at the intricate carving of the feathers, eyes, and beak. "Sofi's heart will break if you do not come for her."

A gentle smile softened his expression. "I'm sure you will do a good job. Find the flat rock at the mouth of the largest cave each day and you will earn crowns in heaven."

The child smiled at him and closed her hand around Sofi.

After leaving the bakery, they went to Calypso's home to collect the few belongings she would need for the trip to Corinth. Adan instructed the carriage driver to take them to the garrison first and then back to Smyrna. Nikolaus and Calais stayed with Calypso in the carriage while Adan went inside. Adan spoke with the commander and learned that they lacked many provisions that they would need if under attack. The two men strolled about the grounds as the commander pointed out structural flaws in the garrison walls and the barracks. Adan made note and told the commander he would include his requests for supplies in his report.

Adan joined the others in the carriage and they were soon on their way. It wasn't long before the carriage reached the pier in Smyrna. Adan paid the driver and they collected their belongings. Calypso and Calais stayed with their knapsacks while Adan and Nikolaus checked with the port master to learn if the *Child of the Ocean* had docked. The man assured them that the ship had not come in yet.

Adan informed the others. "They haven't docked yet but unless they come in this evening, we'll need to find rooms at an inn."

✻✻✻

While the group discussed their options, a man slumped on one of the benches along the pier, suddenly sat upright. After observing Adan for a moment, he hurried away. He walked into a bar and approached two other men drinking honey ale and wine.

"Celsus, you were right," said the man. "They're back. What do we do now?"

Celsus finished off his wine and walked out without answering. The other two men glanced at each other and followed him outside.

"First," declared Celsus, "we find out which ship they're boarding and get ourselves hired as oarsmen. That way we can't lose sight of them again. We can't do anything about the scroll on the ship, but when we disembark, we'll steal it if the opportunity presents itself. If it looks like that won't happen, then we attack."

"Have you lost your mind, Celsus?" hissed one of the men. "We've already gone over this. We can't win against that centurion. Besides, he's got two others with him."

"Don't worry. I'll think of something."

The other two men were doubtful but too intimidated to persist. They had been in a near panic when their ship docked in Smyrna and Adan's group was gone. Celsus was so frustrated, he went to the first bar he could find and proceeded to get drunk. He decided that their mission was doomed, but he couldn't admit that to his companions. Instead, he told them they would wait a few days to see if the centurion returned.

Sleep eluded Celsus that night as he paced the small room he had rented at an inn. He had thought a great deal about his conversation with Commander Lysias. The man must have hated Longinus to even joke about torturing a Roman centurion, the elite in the Roman army. Celsus had heard of the *Lupus Legatus*. The story of Longinus being executed by King Herod's order and then reappearing months later, very much alive, had been circulating for years. The stories had differing details such as the executioner split his heart with an arrow, sometimes a spear, sometimes a thrown dagger, and one version told of an axe as the weapon. Yet, every story told of the heart of Longinus being split asunder, impossible to survive.

Celsus was not easily taken in by myths and legends he assumed were told so many times, they had been exaggerated beyond the truth. He didn't believe Longinus was a werewolf because he didn't believe immortal monsters existed. Every "monster" he ever encountered was all too human. Then an idea came to him. If he could do something amazing that would garner the attention of the people of Rome, perhaps it would give him some leverage against Emperor Domitian if he should fail. If he were to kill the very man others thought to be an immortal, he would be idolized by the masses. The emperor would have to think twice about ordering his execution. The name of Celsus and how he vanquished the legendary *Lupus Legatus* would be chiseled in the proclamation stone that stood at the Colosseum in Rome. Now, all he had to do was kill an "immortal werewolf." He collapsed onto the bed and sleep finally overtook him.

When Adan and the others reappeared in Smyrna, confirming Celsus's prediction, his companions were impressed. They decided not to doubt their leader again. They could see a difference in Celsus. He seemed more confident. There were no more trips to the nearest bar and no more unprovoked outbursts of temper. In fact, Celsus seemed completely at peace with the world. His companions wondered what could have caused such a change in his behavior. However, they knew better than to ask him anything about his life, past or present.

***

Adan and his group found rooms at an inn near the pier. It gave them a chance to relax over a good dinner and a good night's sleep. They hoped that Aurelius and Pomona would return the next day as Aurelius had estimated. Mid-morning, the *Child of the Ocean* appeared on the horizon. Adan and the others were waiting on the pier when the ship docked. Adan nudged Calais and pointed in Aurelius's direction as he stood by his helmsman. Calais grinned to see Pomona standing next to him with her hand shielding her face from the sun. She spotted the group and her posture suddenly stiffened with excitement. She pulled on her brother's sleeve as she waved.

The ship had barely docked and the gangplank pushed out to the dock before Pomona was running to meet them. Calypso saw the joy on Pomona's face and threw her arms open. The two women clasped each other and cried with joy. Calais looked away and wiped at his face with the back of his hand. Adan and Nikolaus smiled at each other and waved at Aurelius. A broad grin graced his face as well.

"I thought I'd never see you again," cried Pomona. "My mother loved you like a sister and I loved you like a second mother."

Calypso let her tears of happiness flow undaunted. "Pomona, my sweet Pomona. Can you ever forgive me? It broke my heart to leave you, but I had to try and find my family. When I found my eldest son, I wanted to come back for you, but then I started caring for the lepers that live in the tombs and I couldn't leave them for as long as it would take to get to Jerusalem and back. Please, forgive me. I never stopped loving you."

"All is in the past. We have the future ahead of us. You will always know that I am safe, here with my brother."

They walked up the gangplank to the ship and sat down to talk. Calypso beckoned to Calais and she described to Pomona's delight, how they found each other.. Aurelius sent Samuel to prepare the passengers' quarters. The new cargo was loaded and Aurelius signaled for the ship to depart. While Adan and the others were getting settled, Junius hired a few oarsmen to take the place of those who wished to stay behind in Smyrna. He was surprised when three of the men agreed to the offered wages without asking about the workload, sleeping quarters, or rations. He figured they must be desperate for employment or were trying to avoid the consequences of criminal activity, as many were.

As the ship headed out of port, Adan and Nikolaus joined Aurelius on deck. He coaxed the brothers to join him in the stern.

"I need to tell you about the excitement you missed," said Aurelius. "Turns out a bounty hunter hired on as an oarsman. He had a copy of the warrant for Pomona in his possession and Samuel found it. The crew tossed him overboard." He told them the details and how Pomona threw the man a lifeline.

"I have never been more proud of any men I've ever known, including my own *centuria* when I was a centurion. They voluntarily paid the man a large bounty in exchange for taking an oath to let her go. It was a wake-up call for all of us. Junius will be more careful in the future when hiring anyone we're not familiar with. I have instructed Samuel to search their knapsacks when they're at the oars. So, this story has a satisfactory ending. That bounty hunter will be no more trouble. If Samuel finds any warrants, he will report it to me immediately."

"Sounds like a good defense," said Adan.

"Are you sure the bounty hunter won't break his oath?" asked Nikolaus.

"No, there are no guarantees when it comes to human behavior," answered Aurelius. "But I put the fear of death in him and I could see he took it to heart. We should be fine."

"I hope so," said Adan. "He knows she's on this ship now and could easily track your progress with one look at every harbor master's records."

"True, but he'll be easy to spot with that blonde hair of his. My regular crewmen call her Mother as a term of affection. There will be many eyes watching for him. He will be convinced to leave us alone."

The trip across the Aegean gave the travelers time to enjoy the beauty of peaceful seas and each other's company. Pomona spent most of her time with Calypso, catching up on each other's lives. Pomona was deeply grieved at the death of Calypso's son, Antipas, but rejoiced with her at being reunited with Calais. Adan and Aurelius stood for hours at the helm, trading stories of life as centurions and past experiences. They made a point to never mention Felix Valentius.

Nikolaus and Calais, at first, had conversed in stiff exchanges, but their conversations gradually grew more sociable. As they neared the Port of Cenchreae, which served Corinth, the two men were willing to put the past behind them. Nikolaus told Calais the circumstances surrounding the death of his family aboard Captain Egnatian's ship, *The Griffin*. Calais told Nikolaus about the death of his father when the Tower of Siloam collapsed and killed him and seventeen others. Both men had suffered great loss and were finally able to sympathize with each other.

Aurelius gave Junius the order to lower the sails and rally the oarsmen. They were nearing the coastline. "I'm glad we won't be going west of Corinth. I won't have to pay their hefty fee to use the *Diolkos*."

"What's that?" asked Adan.

"It's a rail system for transporting ships from the Port of Cenchreae, on the east side of Corinth to the Port of Lechaeum on the west side. That port feeds into the Corinthian

Gulf. It's a great convenience if you need to sail from the Aegean Sea to the gulf without going all the way around the peninsula, Achaea. Shaves a week, at least, off the trip from Corinth to *Italia*. It also eliminates passing Sparta on the southern tip of Achaea. Sparta, has strict docking policies and they charge ridiculously high fees. So, if a storm pushes you into their port, you'll have to forfeit a great deal of your profit from your cargo."

"Do you think you'll find a cargo to deliver in Athens?"

Aurelius shrugged. "I never know what I'll find but it's likely. Athens is a busy city with lots of commerce. Rome takes advantage of the superiority of many Greek items such as bronze and marble sculptures, and ceramics. The Greeks are very skilled artisans."

"I hope we don't have any trouble finding John's friends in Corinth," said Adan. "I'll be very relieved to hand this scroll over to them."

Aurelius glanced at Adan's knapsack. "It must be important. Why haven't you kept it in the cabinet? You did before when we left Patmos for Smyrna."

"Not this time." Adan adjusted the scrap across his chest. "I feel better having it with me."

"What's it about?"

"The end of the world, my friend."

Aurelius thought he was joking until he saw the grim look on Adan's face. "*Ohe*, you're serious. You don't honestly believe it, do you? No human can see into the future. I can make a vague prediction about something and could get it right by coincidence."

"These visions are not vague and not determined by human imagination. These visions come from God; therefore, they will happen. If you check with our historians, you'll see that God's predictions always come true. It's only a matter of time. Nikolaus and I read the entire scroll and we don't understand most of it. How can everyone in the whole world hear the same message or see the same event, *at the same time?* What kind of weapon can destroy a fourth, or even a third of mankind with a single event? Life will have to be very different in the future for these events to happen."

"A fourth of all mankind killed at once? There is no such weapon, Adan, and there never will be. Be rational; no army can move faster than a horse or the wind in our sails."

"If *machinis* were invented that allowed men to fly or live underwater. What then?"

Aurelius chuckled at the absurdity. "Machines that fly in the air? Machines that swim under the sea? These fantasies are beyond ridiculous."

Adan thought of the Prophecy Box. "For now, it sounds impossible but will everything always be the same? Ancient people did not build aqueducts or magnificent buildings like the Colosseum. Now we do. My son, Aquila and my father are always trading ideas on how to improve one thing or another. They've been working on a device that will make water flow up an incline in a greater volume than even an Archimedes screw pump."

Aurelius smirked. "That goes against the laws of nature. Won't happen."

"Archimedes made it happen nearly three hundred years ago. My father and son made a wheel covered with rows of square buckets that carry the water from a lower elevation to the next higher one. The first wheel dumps the water onto the next higher wheel and so on until it comes to a slightly declining channel. It's not perfect but they're working on it. They're always sending letters back and forth with new suggestions and observations."

Aurelius snorted. "I still say nothing will ever surpass the strength of a man's arm or his horse. That's the way it has always been and always will be."

"Perhaps *novum technology* is only limited by the extent of our imagination."

"You're dreaming, my friend," retorted Aurelius. "Have you ever seen a *machina* you couldn't make for yourself?"

Adan wanted to tell him about the Prophecy Box but knew it was too risky. He scanned the sea and the approaching coast of Greece while he put his thoughts together. "You say the impossible will never happen. I agree that men cannot overcome certain things, such as death, but new technology will become reality, given enough time. As for the most impossible thing—remember what I told you about the crucifixion of Yeshua and how I saw him alive that Sunday morning? There's so much more I didn't get a chance to share with you."

Aurelius couldn't help being curious. "I have heard other stories besides yours. I've been wondering when we could discuss them."

"There's no better time than the present," said Adan.

Chapter 15

Targets Turn the Tables

A urelius decided to use the time in the Port of Cenchreae for some ship maintenance while Adan took care of his task in Corinth. Calypso convinced Pomona
that she needed to change her appearance since she had already been spotted
by one bounty hunter. Port cities were known to teem with escaped slaves and criminals,
hence a concentration of the mercenaries. She taught Pomona to braid sections of her
hair and intertwin the braids into the designs wealthy Roman women favored. Pomona
would also need to dress in the Roman style. Since she was half Roman, the clothing and
hair style suited her. The two women decided to shop for new clothing and to resupply the galley with fresh produce from the marketplace. A few oarsmen collected their
wages, having told Junius that they would not be coming back. It was a common way for
men without riches to travel and make money at the same time. However, Junius was
surprised when three of the men he hired in Smyrna already gave notice of departure
only after a few days.

"No wonder they didn't care about the wages or rations," Junius thought to himself
as he paid the men their meager earnings.

Adan, Nikolaus, and Calais gathered the belongings they would need and left the
ship. Corinth was a large city populated with a mixture of mostly Romans, Persians,
Greeks, and Jews. Business was brisk and many streets were dedicated exclusively to
shops, cafes, and bars. The trio questioned shop owners about the location of tent makers
and received conflicting answers, due to the intense competition among the merchants.

Adan curled a lip in frustration. "I didn't think this would be so difficult."

Nikolaus stopped in the next intersection. "Have we tried going that way?" He
pointed in a promising direction.

Before Adan could answer him, a boy of about twelve years approached him. "Sir,
I heard you asking about tent makers. I know the way to their district. There are four
shops on the same street. I could show you the way for only a few *dupondii*."

Adan took two copper coins from his belt pouch. "I'll pay you two now and two more if you lead us to the right shop quickly."

The boy deposited the money in his coin pouch and signaled for the trio to follow him. He moved quickly through the other pedestrians, glancing occasionally over his shoulder to be sure they were keeping up. Adan kept his eye on the boy, but Calais was taking in the sights and sounds of the bustling city. Men were shouting out prices for their wares. Women were haggling to get the best bargains. Children dodged among the shoppers while a few slipped small fingers into distracted shoppers' coin pouches and knapsacks. Occasionally, an irate pedestrian would shout at a wagon driver or a merchant would scream, "Thief!" at a fleeing suspect.

Nikolaus called to Calais to catch up when their guide abruptly turned down a narrow alley wedged in between buildings. Wooden casks along with damaged items littered one side of the alley, forcing them to pick their footing carefully. The mud brick walls on either side were high and interrupted by a few doors that must have been back entrances to shops or villas. Suddenly, the boy took off at a run. He paused near a particularly high heap of wooden casks and vases. A rope was hanging from a vase in the middle of the heap. The boy yanked the rope causing the pile to tumble over, blocking the way. Adan heard a childish laugh from the other side of the debris, and then running footsteps.

A door a few feet behind Adan flew open and three men emerged. Adan and Nikolaus had drawn their swords even before the door opened. The brothers recognized them immediately as the three men who had hired on as oarsmen in Smyrna. One man attacked Nikolaus while two went after Adan. Out in the main street, Calais heard the clatter of the falling trash heap as he approached the alley. He saw three men attacking his friends. He didn't have a sword and had never learned how to use one anyway. He stood paralyzed with indecision as his friends fought to defend themselves.

Adan had his dagger in one hand and his sword in the other as he kept both of his attackers at bay. Nikolaus spun around, blocking the downward cut of his attacker's sword but lost his balance. He went down but stopped his fall with his hand. When the attacker came in for the kill, Nikolaus threw a chunk of a broken urn at his head. The man cried out in pain and dropped his sword. His hands flew to his face. Blood oozed from between his fingers. Nikolaus scrambled to his feet and hit the assailant in the head with the pommel of his sword. The man collapsed, unconscious.

Nikolaus dropped his sword and picked up a dented bronze vase. He bashed one of Adan's attackers on the back of his bald head. The man swayed under the impact. Nikolaus turned around to reach for his sword when something hit him in the back of the neck. Dazed, he stumbled but kept to his feet. He grabbed a cracked vase and threw it at the man's head as he came at Nikolaus with his sword. The man crumpled to the ground this time but Nikolaus stumbled back and tripped. He landed hard on this back and was too dizzy to get up.

Adan had often practiced with multiple opponents since battles were rarely single combat fighting. He slashed and blocked and sidestepped as best he could, but he was growing tired. The tight alley allowed for little maneuvering. When Nikolaus knocked two of the men out, Adan moved in to finish off the last attacker. Then the leather strap across his chest slipped away and the knapsack disappeared from his side. The same childish laughter sounded behind him. He glanced back just in time to see the boy brandish a small pair of scissors and the knapsack before he stepped through the same doorway the attackers had used. Instead of slamming the door shut, the boy stood just inside, watching. His eyes gleamed with satisfaction to see a Roman centurion fighting for his life.

The attacker tried to take advantage of Adan's distracted attention. He stepped closer with his sword raised. Adan shifted his weight and kicked his attacker in the knee, forcing the man's leg to overextend. He howled in pain and dropped his weapon to grasp his knee with both hands. He looked toward the doorway and saw the boy. The sneer on the child's face melted into disappointment. Adan heard the door slam and a bar slide in the metal brackets on the other side. He held his sword in one hand and raised his dagger in the other. The attacker glared in defiance, but instead of delivering a fatal slash across the throat, Adan dropped his dagger and hit the man with his fist. He dropped like a barrel over a waterfall.

Adan panted as he muttered a curse. "Niko! Are you hurt?"

"No. Are you?" Nikolaus sat up and rubbed the back of his neck.

"I'm fine. But that boy stole the scroll." Adan grabbed the man by the front of the tunic and pulled him to an upright position. "This brute was on the ship, Niko. I remember him because he's missing part of an ear. I saw them get off just after we did. He's going to be so sorry when he comes to because I've got some questions and he *will* answer them."

"I wonder how long they've been stalking us," mused Nikolaus.

"They had to have been on Patmos. They probably watched John hand me the scroll."

Nikolaus looked around. "Where's Calais?"

The two men exchanged troubled looks. "I never saw him come down the alley."

"Unbelievable!" Nikolaus fumed. "He ran off! If he had helped with these three, the boy wouldn't have gotten away. How did he get the scroll?"

"He had a pair of *forficulae*. He went through the same door these men did. The shop connected to that door is probably unoccupied and the kid is long gone."

"Whatever we do, we're not wasting our time looking for Calais," snarled Nikolaus.

"No, Niko. I don't believe Calais would abandon us."

"Then where is he?"

"I'm sure he'll tell us when he comes back."

Nikolaus gave him a disgruntled glare. "*If* he comes back."

Adan looked down at his prisoner "If we don't get answers from this useless brute, then I doubt we'll find the scroll." Adan slapped the man across the face. His eyes fluttered open to see the blade of a dagger at his throat.

"Who are you?" Adan hissed.

The man swallowed hard before he answered. "Celsus. I work for Emperor Domitian."

"Where did the boy take the scroll?" demanded Nikolaus.

Celsus looked from one to the other. "Why should I tell you anything. I'm a dead no matter what."

"What do you mean?" asked Adan.

"The emperor hired me to keep an eye on your friend, John. He told me to bring whatever John recorded. So, If I don't show up at the appointed time there'll be a price on my head. If I show up without the scroll, I won't even have a head." The man lowered his eyes in defeat. "Just kill me and get it other with. It doesn't matter now."

"Why does Domitian want the scroll?" asked Adan.

"He's convinced that your friend is a seer. When he tried to execute John and he came out unscathed, Domitian was humiliated and I suspect a bit terrified. I think he exiled John because he was too frightened to try to execute him again. The point is, I was to intercept any correspondence that he sent by messenger. That way, we could be sure John had completed his writings. The emperor said, and I quote, 'as long as the seal is intact, you will richly be paid the full amount you deserve.' A fortune would have been mine." The man's eyes glittered with hatred. "The boy got away but I guess I won't be meeting up with him."

"Where are you supposed to meet him?" asked Adan.

Celsus shook his head. "It doesn't matter. I told the kid to hide the scroll and come find me in the marketplace. I would pay him when he led me back to the scroll. I didn't want him walking around with it any more than necessary. I gave him instructions in case I didn't show up but there's no guarantee he won't try to sell it. Either way, the scroll is out of your reach."

Adan looked over at his brother. "Niko, we don't have to get the scroll back. We can go back to Patmos and John can write everything down again."

Celsus smirked. "Too late. The emperor will know you had it when he receives the message I have already sent. If I don't show up, he'll think you still have it, Centurion Longinus. Yes, I knew who you were as soon as I saw you on Patmos. Domitian will send men after you and your family. He'll use them against you. You've got a target on your back now, just like me."

Adan took a deep breath and considered the situation. "Not necessarily. I've got an idea if you're willing to do your part. It will save both of us and satisfy Domitian. You'll deliver the scroll to him—it just won't be the one John wrote. I'll write an account, in Greek, as John did. You'll meet the boy in the marketplace, collect John's scroll, and we make an exchange. You'll live to fight another day."

"It would be a good plan except for one problem," said Celsus. "The boy saw you take me down. He thinks I won't be coming to the marketplace. I told him that if something went wrong, to take the scroll to the commander of the garrison. If the boy follows my instructions, the commander will send it to Emperor Domitian. Your precious scroll could be in the hands of the commander now. When Domitian gets his hands on it, the order will be given to execute John. Your friend will have served his purpose. There's no way out for any of us."

The brothers knew it was an impossible predicament. Corinth was a big city. How could they possibly find one boy before he made it to the garrison. "Niko, if we hurry, we could take these three to the garrison as our prisoners and intercept the boy." Even before he finished the sentence, he knew it was useless. Incumbered with three unwilling detainees, they could not get there in time. Without the prisoners, Adan could not verify that the scroll belonged to him. John's life was now in jeopardy and the Revelation would never make it to the seven cities or future generations.

Adan lowered his head in despair. He had been outsmarted by a child and a soldier of fortune. He felt like shouting every curse he knew. He leaned his back against the wall and tried to think. Nikolaus made a few half-hearted suggestions but knew none of them would work.

"What are you going to do with me, Centurion?" Celsus cut his eyes over to his dagger which was almost within reach. Adan saw where he was looking and picked up the dagger. He was about to speak when a figure appeared at the end of the alley.

"*Calais!*"

Nikolaus spun around to see their friend walking toward them. He was holding Adan's knapsack. The severed leather strap dangled on either side. He stepped over the two unconscious men and stopped. "I'm sorry I didn't jump into the fight. I just couldn't move." His face reddened with embarrassment. "I couldn't even warn you when the door opened and the boy came up behind you, Adan. Then I saw him go back through the door with your knapsack. I ran around to the street and watched to see if he would come out of one of the shops. I walked slowly along the street until I spotted him. He stepped out of a shop that had a 'For Sale' sign tacked on the door. He slipped the rolled-up knapsack down the front of his tunic and started walking. I caught up with him, grabbed him by the neck, and yanked the knapsack out of his tunic. He looked terrified." Calais lowered his head. "He ran off. I tried to catch him but he got away. I'm sorry."

"You're sorry?" laughed Adan. "For what? Saving one of the most important documents ever written? I'm the one who is sorry. I allowed a child to outwit me—twice. Not only did I follow the kid straight into an ambush, he stole the scroll without so much as a scratch. John said you would be needed, Calais. He was right. You got the scroll back. Niko, tell Calais what this mongrel told us about Emperor Domitian."

While Nikolaus described the details to Calais, Adan pulled Celsus to his feet. "Now listen carefully. You can still get paid if you'll cooperate. You and your friends are going back to the ship. Tell Junius that I need your assistance so he'll hire you back. Tonight, I'll write another scroll. I'll even throw in a few predictions that will keep Domitian happy. I'll seal the document the way John did and use the original spools since he would not have access to anything else. It'll look authentic."

"He's going to ask if I had to kill you to get it," said Celsus. "What do I tell him?"

"Tell him you stole a key to the cabinet in my quarters and slipped a substitute scroll into the knapsack. You were long gone before the switch was discovered."

Celsus smirked with amusement. "That's exactly what I *was* going to do but you always had the scroll with you."

"Really? Interesting," said Adan with a one-sided smile. "It's ironic how things work out. So, do you think you can satisfy the emperor's curiosity? He must be completely convinced."

Celsus grinned with confidence. "In exchange for my life, I can convince a rich man that a hunk of clay is pure gold. It's a good plan, Centurion. I'll wait for you on the ship."

"What about your friends?"

Celsus snorted. "They're not my friends. Let them crawl back under the rocks they came from." He rubbed his bruised jaw. "Tell me something, Centurion. Are you really a werewolf?" He gave a sarcastic laugh and turned his back without waiting for an answer. "I'll be on the ship," he said over a shoulder as he started down the alley.

"*Ohe*, tell me something," called out Nikolaus. "What happened to your ear?"

The man turned around. "A pig bit if off when I was six years old."

"I bet you stayed away from that old sow after that."

"Didn't have to. I ate it. Raw." The man walked away and disappeared around a corner.

Nikolaus and Adan exchanged disconcerted glances before returning their attention to the unconscious men.

"What do you want to do with them?" asked Nikolaus.

"They're lucky I don't have time to drag them to the garrison's pit. Let's go. We still have to find Priscilla and Aquila."

They left the alley and resumed their hunt for the tent makers. After a few more false leads, the trio finally found a tent shop near the outskirts of the city. It was a run-down section of town, but the shop was clean and orderly.

Aquila greeted them. "Welcome, gentlemen. How may I serve you?"

Adan gestured toward Nikolaus. "I am Adan Clovius Longinus and this is my brother, Nikolaus, and our friend, Calais Antipas. We have come from Caesarea, by way of Patmos Island. We are looking for tent makers named Aquila and Priscilla. They were recommended to us by a friend from Tarsus."

"What is your friend's name?"

"Paul. At least, that is the name he uses now. He was once called Saul."

Aquila started to speak, but then recognition made him pause. "I have heard of you. You're the centurion that defended Simon Peter when Herod arrested him." Then his eyes widened with admiration. "And if my memory serves me correctly, aren't you also the one who gave a magnificent pearl to Paul? It helped to keep many thousands from starving to death." The man turned and called to his wife who was working in the back room. "Priscilla, the man who gave Paul the blue pearl is here!"

Calais shot Adan a look of astonishment. "That was *you!* I heard about that pearl."

Nikolaus chuckled softly. "Now you've let the 'rats out of the trap,' Adan."

Calais continued to stare at Adan while a woman came from the back room to join her husband. "I am Priscilla. You are most welcome in our home. You, and your friends."

Adan put a hand on Nikolaus's shoulder. "This is my brother, Niko, and this is Calais, our friend." Adan looked deliberately at Calais. "A friend, I might add, who has done a wonderful thing today. We have something for you from John, son of Zebedee, which was stolen from me, but Calais retrieved it. I owe him a great debt."

Calais's face brightened at the praise but he couldn't think of anything to say. He ducked his head and mumbled something under his breath.

Priscilla smiled good-naturedly at his unassuming reaction. "Calais, you must tell us all about it over the mid-day meal. Will you join us?"

"We would accept if we had more time," said Adan. "But our mission is twofold and most urgent." Adan drew John's scroll out of the damaged knapsack and handed it to Priscilla.

"Considering someone tried to steal it," said Aquila, "it must be very important."

"It is," said Adan. "The first part contains seven letters to the Christian churches in Ephesus, Smyrna, Pergamon, Thyatira, Sardis, Philadelphia, and Laodicea. The rest of the scroll contains the visions that God sent to John in spirit. These visions are events that are to come at the end of the age. Each church must get a copy of the entire document."

Aquila put his arm protectively around Priscilla's waist. "It is an honor that we have been trusted with this task. We will do our best." Aquila looked at Priscilla. "Perhaps this is also the sign we've been waiting for."

Priscilla looked up at her husband and understanding passed between them. "I'll go get it," she said and returned to the back room.

"Please join us for some refreshment, gentlemen. It won't take long," said Aquila as he led them to join Priscilla. There was a small table with two chairs. Aquila pulled three small crates over to the table for them to sit on. "Let me explain. Priscilla and I have been working with a friend of ours and Paul's. He is a devout witness of Yeshua's message. His name is Apollos. Have you heard of him?"

"We have," said Adan as he gestured toward Nikolaus. "Calais?"

He shook his head. "No. Is he also a friend of John's?"

Aquila explained the relationship among the men as Priscilla joined them. She set a scroll on the table and collected five cups and a jug of honey ale. Priscilla filled the cups and offered one to each man.

Priscilla explained, "This is a letter to all the Christian believers in Jerusalem. In the past, God spoke through the prophets. Now we hear God's voice through *His Son, whom He has appointed heir of all things.* We have worked diligently on this essay so that many may learn and believe. We call it The Epistle to the Hebrews. Others have contributed to this essay by carefully editing for accurate content. If you can take that to Jerusalem, you would be doing a wonderful service for all the Christians there."

"I would be honored," said Adan. "Since Niko has spent a great deal of time on adventures with me, I'll ask my father-in-law, Marcus Cornelius, to accompany me to Jerusalem."

Aquila and Priscilla smiled at each other. "Yes, that's right. Cornelius and his household were the first Gentiles to follow the Way of Yeshua."

Adan unrolled the scroll to read the introduction. "What is this scribble on the side?"

Aquila rolled his eyes. "Did you mark out your name, Priscilla?"

"I know you wanted to give me credit but some people, both men and women, might take offense at instruction from a woman, no matter how true or inspired it may be. I don't want to take the chance of losing someone's interest even before he or she reads the first line. Besides, you and Apollos also worked on this and you two didn't take any credit. Besides, we both know that the real author of this message is God."

"There is one thing," said Adan. "We will not be returning to Caesarea directly. There is another task that we must see to and we don't know how long it will take."

They told Aquila and Priscilla that they would be going to Athens in search of answers about the visit of the *Magi* to Yeshua when he was living in Bethlehem. None of them mentioned the Prophecy Box. While he talked, Priscilla used an awl and leather cord to repair the knapsack. Adan put the Epistle for the Hebrews in the knapsack and threw the strap across his chest. He tugged on it to show that Priscilla had repaired it properly. They wished each other well and expressed hope for a future meeting.

As the trio walked through the city back to the eastern harbor, they discussed what Adan should write in the substitute scroll. Calais suggested predicting the collapse of the Roman Empire due to over reliance on slave labor. Nikolaus suggested predicting that leaders of nations would only be elected by the people rather than by royal blood line secession or military might.

Adan chuckled at their ideas. "I don't want to give Domitian an excuse to kill Celsus for being a messenger of bad news."

"Why not?" Nikolaus and Calais demanded in unison.

"It would serve him right," added Nikolaus.

"I confess," Adan replied with a sheepish grin. "The thought did occur to me. The other thought is that I still have to evaluate the garrison before we leave. Why don't you two go back to the ship and I'll hire another carriage. It won't take long."

"Do you want me to go with you?" asked Nikolaus with an involuntary cringe.

Adan couldn't help but laugh. "Thanks, Niko, but I won't put you through that."

The evaluation proved to be more time consuming than Adan had anticipated but he wrote a quick summary of the pros and cons concerning the fort and posted his report.

By the time Adan boarded the ship, he had a good idea of what to write. He checked with the Junius who confirmed that Celsus had returned. The ship maintenance had not been completed so they wouldn't set sail until late the next day. Adan went to his quarters to work. After little sleep, Adan shared the forgery with Nikolaus and Calais the next morning. They had a few suggestions which he thought to be useful and made additions.

Adan found Celsus below deck, leaning against the bulkhead while he ate a handful of figs. "I'm going on deck," said Adan. "Perhaps now would be a good time for you to leave." Pretending not to notice, he opened his hand and a metal object clattered to the deck. "John's name in Hebrew is Yohanan Boanerges. I used that spelling rather than his Greek name in a little note I included. It's from John to the man who inspired him to see the visions and to write them down. His name in Latin is Iesous."

"You put his name in the note? Don't you realize the emperor will find him? He will be interrogated under torture until he is dead."

"I truly hope Emperor Domitian will find Iesous because he knocks on every door, waiting for an answer," Adan stated. He started to walk away but called over his shoulder. "Besides, Iesous has already been tortured to death. He lives forever, now, as he always has."

Celsus stared after him, slack-jawed. Then he shook himself as if from a trance and looked for the metal object Adan had dropped. It was the key to the cabinet in Adan's guest quarters. He knew Adan had "lost" the key to give a ring of truth to Celsus's report. A well-believed liar tells as much of the truth as possible. Celsus's claim of stealing the scroll out of the cabinet using an equally stolen key would be, in essence, the truth. He waited for Adan to disappear up the ladder to the top deck, and then went along the passageway to the guest quarters. Once inside, he pushed the key into the cabinet's lock and opened the door. He removed the knapsack with the repaired strap. He took the scroll out and inspected the seal. It was clay rather than wax. The impression in the clay had the shape of a pebble with YB scratched in the center. Celsus smiled at the attention Adan had given to detail. John's signature ring would have been confiscated.

"Well done, Centurion," whispered Celsus. He slipped the forged scroll into his own knapsack and put Adan's back in the cabinet. He left the key in the lock. He didn't bother to tell the Master of Oars that he would not be staying, after all.

For now, Celsus had a scroll to deliver and his pay to collect. He anticipated getting triple the amount since he abandoned the other two men. Little did he realize that Emperor Domitian literally meant he would be paid 'the amount he deserved.' The scroll came from a prisoner of the Roman Empire; therefore, it was already considered the property of the emperor. He would pay Celsus only what he earned as a prison guard and travel expenses, which was exactly what he "richly" deserved.

Chapter 16

Sins of the Father

Child of the Ocean made good time despite the seas growing rough. As was the brothers' custom, Adan and Nikolaus spent most of their time on the top deck in the bow of the ship. When Pomona sent Samuel to summon them to the captain's quarters, they hoped that Calypso would be with her. They needed to learn as much detail as she could remember before they made port. Adan was concerned about the amount of time they would have to explore Athens for any *Magi* that may have taken residence there but Aurelius had an announcement that relieved his worries.

Samuel opened the door to the captain's quarters for Adan and Nikolaus. Aurelius welcomed them with a hearty wave of the hand. "Samuel, could you bring some refreshment." The boy scurried out of the room. "Come join us." He indicated two chairs at the table next to Pomona and Calypso. "I hope you two were planning on staying in Athens awhile. The port that serves the city, Port Piraeus, has three excellent natural harbors. As a merchant ship, I'll be using the largest harbor called Kantharos. The reason I'm explaining this is because Kantharos has the best *neosoikoi* in the whole Roman Empire."

Pomona looked puzzled. "What is a *neosoikoi*?"

"The best and largest ship shed any captain can find. There are hundreds of them. Long, good width, walled with pillars to allow good ventilation, and roofed against the elements. The ship is pulled up into the shed, stern first, which makes major repairs and maintenance easy to do."

"Dry dock?" asked Adan for clarity.

"That's it," said Aurelius proudly. "I reserved a shed last time I was here so I would be at the top of the list when I came back. The harbor is less than two hours from Athens on a slow horse so you'll want to find a comfortable inn there while my ship has her barnacles and shipworm removed. I want a thorough job done since this prevents waterlogging as well. We haven't been though a great deal of bad weather so hull repairs will be minimal."

Pomona smiled to hear her brother happily explain the logistics of owning a ship. He did love his home on the sea and his happiness was contagious. She enjoyed keeping the records for her brother and overseeing the ship's galley and food supplies. For the first time since their father was arrested and executed for treason, Pomona felt safe. She no longer considered returning to any home on land. The sea, for all its dangers, offered sanctuary far from racial prejudice and unwarranted accusations. The sailors welcomed her as the chief manager of the ship, second only to the captain. The men called Samuel by name, now, instead of Boy, since Captain Hadrian had freed the youngster and Pomona declared that she was now his mother. His thin arms and legs were beginning to show promise of muscular improvement now that she made sure he ate three full meals every day. Pomona had even converted one of the guest quarters to serve as Samuel's own quarters. For the first time since he had lost his family and been enslaved, he had his own bed, rather than a mat thrown onto any spare flooring in the crew's quarters.

Adan listened to Aurelius but he was growing impatient to talk with Calypso. He was relieved when. Samuel returned with fruit and wine, and to inform Aurelius that he was wanted at the helm.

Adan turned to Calypso. "Have you remembered anything else about the *Magi* or anything your father told you?"

Calypso eyed the sliced apple, cherries, and figs on the tray before she answered. "Some. I don't know how useful it will be but I remembered an incident that happened in Athens, many years ago. It caused quite a stir at the time. The chief astrologer was found dead in his home. Some thought he had suffered a calamity of old age and had fallen and hit his head. Others thought he was murdered."

"Murdered? Why?" asked Nikolaus.

"My father served the assistant to the chief astrologer when we lived in Athens. The assistant's name was Balthazar. I would tell you the chief astrologer's name if I knew it. I only knew him as Master. One day, he sent Balthazar to an inn to invite several *Magi* who were visiting from Persia. Balthazar asked my father to go with him. They were to escort the men back so Father and Balthazar had to wait for them to dress accordingly. When they got back to the chief astrologer's villa, Father went to announce that the guests were present. He knocked on the library door, and when there was no answer, he found Balthazar because Father was not allowed to enter the library without permission. They found the chief astrologer, dead, on the floor. Father said the blood had not dried so they knew it had just happened. I was with my mother at the time and did not witness this myself but that's what Father told me." She picked up a slice of apple.

"A suspect was never found?" asked Nikolaus.

Calypso chewed the apple and followed it with a cherry. "No. And no witnesses offered any information. None of his gold or silver was missing. The chief astrologer had no enemies as far as anyone knew. Still, none of the *Magi* believed that his death was natural."

"Why not?" prompted Adan as he selected a fig and several cherries.

"I don't know but you said the Prophecy Box had been stolen. Perhaps that's when it went missing."

Pomona was curious. "What is a Prophecy Box?"

"It was a magical box. The *Magi* kept many of its abilities secret, but a few of the students would discuss it among themselves sometimes. Some young apprentices seem to think people of low status can't hear. Not only did Father overhear stories about the box, he even saw it once."

"You said before that you had never seen it. Was it your father who told you what it looked like?" asked Nikolaus. He had not touched the fruit.

Pomona picked up several figs and placed one beside Nikolaus. He didn't seem to notice.

Calypso held her hands up as if she were grasping a jewelry box. "Yes, Father said it was about this big, made of cypress wood. I think that's what he told me and there were the three stones that we talked about it in Pergamon. One at each top corner and one in the center at the bottom."

Nikolaus could feel his heart pounding. "Did he say what the stones looked like? We didn't discuss that in Pergamon."

"Father said the top stones were 'alive' with light. That's the word he used. He said they shimmered if you moved the box to and fro. The stone at the bottom looked like a picture of desert sand dunes under the open sky but it was not painted or carved. It was a natural stone."

"Have you ever heard of *terrarum* jasper?" asked Nikolaus.

Calypso frowned but Pomona nodded. "I have. Father gave me a small, polished slab of earth jasper once. It was beautiful and looked like someone had fashioned it but he said it forms that way in the ground."

"Did another member of the *Magi* take the master's place?" asked Adan.

"Yes, Balthazar was voted to become the chief astrologer of Athens. He was a great scholar and dedicated to solving the mysteries of the cosmos. He is the one who presented the myrrh to the Child in Bethlehem because the Master could not go. The myrrh was from Saba so it was of the highest quality. It's strange the little details one remembers from the past. But I remember that Balthazar turned twenty while we traveled to Jerusalem. The *Magi* held a feast in his honor in Antioch. There was a great cake covered with honey and bits of spiced nuts. I'll never forget that cake. Father made sure I got a piece of it." Calypso smiled to herself. "He had to sneak it out in a butter dish. We turned south the next day to head for Jerusalem."

"Does Balthazar still live in Athens?" Nikolaus asked hopefully.

"No. He died. The one I told you about took Balthazar's place and he became my Father's master."

"You mean the man named Daniel," asked Adan.

"Yes, he was Balthazar's apprentice. Remember, I told you that Daniel was not his given name. He took that name after Balthazar died. Daniel's ancestors were Israelite captives in Babylon, as I told you before. Daniel loved the stories of his ancestors and took the name of one of the great prophets when Balthazar was no longer alive to interfere."

"Interfere? What do you mean?" asked Pomona. "I don't remember you telling me anything about this."

"I did keep some details to myself," admitted Calypso. "You were very young then. There were also things I simply didn't want to talk about. Balthazar was adamantly opposed to the name change and threatened to cast Daniel out if he took that name. I don't know why but things got very ugly once. One night, Balthazar slapped Daniel and harshly berated him. They must have made amends later because Daniel never left."

Calypso took a sip of wine. "Balthazar was a stern master. My father once said that Balthazar would knock his way through a five-cubit block wall rather than walk around it. He made things difficult. For instance, it was my job to clean Balthazar's villa. When I dusted, everything had to be put back into the exact same spot. One time, a bird flew through the window, as they often do, and distracted me from my work. Balthazar came in just at that moment. I had not replaced a small vase in its proper place yet. He admonished me for my carelessness." Calypso curled a lip. "He was unreasonable when it came to change or opinions that differed from his. However, if you wanted a job done properly, he was the one to do it. When Balthazar set his mind on a task, he would rather die than leave it unfinished."

A sad smile shadowed her features. "Fortunately, he trusted my father and I believe he doted on me. He disliked the 'energy' of young children but I found favor with him. He would take me out on the balcony on clear, moonless nights and taught me the names of the stars and their constellations. A few months before the special star appeared, he told me, 'One day, the brightest, most beautiful star will shine in the east. It will be a great light amid the darkness. It will signal the salvation of all mankind.' Then he said something else that, even now, sends chills through me. Balthazar said, 'Even greater signs will appear. The entire world will see and every knee will bow in worship of the One. Be prepared. Always be prepared.' He said that to me just the one time but I'll never forget it."

"Did he say how he knew this?" asked Adan.

"Not to me. The *Magi* knew many things. Father told me that there were countless records of great events in the Library of Alexandria. The *Magi* were required to spend years studying the scrolls and books."

"When did the chief astrologer die? The one Balthazar replaced," asked Nikolaus.

Calypso sat her wine cup down and gazed at her left hand. She ran a finger along a small, jagged scar on the heel of her palm. "I'm not good with the number of years but it was about the time I cut my hand. There was a torrential rainstorm that hit Athens with high winds and huge hailstones. That's how I fell and sliced my hand open on a broken vase. The storm blew down trees and even killed a few people that couldn't get to shelter. It was terrifying."

Color drained from Nikolaus's face. He struggled to speak and finally made the words come out. "The marble sculpture of Athena in front of the magistrate's villa toppled over."

"Yes. How did you know?"

"My family lived in Athens then. I was six years old." Nikolaus hung his head.

"What's wrong, Niko?" asked Adan as he frowned with concern.

"It was a short time after that storm that Father announced we would be moving to Thessalonica. We were on the road the very next day but left nearly all of our belongings in Athens. We went to other cities before we came back to Athens, back to the same house. That's where we were when Emperor Tiberius hired Father to come to Rome." Nikolaus looked away from their searching expressions. He glanced at Adan and again lowered his gaze. "You know the rest."

Silence hung in the air like a funeral shroud.

Adan licked his lips nervously. It was sounding more and more that Nikolaus's father was involved in the chief astrologer's death.

"Yes!" Nikolaus blurted out as he jerked his head up. "Yes, to the question you're afraid to ask."

Pomona looked from one to the other. "What question?"

"Did my father suddenly find success in his career, that had been so elusive, *after* the death of the chief astrologer?" Nikolaus asked with a sullen tone. "The answer is yes. And it was not long after we were in Thessalonica that a man came to our house, according to Dionysia, demanding that my father turn over something that he had. Something that didn't belong to him."

A gasp of realization escaped Calypso's lips. "You think it was the Prophecy Box?"

Nikolaus massaged his forehead. The misery in his face told the answer. Adan cleared his throat. "Niko, you can't know that for sure. The timing could be a coincidence."

"No. I saw the box, Adan! Remember. Calypso's father described it perfectly to her. Why else would my father tell me that his life depended on no one knowing that *he* had it?"

"Niko, Nicandros was your father. He was a good man," pointed out Adan.

Nikolaus's brow creased in confusion. "Was he? He was terrified that someone would find out that he had that box. Which probably means. . ." He couldn't say the rest.

"Your father killed the master to steal the box," said Calypso.

Nikolaus jumped to his feet. "I can't believe this! Was my father a thief *and* a murderer?"

"Niko, listen to me," exclaimed Adan. "You're making huge assumptions. Nicandros could have bought the Prophecy Box from the real thief. He could have even found it somewhere if the thief stashed it. There's no proof that Nicandros killed anyone."

Nikolaus rubbed at the tension in his neck and sat back down. "You mean, besides circumstantial proof? There's something else I never told you. I didn't want to think about it, much less, say it out loud. Father went into his library the afternoon of the storm. He didn't come out for dinner, which happened at times. That storm ripped tiles off our roof, pushed through the wooden screens we put in the windows, and broke trees all around us. Some villas were flooded and the wind sounded like it did on your wedding night."

Nikolaus stood up again and turned his back on them. They waited in tense silence. He slowly faced them. "Father *never* came out of his library. All night! Mother would throw the door open in a panic and he would yell at her to shut the door! He had that box! The same day the chief astrologer died. Father was never the same from that day on."

Emotionally exhausted, Nikolaus slumped back onto the chair. "He had that box and other people wanted it. My whole family died in one night, except for me and my sister. Captain Egnatian was obsessed with her and that's why he didn't kill her. I was an accidental survivor. You're right, Adan. Egnatian murdered my family and stole that cursed box, probably for someone else who was willing to pay a lot of money. My father's ambition and pride got my family murdered."

Chapter 17

Desperation and Deception

⸺⸺⸺⸺

It was their last night on board the *Child of the Ocean* before making port outside of Athens. Nikolaus had not seen the place of his birth since he was twelve. Now he was thirty-six and he felt as anxious as he did when he first left. He had been devastated when his father announced that Emperor Tiberius had offered him the position of chief architect and he had accepted. It was hard enough that the family kept moving from city to city but they always stayed in Greece. Being suddenly thrown into the heart of the Roman Empire, into the thick of the Roman culture, and directly under the baleful eye of Tiberius was terrifying. Nicandros had told the family that they would have ten times as much money. They would live in a grand villa overlooking the *Tiberis* River. They would have slaves to tend to their every wish. Best of all, they would never have to move again, Nicandros promised.

When his father declared how wonderful it would be to live in luxury, Nikolaus watched his mother's reaction. She never smiled. She tracked Nicandros with a blank expression but said nothing. Nikolaus knew something was wrong but didn't understand why. His brother and five sisters were excited and discussed what they would buy with father's extra money. Even Dionysia eagerly anticipated ordering expensive new clothes from the best seamstresses.

Things had turned sideways fairly quickly after they boarded the ship for Rome. Captain Egnatian hungrily eyed Dionysia as if she was a goddess. Perhaps if she had not dyed her hair red with a concoction of henna and let everyone see her white hair next to her unnaturally pale skin, Egnatian would have turned away. Roman men had a fascination for red hair but dyed red hair on Roman woman looked more like mahogany than scarlet. In contrast, Dionysia's cherry-red hair with her crystalline, blue eyes, and exotic beauty captured the desire of the captain. As an albino, Dionysia was obsessively desired by some and feared by others. It was widely accepted that an albino was a demon from the underworld where there was no light to encourage natural coloring, especially for the demonic hordes of Hades, god of the Underworld.

Even into adulthood, the traumatic memories of his childhood sometimes gave Nikolaus insomnia, as it did that night. He left the ship's quarters to go topside and sat down in the bow of the ship. He thrust his legs through the gaps in the life rails and dangled his feet over the bow. He rested his forehead against the rails and stared into the water. He concentrated all his senses on the smell of the salty air, the soft, moist breeze, and the gentle lapping of waves against the anchored ship. He looked up at the sliver of a crescent moon. Venus was nestled just off the lower tip as if it were a diamond accent on a golden pendant. Mars hovered nearby. Nikolaus wondered what would happen if Mars and Venus ever ran into each other. They were the most opposite of the Roman gods, war and love. Would there be a cosmic explosion or would they melt into one planet? He sighed at such frivolous thoughts and turned his mind back to the present dilemma.

Disjointed thoughts from over the years seemed to come together into one rational explanation. His father had changed after that violent storm when Nikolaus was six years old. Nicandros became distracted and secretive. He would spend long hours in the family library. If any of the children barged in without knocking, Nicandros would whirl around, blocking the view of his desk. He would, contrary to his character, shout at whoever was foolish enough to intrude. The children learned very quickly that Father was to be avoided when he was in one of his moods. Their mother tried to make up for their father's new hostility but without success. Nicandros had become an absentee father, even when he was in plain sight.

Nikolaus heard a footfall on the wooden deck. He didn't even bother to turn his head. "I figured you'd be up here soon."

"Do you mind if I join you?" asked Adan. "I'll understand if you need to be alone."

Nikolaus saw that Adan was carrying a mat large enough for two. "Join me. I'll share the deck if you share your mat. I've been alone with my thoughts long enough, anyway."

Nikolaus got up and Adan unrolled the mat next to the life rail so they could lean their backs against it.

"Niko, I know what you must be thinking. We still have much investigating to do before we can understand what happened to your family."

"Maybe. Probably. There are some things I've never told you."

Adan frowned but Nikolaus missed his expression in the dark. "I'll always listen, Niko."

"Sometimes I find decisions difficult to make," said Nikolaus. "When that happens, I go to Marina. She's always willing to listen as well. She might ask a few questions but mostly she listens. I talk on and on and before I know it, I have my answer. Decisions seem to come easier if someone just listens. It's odd how it works that way. So, I need to tell you a few things."

Nikolaus began his story. "The terrible storm that Calypso remembered was as bad as the one that hit Caesarea on your wedding day. At one point the wind sounded like a thousand chariots racing down a mountainside. It was after that storm; my father became a different man. He would hole up in his library for entire days, not even coming out to eat. Mother took him food. I would sneak in after he would finally leave the room to see what he was working on. Nothing. No designs, no charts, no graphs. His work materials were dusty with neglect. I know he was studying the Prophecy Box. I know this because he started etching predictions on the public stones in the forum. There he would stand chisel and hammer in hand, working away on a slab of limestone. He never chalked his predictions on the public slate. Of course, those were washed off every day. He wanted a permanent record. At first, people laughed at him but not for long. His predictions were always right. Do you know when Tiberius sent Father that offer to be his chief architect?"

Adan looked over at Nikolaus. "Tell me."

"After Father successfully predicted a solar eclipse to the exact day and *hour*. How is that possible? The whole city buzzed like a colony of bees on a hot day. That did the trick. He was soon making more money in a month than he once made in a year. After the sun went black with only a golden ring around it, people thought Father to be a great sorcerer. I never told you about his predictions coming true because I honestly thought you wouldn't believe me. The offer from Emperor Tiberius was delivered to Father within four months."

A flash of light caught their attention. A shooting star streaked across the sky. "What do you think those lights are?" asked Nikolaus. "Once in a while, you can see many of them in one night, but most of the time it's a single flash of light. My mother used to tell me it was stray sparks from the lightning bolt of Zeus."

Adan grunted with amusement. "My mother used to tell me that it was a demon ripping at the black sackcloth that Mother Earth covered herself with every night. The demon always failed to harm Mother Earth because Father Sun would immediately mend the cloth. She said the stars were pin holes that Father Sun left un-mended so Mother Earth would know he was still there, watching over her." Adan sighed pensively. "I miss my mother's stories. I think she made them up, herself. Misha loved them as much as I did."

Nikolaus smiled. "Your mother had quite an imagination. I wish I could have met her."

"She was complicated and unpredictable in everything except her love for family. She adored my father, and me, and Misha. I still miss her, after all these years," said Adan wistfully. "I was fascinated by her when I was a child. You remember how I told you that Misha used to say that she was a tiger transformed into a woman and I was her cub."

"Misha was your aunt, right?"

"Great aunt. She was my mother's aunt," said Adan. "When I looked into my mother's eyes, I could see the tiger in her but she had the heart of a lamb. I could see that my parents cherished each other, but I didn't understand the depth of their connection until many years later. It's amazing how one can see something so obvious, yet completely miss its significance."

Nikolaus pointed to the sky. "I wonder what would happen if they could touch each other, Venus and the moon. And there's Mars."

Adan pointed a short distance away. "And there's Jupiter."

"How do you know that's not Saturn?"

"Jupiter is brighter and looks a tiny bit larger," said Adan as he scanned the inky blackness.

"Ah, I'm always getting those two mixed up," admitted Nikolaus. "Why don't they ever run into each other? All the planets, the moon, and the sun go in the same line from east to west."

"I don't know. Maybe if we can find a scholar from the *Magi*, he can tell us."

A comfortable silence settled over them as the ocean gently swayed the ship to and fro. A pod of sleeping dolphins floated past the ship. The tops of their heads and fins reflected the light of the moon. They moved with the bobbing waves but stayed close together with the smallest dolphins in the center. One dolphin slapped the surface of the water with its tail as if making a course correction.

"Did you see that?" asked Nikolaus.

"Um-hum." Adan thought for a moment. "I think it was dreaming."

"Really. You think animals dream?"

"Dogs do. They start jerking their legs like they're running and make sort of excited barking noises."

"What would a dolphin dream about?" Nikolaus asked with an amused tone.

"Peaceful seas with no sharks or fishing nets." Adan gave his brother a sidelong look. "Just like us."

Nikolaus laughed. "How do you think dolphins and whales sleep at night?"

"I don't know. I never thought about it. But it is curious. Even though their noses are in the top of their heads, you'd think an unexpected wave would slosh over them and wake them up, all sputtering and snorting and such. But that's not what happens. Look!" He pointed at several dolphins that were temporarily submerged by a larger than normal wave. There was no reaction. They simply came back up to the surface.

"You think they just know when to close up their noses," suggested Nikolaus, "as if they can sense the wave coming?"

"How could they do that? They're asleep."

"That's just it," insisted Nikolaus, "maybe they've got some sixth sense that is aware of the motions of the waves and their sleeping brains are on 'duty' in a manner of speaking. Their noses close up automatically in their sleep."

"Umm, you might be on to something. Maybe it's like the way our sleeping brains keep us from falling out of bed. It doesn't matter how narrow the bed is, we never fall out and we're sound asleep." Adan considered another factor. "And why don't they roll around in the water? What keeps them upright?" asked Adan.

"*Ohe*, I got another question. How do they stay together in a group, floating along in the water, asleep? How come they don't float apart? Ships do if you set the rudder in place and don't correct your course. The ships eventually lose sight of each other."

"Well, I guess that settles it. Dolphins are a whole lot smarter than people," said Adan with a grin. They fell into a peaceful silence.

Nikolaus was the first to speak again. "Adan, as much as I hate the idea, I think we have to find Captain Egnatian. He holds the key to this mystery. If he murdered my family to steal the Prophecy Box, he didn't do it on his own, as I mentioned before. I mean, how could he have known about it and how did he know Father had it?"

Nikolaus interrupted the quiet by snapping his fingers. "I just remembered something. Mother had offered to book our passage when Father said we were going to Rome. Father said the arrangements were already made and. . ." He gaped at Adan with a sudden rush of buried memory. "Adan, why didn't I remember this before? Father told my mother that the arrangements were already made and Tiberius had paid for it. Egnatian lied! He said we owned for our passage and that's why we were sold as slaves." Grief washed over him. Suddenly, he was reliving the trauma of being led, shackled and humiliated, to the auction block.

"Niko, I am so sorry. You were in shock from grief. People get confused and forgetful when terrible things happen. You were facing the greatest loss of your life and could barely function. As it was, things turned out the way they should, however, I'm really sorry you and Dionysia were forced into slavery." He paused to let his words soak in and then gently changed the subject.

"I wonder if the man your sister saw arguing with Nicandros was Balthazar and he hired Egnatian to steal the box," Adan suggested.

"Would a *magus* do that?" asked Nikolaus. "Besides, the man confronted Father at our house and left without it. Would a violent man do that?'

"Maybe if Balthazar was squeamish about doing violence himself but not above paying others to do it. Or, maybe it wasn't Balthazar but the man who originally stole it. Maybe he asked Nicandros to figure out how to use it and wanted it back. Nicandros refused so the thief hired Egnatian." Adan considered the possibilities. "I hate to agree with you on this, Niko. But I think you're right. We need to find Egnatian."

✳✳✳

Decades earlier, when Nikolaus was twelve years old, events took place that he never could have imagined. His life was on a collision course with evil men, one of great power, and one barely surviving. The powerful one was an emperor, and the other one leased a ship. They were equally dangerous.

Emperor Tiberius was fascinated with anything of the supernatural. Ever since he learned of the Child King, born in Bethlehem, he was intrigued. Then he was told that the Child King had been killed by order of King Herod the Great. Decades later, stories came to Rome about a man named Yeshua who could heal every illness, deformity, or handicap, and even raise the dead back to life. There were nights when sleep fled and fear wrapped its gnarled hands around his heart, warning him that Death was approaching. He wondered if Yeshua was the Child King who Herod had killed, yet raised from the dead, giving him power over the natural world.

Tiberius was convinced that Yeshua's power was real. He was preparing to send for the Nazarene to make him demonstrate his power by resurrecting Tiberius, himself. Then word came that Pontius Pilate had given the order to crucify Yeshua. The emperor was furious. He left instructions for Caligula, who would succeed him, to exile Pilate to Gaul, a place Romans believed to be primitive and peopled by repulsive barbarians. Caligula was only too happy to comply since he despised Pontius Pilate. There were whispered rumors that Pilate committed suicide because he couldn't bear the humiliation of exile. Others suspected that he died from pneumonia since he was unaccustomed to the cold climate of the northern Alps. Officially, there was no definitive cause of death ever recorded. It simply wasn't important to anyone at the time.

Emperor Tiberius Claudius Nero, son of Augustus, who was one of the greatest generals Rome had ever known. Augustus's conquests had built the foundations for the northern provinces, adding substantially to the empire. Tiberius inherited the most successful and massive empire ever known at the time. By offering citizenship to anyone willing to pay the price, Rome acquired a huge diversity of loyal citizens along with their expertise and manpower.

Emperor Tiberius was able to glean the best soothsayers throughout the empire by offering the highest level of citizenship to the foreign-born and a substantial salary, but he could never find anyone who could predict the future with one hundred percent accuracy. His body turned against him as he aged. He became obsessed with the fear of, not so much death itself, but how he would die. He was convinced Gaius, known as Caligula, wanted to poison him. Gaius was his great nephew who he adopted as his son to ensure the continuation of the Julio-Claudian dynasty. If he knew how and when he would die, he would know how to protect himself.

Tiberius had lost hope until his soothsayers brought him news of a magical device that told the future. It was called the Prophecy Box. Tiberius yearned to test the device and discern its secrets. He waited impatiently for news of its whereabouts from the many spies he employed.

The Greek spies finally brought him good news. There was a man in Athens who made amazing predictions and was never wrong. He had even predicted a solar eclipse to the exact hour. His name was Nicandros Kokinos and he was an architect. When Tiberius heard this, his narrow lips curled into a grim smile as his watery eyes gleamed with hope. He had to entice this Greek to come to Rome. If the man were offered a life-long career, he would bring all of his possessions, including the treasured Prophecy Box if he possessed it. If Kokinos did not have the box, Tiberius would let him live if he told him how he predicted the eclipse. If Kokinos did have the box, the assassin Tiberius had hired would bring it to him and eliminate the family.

An incredibly generous offer, including the highest-level citizenship, was sent to Nicandros Kokinos and he accepted. Travel instructions were conveyed and received. The Kokinos family was to board a ship owned by Captain Egnatian who would make sure they were comfortable and pampered. The captain had other orders as well. The payment offered for his service was astonishing. Egnatian would live in decadent luxury for the rest of his life and never questioned the emperor's intentions.

***

Captain Egnatian lounged against the life rail of his ship supervising his crew as they hauled supplies aboard. He needed to pull anchor soon if he was going to get out of port before sunset. He still couldn't believe how his luck had turned around. He had done other jobs for the emperor but never anything for such a high payment. Tiberius had many assassins under his employment, but he was the only one with his own ship. Egnatian smiled to think what he would do with all that money Tiberius would pay him.

Egnatian straightened up when he saw Nicandros, his wife, and seven children, five girls and two boys, standing on the pier. He frowned when Nicandros stopped and took hold of his wife's arm. She looked at him with surprise and impatience. She started to step onto the gangway but he pulled her back. She seemed to speak angrily to him. He pointed at the bow of the ship where the name was carved and painted in black lettering. He said something that made his wife lose all patience. She turned her back on him and whisked her children up the gangway. Finally, Nicandros followed them onto the ship.

Egnatian had already decided on using poison to murder them. It was the easiest and most popular method of assassination but there was one problem. He had been instructed to make their deaths look like illness. That meant that a few of his own crew would have to be sacrificed. He never considered that the deaths of crewmen would be seen as supernatural events. He thought his plan was foolproof until he saw the eldest daughter, Dionysia. Her beauty was breath-taking. His heart melted as he looked upon her. His breathing quickened at the sound of her voice. The captain knew he could not murder her but surely the death of her family would leave her desperate for a savior. He was convinced that Dionysia would be so grateful for his loving attention after she was alone in the world, she would welcome his marriage proposal. He imagined her fawning over him and seeing to his every wish.

Captain Egnatian was infuriated when he learned that his crew blamed Dionysia for the deaths of the crewmen he had poisoned. He had seriously miscalculated the depths of their superstitions about albinos being demons from the underworld. He didn't hesitate to knife the ringleader when the man nearly threw Dionysia overboard.

When the crewman's dead body was pushed over the life rail into the sea, the rest of the crew backed off. Still, even after saving her life, the bewitching Dionysia rebuffed his affections.

After the family was dead, Egnatian claimed that Nicandros owed for the family's passage and used that against Dionysia and her brother, Nikolaus. No one in the crew knew that Emperor Tiberius was covering all their costs. When the siblings could not pay, he arranged for their arrest in Ostia, the port at the mouth of the *Tiberius* River. They were sold as slaves to pay for their passage.

Luck was still not on Egnatian's side. A prosperous slave trader, representing a few wealthy men, outbid him for Dionysia. Egnatian was desperate. He tried offering the slave trader future free passage on his ship, anytime, anywhere. The man was not interested. Egnatian knew he had one item that no one would resist. He had the Prophecy Box. Just the look of the polished cypress box with the three extraordinary decoration stones told him that this was a priceless treasure. After all, Tiberius had offered a huge sum to acquire the box. Egnatian threw caution overboard as easily as he had thrown his crewman's dead body. He offered the box in exchange for Dionysia.

The slave trader took the box in hand. He studied the stones. He opened the box and manipulated the dials. He was intrigued as the wheels turned with a musical click-click-click. He knew it was far more valuable than one fiery-haired slave and agreed to the trade. They left the inn where the slave trader was staying to walk to the cheap, rundown inn where he kept his newly acquired slaves under guard. When they reached the suite of rooms holding the slaves, Egnatian handed the box over. The slave trader took it in hand just as a guard moved into action. The next thing Egnatian knew, he was regaining consciousness in an alleyway somewhere in Ostia, alone. The Prophecy Box and Dionysia were long gone.

Egnatian was not only livid and lovesick; he was terrified. He had lost everything. What would he tell Emperor Tiberius? He couldn't hide. He would be hunted down if he didn't appear before the deadline. What would he do? He decided he could talk his way out of this mess like he always did. Lies and exaggerated half-truths had served him well in the past. Why would Tiberius react any differently than all the others he had deceived? The emperor was old and probably losing his intellect. He told himself that he had never met anyone he couldn't manipulate. He conveniently "forgot" how the slave trader had tricked him.

The captain took a barge up the river to Rome and made an appointment to see the emperor. When his name was announced, he was shown into the reception hall immediately. Tiberius looked up as Egnatian entered the elaborately decorated hall where all visitors were received. The emperor's gloating smile melted from his face when he saw that Egnatian was empty-handed.

"Where is my Prophecy Box?" shrieked the emperor.

Egnatian knelt on one knee and bowed his head. "Stolen, Your Excellency, right off my ship. I have identified the culprit and received word that my men have him in custody. I will go and retrieve the box and kill the thief for you, free of charge. It is only a matter of time before the box is in your hands."

Tiberius rose from his throne like a cobra rising to strike. "If you are lying to me, I'll have you crucified. Tell me! What was inside the box?"

"There were dials and wheels with cogs and levers. There were instructions written in Greek on the framework of the wheels. Words and symbols and numbers. I swear this to you, Your Excellency, I will have the box for you as soon as humanly possible. As for the architect and his family, I was quite successful in eliminating them." Egnatian's results had always pleased the emperor in the past. Surely, he would give him a second chance.

Tiberius's mouth worked with anger as he struggled to speak. "Tell me the name of the man who stole my property!"

Egnatian swallowed down the bile that rose in his throat. He didn't dare lose his only leverage against the old man.

"Your Excellency, his name would do you no good since it is an alias. Fortunately, you don't need his name since I have the man in custody. I will bring the box as soon as possible. Because of the extra time it will require for you to take possession of the box, I will cancel the debt you owe me for eliminating the family in question."

Egnatian misunderstood the astonished expression on the old man's face. "You remember, Your Excellency, you told me to make it look like they died from sickness. I had to poison a few of my crewmen to accomplish that."

The old man's eyes seemed to bulge out of his head as his mouth gaped open.

Again, Egnatian misunderstood. "Your Excellency, I made sure none of them were Roman citizens, of course."

Tiberius looked at Egnatian as if he had sprouted tentacles from his head. The old man slowly closed his mouth. His eyes dangerously narrowed to slits. If Egnatian had been paying better attention, he would have noticed the slight hand signal the old man gave to his Master-at-Arms. Then he leaned back and gave Egnatian a bitter smile.

"If your men could bring word that the thief was in custody, why didn't they simply bring you *the thief*, along with *my property*?"

Egnatian never got the chance to answer. Four well-armed, huge men lifted him from the ground by his arms and legs.

Tiberius ground words between his yellowed teeth. "You will take them to the thief and get back my property, or they will crucify you on the mast of your ship!" The emperor watched his soldiers carry the horrified man from the reception hall. He signaled his Master-at-Arms to approach. "Tell your men, as soon as they have the box, to kill that disgusting little worm. Tell them, I want to see that box in my hands before the sun sets after the full moon."

The full moon came but the box never did. Years passed, yet Tiberius could never get past his obsession until his death. The power mongers of Rome speculated that Caligula poisoned the old man because he was tired of waiting for him to die. Caligula also knew of his great uncle's obsession with the Prophecy Box but did not see it as a precious treasure. It was something to distract from his own grandiose conception of himself. He was indifferent with things others valued. He routinely dropped priceless pearls into wine to watch them fizzle away or draped strings of pearls around the neck of his horse, Incitatus. Caligula planned to destroy the box if it surfaced. He hated anything or anyone viewed to be more powerful than himself.

The soldiers assigned to escort Egnatian to the Prophecy Box soon learned he was lying. This put them in a precarious position and a very bad mood. They would have killed him if not for his escape, which complicated things. When they returned to the Master-at-Arms, they pointed out that Egnatian was not officially a prisoner, and therefore, they should not be executed. The Master-at-Arms disagreed. Their only consolation before they died was that Egnatian did not escape unharmed.

Chapter 18

The Star of Bethlehem

———⚬⚬⚬———

Calypso and Pomona hugged each other before the four travelers left the *Child of the Ocean.* Calypso and Calais promised that they would return to the ship. Aurelius pulled Adan and Nikolaus aside to tell them that the maintenance on the ship would be delayed a few days, which actually gave him time to run a small cargo over to a nearby island and back. When he returned, the ship would be pulled into dry dock. That would give Adan and Nikolaus a total of eight days before they would need to meet back together in Kantharos Harbor. Adan assured him that the extra time served their purposes as well. The foursome wished Pomona and Aurelius fair sailing and good profit on their cargo.

Adan hired a carriage and told the driver to go to the Roman garrison first. He wanted to get the task out of the way. As usual, Nikolaus and Calais waited in the carriage and chatted with Calypso until Adan came back. He commented on how impressed he was with how the Athens commander was running the garrison and had few complaints. The report to Tacitus was short but informative and positive. Soon, they were on the search for Daniel.

Calypso had no way of knowing where Daniel lived in Athens if he were still there. Adan suggested that they start with the magistrate's office in the city's forum. A few questions revealed that Daniel was a well-known citizen. Directions were given and the four travelers eventually found their way to a villa at the top of a hill. Adan turned to look back at the city when they reached the top of the street. He studied the layout of the sprawling town and marveled at the lack of a systematic pattern. Roman cities were designed with alternative one-way streets to allow for uncongested wagon and pedestrian travel. The one-way streets also left more room for buildings.

Dulcibella sprang into Adan's thoughts as she did every day. He was growing weary being away from her and the family he so dearly loved, despite Herod's threat. He swore in his heart that this would be his last voluntary journey to distant lands. He would see this mission through and, hopefully, help Nikolaus learn the secret that haunted the Kokinos clan of the ruby. After this mission was over, he would go home for good and face Herod, yet again. He dismissed the carriage driver and followed the others to the front gate of the villa.

Someone pulled the bell rope at the courtyard gate and Adan braced himself for whatever came next. Eventually, the gate swung open and a middle-aged woman bowed her head to them.

"Greetings from the home of Daniel. Please state your names and reason for calling?"

Nikolaus smiled at the formal greeting. He introduced the others. "Please tell your master that we wish to speak with him about a most urgent matter. Urgent to me, personally, Nikolaus Longinus."

The woman bowed again and backed away to allow them to enter the courtyard. "Wait here, please, I will tell my master." She trotted off for the front door and disappeared inside.

Presently, the door opened and an older man appeared in the doorway. "I am Daniel. What is your business with me?" He scanned the group until his gaze fell on Adan. He gasped softly and stammered, "Y-you are the centurion."

Adan frowned in confusion. "Yes, I am *a* centurion."

Nikolaus stepped forward despite the awkward moment. He placed his hand over his heart. "I am Nikolaus Longinus. This is my brother, Centurion Adan Clovius Longinus. Calypso, and her son, Calais Antipas. We wish to speak to you about the death of Balthazar's mentor, known only to us as the chief astrologer, or Master. Will you speak with us?"

Daniel studied them with intelligent, deep-brown eyes, but again, he concentrated his focus on Adan. "Centurion Longinus, are you here as a soldier or a private citizen?"

"Both, but only as a private citizen in regard to this visit. I have come to help my brother, adopted brother, learn what happened to his family after they left Athens, decades ago. His family, except for one sister and himself, died mysteriously on board a ship bound for Rome. His father, Nicandros Kokinos had been offered. . ."

Daniel's face drained of color. He jerked his head in Nikolaus's direction. "You are the son of Nicandros Kokinos?"

Nikolaus saw his reaction and hung his head. "It is true then. My father killed the chief astrologer and stole the Prophecy Box, didn't he?"

Daniel raised his chin with determination as color crept back into his face. "Please, come in. Let us go to my terrace to talk. You will find the view quite beautiful and relaxing. I see that you are searching for the truth, Nikolaus, no matter how terrible it may be. I will answer your questions. I even have a few that you might answer for me."

Daniel led his guests to the back of the house to a patio that opened out to a lush garden with a central fountain. The sound of the water splashing into the basin was soothing. The mist from the cascading water cooled the air. There were shade trees along with fig and apple trees. He waved a hand at the cushioned bench that faced the garden. Daniel pulled up a chair to partially face the bench but not block the view of the garden. He clapped his hands when he sat. The same woman soon appeared in the doorway. "Refreshments for my guests. And will you honor me by accepting an invitation to dine in my home tonight?"

They glanced at each other and happily accepted the invitation.

"Tell Cook that they will be staying for dinner."

The woman hurried away.

Daniel turned his attention on Nikolaus. "Tell me how you know Nicandros killed Master Kyril?"

"Kyril? That is the first time we've heard his name," said Adan.

"That is understandable," said Daniel. "He only allowed a select few to call him by his name. I, myself, always addressed him as Master."

Nikolaus told Daniel why he suspected his father. "I don't know if father had anything to do with Master Kyril's death or actually stole the box, but I saw him with the box not long after the storm that nearly wrecked Athens."

Daniel's eyebrows shot up. "Ah! Yes. The storm occurred the very night Master Kyril died. There were those among the *Magi* that believed his vengeful spirit conjured that storm to punish Athens for allowing his death." Daniel touched his hand to his chest. "I, myself, do not believe such things. A storm is an agitation of the forces of nature allowed by Yahweh to reveal his great power."

"Yahweh and Yeshua show their great power in countless ways," said Calais.

"How do you know of Yahweh? You did not learn about the Creator from your mother, Calypso." Daniel looked at her. "Even though you did not go by that name when I knew you, I remember that you did not believe in God."

Calypso smiled at his recognition of her. "You remember me?"

"I do, Kori. Is that not what your father always called you? Kori, the Greek word for daughter. Was Kori truly your given name?"

"Yes, it was. Since Father died, I have not wanted to be called by that name." She explained how Calypso became her name and that she had used it ever since. "I came to believe in Yahweh because of the testimony of my son, Antipas. He taught me the Way of Yeshua."

Daniel smiled approvingly. "I am most pleased to hear that. As for me, you must remember, my name was not Daniel then. Balthazar forbade me to assume it."

"Why is that?" asked Adan.

"Balthazar may have been born in Babylon, but he was not Babylonian. He was an Israelite. His descendants were exiled to Babylon, but he never lost his identity as a son of Abraham. He studied the script of the prophets constantly. His most revered prophets were Isaiah, Ezekiel, and Daniel. He accused me of sacrilege when I chose the name Daniel to honor the 'birth' of my new self when I was baptized into the Way. Balthazar was furious with me when I explained my reasoning and slapped my face. No one had ever struck me before. Then he called me a blasphemer because I had spoken Yeshua's name aloud."

"What!" cried Adan and Nikolaus at once.

Calais glanced at his mother. "John told me that there are those who believe that Yeshua's name was so sacred, it must not be spoken with human lips. They refer to him as Lord, Savior, or Emmanuel, but never by his name."

"Balthazar was a very difficult man to—understand," said Daniel. "Calypso, did you tell them how he was one of the *Magi* that carried a special gift to Yeshua as a child in Bethlehem?"

"I could only tell them what my father heard from others," she said, "since we were not allowed into Mary and Joseph's home."

"I will never forget that day." Daniel paused to gather his thoughts before he continued. "Let me start from the beginning. I was a young boy when I was apprenticed to Balthazar even when he was still the assistant to Master Kyril. I was serving at table when a number of the *Magi* began to discuss the father of all magic, a man named Zarathustra. He was a Persian prophet, religious reformer, and a great leader of spiritual matters. We honor him as the first true philosopher and was a founder of the School of the *Magi*. He recorded a great prediction that followed in line with the prediction in Isaiah's writings. *'The people who walked in darkness have seen a great light; those who dwell in the land of the shadow of death, upon them the light has shined,'* for all mankind."

Daniel smiled at the eagerness in their expressions. "You see, there is a double meaning in the word 'light.' Zarathustra believed that a great Light would be born that would be the one and only true Savior of all mankind. He also believed that a great light—a star—would signal the birth of the Savior, even unto the Gentiles, born outside the descendants of Abraham. Zarathustra said that this Light would be born within the nation of Judea and the family of Abraham. John, son of Zebedee said it best. *In Him was life, and the life was the light of men. And the light shines in the darkness, and the darkness did not comprehend it.* Again, there is a double meaning to 'did not comprehend it.' Nonbelievers refuse to comprehend the Light of Yeshua just like we could not comprehend the presence of the star of Bethlehem, the great light amidst the darkness."

Nikolaus smiled with satisfaction. "The star, itself, was beyond understanding? Then it is true. The Prophecy Box predicted the appearance of that great star."

Daniel's head jerked toward Nikolaus. "Absolutely *not!* The written predictions of the birth of the Savior were given to men by the Holy Spirit of God. No human or human-made object could predict when the great star would appear. The Prophecy Box can only predict the natural movements of celestial objects. The star was a *supernatural* object."

Calais shook his head in frustration. "I don't understand. Doesn't the Prophecy Box hold all the secrets of the universe."

Daniel laughed good-naturedly. "No, Calais. The box is a wonder and was invented by men of amazing genius who discovered the orderly behavior of the heavens. However, it only predicts the natural procession of the earth, moon, and planets in relation to each other. It does not have supernatural power. The box can predict the eclipses of the sun and the moon, decades in advance, even to the exact day and hour. Before the Prophecy Box, most celestial events were a surprise, seemingly random with no pattern or process. With the box we know that all workings of the skies follow an orderly procession of movement. The universe is not a place of chaos. The Prophecy Box is accurate because the earth and the planets orbit around the sun and the moon orbits around the earth *in precise patterns*. Archimedes and Eratosthenes, who determined the circumference of the earth, knew this hundreds of years ago. Archimedes even determined the order of the planets by distance from the sun by simple observation."

"What do you mean?" asked Nikolaus. "Aren't they the same distance from the sun?"

"No, each has its own orbit," said Daniel emphatically. "One must observe their change of position from one night to the next. The faster the change of position, the closer to the sun. The slower the change of position, the farther away from the sun. Apparently, all of the planets orbit at the same speed. Mercury is the closest, Saturn is the farthest, and Earth is third from the sun."

This was amazing news to all of them, except Calypso. Balthazar had explained the distances of the planets to her many years ago.

Daniel looked from one to the other with deliberation. "Don't you see? There was absolutely no explanation for the appearance of that phenomenal star. The *Magi* studied the records in the Library of Alexandria. We know of stars that suddenly brighten for weeks and can even be seen in the day and then disappear. There are comets that appear unexpectedly and then go back where they came, always in the same pattern. The stars stay in their constellations. The constellations move as a whole. There is order in the heavens. Even the bright flashes of light one can see singularly or sometimes many over several nights, appear to come from specific constellations."

"What made Yeshua's star more spectacular than a comet or a day star?" asked Adan.

"It must not have been terribly spectacular," pointed out Calais. "John explained to me that King Herod *secretly called the wise men and determined from them what time the star appeared.* As my mother has asked, why didn't Herod and his councilmen see it for themselves?"

Daniel gestured dismissively. "Because the star was in the east. We lived in the Far East and the star was east of us. Either Herod's astrologers were not paying attention or it simply wasn't visible to them. Let me explain. The planets move from east to west in precise orbits, advancing their progress each night. Yes? The stars are fixed in their constellations but the constellations shift position a little bit each night, also from east to west.. They progress every month until one can observe all of them within a year's time if you always look in the same region of the sky every night."

"Yes, I have observed that," said Adan.

"Then you'll understand what I tell you is truly miraculous. It was the brightest star I've ever seen. It sparkled like a brilliant blue *diamanti*. It was beautiful. More beautiful than the planet, Venus." Daniel raised a finger for emphasis. "Yet, its diamond-like appearance was *not* the miracle." He glanced at each of them.

Calypso felt a chill run up her spine. "What was the miracle, Daniel?"

"The Messiah's star never moved! Night after night, it *never* changed position. Always in the east. Always the same distance above the horizon. We saw it at sunset. We saw it at sunrise. In—the—same—place! That is simply not possible. The sun, the moon, the planets, even the stars appear to move from east to west because *the earth rotates*. Aristarchus proved over three hundred years ago that the earth turns once on its axis every day. That's why we have day and night. Therefore, the Messiah's star was moving directly in line with the specific location of the School of the *Magi*, causing it to appear to be motionless. The star was moving with us. There could be no other explanation. When the caravan left, heading west for Jerusalem, the star disappeared. Then it reappeared as soon as we left Jerusalem. *When they saw the star, they rejoiced with great excitement,* as did I. We did not expect to see it again. There is significance in that the star appeared in the east. It is prophesized that when Yeshua comes to earth again, he will appear in the east. It is written, 'For as the lightning comes from the east and flashes to the west, so will be the coming of the Son of Man.'"

"Why would the *Magi* be blessed with the announcement of Yeshua's birth," asked Calais.

"The *Magi* are the descendants of Abraham exiled to Babylon. We never lost faith in Yahweh and his promise of deliverance out of Babylon. Yet, our descendants stayed behind under Yahweh's watchful eye. We were called to remain as witnesses of Yahweh to the Babylonians."

Daniel clasped his hands together in eagerness to tell them more. "As if the star was not astonishing enough, it took up a new position when it reappeared. It was now south of us, over Bethlehem. It is a two-hour walk to Bethlehem from Jerusalem, as you know. The star seemed to move closer and closer as we approached the city. Then a single ray of light shined down directly upon one house. *And when they came into the house, they saw the young Child with Mary, His mother, and fell down and worshipped Him.*"

Daniel's voice softened. "He was about two years old, no longer an infant. He had the most curious expression I have ever seen on such a young child's face. He seemed to understand why we were there even at his young age. Each of us gave a personal gift to him. Then the gold, frankincense, and myrrh were placed at his feet. When the last gift was presented, he stood up, placed his hand over his heart and said, 'Thank you for these gifts. They will never be forgotten.' I was amazed that such a young child could speak with such distinction. He did not say, 'I'll never forget.' No, he said, 'They will never be forgotten.' We believe our tribute will be recorded in history."

Daniel took a sip of wine, then continued. "King Herod had instructed us to find the Child and report back to him. All of the chief astrologers were warned in identical dreams not to return to Herod. Being unfamiliar with the area, we quickly sought a guide to show us another way. A young man, who was a shepherd since he was a child, volunteered to lead us through the hills which only shepherds use. He amazed us with his story about Yeshua. It turned out that he had been with his fellow shepherds the night Yeshua was born. An angel appeared, shining with the glory of God, and told them their Savior had been born in the city of David. He said that *suddenly there was with the angel a multitude of the heavenly host praising God and saying: Glory to God in the highest, and on earth peace, goodwill toward men!'* After the angels were gone, he and the others found *the Babe wrapped in swaddling cloths, lying in a manger.* We marveled at his story and asked him many questions. His description of the sleeping Child, and his mother, and Joseph touched our hearts."

For a few moments, no one spoke. Adan frowned as jealousy stung his heart. These men had seen Yeshua as a healthy, young child free from agony and humiliation. Daniel and the shepherd witnessed a beautiful moment with Yeshua. Adan's first meeting with Yeshua had been nothing but agony and humiliation. Yeshua was bloodied and beaten, dying from the worst torture, under Adan's supervision. Nausea and a cold sweat made his face grow pale as the image of Yeshua's suffering filled his mind. He looked up to find all of them staring at him.

"Are you alright?" Nikolaus asked with concern.

Adan waved him off, unable to answer.

"Adan, I can see that you suffer a terrible guilt," stated Daniel. "You are not the only one who carries such pain in your heart? There is more to my story. Herod knew that we were not coming back within a few days of our visit. He sent in his soldiers to kill every male child two years old and younger in Bethlehem! He learned of the Child King—from us! He asked when the star appeared to know how old Yeshua was! That's why he ordered the deaths of two-year-old male children." Daniel lowered his head in shame.

Then he continued, "We said, *'Where is He who has been born King of the Jews? For we have seen His star in the East and have come to worship Him.'* As soon as those words were spoken, we could see that Herod was deeply troubled. He knew the prophecy of a coming Messiah, *'For out of you shall come a Ruler Who will shepherd My people Israel'* He thought the Messiah would be an earthly king who would take the throne away from his dynasty." He passed his hand over his brow as if trying to wipe away the memory. "His arrogance knew no bounds since he thought he could overpower God's will."

Daniel's voice shook as he spoke. "Innocent babies, torn from their parents' arms. Men and women screaming and beaten back as the soldiers killed their children." Daniel jabbed a finger in his chest. "We told Herod the King of the Jews has been born! Immediately, he dismissed us so he could consult with his chief priests and scribes. He learned from them that the Christ Child was to be born in Bethlehem. We should have been suspicious when he met with us *in secret* and sent us to Bethlehem. Why did he meet with us in secret? Why didn't he want the people to know that their long-awaited Messiah had been born?" Daniel answered his own question. "Because he intended to murder the Child and greatly feared what the people would do rather than fearing what God would do."

Daniel pursed his lips in anger. "We were so naïve! We even believed Herod when he said, '*Go and search carefully for the young Child, and bring back word to me, that I may worship Him also.*' How could we have been so stupid to think he would want to worship *anyone*, other than himself? For years, we didn't know if Yeshua had been killed, but then word came to us that he and his family were living in Nazareth after Herod died."

Daniel paused and sighed with sorrow. "I still grieve for being involved in the slaughter of those children. Sometimes I feel a terrible misery pierce my heart when I see a young boy smiling into his mother's face, so loving and pure. Countless times, I have wished that we had never declared the birth of the Messiah to anyone in Jerusalem."

"But you didn't know the star would show the way," said Nikolaus. "You said it didn't appear again until you left Jerusalem. How could you have known about Bethlehem if you didn't ask?"

"But we did know!" cried Daniel. "The prophet Micah wrote, '*But you, Bethlehem Ephrathah, although you are small among the tribes of Judah, from you will come forth for Me one who will be ruler over Israel. His origins are from of old, from ancient days.*' We had access to these prophecies of the Messiah at the Library of Alexandria. We knew the Child would be born in Bethlehem but we arrived nearly two years after his birth, so we assumed he would be in Jerusalem, by then. To this day, I cannot understand why God did not save the children yet warned *us* away from Herod. We might as well have put the swords in the soldiers' hands, ourselves."

Adan frowned in concentration. "Perhaps, God warned the *Magi* away from Herod to show that you were not accountable for the deaths of the children. Yeshua saves each of us from our *own* sin but *not* from the sins of others. Everyone has the free will to choose and some will become victims of the choices of others. God allowed the children to be murdered by Herod and his desire to do evil. Their deaths were Herod's orders—not yours. God allowed Yeshua, his own Son, innocent of any evil, to also be murdered for our salvation. And just as Yeshua lives again, forever, so do those children of Bethlehem in heaven. The sacrifice of the innocent children was a foreshadowing of the sacrifice of Yeshua. Sometimes terrible things are required for reasons we may not understand, or accept."

"Like crucifying Yeshua," said Daniel, directing his gaze at Adan. "I know who you are, Centurion Longinus. I know the task for which you were chosen cuts your heart to this day. You see Yeshua's agony in your mind just as I picture the agony of slaughtered children."

Adan solemnly nodded.

"You are the Samaritan in the parable Yeshua told when he defined a true neighbor. When the Samaritan found a man beaten, robbed, and left for dead, he stopped and gave aid. You did that when you stopped and gave aid to Zacchaeus when he was being assaulted and robbed. You chased away the criminals and took Zacchaeus to his home."

Adan was amazed. "How can you possibly know about that?"

"God cannot be silenced. He has ways of spreading messages of good will," answered Daniel. "Yeshua was treated much like the innocent man in the parable. A hated enemy of the Jews gave the brutalized man comfort when his own people left him for dead. You carried out the execution, Adan, but you have been following Yeshua's example to this day. Someone had to be the executioner. God always chooses certain people for certain reasons and you have been fulfilling his plan for you ever since."

Calypso looked from Daniel to Adan. "My son, Antipas, taught me many things about the love of Yahweh. It is not Yahweh or Yeshua that keeps the horrible memories of death in your minds. The Lord forgave you, Adan. He showed it by saving you from Herod Agrippa's attempts to execute you. The Lord forgave you, Daniel. He showed it by warning the *Magi* away from Herod Agrippa's grandfather, Herodes Magnus. Magnus means "great" in Latin but he is really the "least" because he attempted to circumvent God's plan by trying to murder the Christ Child."

Daniel considered her words. The tension in his expression evaporated. "Perhaps, you are right. Perhaps someday, I will visual those children in perfect peace in heaven. Adan, perhaps someday, you will only think of Yeshua as he was that Sunday morning when he greeted you in the garden."

Again, surprise flashed across Adan's face. "Who told you these things?"

"Balthazar told me about your experiences and to expect you. I recognized you when I opened the door, even before I recognized you, Calypso."

She smiled at him in appreciation.

"Why did Balthazar tell you to expect me?" asked Adan.

"To give you instructions. God trusted you with the most horrendous task of all. It is clear that he trusts you with another."

"What is it?" Adan apprehensively crossed his arms.

"A treasure hunt. Let me explain. Balthazar regained possession of the Prophecy Box. He told me everything just before he died. He learned that a street beggar saw Nicandros leave the house, carrying a wooden chest, the day Master Kyril died. The beggar had some dealings with Nicandros after that and learned his name. Balthazar stopped to give him alms and the beggar offered information about Master Kyril for a price. Balthazar followed Nicandros Kokinos to Thessalonica to confront him. It didn't go well. Before Balthazar could convince a judge to issue a warrant on Nicandros, he had sailed to Rome and died on the way there."

"On a ship owned by Captain Egnatian," grumbled Nikolaus. "It was *The Griffin*."

"Balthazar followed. . ." Daniel suddenly stopped. "Did you say the ship was called *The Griffin*? Nicandros Kokinos died on *The Griffin*?"

"Yes. Does that mean something to you?" Nikolaus asked with a frown.

"I'm afraid so. Master Kyril died in the library in this house. The floor of the library is a mosaic of a mythical monster. The master's blood flowed over the creature. It is a griffin."

The others gaped at Daniel in shocked silence.

"That's unnerving," said Adan.

Nikolaus suppressed a shiver. "Please, continue with your story."

Daniel licked his lips. He drank the rest of his wine and set the goblet down a bit too hard. "Where was I? Yes, Balthazar followed your father to Rome and learned that he and most of his family had died. He learned the circumstances and was suspicious. When the ship captain went ashore, leaving his ship in Port Ostia, Balthazar tried to follow but lost him. Days went by with no clues. Balthazar bribed the captain's cabin boy for information. It paid off. It led to a slave trader who had tricked Egnatian. Balthazar offered a great deal of money for the box only to learn that the man had already sold it. He was heartbroken and out of leads.

Daniel rubbed his forehead. He was getting a headache but he continued, "Days later, he went to the slave trader again, hoping to get more detail. When he entered the meeting room at the inn, there sat a man in a heated argument with the slave trader. It was the buyer and he wanted a refund for the box. The slave trader was refusing to comply. Balthazar introduced himself and offered to buy the box. At the sight of gold coins, the man eagerly handed the box over."

Daniel paused to savory the memory. "When Balthazar first came home with the Prophecy Box, he was jubilant. We must have celebrated for a week. Then he sent me on an errand to Thebes. When I came back, the box was gone. I, of course, asked what happened and Balthazar would only say, 'It is safe.' He told me what to do when he was dying."

Nikolaus could not refrain from asking about the thing that haunted his thoughts. "Did my father kill Master Kyril?"

"Only your father, Master Kyril, and God can answer that question."

Calypso gently put a hand on Nikolaus's arm. "Let it go, Niko. Remember your father as he was before any of this happened. Leave judgment to God."

"If Balthazar gave you the box, what do you need me to do?" asked Adan.

"He did *not* give me the box," said Daniel. "He gave me a riddle. He said the solution to the riddle would lead to the hiding place for the box. He said, and I quote, 'You will need the centurion. Only he will be able to solve the riddle.' I asked him, which centurion? He said, 'The one with the golden eyes.' And here you are."

The others turned to look at Adan.

"How could Balthazar know that Adan would come here?" asked Nikolaus.

"Balthazar knew things." Daniel raised his hands in acceptance. "I can't explain it."

Adan took a deep breath and let it out slowly. "What is the riddle?"

Chapter 19

Balthazar's Riddle

———⊷⊶———

Nikolaus hardly heard what Balthazar said about a riddle. He was thinking about coming all this way and spending so much time, money, and effort to learn that his most pressing question could not be answered. Yet, the circumstantial evidence was overwhelming. The chief astrologer did, in fact, die by violence, either accidently or intentionally. Nicandros did leave the villa with the Prophecy Box. No matter what the actual details were, Nikolaus's father took advantage of the situation. His father's actions caused a great tragedy but that ultimately led to Nikolaus being adopted into a close-knit family, being married to a woman he loved, having his own family, and being financially secure with a hopeful future. He had endured the loss of his family and four years of slavery but even that had taught him humility and to never take anything for granted.

Calypso patted his arm. "For your own sake, let go of the past."

"You're right," he whispered. "I don't need to know anything else. There is nothing I can do to change it, anyway." Yet, even as he spoke, he knew his words were empty. He had no intention of letting go of the past if it led him to the Prophecy Box. The power it apparently offered could not be ignored. He would use the box for doing good, he told himself, but ambitious thoughts crept into his mind. Could he be more than just an inn keeper? Could he finish what his father could not? What if the box could do much more than even Daniel realized? What if Daniel was actually lying and knew the box had supernatural power? Nikolaus shook himself and tried to redirect his thoughts. He realized he had not heard what Daniel and Adan were saying.

"Did you write it down?" asked Adan.

"The riddle? No need." Daniel tapped his temple. "I will never forget it. Balthazar said, 'Look to the leg of the mouse and there you will find the box.' That's it."

"What? That's the whole riddle?" chirped Calais. "What does it mean?"

The others looked just as incredulous.

"He must have been ill and feverish," said Nikolaus. "Was he delirious?"

Daniel shook his head. "He told me this riddle weeks before he became ill."

"Look to the leg of the mouse," repeated Adan. "The mouse?"

Daniel made a sheepish face. "Does that mean anything to you? Balthazar said only you could decipher the riddle. He literally meant, only you."

"Only me," Adan muttered. "Then it had to be something unique to me, to my life. Look to the leg of the mouse. Look to the leg of the mouse. What kind of mouse?" Then realization came to him. He leaned his head back and laughed. The others stared at him with concern. Adan ignored them. "Daniel, when you got back from Thebes, was there any new furniture?"

"Umm. New furniture. Not anything that could hold the box. Believe me, I've looked everywhere."

"Don't worry about that. Just tell me about anything new."

Daniel rested his chin on his fist to think. "He bought a new table for the dining room with chairs rather than the reclining couches. He always disliked the Roman custom of lying on one's side to eat. He also commissioned a new bed frame and a cabinet for our scrolls but it only has shelves and no doors. I even checked the grounds to see if he might have buried it. Nothing was disturbed."

"I need to see the furniture," said Adan as he stood up.

They followed Daniel into the library. They entered the room but stopped when they saw the floor mosaic of the legendary monster. Daniel stepped around it and waved a hand at the cabinet. It was a few moments before Adan looked away from the griffin. Nikolaus knelt down and ran his hand over the head of the creature with its yellow eyes and curved, predatory beak.

Calypso took his arm. "It is just some fancy artwork on a floor. People walk on it."

Nikolaus stood. "You're right. It's just a floor." Yet, as long as they were in the room, he kept looking down at the ferocious creature.

Adan turned his attention to the cabinet, took one look, and shook his head. Daniel led them to the dining room. Adan scanned the table and, again, shook his head. They followed Daniel up the stairs to the bedroom Balthazar once used.

"I never come in here," explained Daniel as Calypso ran a finger across the clothes chest and clicked her tongue at the dust. Daniel waved a hand at the elaborately carved bed frame. "It is beautiful, isn't it? Balthazar was quite proud of this bed."

Adan looked at the four legs of the bedframe. They were unusually large with ornate carving along the two sides that faced out. "Yes, I imagine he was. And for good reason. Niko, did I ever tell you about my pet donkey?"

Nikolaus blinked at him as if he'd lost his mind. "Am I actually supposed to answer that?"

Adan addressed the others. "This man in Rome had a donkey that suffered a terrible accident and mangled her lower leg. I nursed her back to health. After she healed from her surgery, I made her a wooden leg. I called my three-legged donkey Musculus,

Little Mouse. Three of her legs were natural, of course, but one leg had a wooden support. 'Look to the leg of the mouse.' And one of those," he pointed to the legs of the bedframe, "holds the Prophecy Box. Balthazar never had to worry about its safety. He slept on it every night."

The others looked more closely at the legs but saw no indication of hiding anything. "What are you talking about, Adan?" asked Nikolaus doubtfully. "They're just legs on a frame."

"Having made a few bed frames when I was working for Serapio, I can promise you, this frame is unique. Help me get the mattress off and turn it on its side."

The undersides of the four legs were exposed. Adan looked at each one until he pointed at a brass ring hidden in the bottom of a leg. There was also space within the leg between an outer wall and an inner core. He raised the ring from its hinged indentation and pulled. The core of the leg began to move. A box made of cypress wood with three stones on the lid came free from the, now hollow leg. A gap in the inner wall allowed for the stones. The others stared in amazement.

Adan set the box on a small table by the window. No one moved to touch it but could only stare in wonder at the ancient object.

"Amazing," mumbled Daniel to himself. "Never in a thousand years would I have thought of that." A struggle of temptation twisted in his heart. Finally, he relaxed and looked at Adan. "I wish I could keep this treasure all to myself, but my conscience won't let me. Balthazar told me that you must take the box, Adan."

"Me! Why? What am I supposed to do with it?" Adan looked at the object and frowned.

"I suggest—as little as possible." He could not hide his coveting expression.

Calypso tentatively extended her hand toward the object. "May I touch it?"

"No!" shouted Daniel. "No one touches it except Adan." He reached into the clothes chest and took out a sturdy linen *loculus*. He handed it to Adan. "This is the same satchel Balthazar used when he brought the box back. Put it in here. Out of sight."

Adan took the offered satchel. "You were right, Niko. The colors in the stones shimmer like sunlight on ocean waves. The golden one symbolizes the sun and the lavender-blue stone symbolizes the moon. Yes?"

Daniel confirmed his observations with a nod.

Nicolaus approached the box. "It's obvious that the stone at the bottom is the earth. It's just as I remembered it. Sand dunes under a starry, green sky. What does it look like inside?" He started to touch the lid.

Daniel stayed his hand and gave Adan an imploring look. "Only he should open it."

Adan carefully lifted the lid to find an array of cogged wheels and dials, pointers, and a central hand crank. There was a main wheel with four, wide spokes. Some of the copper in the bronze had oxidized into shades of turquoise. Adan looked at the instructions written on a plate next to the main wheel. There were symbols on the wheels.

Daniel moved to the side of the table opposite from Adan. Calais stood with his mother and Nikolaus as they stared at the device in silence.

Adan grasped the handle on top of the main wheel and tried to turn it. It wouldn't move.

"Turn it from east to west," said Daniel.

Adan reversed his efforts and the wheel turned causing the dials to shift at differing speeds and click as the cogs fell into place. He saw writing etched on the bronze framework. There were names of the constellations with instructions, names of the planets and astrological terms. Adan realized that it would take much study to learn everything the box could do. He closed the lid and placed the box in the satchel. He muttered to no one in particular, "How can this one *machina* cause so much trouble?"

"It is not the machine's fault," said Daniel. "It neither schemes nor does it desire. It is the lust for power and wealth that causes evil."

"About that," said Calais as he glanced at the others. "We know the box did *not* predict Yeshua's star. But do other people know that? Stories are told and retold and most get exaggerated in the retelling."

"What are you saying, Calais," asked Adan.

"What if others think the box can predict—let's say—the end of the world? No matter what the facts are, people will believe what they want to believe. There's also the matter that my mother told you about. Where there is power or profit, there will be those willing to do evil deeds to acquire it. Unexpected events could always sabotage their good intentions."

"Enough of all this gloomy talk," announced Daniel as he spied his chief cook in the doorway. He consulted with the cook for a moment and turned to the others. "It is time for us to enjoy a fine dinner of baked dormice, dipped in honey and rolled in poppy seed along with smoked and seasoned duck prepared by my excellent cooks. My steward tells me that *calda* will be served, made of the purest water, fine wine, and spiced with cloves, nutmeg, cinnamon, and a touch of cardamom." He instructed his servant to seat the others in the dining room but turned to Adan. He gestured at the bedframe and the two of them set it back properly on the floor. "You must never let the box out of your possession." He looked over Adan's shoulder and stared intently.

Adan turned to see what had his attention. Nikolaus was looking back from the doorway.

"Centurion, I beg of you," whispered Daniel, "never let anyone touch it. It is only safe with you." He walked around Adan and followed Nikolaus out of the room.

After dinner, Daniel insisted that the four travelers accept his hospitality until they left Athens. It would be a few days before Calais and Calypso would need to rejoin Pomona and Aurelius to head east back to Pergamon. Adan and Nikolaus would go with them to bid farewell to Aurelius and Pomona before the brothers boarded a different ship headed south to Caesarea.

As the men discussed politics and the brewing turmoil in Jerusalem, Calypso thought back to the day Adan and Nikolaus came looking for her. She came so close to refusing to talk to their friend about her son, Antipas. If she had refused, she would never have known that their friend was her youngest son. She smiled to herself as she looked over at Calais as he and Daniel talked with the others over a game of *Petteia*. The checkers-like game was popular in Greece, but she hadn't seen anyone play it in a long time. It pleased her to see that Calais was winning, having captured nearly all of Daniel's game pieces. Adan and Nikolaus watched the progress of the game, sipping wine, and enjoying the cool, night breeze drifting in from the open balcony doors. There were delicate clouds, like sheer lace, floating across the waxing moon. An iridescent circle of pale rose and citrine framed the face of Luna.

"I wish we were going home on Aurelius's ship," bemoaned Nikolaus.

Adan agreed. "Yes, it has been good traveling with friends."

"I feel as if I've been away from Marina and the family for years but it's been only a few months. Adan, I've been thinking about what Calais said. About what other people may think the box can do. It would only take one determined person to put your whole family in danger. I could keep it at the Inn. It would be safe there until you decide what to do with it."

Adan upended his goblet and drained it. "Wouldn't that be putting you and your family in danger? I'll figure something out or something will figure it out for me."

Nikolaus gave Adan an annoyed look. "What does that mean?"

"Nothing." Adan tried to ignore the sting of suspicion he felt at Nikolaus's offer. "It just sounded like the thing to say. Right now, the only coherent thought I have is that I want to go home. Then I'll still need to take the epistle to the Hebrews to Jerusalem. I'll write a copy, first, to keep in Caesarea."

"I wish we would have had time to make a copy of John's Book of Revelation," said Nikolaus, trying not to be irked that Adan had abruptly changed the subject. "I know John told us not to make a copy but I already can't remember all the details. Maybe a copy will make its way to Caesarea." He stood up and stretched. "I'm tired. I'll see you in the morning."

Adan looked at the sleeping mat Daniel's servants had set for him on the balcony. Nikolaus had told them that his brother liked to sleep in the open under the stars. Foot-steps sounded at the balcony doorway and Adan glanced around to see who it was.

Daniel motioned for him to come inside. "Adan, I need to speak with you alone. Do you mind?" They sat at the small table in the library.

"It is most important. I couldn't tell you before because this is meant for you only."

"I imagine you're going to warn me against using the machine," said Adan.

"It would be wise. But you need to know that there was a journal with the Prophecy Box. Nicandros didn't know about it, of course. Each guardian recorded his experiences with the box until he died. Then it went with the box to the next guardian."

"Do I need to take the journal as well?"

"No. Balthazar burned it."

Adan was startled. "Why would he do that?"

Daniel pressed his lips into a tight line. "I don't know. He wouldn't explain. He didn't plan on telling me but I saw him do it. I had gotten back early from running errands." He paused and licked his lips nervously. "The journal was also a recording of each guardian's death. Some appear to be accidental. Others were murdered. But all died unexpectedly. Except for Balthazar."

"Are you telling me the curse is real?" demanded Adan in disbelief.

"Curses are just words," retorted Daniel. "Curses have no power. But *belief* in curses can be very powerful. I will tell you this; every man who learned to use the box did not die of natural causes—except for Balthazar, as I said."

"And now I have the box." In spite of himself, Adan felt a tinge of alarm.

"I don't believe you have anything to worry about," assured Daniel. "The box might tempt you but you must not listen to its enticing voice. If you ever use it, the temptation to continue may be more than you can resist. Do not forget that Balthazar put his trust in you instead of me, despite having never met you. I believe he heard of you from other followers of Yeshua. Perhaps they also told him about your pet donkey."

Adan smiled at that. "There are some good people who know about Little Mouse."

Daniel's expression lightened. "It is hard to imagine a future Roman centurion tending a useless donkey back to health. However, Balthazar must have taken the story to heart. That is why I have set my pride aside and have faith that he made the right decision. Does it disturb me that he did not trust me? Did it anger me that he gave me a riddle, instead of the box? Yes, to both questions. Now it gives me comfort. I don't carry the burden. You do. Adan, take the box to a safe place and leave it there. Let the future deal with it as it may."

"You said every guardian, except for Balthazar, died unexpectedly. Does that include the inventor?"

"Excellent question. The answer is yes. The chief inventor was Archimedes, the greatest scientist of the age. Members of the *Magi* contributed but he was the main genius behind this machine. The Greek mathematician and philosopher, Pythagoras, also contributed, in absentia, of course. He died hundreds of years before Archimedes was born. Archimedes invented and discovered many great things, but sadly not everyone understood his incredible abilities. The Roman army besieged the city of Syracuse hundreds of years ago, as I'm sure you've been taught. A Roman soldier invaded Archimedes's home when the Roman army finally broke through after two years. Archimedes ordered the man to stay away from his charts and drawings and leave him alone to finish his work. The soldier demanded that he stop what he was doing but he refused. Archimedes was probably the greatest genius of the age, but despite orders to not harm him, the soldier killed him. It was like a common rock crushing a beautiful pearl because the rock was too stupid to appreciate the beauty of the pearl. What a loss to mankind." Daniel lowered his head into his hand.

Adan curled a lip in disgust. "Every soldier knows this story. The soldier you speak of was crucified for his disobedience. His Roman citizenship did not save him from the rage of Proconsul Marcellus. Ever since, when our commanders want us to spare any citizens, they include a warning. Do not kill Archimedes—or you die."

Daniel raised his head. Deep sadness tempered his voice. "After Archimedes was killed, the Prophecy Box passed to his assistant, and then to his assistant and so forth until over a hundred years later, it ended up with the School of the *Magi*. It became clear as the decades passed that whoever used the box for any length of time died tragically. There is no record of previous owners' deaths, but none of the *Magi* who took possession surrendered it while they lived. Only Balthazar. He bequeathed it to you and made me promise before God and man to fulfil his wishes."

"Does the School of the *Magi* know you are giving this to me?"

"No," stated Daniel emphatically. "Balthazar's official report states that he could not find it after it was stolen from Master Kyril. I imagine that was the only lie he ever told in his entire adulthood. He must have had a very good reason to deceive his fellow *Magi*. He did not share his reason with me but I suspect it has something to with the temptation to misuse it."

Adan bowed his head and muttered, "I wish Balthazar had shared one thing—instructions on what to do with the thing. I am at a complete loss."

"Do not be concerned, Adan," assured Daniel. "Whatever happens will be as it should."

Adan looked at him sharply. "Whatever happens will be as it should. Interesting that you would say that. Since we're sharing private information, I wonder what you can offer about a situation I am in with King Herod." Adan told him the details about Aurelius.

Daniel lowered his head and closed his eyes. Adan did not interrupt. Finally, the *magus* spoke. "If you protect this man's life and suffer the loss of your own because of it, you have done nothing more than what Yeshua did for all humanity."

"Except for one insurmountable difference," countered Adan. "Yeshua lived again on the third day."

Daniel smiled. "You won't even have to wait *that* long. You will live again, instantly, in heaven. Do not grieve for your loved ones. They will follow you soon after. It is the brief time when loved ones are left behind in this world that causes them grief, but not in heaven. There is no grief in heaven."

Chapter 20

The Kraken's Captain

———— ⦿⦿⦿ ————

After a few days of rest and long talks, Adan and the others said their farewell to Daniel. Calypso was especially sad to leave him since they shared so many good memories of her father but she was equally excited about going back to her home in Pergamon with Calais at her side. She would always grieve for the tragic loss of her husband and eldest son. However, being reunited with Calais was a blessing that eased the pain.

Adan hired a carriage to take them back to the harbor of Kantharos. The road bustled with pedestrians, carriages, and commercial wagons taking cargo to and from the city. They were delayed several times when the traffic snarled, but their driver was well experienced with Athenians' pursuit of commerce and managed to disentangle the carriage when gaps in the traffic appeared, no matter how briefly.

They found Aurelius shouting orders and waving signal flags to the men maneuvering his ship into the water from the *neosoikoi*. The ship's hull was clean and freshly coated with the water-resistant paint so necessary to prevent the wooden beams from getting waterlogged. Adan and the others watched in fascination as levers, pulleys and ropes were aptly applied to slowly return the ship to the sea. After the *Child of the Ocean* was safely released into the waves, and everyone had boarded, Aurelius strode over to them. He greeted them enthusiastically and took their relaxed manner as an indication they had been successful in finding their mysterious *magus*.

Calypso hurried over to Pomona for a hug. The two women went below deck to Pomona's quarters to share their mutual adventures. Calypso , again, warned Pomona to be ever watchful for the fair-haired bounty hunter. She had hoped that Pomona would never be spotted since she stayed on the ship.

"You don't need to worry, Calypso. We won't be seeing that one again. Aurelius convinced him that pursuing me was not in his best interests." He eyes filled with tears of gratitude. "You should have seen them. Samuel offered up the little he has saved and then the rest of the crew pitched in to pay my bounty. Who would not be moved by such compassion? They defended me without question. No, we've seen the last of that horrible man." Calypso hugged her again and thanked God that her beloved Pomona was safe.

Up on deck, Calais left the other three men to talk and went in search of a snack in the galley after stowing his and his mother's knapsacks in the guest quarters. Aurelius pulled Adan and Nikolaus away from the bustle of the crew who were preparing to set sail. He asked for details of their search for answers. Nikolaus gave him a summary and especially enjoyed telling how Adan solved Balthazar's riddle. He did not avoid describing his father's apparent involvement in the mystery, which surprised Adan but he hoped that meant Nikolaus was beginning to accept the situation. Their conversation gradually turned to other topics.

"Adan, I know you and Niko must be eager to head for home so I managed to find passage for you. The captain of the ship, over there," he pointed to the vessel to the left of them, "introduced himself to me, finally. I've been seeing his ship for years but until the other day, I hadn't met the man. He wanted to know what I paid for different phases of the overhauling. Said he suspected he was being overcharged. Turns out he'll be going to Caesarea and I took the liberty to say you two needed transport. He asked a few questions to make sure you could pay and agreed to take you on board. He said he would be sailing tomorrow after his cargo is loaded. He'll be going south to Fair Havens, then Paphos, then east to Caesarea. You can see his ship is not as grand as mine, of course, but she looks seaworthy. She's called *The Kraken*. Can you believe anyone would name a ship after the most dreaded sea monster?"

Adan shrugged with unconcern. "It takes all kinds. Some people enjoy tempting fate."

Nikolaus smirked. "Like we've never done that, ourselves. What is this captain's name?"

"Tullus. Captain Vinicio Loukios Tullus. Like I said, I've seen his ship many times over the years. We take similar routes, as do all cargo captains. It's understandable why I've never met him, considering." Aurelius gave a slight shudder but didn't explain. "I guess, his suspicion of being swindled outweighed his reclusive nature."

Aurelius gestured toward the pier. "I have a favorite restaurant on the pier that serves the best sea urchins with just the right spices, honey, and egg sauce. Dine with us tonight. I'm sure Calypso and Calais will join us as well. You'll love it. I challenge you to a game of *Tali* after dinner, and then you can sleep in my guest quarters. You can board *The Kraken* tomorrow after a good breakfast. How does that sound?"

"Sounds great," said Adan after a quick look to see that Nikolaus agreed.

Aurelius's restaurant choice turned out to be just as good as he promised but Adan was unusually quiet. He was content to let the others tell Aurelius and Pomona about Daniel and the stories of the *Magi*. Adan tried to follow the conversation but found himself thinking about the contents of the locked cabinet in his quarters. The mysterious Prophesy Box drew his thoughts as if beckoning him to retrieve it. Nikolaus noticed

A. E. Smith

Adan's distraction and tried to pull him into the conversation. He wasn't successful. He felt bad for his brother, burdened with the responsibility of two highly valuable articles: the Epistle to the Hebrews, and the Prophecy Box. Nikolaus had offered to keep the box in his quarters to lighten Adan's burden but his offer was flatly refused. His brother's curt response startled him but he accepted Adan's immediate apology. Nikolaus decided that now was not the time to get into an argument. He would, again, offer to help once they were on *The Kraken*.

The evening was still young when they left the restaurant. While the others decided to head back to the ship, Adan suggested that he and Nikolaus take a walk along the pier. Adan was not ready to confine himself to the *Child of the Ocean* just yet. He wanted to stretch his legs and see the sights of the harbor. Adan suggested that they might even find a trinket or two that would please Dulcibella and Marina, especially since the best shopping was down at the pier.

The brothers had walked for over an hour from shop to shop, café to café. Oil lamps were lighted and hung from hooks in walls and open display windows. People milled about talking, laughing, and grumbling curses at careless pedestrians. Nikolaus was about to suggest that they head back to the ship when shouts and screams came from a bar several shops away. Adan and Nikolaus moved through curious observers and found two men lying in the street. The brothers pushed their way through the crowd to approach the injured men.

One of them, a Roman with a swarthy complexion and missing teeth was dead. His gaping mouth and wide, staring eyes were unfocused. Blood had poured from an injury in his neck but it had stopped flowing, indicating that his heart had stopped beating.

"What happened here?" demanded Adan from a wizened, old man who was wringing his hands and sweating profusely.

"It wasn't my fault," the man cried. "They were drinking at different tables in my bar, right there." He pointed over his shoulder. "Then one of them got up to get more ale. He was staggering and bumped into that one." He pointed to the other man who was lying on his stomach. His face was hidden under a mane of hair. "Next thing I knew, the two of them pulled knives and started to go after each other. It wasn't my fault, Centurion." The man waved his open palms defensively and backed away.

Adan and Nikolaus knelt next to the man lying in a spreading pool of his own blood. They carefully turned him onto his back. The man's eyes fluttered opened.

"I'm a *medicus*," exclaimed Adan. "I can help you. What is your name?"

"Folke, it means 'chief,' in my country," the dying man managed to say. "Some chief, I am, eh?"

"Why are you here in Athens, Folke?" asked Adan as he drew his dagger and ripped open the man's tunic.

"I hunt humans." He clutched his stomach as blood flowed freely between his fingers.

164

Adan and Nikolaus pried Folke's hands away from the wound. The cut was short but the knife had penetrated the aorta, the biggest blood vessel in the body. Adan cut out a section of the man's tunic, wadded it up, and pressed it into the wound. He applied pressure with the heel of his hand. The man groaned and his eyes momentarily rolled back in his head. Making a supreme effort, he refocused his attention on Adan's face.

"What are you doing? Trying to save my life like that little sorceress did on the ship?"

Adan felt the back of his neck tingle. "What ship? What are you talking about?"

"That little half-breed thought she was winning my favor by tossing me a rope." He turned his head and spat on to the street. "Since when did I ever need a woman's help?"

Adan and Nikolaus exchanged startled looks. This had to be the bounty hunter Aurelius told them about.

"I tracked them here to Athens but they had shipped out by the time I got here. Harbor master said they would be back to overhaul the ship in a *neosoikoi*. Luck would bring them back to me."

The man coughed and sputtered at the effort it took to talk. His lips were beginning to show a bluish tint. "I went to the bar to meet with a woman who could help me lure my prize away from that brother of hers, the ship captain. She never showed. I should have left."

The man's breathing was becoming shallow. Adan placed two fingers on his wrist. His pulse was weak and his heart was racing. He felt cold to the touch despite the balmy weather. Adan looked up at Nikolaus and shook his head. He knew Folke would be dead soon.

"The oath you took meant nothing?" asked Adan. "Have you no honor?"

Folke curled a lip. "Honor. It's just a word." He frowned and focused on Adan. "Wait. How would you know about that? Never mind. I don't care. Leave me be. Let me die as I see fit!"

"You should stop talking. You'll only make the blood flow faster," cautioned Adan.

"Who cares? I don't. Besides, I don't even feel any pain. I don't feel anything."

On-lookers tried to crowd in until Nikolaus stood up with Adan's sword in hand. Most decided they had seen enough and moved away. Nikolaus continued to "stand guard" to let the man die without the insensitive curiosity of the townspeople.

Adan pressed harder on the wound. "Folke, you are about to die. Pray to God. He will forgive you."

Folke tried to laugh but only a gurgling sound came from his mouth. His face contorted with the effort. "Spare your words. Ever since my mother kicked me to the curb and my father forgot my name, I've known that nothing matters but myself."

"Please, listen to me. You can pray to Yeshua, the Son of God. I know that. . ."

"Save your breath! I know all about your pathetic Yeshua. I was in Jeru. . ." Folke winced and struggled for his next breath. "Jerusalem. I was there. They cried and whimpered at the sight of him. Claimed he rose from the dead. Fools! It was obvious he was nothing but a trickster."

"Folke, he was dead, but death could not hold him. He is alive and always will be."

"You are as deluded as they were. No one comes back from the dead. Except maybe me. Maybe I'll haunt that little half-breed." He narrowed his eyes. "What was her name? I can't remember her name. Did I tell you my name? It's Folke. It means chief."

"You're dying, Folke," pleaded Adan. "Yeshua did not trick anyone. He was dead while he was still on the cross."

"How would you know?"

"I know because I'm the one who put him on that cross. I'm the one who saw his lifeless body hanging there, unmoving, no longer struggling to breath. I'm the one who sliced his heart in two with my spear. I buried him in a tomb and sealed it with a stone."

Folke looked into Adan's face. "You're lying."

"For what purpose? Why would I lie to you—a dying man who I don't even know? Listen to me, Folke. If God doesn't exist then you have nothing to lose. If God does exist, then you have everything to gain, depending on what you do right now. Call on Yeshua. He has already saved you if you will only accept it."

"How stupid do you think I am? I have lived a life of pure *evil*," he gritted the words between his teeth. "It felt good to grind my heel into the face of every pathetic fool I could."

The flow of blood was slowing as Adan continued to press the wad of linen into the wound but Folke was also bleeding internally. There wasn't much time left.

"The thief crucified with Yeshua was guilty. Yet, he believed in Yeshua and said it aloud. I heard him. Yeshua answered him, *'Truly, I tell you, today you will be with Me in Paradise.'* The criminal had no time to do anything else but believe. You can do the same. Just call on. . ."

"Stop! I don't care about your miserable Messiah. I've lived the same way my whole life and I see no reason to change anything now." The man's eyes unfocused. A soft gasp of air escaped from his lips. Adan felt the tension melt away from Folke's body. His pale, blue eyes darkened as the pupils dilated. The man was dead.

"Why didn't he call on Yeshua? That's all he had to do."

"No, Adan, that is not all he had to do," said Nikolaus as he replaced Adan's sword in the scabbard. "He also needed a change of heart, and mind, and to truly believe. He could have called out Yeshua's name a hundred times and it would not have mattered if his heart and mind were still buried in sin." Nikolaus placed a hand on his brother's shoulder. "Adan. He's gone. Get up. We have to go."

"We just leave him in the street?"

"Soldiers are coming. We don't need to get tied up in questioning. You did all you could. Even people who saw Yeshua bring dead Lazarus back to life, rejected him. Get up. They're coming!" Nikolaus took Adan's arm and pulled him to his feet. He dragged him along until they could turn a corner. They heard the soldiers shouting for the persistent on-lookers to get out of the way.

***

That last night on *Child of the Ocean*, Adan didn't sleep on the deck as was his habit. He needed to guard the box. He even hid the key, fearing someone would steal it while he slept. He spent a fitful night, hampered by disjointed dreams. Finally, desperate for relief, he went up to the top deck and stood in the bow.

Adan looked into the heavens, the multitude of glittering stars, and the hazy "dust" of the Milky Way. "My Lord God. You know what Herod has ordered me to do and you know his only motive is to execute me. Twice, you have caused others to save my life. I ask you now, for a third time, to protect me from this man's evil intent. Yet, if it is your will for me to die by his hand—then so be it. I only ask that you give comfort to my family." Adan felt his anxiety lift. He took a deep breath of the sweet, sea-spun air and returned to his quarters. He was finally able to sleep.

He looked tired the next morning and the others were concerned. Adan assured them he just wanted to get home. After breakfast, Adan and Nikolaus took their leave amid well wishes and hearty back slapping for the men and tender hugs for Pomona and Calypso. Adan asked Calais to send a letter as soon as they got back to Pergamon to let him know they arrived safely. The brothers thanked Aurelius for supplying safe passage throughout their travels.

Adan pulled Aurelius aside. "Don't forget you and Pomona must always be careful. Arrest warrants stay in effect for ten years. Make sure Pomona never steps foot in Judea again. Since you abandoned the army two decades ago, no one has high expectations for your arrest. In fact, I don't think Herod really expects for you to be found. The two of you should be safe as long as you keep to the sea."

Aurelius saw that Adan looked distressed. "You're still worried about Pomona, aren't you? At least, we've seen the last of that bounty hunter."

"Yes, you have," said Adan but he added no detail.

Nikolaus clamped his mouth shut and looked away.

"Pomona is a blessing to you, Aurelius," said Adan.

"Yes, she is. She insists on treating the crew as if they are family. I thought she was wasting her efforts and my money, but I see now that she was right. I know others will not always appreciate our diligence, but so far, every extra *denarius* has been well spent."

"Calypso has also helped," added Adan. "Her aid in changing Pomona's appearance is most effective. I barely recognize her now. She looks like a Roman woman of sophistication and means. She needs to drop the name Pomona, however."

"She was resistant to a change but she's decided to answer to Hadriana now."

"Next, you'll be calling her Ana, like Fabiana's nickname." The thought of his friends added to Adan's longing for home, despite what Herod had planned for him.

"Thank you for your concern about our safety." Aurelius gratefully patted Adan's shoulder. "And I hope everything works out well for you. Get home quickly and safely, my friend."

Aurelius was unaware that a port worker unloading supplies was listening to every word. The man, one of Herod's spies, had kept the centurion under surveillance since he arrived in Athens. His orders from King Herod had been to watch for the *Lupus Legatus* in case he showed up. The spy had hired street urchins to watch every ship coming into dock. Finally, one of the boys reported that the wolf-eyed centurion had arrived and several boys were tailing him.

Herod's mercenary had taken over the surveillance. He heard the captain tell the centurion he had booked passage for him on *The Kraken* and to, 'Get home quickly.' He hurried to the harbor master's office to find a ship scheduled for Caesarea and to make sure *The Kraken* would eventually dock there as well. No ships were slated for a non-stop voyage but Herod had sent a letter of authorization to pay any captain to by-pass his usual route and sail straight for Caesarea.

On the promise of a substantial reward, a ship captain agreed to the spy's terms. They departed from Athens, skirting the western coastline, and docked in Caesarea well before Adan and Nikolaus. The captain and the spy reported to Blastus upon arrival. Blastus paid the captain and dismissed him.

"Now it's my turn," said the spy. "Take me to the king."

Blastus held up a hand. "King Herod is quite busy with a number of delegates from the coast. You'll need to report to me."

The spy told him everything he knew of Adan and Nikolaus. "We had to stop and take on supplies in Rhodes and Paphos but the centurion's ship would be stopping to ex-change cargo in several ports. He should be arriving in about a week, or two, I estimate."

Blastus took the spy to his office and removed a small scroll from his desk. "Take these orders to Commander Lysias of the Antonia Fortress in Jerusalem. Come back with him and you will be paid double what King Herod promised you."

***

Adan and Nikolaus plodded down the gangway and turned to wave one last time to their friends. The brothers walked the short distance down the pier to *The Kraken*, dodging crates, barrels, and other articles of cargo. They approached the ship and hailed the officer of the deck who gave them permission to come aboard. Adan gave the man their names and paid the customary rate for passage. They saw that the ship seemed sturdy and well-maintained. As Adan scanned the deck, he noticed that a man, somewhat older than himself, was staring at them. Adan instinctively laid a hand on the knapsack holding the Prophecy Box. He told himself that no one could have learned that he had it but a tinge of fear surged in the pit of his stomach. He turned back to the sailor at the gateway.

"Who is that by the helmsman?"

Nikolaus looked where Adan was pointing.

"That is the captain, Sir," answered the sailor.

"I see," said Adan. "Captain Tullus, is it?"

"Aye," answered the sailor.

"Which quarters should we take?" asked Nikolaus.

"There's one in the bow. The other is in the stern. We only have the two guest quarters."

Adan gestured toward the bow. "Let's go. You pick the one you want. I'll take the other."

The room in the bow was small with a low ceiling. It had a narrow cot, a chair, and no table. It smelled of musty wood, resin, and stale air. There was the usual small cabinet bolted to the floor with a lockable door. The key was hanging from a hook on the door. "You want this room, Niko?"

Nikolaus gestured disinterestedly. "Doesn't matter to me. You take it."

Adan set his knapsacks on the cot. He opened the cabinet and tested the lock. A flaw inside the lock resisted the key. Adan withdrew the key and inspected it. "Umm. Looks all right."

"Try it again. Jiggle the key or something," suggested Nikolaus.

Adan took his advice but it still wouldn't turn. He gingerly slipped the key most of the way in and gave it a light turning pressure. The lock opened. "*Ohe*, there's a trick to it."

Adan placed the Prophecy Box, still in the satchel, inside the cabinet. It fit with no room to spare. He locked the cabinet and put the key in his belt pouch. "I hope you have a locked cabinet. We'll have to put the Hebrews' epistle in it since there's not enough room for both in this one." He handed it to Nikolaus. "Otherwise, one of us will need to carry it around and that might attract attention we don't want."

"Or I can take the box and you can keep the scroll," said Nikolaus.

Adan leveled his gaze at his brother. "Why? The box is fine right here."

Nikolaus was startled at his sharp tone. "It was only a suggestion." He was irritated at Adan's consistent refusal of his help. It felt like Adan did not trust him, which only made him more determined. It wasn't as if he was desperate to open the box and see how the machine worked, he told himself. Nikolaus was startled when Adan tapped his arm and repeated that they should go. He had been staring at the cabinet and was unaware Adan was talking to him.

They left and walked the length of the ship to the stern. They entered the second guest quarters. It was identical to Adan's room. Nikolaus unlocked the cabinet and slipped the scroll, rolled up in the knapsack, inside. He put the key in his coin pouch and left his travel knapsacks on the cot. The brothers decided to introduce themselves to the captain.

They walked back to the ladder to the top deck. The captain was still standing by the helmsman at the wheel. His back was to them as they climbed the ladder to the bridge. Adan immediately noticed the dagger resting in a bronze sheath at the man's belt. The pommel was a rendition of an octopus. The tentacles twisted about each other to form a long handle. The head of the octopus formed the pommel and had glaring, red fire agate eyes. Many a sailor's tale told of the wicked, red-eyed stare of the kraken. The man glanced over his shoulder but did not turn around. Adan and Nikolaus stood, waiting, but the captain ignored them.

Adan cleared his throat. When the man still did not acknowledge them, Adan spoke up, "Captain Tullus, if we may have your attention for a moment."

The man slowly turned to face them. His face was severely scarred on the left side, giving it a melted-wax appearance. The left eye was nearly obscured by the damaged eyelid. His dark, wavy hair was long, contrary to the Roman short-cropped hair style. Long hair on men was considered unseemly to Romans since it was the style among men they considered barbaric.

The captain peered at Adan and Nikolaus with unsettling hostility. His hand dropped to the handle of the dagger sheathed on his belt. Seeing the aggressive gesture, Adan gripped the scabbard of his sword and moved his other hand closer to the hilt. The captain saw the maneuver and dropped his hand to his side.

Adan wondered if he and Nikolaus had made a terrible mistake. Perhaps *The Kraken* lived up to its name in a manner far more realistic than the fantastical sea monsters ever could.

Chapter 21

Sacrifice to Salvage

———— ✦ ————

A dan extended his hand to the captain. He refused to take it but instead offered his hand to Nikolaus. When Nikolaus complied, the man grasped his hand more tightly than necessary and held on too long. When he let go, he hooked his thumbs in his belt and stared at Nikolaus. Apparently, social graces were not a high priority for the captain.

"My name is Centurion Adan Clovius Longinus," he said to break the awkward silence as he waved a hand at Nikolaus. "And this is my brother, Nikolaus Kokinos Longinus. Thank you for taking us aboard, Captain."

"Why thank me? You paid for your passage, didn't you?" He glanced at Adan with a sullen expression but returned his gaze to Nikolaus.

"Will you set sail today, Captain Tullus?" asked Nikolaus, hoping to gloss over the tension.

"Aye." The man turned his back on the brothers and walked away.

Adan gave a questioning look at Nikolaus. They decided to leave the taciturn captain to his work and left the bridge to stand in the stern of the ship.

"What do you make of that?" asked Adan.

"It's understandable that the man is not eager to make conversation as disfigured as he is, but he particularly does not like you. I can't image what caused those scars."

"I don't need to imagine." Adan clenched his teeth and avoided his brother's eye. "My centurion's belt and *caligae* told him all he cares to know about me. Perhaps, I'll leave my weapons in the guest quarters. Maybe my 'appearance' will be less intimidating for him that way."

"And all I care about him is getting us to Caesarea."

The oarsmen of *The Kraken* were soon put to work to maneuver the ship out of the harbor. The sail of the single mast was unfurled and they were under way. The sky was clear with only a few clustered, cumulus clouds that signaled fair weather. The sea breeze was cool and fresh, being far away from dusty roads. The sight and scent of the ocean always reminded Adan of home.

As was the brothers' usual habit, they spent most of their days in the bow, watching the ship slice through the water as they talked. The occasional pod of porpoises frolicking just ahead of them was always an entertaining encounter.

After a few days, *The Kraken* passed the southern tip of Achaea, the largest of the Greek islands. The cabin boy approached the brothers as they sat in the bow and delivered an invitation to the mid-day meal in the captain's quarters. They discussed the curious change-of-heart of the unsociable captain but welcomed the change of activity.

Adan knocked on the captain's door.

"Enter," growled a low voice.

The chamber was nearly as cramped as the guest quarters, except there was a round table set with four chairs, a more substantial bed, a desk, shelves for scrolls along one wall, and a larger lockable cabinet. The captain nodded once at the brothers and indicated they should take a seat at the crude table which was already set with bread, olive oil, dried mutton, and fruit. There was a wine bottle and goblets already half filled with water so they could easily mix in the wine. The table was fitted with braces for the bottle and goblets to prevent spills in case the ship hit rough seas.

"Gentlemen, I hope you forgive me for not welcoming you previously and for serving dinner at a table, which I'm sure you're not accustomed to doing," said Captain Tullus. "As you can see, there's no room for dining couches. I find reclining while eating to be uncomfortable, anyway. It's a show of self-indulgence."

The brothers didn't respond to the captain's unfavorable observation of typical Roman behavior. They didn't think it worth the effort.

Nikolaus changed the subject. "How long have you been in the shipping business?"

At first, the man stared without answering. "Many years. I inherited my first ship when I was still quite young. The ownership of that vessel ended with a tragic mishap," he lightly brushed his fingers across the left side of his face, "but as you can see, I recovered and eventually I was able to buy this ship."

"You must be a fearless sailor, Captain," said Adan. "Aren't you tempting fate to name your ship after a sea monster?"

The man's lips curled into a sly smile. "What can I say? I have an obsession for monsters." He cut his eyes over to Nikolaus and his smile faded. "So, tell me, have the two of you been on vacation or business? I assume Caesarea is your home."

"It is," said Adan. "I have been on official business for my commanding officer, *Primus Pilus* Tacitus. Nikolaus was gracious enough to join me since he also had business abroad."

"Were you both successful?" Tullus's gaze restlessly danced between the brothers.

"We were," answered Adan with growing unease. "Have we ever met before?"

Tullus jerked his head in Adan's direction. "Why would you ask that?"

Adan frowned at the man's curt response. His own tone sharpened, "Because I wish to know if we have met. If we have, I don't remember the encounter. Are you acquainted with Commander Lysias at the Antonia in Jerusalem, by chance?"

The man took a long drink from his wine goblet, refusing to look Adan in the eye. "No, Centurion. I do not know this Lysias you speak of." Tullus smirked. "All the Roman soldiers I know are dead. Until now, of course, since I'm making your acquaintance this very moment. I will never forget meeting you, Centurion. I never forget a face."

Nikolaus shook off the uncomfortable moment and reached for more bread. "We were fortunate to book passage on *The Kraken* since you're headed for Caesarea. I will be glad to get home. I have an inn and several other businesses to run. My managers are taking care of things while we're gone, but I want to get back to my family." Nikolaus looked up to find the captain watching him with barely subdued hostility.

Silence hung in the air. Adan was trying to think of something to revive the conversation when the ship suddenly lurched, knocking everything on the table to the floor, despite the table restraints.

"By the gods!" shouted Captain Tullus as he jumped to his feet.

The three men ran from the room and hurried up the ladder to the upper deck. Crewmen were scurrying around while the helmsman was frantically trying to turn the wheel but it made no difference. The ship's Master of Oars roared at the crew to reverse course.

Captain Tullus bellowed at the helmsman. "What happened?"

"We've hit something, Captain! It looks like the bow of a sunken ship. By the sound of it, I think it ripped into the hull. We're taking on water!" The captain ran to the bow and peered over the side. Adan and Nikolaus could hear him savagely cursing his bad luck.

"Captain, should we lower the skiffs?" shouted one of the crewmen. When Tullus didn't respond, the man motioned to the other crewmen to lower the lifeboats. As activity swirled around them, Adan and Nikolaus tried to stay out of the way until they realized that the bow of the ship was starting to dip downwards.

Captain Tullus spun around and faced Nikolaus. "This is *your* fault, you pampered little worm! I should have finished you off the *first* time!" The man shouted frantic orders at his crew.

Adan and Nikolaus gawked at the man in shock. Nikolaus could only stare in confusion. Adan realized he had misread all the clues. Tullus was focusing his hostility on him to avoid giving himself away to Nikolaus.

"Niko, what did Egnatian look like?"

Nikolaus gasped with disbelief. "No! It can't be." He looked toward Tullus and tried to think. "His voice. I thought his voice was familiar but I decided it was only my imagination. He doesn't look anything like I remember him but it's obvious why."

"His other ship was *The Griffin*. Now this one is *The Kraken*. He said he had an obsession for monsters. I don't think he was kidding." The descent of the ship's bow began to accelerate. "Niko! The epistle! It's in your quarters! We have to get it before the ship goes under."

Nikolaus angrily pointed at the bow. "We have to save the box! There will never be another one. You go to the stern and get the epistle and I'll get the box."

Adan grabbed his arm. "There's no time to get to the box. Look how fast the bow is sinking."

"Just give me the key to your cabinet!" shouted Nikolaus as he shook off his hand and thrust out his palm. "Give me your key!"

"That letter to the Hebrews is far more important than predicting eclipses and moon phases, Niko." Adan looked at the sinking bow. "My quarters is nearly under water, anyway. Give me your key and I'll get the epistle."

Nikolaus dug the key out of his belt pouch and held it up. "Give me your key first. I'm not leaving the box." He pointed at the bow which was quickly tipping into the sea. "It's not under yet! I've still got time!"

Adan grabbed his brother's arm and wrenched the key from his hand. "It's already too late, Niko! By the time you get there and unlock the cabinet—even if it opened easily—you'll drown." Adan looked back at the stern of the ship which was slowly rising out of the water. "I'm going for the scroll. There may never be another copy."

Nikolaus reached for Adan's coin pouch. "Give me your key! I won't leave the box. We can use it, Adan. Neither one of us will have to work another day. Besides, your weapons are in there. I'll grab them, too!"

"There's nothing on this ship worth more than your life." He grasped Nikolaus's arm. "Get in a skiff! Now!"

"Let go of me!" Nikolaus jerked his arm free. "That box belonged to my father. He risked everything for it. He used it to provide for the family. To provide for *me*. It's too valuable to lose!"

Adan tried one last time to reason with him. "Niko, the box is my responsibility. Daniel relinquished it to me. He said no *one else should touch it!* Why do you think he said that? Let it sink to the bottom of the sea. We have to let it go!"

"I can get it before *The Kraken* sinks!" shouted Nikolaus as he tried to push past.

Suddenly, the image of a dream flashed through Adan's mind. It was the night in Emmaus when Nikolaus had briefly run away. He was seventeen, at the time, and still a slave. That same night, Adan dreamed that a sea monster dragged Nikolaus from a ship and pulled him under tumultuous waves. Adan could not save him in the dream.

"Not this time, Niko." Adan smashed his fist into his brother's jaw. Nikolaus crumpled to the deck. Adan shouted at several crewmen to get him into a skiff.

Adan hurried to the hatch and down the ladder to the lower deck. He struggled against the upward tilting passageway to make his way to Nikolaus's quarters in the stern. He unlocked the cabinet and grabbed the knapsack holding the scroll. He snatched his brother's travel knapsacks as well. With the knapsacks slung across his chest, he hurried back to the ladder and climbed to the upper deck.

To Adan's horror, Captain Tullus was crouching behind Nikolaus with his dagger at his throat. Tullus had forced his dazed prisoner into a sitting position by grasping him with his other arm. Nikolaus's head lolled against the captain's shoulder. His hands lay uselessly on the deck.

Tullus looked up at Adan. "I'll have my revenge now," he hissed. "Dionysia escaped from me, but this filthy mongrel will not!"

Out of habit, Adan slapped a hand to his belt before he remembered that he was unarmed. Without taking his eyes off Tullus, he inched forward. "Egnatian, you killed Niko's family. You poisoned them to steal the Prophecy Box. You got Niko and Dionysia arrested and sold into slavery. But *you* want revenge? Whatever you suffered, you brought on yourself."

"You're wrong! If his sister had only married me, *this* wouldn't have happened!" he brought his hand to his scarred face. "But no, Dionysia refused me. That slave trader double-crossed me. He took the box *and her*. Tiberius sent soldiers with me to find that cursed box. I told them who had it. I told them where to find him but they tortured me, anyway. Too bad for them, I got my revenge. I escaped. They got executed—just like I'm going to execute him!"

Tullus twisted his fingers into Nikolaus's hair and jerked his head back. Nikolaus moaned and tried to move. The captain pressed the dagger against the beating artery in his captive's neck. A line of blood oozed from around the blade.

Adan's voice deepened with malice. "If you harm him, I will kill you."

A bitter laugh escaped the captain's lips. "*Ohe,* please do! I have craved death ever since Dionysia rejected me because that little demon will be mine in Hades." Tullus cried out, "I will deliver his dead body to my beloved as a wedding gift!"

Nikolaus reached across his chest with his fist and hit Tullus in the eye. Adan launched himself at them. He grasped Tullus's wrist and buried the point of his thumb into the hollow above the wrist joint. The captain snarled in pain as the pressure forced him to drop the dagger. Nikolaus twisted away and punched the man a second time. Adan pulled him up by the front of his tunic and hit him again. Tullus fell unconscious to the deck. Adan picked up the kraken-headed dagger and threw it as far as he could. It splashed into the sea and sunk out of sight.

"Niko, jump! Swim to a skiff."

"What about you?"

"You go first and I'll toss you the knapsack! *Go!*"

Nikolaus took one last look at Tullus and jumped. Adan shouted encouragement as he dog-paddled away from the ship. A crewman helped him into a lifeboat. Adan rolled the knapsack into a tight bundle, securing the scroll inside. He tossed it. Nikolaus caught it with one hand. Adan jumped overboard and swam to the skiff. He handed the soaked knapsacks to a crewman and clambered into the boat.

Adan yelled at the crewmen who were lowering the last skiff into the water. "Get your captain!" The crewmen didn't respond. Adan shouted again but they still ignored him.

"Centurion," said one of the men. "We have orders to let him die with the ship if it ever sinks. He said if he is forced off the ship, he would kill the men responsible."

"What? You can't be serious," Adan exclaimed in disbelief.

"Deadly serious. He told us there was a fire-haired *daemon femina* waiting for him in Hades. He craves the demon woman even though she scarred his heart ten times worse than the soldiers scarred his face."

The remaining crewmen jumped overboard and climbed into the last skiff. Even if Adan had been able to get back on the ship, it was too late. The stern of *The Kraken* rose out of the water. Unconscious, Tullus began to slide along the deck toward the submerged bow. He silently slipped into the churning water and disappeared. The sailors used all their strength to row as far from the sinking ship as they could. The waves boiled in the wake of the stern as it was swallowed by the sea. Adan marveled at how quickly the water calmed as if the ship had never existed.

"Niko, I'm sorry I had to hit you," murmured Adan as he gripped his brother by the arm. "It was the only way to save you from the—monster."

"Egnatian was a monster." Nikolaus put his hand to his neck. He looked at his blood-stained fingers. "He would have killed me if you hadn't. . ." He frowned at Adan's odd expression. "You weren't talking about Egnatian when you said 'monster,' were you?"

"Sometimes there's more than one." Adan looked at Nikolaus's injury. "Are you alright?"

"I guess. The salt water made it bleed more, but it's all right."

"I couldn't let you risk your life, Niko. I lost Martialis, my little brother, when I was a child. I can't lose you as well."

"You haven't. I'm right here." He held up the scroll. "And you saved the epistle. We'll get this to Jerusalem. The Christians there are desperate for encouragement."

"What happened to you, Niko? The Prophecy Box was getting to you, wasn't it?"

Nikolaus gazed where the ship had disappeared. "That doesn't matter now. It's gone."

"Yes, the sea owns it now. It is gone for good."

"No, that's not what I mean. That nagging urge to get my hands on that thing is gone. I feel like a weight has been taken off my back."

"What about your father, Niko?"

Nikolaus exhaled slowly. "No matter what I find out, it won't change the past. Knowing the truth only satisfies my curiosity. It doesn't change me. It doesn't affect me. Sometimes, it's best to leave the past alone."

The sailors headed the skiffs toward the only land in sight. It was the island of Kythira.

Chapter 22

In the Shelter of His Wings

⸺◦◦◦◦⸺

T he crew manned the oars diligently and the skiffs sped through calm seas into the harbor on the island of Kythira, a twisted, tortured landscape of opposing geologic forces. Sudden invasions of volcanic rock interrupted the layers of limestone deposited over millennia. Struggling pockets of vegetation looked to solitary trees for inspiration. Rocky cliffs and sandy beaches told a story of building and breaking down in constant conflict. The violent eruptions of lava were tamed by the gradual accumulation of sediment and sand. It was a landscape of contradictions that compromised with a promise of mutual co-existence.

Adan could see a ship being pulled into the only *neosoikoi* available at the port, which revealed a scant population and a relaxed way of life. After giving a statement to the Quarter Master about the sinking of *The Kraken*, the brothers made arrangements with another captain who would eventually dock in Caesarea. It would be a few days before the ship sailed, which made Adan impatient and Nikolaus irritable. They took rooms at an inn while they waited for the departure date and decided to make the most of their delay.

They ate a quiet dinner and went to bed early the first day but greeted the morning well rested. Adan suggested that they explore the village to while away the time. He hoped their explorations would help distract him from thoughts of Herod's intentions. Since they were finally on the last leg of their voyage, they made a few purchases to take home to the family. Adan found a delicately carved vase of alabaster infused with lightning-like streaks of vermillion-colored cinnabar. The exquisite carvings featured hummingbirds, some perched on branches, some drinking from calla lilies. Adan was tempted to forego the usual price negotiation. He knew Dulcibella would love the beautiful vase and he had his own money separate from the government funds. He made a few offers but in the end, he paid the original price. The merchant had watched the way Adan studied the vase and knew he would not leave without it.

Nikolaus found a tunic of fine, purple linen shot through with gold thread. He knew Marina would be delighted with such an elegant garment. After they found gifts for the rest of the family, they stopped for dinner at a café with a rooftop patio overlooking the sea. They selected and paid for their food. The owner waved a hand toward the stairs leading to the patio and invited them to select a place to eat. He followed them with goblets filled with *Mulsum*, a honey and wine mixture. He placed a small bell next to Adan so they could summon him if they needed anything else. The air was crisp with the tangy scent of the sea and honeysuckle vines that grew along trellises adorning the low patio walls. Bees peacefully buzzed from one succulent blossom to the next, completely unconcerned at the closeness of humans. When a flash of iridescent turquoise and deep rose caught their attention, they smiled to watch a hummingbird flit among the nectar-rich flowers. Adan carefully unwrapped the linen protecting the alabaster vase and marveled at how perfectly the artist had captured the beauty of the tiny birds. He re-wrapped the vase and put it back in the knapsack along with the epistle to the Hebrews.

Nikolaus closed his eyes for a moment to listen to the call of the seagulls and terns as they competed for perches. "I've been thinking about the Prophecy Box." Adan shot him a look, hoping he wasn't going to ruin the tranquility of the moment. "Take that dismay off your face, Adan. I'm sure if we were meant to keep the box, we'd still have it. It is a terrible loss but perhaps it's for the best. No telling how many other people may have been murdered for that *machina*."

Adan sighed with relief. "I'm really glad you feel that way, Niko. We couldn't save both the scroll and the box. It is a shame. The sea will dissolve the machine but its wonders will not be lost forever. If it was invented once; it will be invented again."

The brothers fell silent as they gazed out over the sparkling sea. The sun was low in the western sky and cast crimson tones across the peaks of the waves.

Nikolaus twisted his lips in contemplation. "I wonder how long it will take before someone invents another device as ingenious as the Prophecy Box."

Adan grunted. "It was invented hundreds of years ago. There will be other smart people inventing other amazing things. Maybe even more spectacular than the box." He studied Nikolaus for a moment before he spoke again. "Perhaps we should talk about something more personal. Something that affects you and those around you."

"Like what?"

"Egnatian," Adan said the name tentatively.

"What about him?" Nikolaus's expression went rigid with annoyance. "The man's dead."

"We talked about this once before, Niko. You can still forgive him in your heart and free yourself of his ghost. He will haunt you as long as you allow it."

Nikolaus grumbled, "You had to go and spoil a perfectly peaceful evening."

"Better to spoil one evening than the rest of your life."

"Adan, he murdered my family for money. He caused me and Dionysia to be sold as slaves. He tried to kill me—twice. How do I forgive that?"

"How did Yeshua forgive me when I ordered my men to torture him to death, despite the fact that he was innocent of any crime or immorality?" Adan leaned closer. "And I wasn't the only one who put him on that cross. All of humanity's evil, put him on that cross—including yours. Yet, he forgives us for the asking."

"I don't want to forgive Egnatian. Ever!"

"Then you will suffer."

"I'm not suffering! I like hating him," snapped Nikolaus. "It makes me feel powerful to hate him. Why would I deny myself that feeling?"

"Powerful? Is it powerful to feel frustrated? Is it powerful to feel anxious and desperate to get revenge? Revenge you can never have." Adan took in a deep breath. With a softened tone, he added, "If you really want to have power over Egnatian, give him to God. If you keep Egnatian locked inside your heart, he will gnaw on you like a parasite. He will be in control, not you."

"What are you talking about? You're not making sense," grumbled Nikolaus.

"I'm making perfect sense." Adan took a sip of wine and set the goblet down. "Hating Egnatian proves that he still has a hold over you. If he were alive, knowing that would give him great pleasure. The worst thing you can do to him is to *not* think about him. And the only way to banish him from your mind is to hand him over to God."

Nikolaus slapped his hand on the table. "You don't understand! You were never a slave, chained and caged like an animal."

Adan leaned toward his brother. "Wasn't I? You have no idea what I endured with Valentius. My chains were invisible but there were just as binding. My cage was the authority Valentius used against me. Yes, you faced humiliation and abuse at the Antonia. I faced death by Valentius's design. He arranged 'special' assignments, just for me. He sent me on details alone. In Judea! A solitary Roman soldier trotting around the countryside without a single squad. Not only was that against protocol, it was downright malicious. He knew I wouldn't break the chain of command and go over his head to complain. He actively tried to turn my own men against me. Valentius did everything he could to get me killed and he did succeed at getting fifteen other soldiers killed while under my command. Don't you think I feel guilty about that? I sacrificed their lives to protect Simon Peter from Lucius Octavean! It was the right thing to do but it cost fifteen lives! Don't you think I *loved* hating Valentius for putting me in that position?"

Adan let the statement soak in and then he spoke again. "And while I'm talking about hating someone, don't you think I should hate Herod Agrippa? I haven't talked about my death sentence to you on this whole trip because we've been busy finding your answers, doing John's biding, protecting Pomona and Aurelius, helping Calypso and Calais be a family again, and sending reports back to Tacitus so Emperor Domitian can attack Jerusalem. I haven't spent one word on what's going to happen to *me* as soon as I step foot in front of Herod without Aurelius's head dangling from my hand!" Adan leaned back in his chair and looked out over the sea.

Nikolaus sat in guilty silence. "I admit I pushed that out of my mind. Adan, I am so sorry. What are you going to do?"

Adan ran his fingers through his hair. "What I've always done, I guess. Face him. What is to be, will be done. There simply are times when one does nothing. Isn't that what God says to do sometimes? Be still and wait."

Nikolaus stood up in frustration. "How do we deal with this? Even after twenty years, Herod *still* figures out a way to execute you. And what about me? Egnatian murdered my family! I was only twelve. I needed my family. Finding out that they didn't die from some random illness gives me even more reason to hate Egnatian. You put that in my head! And now you want me to forgive the man that murdered them? Herod wants you dead for no other reason than to satisfy his malignant pride and you tell me you're just going to 'stand and wait' like a chained slave? Why aren't you going after Lysias? He set this up. Why don't you figure out some kind of counter accusation to make Herod back off? You beat him twice before. And why, for pity's sake, did you have to suggest that my family was murdered! I seriously, really, *didn't need to know that!*"

Adan swallowed hard and lowered his gaze. "You're right. I have forced you to face terrible grief but it was the lesser of two evils. I was afraid that someone who knew your father had stolen the box would think you had it because of your success. The box belonged to the *Magi*. They have long memories and jealously guard their interests. Eventually, they would track you down and could have been hunting for you all these years. If we learned that your father was *not* guilty of stealing the box then we would know that you are safe from avengers of the *Magi*."

Nikolaus frowned at the explanation. "That may be the good reason you tell yourself but there's more to your motive. You wanted to know if you were right! You figured they were murdered and you wanted proof that you had worked it all out. You always need to be right, Adan. You don't let it go until everyone accepts your version of events."

Adan stared at his brother in dismay. "Is that what you think? You think I left my home and family to prove how smart I am?" He stood up and walked to the railing.

"Adan, I'm sorry. It didn't sound so awful in my head. I know you mean well. I'm just tired and frustrated and disappointed. I was hoping to prove my father's innocence."

Adan returned and sat down. "You're right, though. I should have thought it through better. Dulcie tried to warn me about what it would do to you. I guess I was too stubborn. But one thing I need to say is that *I* did not beat Herod. God did. But maybe not this time. As sad as it is, everyone has to die. If it is my time, then it will be so."

"You can't just give up!"

"Yes, I can."

Nikolaus rubbed his forehead in frustration as he tried to put his thoughts in order. After a few moments, he sighed and shook his head. "Learning that my family was murdered—that's not on you, Adan. I think I knew all along that they had been poisoned. It was so much easier to pretend that their deaths were unpreventable. I crawled into denial to save myself. As an orphaned, twelve-year-old, I simply could not bear the truth. Remember, I told you that we were sold as slaves to pay off the *medicus* who treated us? I lied, mostly to myself, because I didn't want to blame Dionysia for what happened."

Nikolaus gestured in frustration. "Dionysia tried to tell me they were poisoned while we were still on the ship. I covered my ears and screamed at her to stop. But maybe now, I can accept the truth for what it is. Murder for money. And I will never forgive the murderer."

"Then Egnatian will poison them over and over, just like he's poisoning you now. You are giving him permission to exist, in your memory, in your nightmares, in your life."

"That doesn't make any sense to me!"

Adan gazed at his brother patiently. "I can explain this to you in a hundred different ways, but I cannot understand it for you, Niko. Peter tried to explain it to me. I didn't understand him, either. Until I did. When I forgave Valentius, I set myself free."

"I *am* free. Free to hate whoever I want. Anger makes me strong. It was anger that kept me alive when they put me on the auction block in chains."

"And you're still in chains. You just can't see them anymore." Adan stood up. "I'll be at the inn." He left Nikolaus staring out over the ocean.

It was hours before Nikolaus knocked on the door to Adan's room at their inn. "Come on in. It's not locked," Adan called out.

Nikolaus came in and dropped into a chair. "How did you know it was me?"

"I didn't," said Adan as he sat down on the edge of the bed.

"Is that a good idea?" drawled Nikolaus. "You don't have your weapons anymore."

Adan shrugged. "True. But I'm not defenseless. I've learned not to depend on something I can lose."

"Spoken like a true believer—and a well-trained soldier. So, I've been thinking about what you said. I'm just not ready to let go. I don't even know where to start. And I've been thinking about Herod, too. You can't just let him have his way. We've got to do something. What if you appealed to the emperor? He'd have to let you go to Rome. You'd be in chains—real ones—but you'd be alive."

"And then Aurelius's deception would be made known to the emperor. He would be forced to do something public to discourage others from following Aurelius's example. No. I will not do anything that puts a torchlight on Aurelius, which also would affect Pomona."

"I can't think anymore. I wish I could run a sword through Herod and Egnatian but both of them are out of my reach. I don't know how to deal with this, Adan."

"You'll figure it out. Egnatian is at the bottom of the sea. He truly is beyond your reach. Leave him to the eels and the sharks, Niko. Let God be your avenger. Herod is beyond our control but not God's. Don't you think I've been anxious? Don't you realize how the 'Sword of Damocles' has dangled over me all these weeks? I'm not immune to worry and fear. I have to concentrate every day on not giving in to despair."

"I suppose you want me to forget what that bloated toad they call a king has done to you already? Malchus put an arrow into your chest by Herod's order."

"And God gave you and my friends the power to save my life."

"Then why didn't God give me the power to save my family?" Nikolaus demanded.

"I don't have an answer for you, Niko. But God does. One day, you will know it."

"In the meantime, I will keep that question in my heart. You can't ask me to forget my pain."

"No one could forget that, Niko. Time will dull the sharp edges of grief but no one forgets the trauma."

Nikolaus dropped his gaze to the tile floor. He stood up and headed for the door. He paused as he turned the door handle. "I'll make a vow to you, Adan. I'll forgive Egnatian—over Herod's dead body." He left to go to his room across the courtyard.

A messenger came the following morning to say the ship was ready to depart. Once they were on board and under a full sail, the brothers tried to put their argument aside. They were more than homesick and ready to be done with traveling. After a few days in the harbor at Fair Havens and a few more in Paphos, they were finally headed for Caesarea. The death sentence hanging over Adan's head was not brought up again.

Adan and Nikolaus were overjoyed when they first saw the Judean coastline appear on the horizon. It seemed to take forever for the ship to dock in the harbor. They were in for a happy surprise when they saw the whole family waiting for them at the pier, including Serapio, Fabiana, and Nebetka's family. Dulcibella ran into Adan's arms and nearly knocked him over. Marcus and Iovita hugged both of them at once. Marina ran to Nikolaus and hugged him as if he might vanish if she let go. The children impatiently waited for their turn to share hugs. Serapio nearly caused bodily damage when he hugged Adan and Nikolaus, he was so happy to see them.

"You should see the new house and my grand new shop as soon as you can," Serapio announced. "Nebetka's house is nearby and just as fine. A small gift from a kind-hearted woman made it all possible. In fact, neither Nebetka nor I need work another day in our lives but I would die an early death from boredom if I retired now. It's amazing how much money some men will pay for an object produced by an ugly little oyster." The others laughed and Adan congratulated Serapio and Nebetka on the completion of their new homes.

Marina pointed to the top of the ship's mast. "I'm so glad you didn't lose it!" she cried with delight. "I thought for sure you would."

A bright, blue banner with a central, white L waved at them in the breeze.

Marco excitedly exclaimed, "I was the first to see the flag from our terrace. I just happened to be sitting on the bench under the tree and I saw a ship's mast coming over the horizon. I squinted up my eyes but I couldn't see well enough for ages, it seemed. Finally, something flapped in the wind at the top of the mast and I saw that it was blue."

"He ran through the villa like a madman, yelling that a ship with our flag was coming in," said Marcus. "I've never seen horses saddled and the carriage hitched up so quickly."

Adan playfully threw an arm around Marco's neck and ruffled his hair. He turned to Aquila and his daughter, Longina, to assure them that he had surprises for all three of them. They grinned at each other and back at their father. Adan reached for one of the knapsacks.

"Dulcie, I brought you something that I know you will like." Adan held the gift for her as she unwrapped it. She cried out with surprise when she saw the alabaster vase.

"It's so beautiful!" she exclaimed with delight. "The hummingbirds are exquisite." She turned to the others to show them the vase. They uttered sounds of amazement and approval.

"Marina, this is for you," said Nikolaus as he handed his wife her gift. Everyone watched as she carefully unwrapped it. She gasped at the softness of the silk, the deep purple color and the glittering gold threads woven into the cloth. The joyful look in her eyes told Nikolaus that he had made an excellent selection. Dulcibella and Marina handed their gifts to Iovita and Fabiana to admire and to share praise for their husbands' thoughtfulness.

Adan looked back at the waving blue flag. "Niko, I never asked you how you talked the captain into putting that up there."

"I had to pay him a *denarius* before he would order a crewman to climb to the top and tie it on," Nikolaus explained. "It was well worth the expense to see everyone here. Besides, it's a tradition for wayfarers to signal their return. We couldn't ignore tradition, now could we?"

"No, we could not, but a whole *denarius*?" chuckled Adan. "That's a week's wage for a sailor. You must have been carrying more money than I thought."

Nikolaus grinned sheepishly. "I kept a few well-hidden coins stitched into my tunic."

Marcus gathered the knapsacks and set them in the carriage. He frowned at how few there were. "Where's the rest of your gear? In fact, where is your sword and dagger?"

Adan's smile faded. "There was a shipwreck. We lost a few things." He looked at Serapio. "It couldn't be helped, my friend. I'm sorry to lose such magnificent blades. I know what it meant to you when you gave them to me."

Serapio threw his hands up. "They were made once before—even better ones can be made again. Besides, I'm a rich man now and I will be delighted to design something even more special and spectacular." His eyes sparkled with anticipation. "And I know just the craftsman to make them."

Dulcibella laughed to see Serapio's enthusiasm. "Well, I'm grateful that's all you lost. Better to lose a few things rather than your lives."

"A few things," said Nikolaus pensively. "Yes, we lost a few things. Perhaps because we weren't meant to keep it." The two brothers looked at each other and understanding passed between them. Dulcibella tilted her head with curiosity as she watched them. She knew that whatever they lost was more significant than a tunic or a pair of sandals.

"That's enough talk for now," announced Iovita with a brisk clap of her hands. "Let's go to the house. Cook is preparing a special feast for our returning adventurers."

Adan caught Marcus's eye and stood back from the family. Marcus knew what he was going to say. "Adan, I know you're thinking about Herod. The whole family knows including Serapio and his clan. They're doing their best to put their fear aside. Tonight, try to do the same. Rejoice in being reunited with your family and we'll all face Herod tomorrow. I don't know what will happen but we're all going with you."

✳✳✳

The next morning came all too quickly after the family had tried to get some rest. None of them were successful. No one was interested in breakfast. Horses were saddled and the carriage was again prepared. The Longinus and Cornelius clan slowly made their way down the switchback road and plodded along the short distance to the Ocean View Inn to gather Nikolaus's and Serapio's families. Adan and Dulcibella rode in front. Adan on Blackfire, Dulcibella on Venustas while the others followed behind.

"Adan," Marcus called out as he urged his horse to catch up, "Tacitus wants to join us. I know you asked me to do nothing but I went to him and we discussed the situation. He wants us to stop at the garrison first so he can go before Herod with us."

Adan nodded but made no comment. He glanced back at Aquila and Marco and they each nodded once in solidarity with their father.

No one spoke as they rode along. Even as they approached the gates of the garrison, Adan didn't bother to acknowledge the sentries on duty. They started to step forward to welcome Adan back but Marcus shook his head at them. They looked at each other in confusion but stepped out of the way of the somber procession.

The sound of galloping hooves came to them as they passed through the gates of the fortress. Adan glanced over his shoulder to find that Commander Lysias and his escort of soldiers had just reined in their horses.

Lysias called out to the sentries on duty. "I am Commander Lysias of the Antonia Fortress. I was summoned by King Herod." He urged his horse to enter the garrison before the sentries could respond. The man and his escort trotted their horses past Adan's group, all the while, leering at Adan with self-satisfaction. They reined their horses to a stop outside the stables and dismounted. Lysias ordered the stable slaves to see to their horses and stood watching Adan's group. His feet were planted wide apart and his arms were crossed. He smiled with anticipation of fulfilling Herod's order.

"I've been watching for you Centurion Longinus," shouted Lysias loudly enough for Adan and his group to hear. "We made camp right there on the hill." He pointed to a small mesa that overlooked the road. "You didn't even keep me waiting long. How considerate of you. Herod summoned me to perform a task for him. Perhaps you can guess what it is." He laughed and his men joined in.

"Is that the man who wrote the letter to Herod?" whispered Dulcibella.

"Yes. He is."

They reined the horses to a stop in front of Tacitus's office. Adan dismounted and walked purposefully to the door and knocked. The door flew open. Tacitus stood in full formal attire, reserved for only the most ceremonial affairs. His armor was polished and gleamed in the sunlight. His red cape was expertly secured and he held his red horsehair-crested helmet in his hand. His sword and dagger were prominently displayed on his belt.

"Sir, reporting for duty," said Adan with his chin up and his shoulders squared. "Sir, will you be joining us at Herod's palace?" Adan wondered how Tacitus knew they would be coming since he was already dressed for the official proceedings.

Tacitus looked startled. "Well, it is certainly good to see that you're back, Centurion. We've sorely missed you. But I will not be going with you to see King Herod. Please accept my apology." He glanced to the side and saw Lysias watching.

"Where are you going, Tacitus?" demanded Marcus. "I thought we had an understanding."

"We did, Marcus. But you see, I have to attend a funeral."

"Whose funeral is so important that you break your promise to me?" growled Marcus.

Tacitus smiled up at Marcus. "Whose funeral? Why—King Herod Agrippa, of course. He died late last night. According to Blastus, *on the appointed day Herod, wearing his royal robes, sat on his throne and delivered a public address to the people. They shouted, 'This is the voice of a god, not of a man.' Immediately, because Herod did not give praise to God, an angel of the Lord struck him down, and he was eaten by worms and died.* Apparently, Herod developed gangrene of a certain extremity and somehow he became infected with maggots. Or so I was told. Now, if all of you will excuse me, I'm off to the palace."

Tacitus started to leave but stopped and clapped a hand on Adan's shoulder. "I asked Blastus to go through any written edicts Herod left behind. None of them had anything to do with a certain centurion who drowned in a storm while aboard the *Scarlet Jade*. I'm not really sure why I thought you needed to know that but. . ." He smiled. Contrary to his normal demeanor, Tacitus gave Adan, who was stunned to speechlessness, a great, heart-felt hug, and then marched off toward the stables.

Tacitus shouted as he walked. "Lysias! Get your flea bitten hide in my office! Now!"

Lysias pulled a small scroll from his under his belt. "No, Sir. I will not. King Herod sent this order for me to carry out the execution of Adan Clovius Longinus. I will report to King Herod for duty before I do anything." He brandished the scroll. "It has King Herod's official seal."

"Then you might as well stop breathing so you can keep that oath. Herod is dead. He left no record of any orders pertaining to you *or* Centurion Longinus." Tacitus gestured at the soldiers standing behind Tacitus. "Arrest that man for disobeying a direct order and violating the chain of command. Lysias, you are hereby relieved of duty, *indefinitely!*"

A spontaneous cheer erupted from Adan's entire group. Before he could find his voice, Dulcibella was hugging him and sobbing with joy and relief. Suddenly, she slapped him across the arm.

"Don't *ever* make me do this again!" she cried and threw herself back into his arms.

Joy erupted as family and friends jostled Adan with embraces, back slaps and shoulder smacking. Somehow, the entire group managed to find their way back to the Cornelius estate for the biggest, hardiest breakfast any of them had ever thought possible.

* * *

After several months, Adan received a letter from Calais. He found Dulcibella on the cliff-top terrace under the shade of the ancient oak tree. She was sitting on her favorite bench. He sat next to her and read the letter aloud.

Greetings Centurion Adan Clovius Longinus:

I am happy to inform you that Mother and I made it home to Pergamon without too much trouble. Before we said our farewells to our mutual friends, they gave Mother a wonderful gift. Mother's 'daughter' pressed a small leather purse into her hand. Her tears of happiness convinced us that this gift must be very special. We were shocked when we opened it and a beautiful pearl rolled out. We are so grateful to them for bestowing such a blessing on us. We were able to find a buyer for the pearl and now will be quite comfortable for the rest of our lives, and then some. Still, it was very sad to tell the sister and brother farewell. Mother cried and cried but she's recovering.

Now I have to tell you something even more amazing. Remember the slave girl that you hired to take bread to the lepers? The lepers confirmed that she fulfilled her duties diligently. You should have seen how proud she was to return Sofi to me, the little wooden owl Marco also gave back to me when Vesuvio was threatening our lives. Then, about a month later, we learned that she was very ill. She did not have leprosy as we first feared, but was ill with the coughing disease, instead. We went to her. Mother and I prayed to Yeshua to heal the child. We stayed with her all day and night, praying. She wanted to know who we prayed to and we told her about Yahweh and Yeshua.

Then a voice spoke to me in my head. "Hold her hands and pray one more time." I was startled and asked Mother if she heard the voice. She shook her head, then smiled so sweetly and said, "Do what He told you to do." I was afraid. What if nothing happened? Mother must have read my mind. She said, "If you don't obey, I assure you, God will not relent until you do." I took the child's hands in mine and I prayed one more time.

Adan, I wish you could have been there. Immediately, I felt her small hands cool as I held them. Her struggles to breath stopped. Her complexion grew healthy and her eyes widened, first with amazement, then fear, then joy. Adan, could it be possible that God has chosen me to take my brother's place? Is this what John meant when he said I would be needed? Life will not be any easier for me than it was for Antipas. The Nicolaitans are still here. They are grumbling behind their hands about my presence. So be it! I have been given a new life. I will not waste it. Mother and I go to the lepers every day and tend to their suffering, both physical, emotional, and spiritual. Perhaps in time, God will use me to heal more people. For now, Mother and I bake bread together and rejoice in being a family again.

I want to thank you, again, Adan, for refusing to leave me on the dock in Herculaneum and saving me from Vesuvio. Who knew it was a flaming mountain? It is crazy the way the most unexpected things can occur in the most unlikely way.

Give my sincere regards to Nikolaus. I pray that you and your family will always be as blessed as I am. I also have wonderful news for you which I have saved for last. John has been pardoned from exile. He has left Patmos and gone to Ephesus. If you are ever in that city, you should look for him. If you're ever in Pergamon, come find us. You will always be welcomed in our home.

Your faithful brother in Christ,
Calais Antipas

***

Dulcibella smiled and curled her hand around Adan's arm. "I also have some good news for you, my love," she said with a sparkling eye.

"What would that be, Little Elf?" He leaned over to kiss the top of her head.

"Serapio says your new weapons have arrived but he wants you to come to his shop so he can present them in a proper fashion. His words, 'proper fashion,' and he says we are to go this afternoon."

"Ah, I can't wait." He grinned with anticipation. "When Serapio does anything in a 'proper fashion' it is memorable. I might need to wear my armor in case he wants to demonstrate how effective these weapons are."

Dulcibella snickered. "I'm sure Serapio would tell you that all the armor in the world would not protect you from this sword and dagger. He's quite proud of them. *Ohe,* I almost forgot to tell you; I saw Marina yesterday and Niko had a message. He said to tell you, 'I have kept my promise that I made to you on Kythira.' He said, 'I have escaped the tentacles of the Kraken.' His exact words."

Dulcibella leaned back and studied her husband's reaction, "Ah, I see you know what that means. Maybe you'll tell me someday." She smiled to see Adan smile.

"Speaking of that ship sinking and you two getting delayed on Kythira. Do you realize that if you had come home just a few weeks sooner, Herod would have been able to order Lysias to carry out his edict against you? If your ship hadn't hit the other sunken ship, you might have. . ."

She left the sentence unfinished. "Three times Herod has tried to end your life. Three times God caused him to fail." She sighed and nuzzled against him.

Adan sighed. "Have I told you, today, how much I love you?" He peered into her turquoise eyes and gently urged a stray lock of hair behind her ear.

"You have now." She caressed his face with a gentle hand. They shared a kiss and nestled into each other's arms. The family was, once again, reunited. Dulcibella gazed out over the sea. She whispered a prayer of gratitude that Adan and Nikolaus were safely home. Adan drank in the beauty of the moment and added a prayer of gratitude of his own. Adan and Dulcibella were exactly where they always wanted to be—together.

The heart yearns for home when home is where love is the greatest treasure.

Epilogue

The Year 2019

———— ❦ ————

The curator of the Archaeological Museum in Athens opened the door to allow a journalist to enter the testing lab. The curator cleared her throat. Two people looked up who had been staring at a chart spread on a table.

"Elizabeth Ventura here to see you, Dr. Latham, Dr. Hampton," announced the curator. She beckoned the young woman to enter and smiled. "I'll leave you to it."

The two doctors were married to each other but Dr. Latham was required to use her maiden name, which she had when she earned her doctorate.

Elizabeth, a tall, blonde with gray eyes, thanked the curator and shook hands with the two doctors. "On behalf of *International Archaeology*, I want to thank you both for this interview on the Antikythera antiquities."

"We're thrilled to have the opportunity to discuss any of our artifacts," said Dr. Latham. She was a stately woman with curly, red hair and ocean-blue eyes. "And please, call me Sandra." Her welcoming expression spoke of a zest for life and love for her work.

Elizabeth immediately felt at ease. "Ok. Then call me Evie if we're going to be informal. E.V., as in my initials. E-liz-a-beth is just too many syllables."

The doctors chuckled in agreement.

"Where would you like to start, Evie?" asked Dr. Hampton. He had a thatch of white hair and full beard with a cheerful demeanor. Evie suppressed a grin as she visualized the scientist in a Santa Claus suit, singing Christmas carols. "And you should call me Jim. Everyone does."

"Ok, Sandra, Jim. How about we start with some background on the Antikythera Device to be sure I have my facts straight."

"Sure. Most of the device was found in 1901 by sponge divers," explained Sandra. "More pieces were discovered later by the Jacques Cousteau expedition. Everything was turned over to the archeologists here in Athens and as time went on, more and more discoveries were made about the device. It is actually a computer and, most likely, the very first one ever invented. Some prefer to call it the Antikythera Mechanism but we just call it the device."

"It was found amongst the cargo of an ancient shipwreck off the island of Antikythera, Greece, correct? Hence the name," Evie clarified as she jotted a few notes.

"That's the modern name for the island but in ancient times, it was called Kythira." Sandra continued, "One theory for the sinking of the ship is that it was overloaded. It included a large trove of full-sized statues along with stone and ceramic artifacts. It was a huge find."

"Sandy and I have a different theory on the unusually large number of artifacts," replied Jim. "Since the objects were in such a tight area, we think that the sea was calm when it sunk. It was shallow water and it would have been even more shallow two thousand years ago. Climate change has raised the sea level about six feet since ancient times. A storm would have sloshed things around at that depth. Also, the ship captains knew exactly how much weight their vessels could haul just as well as they do today. They wouldn't chance losing everything by overloading. Ship owners could pay into an insurance program, even back then, to recover the cost of lost cargo but they certainly didn't want to make a habit of collecting. Their insurance premiums went up after a claim, just like they do now."

"An insurance program? Really?" Evie made a doubtful face.

"They were called benevolent societies," said Jim. "Insurance against risk goes back to Chinese and Babylonian traders in the 3rd and 2nd millennia BCE. Ship captains faced the greatest hazards and caused the benevolent societies to become a mainstay."

Sandra commented with amusement. "It's not like they could radio the Coast Guard if they got in trouble, could they?"

Jim laughed and pulled on his beard. "Exactly. So, we thought that maybe there were two ships that went down in the same area. That would double the cargo."

"You think they collided? Maybe at night or in a dense fog?" Evie twirled her pen between two fingers.

"Not likely," said Jim. "When they couldn't see where they were going, they dropped anchor. So, no sailing at night or in a fog. There would be ample visibility during calm weather. So, we think a ship crashed into another ship that had already sunk. It would have been just under the surface. They wouldn't have seen it until it was too late. It could have ripped the hull open much like the submerged edges of the iceberg that sunk the *Titanic*."

"Ah, good theory," said Evie. She made a note. "You said the device is a computer?"

"An analog computer. X-ray tomography revealed that the device is based on physics and mathematics because the numbers 76, 19, and 223 are used." said Sandra. "It's a complicated clock-like mechanism made of thirty meshing bronze gears. Maybe more. There were thirty-seven gear wheels. All of these parts were powered by a small hand crank. It showed how the orbit of the Earth and the Moon interacted with the planets as they orbited the Sun. It traced how the sun appears to move through the zodiac."

"What exactly is the zodiac? I know it is twelve constellations, but why those particular ones?" asked Evie.

"The sun is surrounded by stars of twelve constellations throughout each year," explained Sandra. "The sun 'stays' in each constellation for one month. We would be able to see each constellation that the sun passes through if the stars were visible during the day. The constellations that the sun appears to 'travel' through are called the zodiac. Let me illustrate. Imagine the sun is surrounded by twelve picture frames. You are standing between the frames and the sun. If you keep your eye on the sun as you orbit around it, you will see the sun 'move' into the next frame. Once a month, the sun will be in the center of each frame."

Jim continued the description. "The Antikythera Device could predict, decades in advance, solar and lunar eclipses and even accounted for the irregular orbit of the Moon. Tomography also revealed instructions pressed into the bronze outer casing. There are 3,400 characters etched in the bronze which amount to a manual on how to use the device. The largest gear, at five and a half inches, has 223 teeth, revealing that the exact movements of the moon were understood about twenty-two hundred years ago. This knowledge was apparently lost well into the Middle Ages. The device was found in the remains of a wooden box that would have measured 13.4 inches, by 7.1 inches, by 3.5 inches. It's astounding that it was so small. We're still discovering things about this masterpiece of genius. Fragment F was found in 2005, tucked away in storage. So far, we have 82 fragments. As our technology increases, so does our understanding of the device. Some investigators have made replicas, using only hand tools, and they actually work."

"Sounds amazing," replied the science journalist. "How old do you think it is?"

"It pre-dates the birth of Christ by hundreds of years," said Sandra. "Could be as early as the third century BCE."

"Wow. There were geniuses back then. Go figure," said Evie with a tongue-in-cheek smile.

Jim gave a hearty laugh. "Yes, shocking, isn't it?"

"Actually, what is shocking," said Sandra, "is how arrogant many people are when it comes to ancient discoveries. Conspiracy theorists think extraterrestrials must have popped in just to share their superiority with us stupid humans. There have always been inspired inventors in every age. There's no telling how much knowledge was lost in the fire at the Library of Alexandria, alone."

Jim continued, "One such genius was Archimedes who might have actually built this device. He was a phenomenal inventor and scientist who lived from 288 BCE to 212 BCE. Some speculate that the charts he was working on when he was killed, may have been improvements for this device. Another clue is the manufacturer's stamp among the instructions. It stated, 'I am a Pythagorean.' Pythagoras, a Greek philosopher and mathematical genius, lived from 570 BCE to 495 BCE, over five hundred years before the birth of Christ. Others used the records of his knowledge to good use. There's no telling how many other amazing devices and tools were invented in the past. For example, do you think there were only fifty T-rex dinosaurs running around for sixty-six million years? Of course not, but that's about how many partial skeletons we have. In fact, there are only three complete skeletons of dinosaurs on record. It was a single Scelidosaurus and two Changmiania skeletons of burrowing dinosaurs. Just because this is the only ancient computer we have discovered, does not mean it was the only one that existed."

"Think about this," exclaimed Sandra, "at least three centuries before the birth of Christ, scientists knew that six planets orbited the sun. Aristarchus taught that the Sun was the 'central fire' of the universe. He even knew the correct order of the planets from the sun. Mercury, Venus, Earth, Mars, Jupiter, and Saturn. Aristarchus and others knew the moon was closer to Earth relative to the Sun because of solar eclipses. Using Pythagoras geometry, he used the triangle to estimate that twenty times the distance to the moon was how far away the Sun was from Earth. He was short by nearly ninety million miles but he had the right idea. Then he estimated the size of the moon as being one third the size of Earth, based on the timing of lunar eclipses. Pretty close. It's about one fourth. Around 2,200 years ago, Eratosthenes correctly calculated the circumference of the Earth. They knew then that the earth is a sphere, not flat. We believe all this knowledge was applied to create the Antikythera Device. All you had to do was turn a handle and set a few dials to predict celestial events like eclipses. It revealed the future positions of the planets, even accounting for observable retrograde motion of Mars, Jupiter, and Saturn."

Evie looked up from her notes. "Retrograde motion?"

"It's an optical illusion of the planets' motion as viewed from earth," explained Sandra. "It looks like the outer planets move backward for a short period, but actually it is us moving faster, due to a smaller orbit. We see the outer planets moving forward as we catch up with them. When we speed past, they're still moving forward, but they will be left behind and will appear to back up. The concepts of a spherical Earth, a Sun-centered solar system, and retrograde motion were not fully accepted until the 1500's"

Evie raised her eyebrows. "Wow! Guess that makes the rest of us slow learners. That's about 1,800 years for the general public to fully grasp these basic concepts. Why is that?"

Jim offered an explanation. "One must look at the difference between our modern culture and the ancient culture of the past. If a ghost floated into this room, we would say, 'How is this happening? What is it?' Right?"

Evie knew her response would be more dramatic but didn't argue. "Probably."

"But if a ghost floated into a home of ancient people, they would say 'What does this mean? What should we do?' You see the difference? Most ancient people cared about the *meaning* of events, not their *cause* or logistics. Most people in ancient times and even many people today, see an event they don't understand and decide it must have a supernatural cause or meaning. Actually, natural phenomena can be mind-boggling and sometimes, frightening, but it's still a natural process."

Secret of the Ruby

"The Antikythera Device would have been seen as a supernatural instrument," said Sandra. Many inventors in ancient times were seen as sorcerers and mystics. No, they were just smart and educated. This is why we love finding and analyzing artifacts. They provide a window into the knowledge of a culture long gone and, literally, buried."

"Why do you care about the past? How can it affect us now?" asked Evie.

"The motto for every archeologist," said Jim, "is the past is the key to the present. Sandra and I see things in a broader sense. We think the past reveals the *promise* of a future."

"Please explain that." Evie set her pen to a page and waited.

"No matter what terrible things befall humanity, someone, somewhere, always rises to the emergency. Pandemics were a fact of life, so scientists invented antibiotics and vaccines. Starvation was a fact of life, so scientists invented fertilizer and pesticides. Travel was difficult and dangerous so engine-driven modes of transportation were invented. The barter system was cumbersome so paper money was invented. It goes on and on."

"The problem with 'necessity is the mother of invention' is the ripple effects," said Sandra. "Germs are constantly developing immunity to antibiotics and vaccines through mutations. Fertilizers also feed harmful algae and pesticides also kill bees, which we need for the pollination of crops. And we all know what fossil fuels are doing to our climate, even though methane is far more harmful than carbon dioxide."

"Ok, hold on there a minute," Evie exclaimed. "I thought carbon dioxide is the problem."

"It is the problem," said Sandra, "in that it is causing temperatures to rise, which melts the permafrost, which releases massive amounts of methane. It takes a great deal less methane to cause the same damage as carbon dioxide."

"I know I'm getting off track here, but hasn't the same amount of carbon dioxide always existed on earth?"

"Here's the thing," said Jim. "If you have a square foot of coal that has, let's say, one thousand units of carbon dioxide in it and you let it decompose into the environment over one hundred thousand years, that doesn't cause any harm. If you take that square foot of coal and burn it, those thousand units of harmful gas goes into the air in a number of hours. The carbon dioxide trapped in coal and oil gets released millions of times faster than if it decomposes by natural processes. Does that make sense?"

"Unfortunately, yes," admitted Evie. "We really are causing climate change, aren't we?"

"We aren't *causing* the change; we're *accelerating* the change," clarified Sandra.

"We never solve the problems of this world," said Jim. "The problems just change into new problems. When we discover an ancient artifact, we learn how early humans adjusted to their problems. Those adjustments led to new problems, yet, we're still here—adjusting."

"Interesting. Were there other unusual objects in the Antikythera find?"

"None so astronomically amazing," quipped Jim.

Sandra snickered good-naturedly. "Really, Jim?" He grinned at her.

"But we did find some beautifully crafted, very unique weapons," volunteered Jim. "Want to see them? And then we'll show you the Antikythera Device."

The scientists led the way to a large room with the usual display cases and cabinets. They walked over to a display and Jim unlocked the case. He donned cotton gloves and carefully lifted a sword and two daggers out. He set them on a felt pad Sandra placed on a table.

"Oh! They're beautiful. Those wolf heads are exquisite." Evie pointed to the pommels of the sword and one of the daggers. "And what is that?" She pointed at the other dagger. "An octopus? Look at its red eyes. They seem to be watching me. Is that a trick of the light? It was clever how the craftsman made the tentacles form the handle."

"Sure was," said Sandra. "Look at the expression on the wolves and the way the ears are turned. The eyes are made of amber. That, in itself, makes the weapons one-of-a-kind. Amber is very soft, meaning it is easily scratched. Something you never find on a weapon. There must have been a special reason why amber was used. Various types of quartz, ruby, sapphire, jade, and varieties of feldspar were most commonly used."

Evie studied the wolf-headed weapons with interest. "The workmanship is superb. They must have cost a fortune. Tell me about how such a weapon would be made."

The scientists explained how metals and alloys were refined and forged. They showed Evie pictures illustrating the process of metal crafting done thousands of years ago. She questioned them on the step-by-step process and they pointed out that metal forging was not much different today. Jim and Sandra discussed how the three ancient weapons were examples of not just craftsmanship but the high status of the owners.

Jim turned the octopus dagger back and forth to amplify the shimmer of light in the eyes. "The eyes are made of red fire agate. The crystallization of the stone plays tricks with the light and has a high degree of hardness. Much more suitable for a weapon. As Sandy pointed out, these weapons would have been highly prized, not just for defense, but as objects of prestige and authority. They are truly rare finds. People always value anything that is rare."

Evie pointed at three ornamental objects that were also in the case. "What are those?"

"Semi-precious gemstones fashioned as cabochons. As you can see, a cabochon has a smooth surface with no facets like a star ruby or a star sapphire." Jim lifted them out and set them with the weapons. "The iridescent red and gold one is called a sunstone, a type of plagioclase feldspar. The blue one is a moonstone, which is also a type of feldspar." He tilted the cabochons back and forth to reveal the light diffraction that made their colors shimmer. He picked up the third stone. "This is a picture jasper, a type of quartz called chalcedony. We think they must have been on a leather belt or a jewelry box since they were not in a metal framing with eyelets for stringing on a necklace. These stones would have been highly prized."

Evie asked questions about the properties of the stones and their availability in ancient times. That information led her to ask about mining techniques and how slave labor was used. Sandra and Jim explained how mining was always done by slaves and the life expectancy was about eight to ten months. Wars were fought sometimes to enslave the population to gain new workers for the mines. She took notes and then returned her questions to the artifacts.

"What do these weapons say about the owners?" Evie asked.

"The owner of the wolf weapons," said Sandra, "was most likely a military officer of high authority, definitely a centurion. They were the Special Forces in the Roman Army. He might have held the rank of a general or an admiral."

"Wait, how could he have been both a centurion and a general?"

"Being a centurion was not a title of rank. A centurion could have been the equivalent of a captain or a colonel or a general. Just like you have different ranks of soldiers in the Navy Seals or Army Green Berets."

"I see." She imagined a Roman soldier in full regalia. "What of the owner of the octopus dagger? A soldier as well?"

"Well, he certainly was not a sailor," said Sandy emphatically.

Jim agreed. "Many ancient sailors were terrified of octopus and squid because they thought they were infant krakens and mom or dad might be lurking nearby. They believed a kraken could sink a ship and devour the unfortunate sailors, alive. In fact, we've rarely ever found an object in a shipwreck with an octopus motif. I'm surprised the captain even let him come aboard, as universally superstitious as they were then. The owner must have smuggled it in his luggage."

"If the ship did sink in calm weather and shallow water," asked Evie, do you think the people could have made it to Antikythera Island?"

"Most likely. They should have had time to lower the lifeboats. The ship was not far from land when it sunk. Why?" asked Sandra.

Evie arranged her thoughts. "Just speculation. Do you think there was a reason a centurion would leave such extraordinary weapons behind? Could there have been something he needed to save which forced him to sacrifice these." She pointed to the sword and dagger. "I mean, wouldn't these weapons be his most important possessions on that ship? He would have had time to retrieve them. As for the other dagger, maybe the captain wouldn't let the owner in a lifeboat. Maybe the octopus guy was blamed for the ship sinking and they let him drown. In fact, maybe the centurion owned all three weapons and was refused a place in a lifeboat and drowned."

Both scientists shook their heads. Sandra explained, "The dagger was the only item found at some distance from the rest of the cargo as if it was thrown from the ship. The captain could have thrown it off the ship out of superstition—a tad too late since the ship was sinking."

"Along those same lines," pointed out Jim, "the device and the wolf head weapons were found together. If the owner survived, why was the device also left behind? Why would anyone in their right minds forfeit such valuable treasures, including the gemstones? They were all found together. Only the octopus dagger was separate from the rest."

"Could the gemstones have been decoration for the box that held the device?"

The scientists grinned at each other. "That's what we think," said Sandra, "but we like to wait and see if others suggest the same idea. It would make sense. A sunstone, a moonstone, and jasper that looks like a landscape on earth."

"Sweet! But that brings us back to the question of why these treasures were left behind."

Sandra tapped a finger on the sword. "The weapons, gemstones, and the Antikythera Device were all found together. Let's speculate that the same man owned the wolf weapons and the device adorned with the gemstones, *and* he made it to shore. As you questioned, what did he value more than these items? Could it have been his or someone else's life?"

"Maybe so. The device and the weapons could be replaced. A life, not so much."

"If he did survive the ship sinking," said Jim, "clearly, something else was much more important. Too bad we don't know who he was. If we did, we might figure out what motivated him to let these treasures sink into the sea."

Evie jotted down their comments. "I guess we'll never know."

Sandra and Jim shared a meaningful smile.

"I think there have been events," said Sandra, "both wonderful and terrible, which were never recorded in history. That doesn't stop us from 'filling in' the gaps with creative logic. It makes history much more interesting; don't you think?"

"I think so." Elizabeth Ventura grinned. She suddenly thought of a new project and set her pen to paper. "One can always use 'creative logic' as you say. And who knows? It might even be true."

www.ingramcontent.com/pod-product-compliance
Lightning Source LLC
Chambersburg PA
CBHW080728020726
47503CB00010B/2829